To Jeanette

READY FOR FLYNN

Part 1

K. L. SHANDWICK

Love K L Shandwick

First Editor: Amy Donnelly

Second Editor: Traci Sanders

Proof Reader: Lisa Perkins

Cover Design: by Russell Cleary

Photograph: Eric David Battershall

Cover Model: Burton Hughes

Beta Readers: Elmarie Pieterse, Sarah Lintott, Emma Moorhead & Lesley Edwards

❀ Created with Vellum

Since my first series, I've always strived to bring my readers characters who have flaws and real-life situations, but in a fictional setting. Some of the stories may seem far-fetched and too unbelievable at times to happen in real life, but for a small minority of people, the unbelievable is their every day. Writing rock star romance allows me a degree of poetic license to use these characters in bringing forth stories that, on the surface, may not seem realistic. However, just because it's never happened to someone we know, doesn't mean it's not possible. No one is born thinking they are going to be famous, or have unbelievable things happen to them. People become amazing through their raising, or they stumble across something that makes them stand out in a crowd.

Alfie Black, Gibson Barclay, Jack Cunningham are some of the book boyfriends I've shared with you so far. Now I give you my latest. I hope you will take Flynn Docherty into your hearts in the same way you did the others. Thank you to all of you for your constant support and kind words, reviews, and for sharing my work. I appreciate every comment I receive.

Social media plays a huge role in spreading the word about KL Shandwick, and in my view, no one does that better than my team of dedicated followers. This book is, therefore, dedicated to a very special lady, Jacquie Dennison, who has been part of the team since day one. Jacquie has always been there in Australia, shouting out my work, while I am asleep in the UK. We are like ships passing in the night. An Aussie with a wonderful sense of humor, Jacquie is there offering sensible and sound judgements when I want to talk about book-related things, but she's so much more than who. She has become a good friend. Thank you, Jacquie, for choosing to read my work, because I'd be lost without you and the rest of the team.

As for the rest of my team, as always, I am forever indebted to you for all the hard work you put in on my behalf. You are all very special ladies, and I am truly thankful to each one of you. KL.

Some of the team are already mentioned as beta readers, but everyone who had a hand in this creation deserves to be included here.

Ashley Appleby, Debra Hiltz, Samantha Harrington, Janet Boyd, Angela Wallace Kawauchi, Donna Salzano Trippi, Leigh Black, Isabel Adams, Ann Meemken, Tammy Ann Dove, Jennifer Pierson, Louise Husted, Ellie Aspill, Michelle Lov Engler, Lacey Smith, and Nancy Pracht.

Chapter One

GOING HOME

*T*earing down the stairs, I was breathless by the time I reached Aunt Joan's old melamine wall-mounted phone in her kitchen.

"Valerie, it's lovely to hear your voice, sweetheart. You haven't called for a week. Are you okay?"

"Oh, sure Mom. Sorry. I've been busy with Auntie Joan. We've been cleaning things out here. She felt it was time to sort through Uncle Terry's things, and one thing led to another. You know how she is. It's been great reminiscing about their lives, though. There is so much I never knew about them, both as a couple, and their lives before they met each other."

Uncle Terry met my Aunt Joan after his first wife died. They married in their forties, and neither had any children. My uncle was an only child, and we were the only family Auntie Joan had left.

"I was talking to her last night, Valerie. Didn't she tell you she called?"

"She did? She never mentioned it to me. I wonder why?"

"Seems you may have outstayed your welcome, honey." Mom chuckled, and I knew she was only teasing. My aunt would have kept

1

me forever if she'd had her way. I knew she'd worried about home-schooling me for a while, but to be honest, I'd welcomed the opportunity to get out of town after the whole situation with Bradley, my ex. Talk about humiliation. I was even more embarrassed by the number of well-wishers who stopped me in the halls—on a daily basis—to tell me what an ass Bradley was, and what a slut my best friend Heidi was for hooking up with him.

"Oh well, I guess I'm coming home," I said, pretending to feel hurt. But I was excited. I'd been missing everyone, and it was only a few days before Thanksgiving. And best of all, Martin was going to be home.

Martin, my second oldest brother, was my best friend, and had always been. He'd been in college for the past three years at St. Cloud's in Minnesota, and I missed him every day. After he moved out, we didn't see him unless it was a holiday.

I realized I'd drifted off at the mention of Martin's name, and tuned back into my mom's call.

"I think she just wants to try to put some normalcy back in her life. Or a new normal, as it will be. It's early on, but she seems okay. She's being practical about the next chapter of her life and wants us to help her with that. Has she told you she's selling the house and moving closer to us, or is that news to you also?"

Aunt Joan was much stronger than we gave her credit for, but she had recognized the benefits of having her family close by. Over the previous nine weeks, I'd seen her grow from a grieving widow, to slowly regaining her sense of identity. Selling her house and moving meant another period of adjustment, but if anyone could move forward with life after something like that, it would be her.

Uncle Terry's passing wasn't totally unexpected. He'd been chronically ill for a long time, and there were constant references about his health over the years. The initial daily conversation for the previous three months, when my father returned from work each day, had been to ask my mother if Uncle Terry was *still with us*.

When my mom suggested I go to Michigan and support Aunt Joan after her husband's passing, I'd appeared selfless by agreeing immediately to go. But, I had an ulterior motive for packing up and living with the drudgery of home-schooling for a while. I was running away.

Everything happens for a reason, or so I'd heard. My uncle's timely death gave me the ideal excuse to step out of my life and look at it from the sidelines. Or in this case, Michigan. Brad's crappy behavior had humiliated me, and staying with Auntie Joan gave me an excuse not to face anyone.

That was the only downside to going home—facing everyone at school again. Trying to hold my head high after Bradley hit a home run with Heidi, and their sickening relationship going viral on the high-school intranet, was pointless. After nine weeks away, I was ready to tough out any comments, but at the same time, I hoped enough time had passed and everyone had moved on.

At least I'd sent a clear message to the boys that, at barely sixteen, I wasn't ready to have a sexual relationship with any of them. Unlike Heidi, who lost her virginity only three days after her sixteenth birthday.

Mom talked for another ten minutes and, during that time, I'd argued and won my case to travel home by bus. Auntie Joan wasn't leaving until the day before Thanksgiving, and Martin would be home on Monday. If I'd stayed and traveled with her, I'd only have had two full days to spend time with him before he flew back on Saturday.

At six, the Sunday before Thanksgiving, I was climbing on a Greyhound bus, headed for home. An hour later, I questioned my decision to take the bus.

Fat raindrops splashed against the window and were washed away in quick succession by others. My vision was disrupted by the constant stream of new strands from the relentless shower against the glass. The heavens had opened, and the sound of the wet storm battered down on the bus roof as it grew. The force behind it was deafening.

Staring at the tiny rivulets of water against the windowpane, I allowed my mind to wander, contemplating what the holiday would be like. My lips curved into a smile when I saw Martin's face in my mind's eye and wondered if he'd had his hair cut shorter since the last time he'd been home. Dad had given him a hard time about looking like a girl.

I chuckled at that memory.

Martin had always been different. He was studying Theater Arts. He wanted to do stage design and production for large live events. My father said he'd be better off learning to drive a truck than any of that stuff, but he was secretly proud of his achievements so far.

It had been almost three months since I'd seen Martin. He was upset he couldn't make the memorial service for Uncle Terry, due to a college exam.

The rain gave way to a spectacular sunset, and was enthralled by the iridescent sky as we traveled along the open highway. Glorious oranges, blues, and yellows lit up the horizon. After a while they made way for purple, ruby red, and violet hues until eventually darkness fell.

I arrived at our hometown bus station and my heart leapt at the thought of seeing everyone again.

I saw my oldest brother Kayden before he saw me, as I stepped off the bus. He was on his tiptoes, neck extended, while his head moved left and right, looking past some of the passengers in front of me. I smiled widely when he caught sight of me and pushed his way past people to reach me.

"Valerie!" Kayden called out. When we made eye contact, his face broke into an infectious smile. All the girls thought Kayden was adorable, and his facial features looked similar to Martin's. They had the same eyes and mouth. However, Kayden's hair was light like our dad's while Martin and I were the only two siblings with dark hair. We resembled my mom. All four of us had Mom's dimples.

Reaching me, Kayden wrapped a strong arm around my waist and lifted me off my feet.

"Holy hell, Sis, look at you. We're going to have to lock you up now that you're back. You get more beautiful every time I see you. I'll have to beat the boys back with a stick," he said, then chuckled.

I swatted his chest and hugged him tightly. Kayden's warm embrace and the familiar aroma of his body-wash, paired with the faint smell of engine oil on his clothing, was comforting. Familiar. Kayden put my feet back on the ground and picked up my bag. We waited around for my luggage to be unloaded. Kayden seemed surprised to see me traveling so light, until I explained that Auntie Joan was bringing the rest.

While we walked to Kayden's car, he filled me in on the town gossip, and I sensed he was avoiding the issue of Bradley and Heidi, so I brought it up.

"They're not together," he said to reassure me.

"I'm over it. I just want everyone else to be over it as well, you know?"

Kayden nodded and glanced up. "She dumped him when she found out he'd filmed it, and no one else will go out with him. I'm proud of you, Valerie. If you'd have let that fucker into your panties, I'd—"

"Kayden! Stop. This isn't the kind of conversation I want to have with my big brother ... and no one is getting into *my panties*. I'm fifteen. I want a life first, not a baby."

Kayden chuckled and had the grace to look sheepishly back at me. "Sorry. I got carried away with the sick thought that someday some..."

"Enough, already." I smirked as my cheeks flushed with color. I'd been given "the talk" by Kayden and Martin several times in the past about saving myself. They were always on my back about it.

Of all my siblings, Martin was the most like me, and we had this effortless bond. I was close to all my brothers, and although I wasn't supposed to have a favorite, Martin and I had spent a lot of time together, and we were the most alike. Most of my friends thought it was weird that we hung out so often. But after a while, my girlfriends thought it was cool because they'd all had a crush on him.

Martin's buddies used to get annoyed if I turned up and Martin didn't let me tag along with them when they had something planned. I'd only hang out with him when they were sitting around in the park, or when they came over to hang out in our yard. Martin saw no harm in my being there at those times. He told his friends that, although I was his little sister, we were also friends, and just because I was younger than them, it didn't make me any less interesting.

I looked older than I was, and I had no interest in hanging out with kids my age. I wasn't shy, but when I was with Martin, I felt relaxed, like I could be myself. I'd led a sheltered life, compared to a lot of girls my age, and I lacked confidence when I went out in public, because most of my social life had taken place at home.

Hanging around a large group of adolescent boys meant I heard stuff I knew I shouldn't have had any idea about. I was around twelve when I'd started hearing about my brothers'—and their buddies' sexual encounters. I found out what a virgin was and listened to the boys talking about girls "putting out." Consequently, I'd learned which girls in high school were *easy* and *hot*.

Just after one of those conversations, Martin, and my eldest brother Kayden, taught me how a *nice* girl didn't let boys into her panties. Afterward, what I took away from that conversation was, while it was okay for all boys to take a shot at a girl, it was *my* job to say *no*.

At fifteen, I had the body of a woman. I had obviously developed earlier than most girls my age. I never had the slender, boyish-girl thing going on that a lot of teenage girls had when going through puberty. It felt like I'd gone to bed one night and had woken up the next day with a pair of 32DD breasts and curves in all the right places.

My brothers' friends had made comments on how I looked, which made all my brothers nervous. Kayden said I was the kind of girl men looked at twice. A "head turner," my dad called me. When I'd look at myself in the mirror, I thought they were biased, because I couldn't see what the fuss was about. I thought I looked quite plain.

One of my dad's cousins once commented that my emerald green eyes, with their flecks of hazel were "bedroom eyes." My dad flew off the handle and became irate at his statement. His cousin retorted with, "Just sayin'," right before my dad threw him out of our house. I never saw his cousin at our house again after that.

Growing up the youngest, and the only girl in a four-kid family, had its benefits and disadvantages in equal parts. Living with three older boys was great training for how to take care of myself, but they were all fiercely protective of me, and that sometimes drove me crazy.

Being the only girl, I'd learned to keep house from an early age, and I was organized and capable. None of the males in my family did anything for themselves. All their chore allocations involved being outdoors—stacking the woodpiles, mowing lawns, or washing the cars. My parents both worked, so it fell on me to learn how to use the washer/dryer, the stove, and my least favorite small appliance—the iron.

Martin did what he could to help me when he wasn't playing baseball, acting in the local theater, or working his paper route. Martin was the most like me in many ways, apart from him being a boy.

Chapter Two

AN EXTRA MOUTH TO FEED

*B*rittle, leafless trees greeted us as we crossed the street to Kayden's car. His old Ford Falcon was his pride and joy. From the age of thirteen, I'd seen more of Kayden's legs than his face. He'd spent every waking moment underneath the damned thing, up in the old barn behind the house, where he kept it parked.

"Looking good, Kayden," I commented as I patted the hood. Kayden's face lit up as he flashed a wide smile, showing off both of his dimples. He pulled his sleeve down, grabbed the edge with his fingers, and huffed out a breath on the hood to rub away an imaginary smudge he assumed I'd left behind. The black metallic paint gleamed.

"She's still my number one girl, Val." The way he'd said it made me stop and take a hard look at him. Kayden's face flushed a little, and I instinctively knew he was in love.

"Okay … and number two is?" Kayden reached down and pulled on the chrome handle, opening the door for me.

"Get in. I'm not talking about her in earshot of 'Sexy Susan' here."

"Kayden, it's a Falcon, not a nightclub stripper." I smirked and glanced at him, while he slid into his seat and turned the key in the ignition. The car purred to life, and Kayden smoothed both of his hands down the wheel to the bottom of it. He was about to release the hand brake when he turned and looked at me. His brow was furrowed in irritation.

"She's not an *it*, Val," Kayden admonished with an annoyed look, because I wasn't going along with him *gendering* his vehicle. Silence had fallen between us, and I stared out the window at the familiar landscape I'd known all my life, that I'd run away from. I leaned against the window, and my thoughts turned to how Kayden had always known what he'd wanted from life, and how I had no real clue about my direction. I knew I wanted to take pictures and had been thinking about photography, but I wasn't sure how much scope there was for earning a living taking pictures in our little town. Cars were Kayden's *thing.* He'd decided not to go to college, and instead took an apprenticeship with our dad in his car repair shop. I'd never understood why it fascinated him to lay under a smelly car all day, getting covered in oil. All I'd ever seen him do was tweak a few bolts here and there.

Apart from my brothers, I hadn't taken much notice of boys until I met Bradley Sutton. I developed a crush on him when I was fourteen and was amazed when he'd asked me to go to the movies just after Valentine's Day that year. I'd suspected he might have been interested in me when I caught him stealing glances at me every day at lunch. From the day I'd entered the school cafeteria, I felt his eyes on me.

Coleen, a friend and classmate, noticed him as well and began teasing us both. It was mortifying. We'd checked each other out for another two days before he got the balls to ask me out. For me, it had been deadly puppy love, and I'd somehow convinced myself we'd be together forever. However, Bradley began pressuring me about sleeping with him. Even though he was my world, I knew I wasn't ready.

I understood his need and my refusal was tearing us apart. I'd stupidly confided about it to Heidi, my best friend from school. She'd been incredibly supportive, and I felt relieved when she agreed Bradley was being "a selfish pig for pushing." I never considered she'd snag him for herself by doing what I wouldn't.

Breaking the silence, Kayden smoothly changed the subject.

"Adam and Jim are both playing later. Fancy coming to hang out on the bleachers with me?"

"How's Adam shaping up?" I asked with interest. Adam was the brother closest to me in age. At seventeen and a half, there were less than two years between us. Adam played on the high school football team with his best friend Jim. Both had already been offered full scholarships to a few colleges. Adam was looking forward to accepting his at the University of Chicago.

"Yeah, he's doin' good ... closing in on Jim's school record. I think Jim will be relieved when he moves on to college next year. Adam's proving himself to be stiff competition."

As Kayden answered, he swung off the road and down the long, tree-lined dirt driveway that led to our home. We had seventy acres of nothing but overgrown grass, except for the area of well-kept lawn nearest the house. My grandfather, my dad's father, had left it to my parents when he died. The house was amazing; it was more than a hundred years old and stood proudly at the top of a small hill.

The rest of our land was as flat as a floor and had given us kids an amazing amount of safety and freedom to play when we were little. Cookouts and campfires were a regular event at our place, and my parents had a lot of friends, some going back to their childhood.

I vaguely remember my father, Kayden, and Martin fencing our yard area. That was when Mom had decided we needed a defined picnic area to accommodate everyone during our family barbecues. As we grew up, home became the safe place for us to hang out and have parties with our friends.

Kayden muttered about the dust the car wheels kicked up from the driveway as we reached the house and he stopped the car. Buster, our nine-year-old collie, came bounding up when he saw us, and his claws made an excited tick-tac noise as he jumped on the window of the car on my side.

"Aww, Buster. Get the fuck down! You'll scratch the paint," Kayden complained.

He started to say something else, but it barely registered with me as I flung open the door and pushed myself out in the direction of my mom. She'd just opened the screen door on the porch and shrieked out to my dad that I'd arrived.

Bounding down the stairs, we ran toward each other at full speed. We met right as she reached the last step, and we threw our arms around each other. It felt great to hug her. A lump formed in my throat. I'd missed her a lot. Buster tried to get in on the act, jumping up on us; and when he couldn't get between us, he began licking Kayden.

"It's so good to have my baby back," my mom cooed. "You have no idea what it's been like around here as the only female in the house. None of these men know how to put the seat down on the commode, and I have a basket full of smelly boys' clothes to wash every day."

I glanced at Kayden. He shrugged his shoulders and smiled, leaning toward her and kissing her cheek. "One day you'll complain that there's no one to leave the seat up around here, apart from Dad, so enjoy it while you can, Mom."

Our mom's face registered the impact of Kayden's words and her smile instantly fell. Kayden reached out and pulled her into his chest, grinning down with affection at her. "I'm joking, Mom. I'm going to be one of those boys who still lives in the house when I'm fifty. All I'm saying is I may have learned to drop that pesky seat back in place after I've peed is all." Mom's face brightened into a loving smile again as she patted Kayden's chest.

"Now don't you go threatening me, young man. I'm dreading when your father becomes a grumpy ol' man, never mind having the both of you bugging me here when I'm in my twilight years."

Kayden released my mother from his hold and threw his arms around both of us. "Let's get Valerie settled before she remembers what life is really like here. We don't want to expose her to too much before she's unpacked her stuff. I'd hate to have her so ready to leave she'd run to the bus station under her own steam."

I shook my head, chuckling at their banter. I was finally home to stay. The nine weeks I'd stayed at Aunt Joan's place had been quite somber, given what had happened to her husband. Being back here—the one place I felt truly at peace—was amazing.

After we entered the house, Kayden ran upstairs with my luggage and then reappeared in the kitchen doorway as Mom was making coffee. Hanging on both sides of the wooden doorframe, Kayden cleared his throat. "Martin is getting in later tonight. They're driving down this time."

My heart raced with excitement at the unexpected early arrival, and then I realized what Kayden said and thought he may be bringing a girl. "They?"

"Yeah, Martin has a new roommate in his apartment. He moved in at mid-term, and he's bringing him here for Thanksgiving."

"Doesn't he want to go to his parents?"

"Some kind of orphan or something ... I can't remember what he said. Mom?"

Both of us glanced at our mom, who was over by the sink. She turned, wiping her hands on a kitchen towel.

"His name is Flynn, and stop calling him an orphan. He was in the foster care system. His foster mom died last year, and he moved to St. Cloud's for a clean break from the area. You know what a kind boy Martin is. He called asking if he could bring the boy back to spend Thanksgiving with us. Poor kid was going to be staying alone at college over the break. And, apparently, they have extra time for self-directed study, so it fits in for them to be here for an extra day or two."

Shortly after our brief discussion, Mom asked Kayden to run some errands. Pulling out his car keys, he asked, "Want to come, Val?"

"To be honest, Kayd, I need a shower, and I'm a bit sore from sitting on a bus for hours on end. I'm going to stay here and clean up. I think I'll fill the tub and soak for a while."

Kayden nodded and left to do the errands, while I went upstairs and relaxed in the bath. Twenty minutes later, I got out and wrapped myself in a huge, fluffy bath sheet, then wrapped a robe around that. With a smaller towel, I wrapped my hair turban style and walked over to my lovely, four-poster bed. I slumped onto the mattress and lay staring at the ceiling. It was great to be home.

I must have dozed off and was a little disorientated when I heard Martin's voice. "Are you intending to lie there all night, or can a brother get a hug around here?"

At first, I thought I was dreaming, but when my eyelids fluttered open and I saw Martin, my whole body sprang to attention. I squealed my delight at Martin, standing over me at the side of the bed.

"Martin! I'm so glad to see you. You made it home!" I leaped off the bed and flung my arms around his neck, hugging him tightly. I pulled back to study my gorgeous brother, noting his hair had gotten longer. I told him it was a good look on him. In fact, I bet it attracted more girls than even *he* could have coped with.

"As if I wouldn't? Mom's roast turkey and my favorite girl? I'd be dumb to pass that up. I mean, it's not that far to drive home." Martin smirked wickedly at his use of sarcasm, and I sat down on the bed with my arms behind me.

"You need to get dressed, honey. There's someone I want you to meet. I brought my roommate home with me. He's a nice guy, just had a shitty life, Val. I know I don't have to tell you to be sweet to the guy, but it would make it easier for me if everyone made him feel welcome. I'd like him to have a great family holiday for the first time in his life."

"Jeez, Martin, you'd think we were entertaining the Queen of England," I said, rolling my eyes.

Martin shoved his hands into the front hip pockets on his jeans, and stared at his feet for a second before looking me straight in the eye.

"Nope, he isn't; he's much more important than her. She's got plenty of family, he doesn't. I couldn't leave him in the apartment on his own during the holiday, but now that I've dragged him all the way here, I'm kind of responsible for showing him a good time."

I felt a small pang of guilt for his friend, and I nodded. Martin smiled widely, grabbed me, and kissed my cheek. "I love you, Beatnik," he said as he left the room. Staring at myself in the long, freestanding mirror, I giggled at the mess my hair was. It was almost waist length and curly, but it had dried under the towel, and I looked like a 70's poster for big hair.

I quickly pulled on some sweat pants and bra, and then took a checkered work shirt from the wardrobe and popped the snap buttons closed. I finger-combed my hair and put a little gloss on my dry lips. I figured it wouldn't matter what I looked like anyway, because no friend of Martin's would be interested in me, a kid of fifteen. Also, from what Martin had said, it sounded like he had an isolated upbringing and he might be socially awkward, not having anywhere to go for Thanksgiving and all.

Chapter Three

I WASN'T EXPECTING THAT

*F*eeling pleased about Martin being home, I hurried downstairs and had just about reached the living room when Mom called me to the kitchen.

"Valerie, is that you? Can you come here and carry a tray for me?"

Pushing the door to the kitchen open, I saw Mom had made sodas and coffees for everyone. A huge coffee cake was on another tray with small cake forks.

I smirked and wondered what Martin's friend Flynn would make of my mom's afternoon coffee. At twenty, I imagined he'd rather have been offered a beer than a cream soda float, or coffee and cake. I picked up the tray and left Mom shooing Buster outside so he wouldn't eat the rest when no one was looking.

While walking from one room to the other, I concentrated on the tray of drinks in my hand. I was standing in front of the coffee table when a soft, veiny male hand reached out and grasped one side of the tray. Another hand caught the other side in front of me. Long legs, belonging to someone slender and tall, were now within my sight. My eyes continued to trail upward, over the faded denim and taut navy-blue t-shirt, as I straightened. I almost fell over when I finally got a full look.

"Ah, at last. You must be the beautiful Valerie who Martin talks about all the time. I can see why now," he said in a soft tone, as his eyes raked slowly over me. Instantly, he had my undivided attention.

Flattery will get you everywhere, I thought, staring openly at Flynn in front of my family. I kind of froze on the spot. It was suddenly way too hot in that room. I knew my parents and brothers were all watching me, but I was speechless. Flushed and self-conscious, I was horrified at how frumpy I must have looked. When I looked up at his face, I saw a perfect mouth, attached to a perfect face, on the most perfect-looking guy I'd ever seen. *Perfect* was the only word to describe him. No one had prepared me for extent of this man's hotness.

As soon as we made eye contact, the genuinely soft smile he gave me instantly melted my heart. I was toast. Flynn's piercing green eyes were almost the same color as mine, but his were hypnotizing. All it had taken was one smile and our eyes connecting, for a current of electricity to create havoc within my body. My heartbeat soared, and I almost fainted with the heady feeling of instant attraction toward him. In a nano-second, I had developed a huge crush on Flynn, and I hadn't even spoken to him.

"I'm Valerie. Flynn, is it? Nice to make your acquaintance," I said in return and cringed inside at my less-than-sophisticated response. I sounded like someone from a historical romance movie, set in the deep South. I was almost sixteen, but my answer sounded like something a sixty-year-old woman would say while chatting with someone in the doctor's office.

He reached out his hand, and I slipped mine into it. Flynn's long, warm fingers curled around my hand and he squeezed it gently. I couldn't tear my eyes off him. Goosebumps crept over my body as the full effect of meeting him, and now touching him, sank in.

The guy should have come with a warning label. I was almost drooling as my unblinking eyes remained locked with his. Mentally, a little fantasy took hold, and I imagined my hands running frantically over his smooth cotton t-shirt.

Buster barking at the door brought me back to reality, and I remembered my parents and siblings were in the room. Luckily, they had begun talking about everyday things like football and stage sets, and something else I missed because I hadn't been paying attention. I pulled my hand back and sat heavily on the chair, still buzzing from his touch.

Try as I might, I was off my game in the room after that. I stared at him, drinking him in, while my brothers chatted naturally and tore each other up about things that had happened since the last time we'd all been together. Normally, I'd have been just as rowdy, but I found myself tongue-tied by the guy with the dark brown hair, athletic build, and mysterious smile, who was observing my brothers cut up. I couldn't stop watching him watching them with a twinkle of amusement in his gorgeous dark-green eyes.

"Earth to Valerie. Can you hear me?" Adam was waving a hand in front of my face, and I felt myself being drawn back into their conversation. I'd only heard background noise, and I had no clue what they'd been talking about. My mind had eloped with the hot new friend of Martin's somewhere along the line.

"Sorry, Adam. What did you say? I was wondering how Auntie Joan was coping on her own," I said, and prayed God wouldn't strike me dead for lying. Adam nudged my shoulder and smirked.

"I was just telling Flynn you play a mean tune on the guitar."

"I'm not playing the guitar, Adam," I said dryly, indignant that he should even mention that in front of our new guest. My parents used to make me sing and play for the neighbors sometimes, or at family cookouts. Kayden was a kickass drummer, and Martin sang a bit as well, but I was regarded as the musical talent in the family.

"Jeez, Val, I wasn't asking you to sing, just telling Flynn here you have something in common with him."

"I do?" Good grief, I really hadn't been listening.

"Have you been listening to anything we've been talking about?"

I must have looked like a complete airhead. I hadn't joined in any conversation. I glanced over at Flynn, who was obviously enjoying how distracted I was. His intent stare was fixed on me, and the twinkle in his eye was brighter as his grin grew even bigger. He looked relaxed with every one of my brothers, but he hadn't said much to me since our introduction. I was certain anything he said would have registered with me if he had.

As the evening wore on, Adam's friend Jim arrived. He and Adam left to prepare for the game. Kayden had already spoken to Martin, and when I'd found out he and Flynn were going to the game with us, I'd gotten a little flustered. I'd planned to go with Kayden dressed as I was, but there was no way I was going out with my hair looking like I'd been dragged through the bushes and then treated with a humidifier, with Flynn there.

I excused myself and ran upstairs. At lightning speed, I straightened my hair until it hung down my back, looking sleek and glossy. I applied mascara and the tiniest amount of blush. The final touch was some lip gloss after I'd changed my entire outfit. Twice. I knew it was pointless. I was too young, and he'd never notice me in any romantic sense, but I'd never met a guy who'd had such an impact on me.

I pulled on some black skinny jeans and a dark, ruby-red top, and grabbed a black sweater, because it always got chilly sitting in the bleachers. Martin knocked on my door just as I was tying my sneakers.

"We're heading out. Are you ready?"

I stood and flicked my hair behind my shoulders with both hands. "Yup, was just making myself look human again."

"Hmm, let's hope it's the opposing team's attention you attract and not our players, Val. You're gorgeous. I always worry about the effect you have on guys."

I smirked at Martin. "You're only saying that because everyone says I look like you, aren't you?"

Martin chuckled and nodded at my chest. "Val, if I looked like you, I think I'd have even more friends than I could handle."

I swatted his arm and strode past him.

"Martin, I'm your sister. That's inappropriate."

Martin chuckled and caught up with me, throwing his arm around my shoulder.

"I know. I'm just pissing you off so that you'll scowl at anyone who looks at you when we get to the stadium."

Flynn was downstairs when we went back to find him and Kayden.

Kayden smiled and picked up his car keys from the bowl on the console table behind the sofa. "Ready? I'll just go warm up Susie."

Raising his eyebrow, I could see Flynn was puzzled. "It's his car, Flynn. Susie's his car."

Flynn chuckled., "Cool, I was wondering if it was pay-per-view."

I didn't know how to react to Flynn's suggestive joke, and Martin smacked Flynn upside his head. "Sister," he growled.

Flynn shook his head, smirked, then raked his eyes the length of me. "Goodness, Valerie. I didn't realize we were supposed to dress up for this. You look beautiful."

Martin chuckled. "Flynn, trust me. You'll never get used to how our little Beatnik looks. Us Darsin boys spend most our time shooting menacing looks at anyone who comes within thirty feet of her."

"Glad I'm on the right team then, Marty. I'll have to remember that."

"Hello. When you're both done trying to get a rise out of me, are we going to see my brother demolish this other team or not?"

Martin smiled mischievously and shook his head. Then he spun me toward the door by the shoulders, and we headed out to join Kayden in the car.

Opening the back door for me, Martin ushered me to climb in first. I thought he would get in beside me, but he opened the front passenger door and got in there instead. Kayden and Martin struck up a conversation about Dad's workshop as Flynn slid in beside me in the back seat. His hand brushed the side of my thigh absentmindedly, while his other hand closed the door. My heart pounded with excitement at the thought of us sitting together in the back.

"Oh, sorry." He chuckled and grinned as he moved his hand away and straightened his jacket from behind him. He tugged on the seat belt and reached down to fasten it before he looked up, straight into my eyes.

I'd been staring at his head the whole time. He raised an eyebrow, smiled slowly, and pulled his bottom lip into his mouth. I blushed because he'd caught me watching him, and the sexy way he was chewing his lip. Every muscle in my body tightened, and I tried to control my heart as it hammered in my chest. He never made anything of it and stared ahead of him, listening to Martin and Kayden talking.

Once I settled from my reaction, I tried to relax into the seat. I drifted off into my thoughts about how handsome he was. My body sat limply as I looked out of the window, marveling at Flynn's closeness. Kayden suddenly took a sharp turn, and I was instantly hurled toward Flynn, flopping heavily into his side. My face brushed the side of his head as his strong hand reached out to steady me. He twisted to face me and for a second, I thought he was going to kiss me.

"Whoa, Val. No need to throw yourself at me, babe. You've already got my attention." Then he gave me a panty-melting smile. His mouth was so close to mine I'd felt his breath on my face when he'd spoken.

Heat rushed through me as I considered his flirtatious comment. There was no doubt about it, my initial assumption had been correct; I had an instant crush on Flynn. I stared at him a bit too long and saw a fleeting discomfort in his eyes when they darted back to the front seat, and Martin.

My brother's head snapped around in our direction, and from the startled look on his face, he'd noticed Flynn's comment had affected me. I knew I was blushing but I didn't comment. Fortunately, we were distracted as Kayden pulled into the stadium parking lot. Martin climbed out of his seat and closed the door. Kayden got out and opened my door while Flynn slid out the back on the other side. Martin grabbed Flynn by the shoulder and pulled him back. I don't think I was supposed to hear him, but I did anyway.

"Dude. She's my little sister, remember? I told you she's not like the girls you've hung around, Flynn. Stop fucking hitting on her. Last guy who did couldn't walk for a couple of days after Kayden kicked him in the balls. She's a bit innocent and has only ever had one boyfriend. You'd do well to remember that," Martin said through gritted teeth, warning him. The anger in his voice was primal.

Kayden walked toward them, chuckled, but reinforced Martin's warning. "Val's quite special to us, Flynn. Don't go pissing us off. Otherwise, your beautiful friendship with Martin will end as abruptly as it started."

Flynn shifted uncomfortably, dipped his head, and looked briefly sideways at me before he turned back to my brothers.

"Jeez, guys, I was only trying to make her feel good. She's only fifteen, for Christ's sake."

I was instantly crushed by his comment. His words stung, but he had the grace to look embarrassed when he glanced back at me.

Martin slapped Flynn on the back. "So long as we're clear—Val's off limits." He chuckled and pulled him in for a one-armed man hug. I'd been standing on the other side of the car watching the whole thing, and I was furious. I'd seen my brothers do that before, but that was the first time I'd felt belittled by them.

I was mortified that I'd fallen for Flynn's insincere flirtations as well. Hearing his comment about making me *feel good about myself* had done the opposite. I suddenly realized he saw me as an immature girl, and instead of wanting to go and cheer Adam on, I just wanted to go home.

Tears threatened to burst past the lump in my throat. I swallowed several times in succession as I fought to stay in control of my feelings. The last thing I wanted to do was flip out because I knew they'd guess I had a crush on him, and they would have highlighted my immaturity to Flynn.

My pace was slower than theirs after that, and I hung back, suddenly reluctant to be around them. Kayden turned and called out to me, "Come on Val, move it. Only five minutes until the game starts," and I knew there was no way out. I had to suck it up and put on a brave face for everyone's sake, including my own.

Heidi was one of the first people I recognized when we reached the bleachers, and my stomach formed knots.

"Oh, great. That's all I need," I muttered, slowing my steps as I hugged myself. Kayden gave me a pitied look, which annoyed me.

"Ignore her," Martin said flatly.

"What's the deal?" Flynn asked.

I could have died when Martin straight out told him what had happened, and I was humiliated all over again.

"Fuck. Way to go, Valerie. You need to pick your friends and boyfriends more carefully in the future," Flynn said.

I glared at him, shocked that he'd actually had the balls to state the obvious. He didn't even know me. I sneered.

"You think? Thanks for your advice. I may be young, but I'm not stupid. I'm not one for making the same mistake twice."

Stepping into me, he put his arm around me and I immediately felt comforted. "I'm sorry. That was a stupid thing to say. I didn't mean it like that. I was just mad at the thought of someone hurting you like that."

Flynn tilted his head and looked over to at Heidi before turning to Martin and Kayden. "I think that girl needs to be taught a lesson."

Martin immediately bristled in his stance, narrowing his eyes as he warily glanced at Flynn.

Turning to me, he said, "You've been out of town since this happened, right?"

I nodded but felt embarrassed and horrified that he knew my business.

"Alright. What better way to get back at her than to get even? She did you a favor by exposing that douchebag. And you weren't all that bothered, were you? Because you moved on with *me*."

"Hey, that's not happening, Flynn," Martin protested.

Kayden was nodding and smiling with Flynn. He obviously thought it would be a great idea, but Martin continued to argue his point.

"Nah, dude. I don't want our sister to look like she's dating a much older guy, or you with a young girl for that matter. It doesn't look right."

"Jesus, Martin. She's what ... four years younger than me?"

"Nearly five," Martin corrected.

"Lighten up, Martin, this is pretend. You don't have to worry. I'm not going to fuck your sister. I'm supporting her so that when she goes back to school, she does so with her head held high, and it kills the buzz around what happened."

My mind was centered on Flynn's comment: "I'm not going to fuck your sister." Hearing him talk in sexual terms about me made my heart flip in my chest. Even though he'd said it was something he wasn't going to do. *Why did he choose to say that?*

Kayden slapped Martin on the back and tilted his head. "Sounds like a plan to me. Let him do it. Heidi needs to be taught a lesson. Bradley too. It will send a message to everyone that Valerie has moved on."

"Better that it's Flynn, right?" Martin said, his voice still sounding less than impressed with Flynn's plan.

"Hello? This is *me* we're talking about?" Flynn turned and grinned widely. There was a playful look in his eyes, and my heart flipped over inside my chest again then raced excitedly.

"Exactly, Valerie. Do you want to face them when they're still ambiguous about your feelings, or do you want to send them a *fuck you, look-at-me* message?"

There was a plea in his eyes, as if he was willing me to say yes, and I'd wondered why he was so eager to make a show of himself on my behalf. I wondered if it was to impress Martin and Kayden rather than anything directly to do with me.

"Yes. I want that," I heard myself say decisively.

"Which one? Pick one."

"I want you to be my boyfriend." I blushed because, although the situation wasn't real, my feelings about it—and him—were.

Chapter Four

UP CLOSE AND PERSONAL

Seven minutes before the game started, we climbed the bleachers. Martin filed in first and sat down, followed by Kayden, Flynn, and then me. I'd never sat on the aisle seat before, and it felt weird not sitting next to Martin. Flynn served as a buffer zone between my brothers and me, probably so I would have the confidence to play my part with him. I just wasn't sure I was playing.

As we settled down to watch the game, Flynn slipped his arm around my shoulder and pulled me tight against him. His swift move took me by surprise, and I glanced up at his face. He wore the sexiest smile I'd ever seen as he winked and said, "Better make the most of the situation. We want this to have the maximum effect. This is how couples do it, right?"

Heat rose to my face. A rush of excitement flooded my insides and I clenched my thighs together. My panties were soaked, and I smiled slowly and nodded. I was speechless and too mesmerized to answer. Flynn chuckled and planted a quick kiss atop my head before settling down to watch the game. I, on the other hand, sat trying to cope with the tingle in my scalp from his kiss, and my pulse racing to keep time with my breath.

The thrill of my surreal situation at sitting in the bleachers of my high school, wrapped in the arms of the hottest guy I'd ever seen, was the biggest turn-on of my life. The downside of it all was I had the hugest crush on him, and he was almost five years older than me. It wouldn't have been so bad had I been eighteen or so, but he was a man, and I was still only a girl. And he was my brother's friend.

Colleen, another friend from school, walked up the bleacher stairs with Simon Hutton, who was also in our same grade. From the way they were hanging onto each other, I suspected they were a couple. Then again, that's what Flynn and I wanted people to think about us, so it could have been an act too.

I'd watched her scanning the bleachers looking for familiar faces, and then her eyes settled on me and widened. "Valerie. Wow. When did you get back?" Her curious eyes flicked between Flynn's and mine, as she began to stalk her way further up the wooden steps toward us.

"Only got back today," I said, not sure of what else I should add.

Flynn tugged me closer and kissed my head again. "Don't I get a mention, babe?" he murmured softly into my ear. I shivered. The heat of his breath tickled my ear as his intimate comment stole *my breath* for a moment. My heart pounded in my chest and accelerated when his thumb rubbed absent-mindedly against my bare arm.

"Of course," I stammered, turning toward him while I tried to clear the sudden fog in my brain. I found it hard to concentrate with his arms around me.

"This is Flynn... my..."

"Boyfriend," he explained, when I struggled for what to introduce him as.

Colleen was suddenly very interested in Flynn and focused her attention on him. Her eyes raked up and down his body as she introduced herself as one of my *best friends*. When she smiled at him again, it was much different than the one she'd given me. It was salacious.

"Hey, Flynn," she cooed, her voice almost an octave lower. Reaching up coyly, her hand found her hair and she twirled it for good measure. I couldn't believe she would flirt with him right in front of me, and after all the stuff with Bradley, not to mention poor Simon.

Flynn ignored her and looked out at the field where the boys were lining up to start the game.

"Oh, you won't get a response from him now, Colleen. Football is Flynn's passion. Isn't that right, honey?" I said, trying to sound as if I knew him that well.

"That and you, *babe*, but in the reverse order," he responded with a seductive growl as he turned to stare into my eyes for a second. His intense gaze almost melted my bones where I sat, and I sighed audibly.

"Well, I guess I'll leave you two lovebirds alone then," Colleen said wistfully, stumbling down the first step as she headed back to Simon. The poor sap had been waiting patiently at the bottom of the stairs for her. When she reached him, she glanced back up at us. I saw her take a deep breath and sigh heavily, and then turn to look at Simon in disappointment. I couldn't blame her for the effect Flynn had on her; he made me sigh, too. Watching her link arms with Simon, they began making their way over to Heidi, and I looked at Flynn. A smile curved my lips when he smiled back.

"Thank you," I said, and reached over to squeeze his thigh. It was solid muscle, and intense heat surged through me at how bold a move I'd made.

"Anytime," he replied, holding my gaze a bit longer than I felt comfortable with. I'd almost begun to look away when he winked and squeezed my arm. My heart skipped a beat. The guy tortured me with his flirting as I sat there with him, but I gave it my best shot and tried to focus on the football game.

Adam was amazing during the game, and I could see what Kayden meant about *matching Jim's ability*. Each time he got the ball, he was a blur running across the field. Extremely agile and fast, he twisted and weaved his way to score several touchdowns, much to the delight of the crowd.

Flynn never took his arm from around me during the game. Even when he reacted to Adam or the team making a good play, he'd take me with him as he stood up and cheered.

By the end of the game, most of the kids in my grade—even the ones above us on the bleachers—had noticed us together, and I saw pure envy on most of the senior girls' faces. If Flynn had seen them looking, he never let on. He kept his attention squarely on me.

It wasn't until we got back into Kayden's car that Flynn let the pretense go. Once he was sure no one was around, his arm trailed down my back and fell away. The loss of his touch made my heart sink. Flynn started to get into the car beside me, but Martin held him back saying he wanted some time with his little sister, and directed Flynn to the front seat. Once Kayden began to drive, Martin said what was on his mind.

"Well, you two sure put on one hell of a show out there tonight," he said, his voice not disguising how annoyed he was.

Flynn chuckled but didn't respond. There was an awkward silence between us all, so I answered because the tone of Martin's voice was angry.

"Yeah. It was fun. I bet all the girls will be questioning me on Monday about you, Flynn. I'm going to have to figure out some stories for them. Otherwise, they'll know we were fooling them."

I'd made light of what Flynn and I had done but wished for that time again, because I was already missing his arms around me. Martin seemed to relax into the seat at my comments, and I figured I'd done just enough damage control to convince him that I hadn't taken it seriously. Flynn had made it abundantly clear he wasn't interested in me, when we'd first arrived to watch the game. Even knowing that, I'd still enjoyed sitting there, allowing everyone to think we were an item. We'd certainly given them something else to talk about, other than my rejection by Bradley.

Kayden and Martin went straight from the car to raid the fridge for snacks as soon as we arrived home. Flynn surprised us when he suddenly asked if it was okay for him to take a shower. Martin turned and stared at him for a second, totally thrown by his request, then nodded.

"Sure, use the one in my room. Your room doesn't have its own bathroom, and the one in the hall is next to my parents' bedroom. I don't want you to wake them. Towels are in the cabinet beside the sink."

Martin went back to selecting things from the fridge, and Kayden was busy buttering bread rolls. The thing I usually loved about all the boys being home was that none of us were in a hurry to go to bed. We weren't all together often, so our routines would go crazily out of whack just to make up for lost time.

"Is everyone having beer, or am I making lemonade?" I asked. Dad was fairly liberal and allowed the boys a few beers at home, as long as they were sensible about it. At fifteen, I'd never had that privilege extended to me.

"Yup. All beers, Beatnik, except for you," Martin clarified.

My eyes sliced through him. For the second time that day, I'd felt a gap between my brothers and me, that had grown wider since I'd been gone. It was like I was suddenly not old enough to hang out with their friends, and I wasn't being treated as an equal.

The incident with Flynn clarified that. In their eyes, I was too young for the one guy who had caught my attention since Bradley. My feelings for Flynn were like nothing I'd ever experienced. Not that I *loved* Flynn—I wasn't that naïve—but I'd never had stronger emotions as those that bubbled up when he was near.

I stood motionless while everything ran through my mind, and the wedge that was forming between my brothers and me made my heart hurt. I'd never been upset by anything they'd said before.

"Actually, count me out. I'm tired. I'm going to bed. The bus ride must have taken more out of me than I realized," I said, wanting to escape to my room before I broke down in tears.

Martin stopped and turned to face me. "Are you okay, Val?"

Trust Martin; he'd always been so perceptive about me.

"I am. Just beat. I'll be better tomorrow," I'd said, trying to sound as if I would. Martin strode over and hugged me, as if he sensed my true pain. Taking a sharp breath, he hugged my head to his chest, and his strong heartbeat soothed me.

"It's so good to see you, Val. Sorry I've been aloof tonight. I've missed you, honey. We need to spend some time together tomorrow. I want my favorite girl to tell me all her latest news."

I looked up at him, and he smiled affectionately, which soothed my heartache a bit. "You bet, Martin. I'm looking forward to all those stories about the *hot* girls you've discovered at college."

Martin looked a little sheepish and replied, "Um, have I done that before? Sorry."

I smirked as I pushed away and headed for the kitchen door. "Don't worry, Martin, like you and Kayden wanted, I've got my built-in radar for guys like y'all. I've learned to spot them, so I'm good."

Kayden started chuckling, when Martin tried to protest that he wasn't really like that, and put him straight, "Come on, Marty, us men are *all* like that, to some extent."

I was thankful for Kayden's interjection because it gave the perfect distraction to excuse myself. I headed up the stairs and was turning the handle on my door when I heard another door open. I looked up and there he was. Flynn was leaving Martin's room. He was naked, apart from a white towel slung low around his hips. My jaw dropped at how beautifully sculpted his upper body appeared in the low light glowing from the open bedroom door. When he turned his head in my direction, I let out a loud gasp.

"Sorry, Valerie, I didn't mean to startle you."

"You didn't. I mean you did, but..."

I knew I was babbling because I wanted to tell him it wasn't the element of surprise had torn my breath from my lungs, but the half-naked specimen of a man before me.

Flynn stood silent, rolling his eyes the length of me, and an awkward vibe fell between us that hadn't been present earlier. The air between us grew thicker. I cleared my dry throat, and Flynn checked the tuck in his towel. He began to turn away from me.

"Sorry. I shouldn't be standing here half dressed like this. Are you going to bed?"

"Yeah. Tired," I muttered. Tingling feelings in places I didn't know I had, made my body hum with need. I wanted to wrap my arms around him, because I wasn't tired in the least.

Flynn stood there a moment longer before he nodded slowly. "Yeah, I'm feeling a little drained right now too. Go to bed, babe. Sweet dreams," he said, turning and making his way inside the bedroom.

"Thanks," I blurted out.

He hesitated and turned his head.

"For?"

"Tonight. The game ... you ... Colleen—"

"Anytime, babe," he said, smiling. I knew I shouldn't have read anything into him calling me *babe*, but at my tender age, I did.

I stood there watching him until he was gone, and the door handle clicked. I opened it and stepped inside. I closed the bedroom door and I leaned back heavily against it. I exhaled low and long, and couldn't believe the effect that man had on my body. Emotions ran strong through me, sad and unfair ones. No one had ever captured my heart and tugged on it as hard as Flynn, and I'd only known for less than a day.

Memories of being in the bleachers floated around in my mind, replaying visual images the whole time I prepared for bed. I knew, as hard as it was to admit, Flynn was almost twenty-one and I'd not even turned sixteen. That age difference didn't seem like much if I were older and less innocent, but I was neither of those things.

As I got into bed, the cold sheets distracted me from thoughts of him. The temperature outside had dropped toward the end of the game, and frost had made the grass glisten by the time we'd arrived home. The forecast was for snow the day after Thanksgiving, and my mind turned to Martin. I knew he'd have to drive back to school in that. My heart sank at the thought of them leaving, and my thoughts stayed with Flynn and Martin until I eventually fell asleep.

Chapter Five

CRUSHED

ootsteps on the landing woke me. The old oak wooden floorboards made it impossible for anyone to move around without being heard from my bedroom. My brothers used to sneak out their windows and climb down the rain gutters, because of that very reason. I sat up and scooted my way over the mattress until my legs dropped and my feet touched the old, cold, polished boards.

Remembering what had happened the night before, I'd decided to let my thoughts about Flynn go. I couldn't make myself older, more sophisticated, or *not* Martin's sister. I tried hard to accept that Flynn was just being kind, and that's all there was to what had gone on the previous day. To make the point to myself, I'd gone downstairs in my old flannel pajamas with my hair braided as it was before I'd gone to bed.

It was still dark outside, and the boys had only come to bed around five, so I'd expected to see my mom in the kitchen. The light was on but the room was empty, so I started to make a fresh pot of coffee. When I lifted the glass jug, it was still warm and there was a small amount in the bottom of it. Deciding to make toast, I grabbed a couple of plates from the cabinet under the countertop. When I stood up, Flynn was standing on the other side, staring straight at me.

"Holy fuck," I cursed, and dropped one of the plates to the floor. It smashed in half, straight down the middle.

Flynn's eyes widened. I wasn't sure if it was because the plate smashed, because I'd startled him by cursing, or because I'd unexpectedly popped up in front of him.

"Jesus. Don't move. I'll get a dustpan."

"Stop. Will you stop treating me like a kid? I can clean up after myself," I snapped.

Flynn froze where he stood and held up his hands. "Alright already. Sorry."

I stomped over to the utility room and came back with everything I needed to discard the plate, and clean the floor.

Flynn wandered out of the kitchen, and when I'd finished clearing up, I followed him into the living room. *Wow, bitchy much, Val?* I turned to him with apologetic eyes. "Sorry. I shouldn't have snapped at you."

"It's okay. You're upset. Want to talk about it?"

Did I? What was I going to say? *It sucks that I have the hots for you, and I'm only a kid? It sucks that you can make my body feel crazy things without even trying, things I can't do anything about?*

"Is it that Bradley guy? Are you still sweet on him?"

I rolled my eyes. "Bradley is a grade-A douche. He doesn't even figure into my thoughts anymore."

Flynn chuckled at my choice of words to describe my ex-boyfriend.

"Good. He doesn't deserve to be there, babe. I'm telling you, any guy who's nuts enough to cheat on you needs therapy."

Heat flushed my cheeks at his compliment, and suddenly I was glad I was near the sofa. Every time he called me babe, my head whirled. I sat down slowly, collecting my thoughts, before I glanced up at him. The last thing I'd expected him to do was come and crouch near me, leveling his face with mine.

"Valerie, you're a very beautiful girl. Any man would be proud to call you his one day, and believe me, I'm not saying that to make you feel better. Just make sure it's not one of the Bradleys of this world. You deserve to be treated like the princess you are, and if the lucky guy who gets you doesn't, I'm sure your brothers will straighten him out."

Flynn traced my face gently with his finger and placed his palm on my cheek. I leaned into it and reveled in the warmth from the coffee mug he'd been holding. A slow smile played on his mouth and then he narrowed his eyes, dropped his hand, and stood back up.

Despite the fact I was sitting on a huge sofa, he chose to sit on the sofa on the opposite side of the room. I stared at his back as he walked away, wondering if I'd imagined he'd made that intimate gesture, or whether it was what I'd wanted to happen. I stood and made my way back into the kitchen, because I had no idea what to do after he'd said that.

After everyone else got out of bed, the day passed without any further incidents to suggest that Flynn liked me. I began to relax and felt comfortable again sitting with everyone. They talked about an eclectic range of things—from stage settings and technology, cars, and football—to the benefits of the latest smartphone Kayden had bought.

Adam got Flynn on the subject of music and Flynn told us he was studying classical music at college, but he said he loved all genres. Adam dragged me into the conversation when he told Flynn I played the guitar. I wanted to punch him for telling Flynn it was my "party talent" when there was a cookout at our house. Flynn glanced at me and smiled.

"Maybe she'll play something for me someday."

"And maybe Adam will have that loose tongue of his frozen and stuck to a metal pole if the weather permits," I responded, scowling at them both.

Flynn and Adam chuckled, and Adam asked Flynn if he'd play something for us.

As soon as the spotlight fell on Flynn and his music, embarrassment painted his face.

"Sorry guys, I don't do public performances unless it's a necessity for a grade. My college gigs are bad enough. I'm more of a one-on-one performer. That's why I chose to study to become a mentor. I'd die if I had to get up on stage and play for a living."

I stared in disbelief, thinking he was joking. Until that moment, he'd seemed like one of the most confident people I'd ever met.

Martin had been on his laptop and was obviously well out of the conversation, but he tuned in when he heard Flynn talking.

"My mom and my grandpa died within seven months of each other. I went to live with my uncle for a while but—"

Something held him back as he sat silently, as if in deep thought.

"Where's your dad?" Adam asked, with a complete lack of insight into Flynn's foster care history.

"Don't be so nosy, Adam. Flynn pushed himself to learn music as a form of therapy. He doesn't like talking about his past," Martin warned.

Seeing how uncomfortable Flynn was, I tried to distract Adam from asking any further questions. "Anyone want a soda or anything?"

Flynn nodded and gave me a half smile before swallowing, and I watched pain pass over his face. A dark look settled in his eyes.

"Let's just say my dad isn't a very nice man. Anyhow, I ended up in foster care and after a few years in a children's home, I was placed with some awesome foster parents. They were much older, in their late sixties, when I was placed with them. I was a hard-to-place kid, but Yvette knew exactly what to do to get the best out of me. I had my grandpa's old classical guitar, and instead of sitting, questioning me about my life, she decided I should try music as a way of connecting with the world."

Staring straight at me while he spoke, I felt a little unnerved, like the conversation Flynn was having was too intimate to share for the short time we'd all known him. I'd heard someone say it was easier to talk to strangers on a late-night radio station program before, so I wondered if that's how Flynn was viewing it all. He went quiet for a few minutes and then he spoke again.

"I'll admit, I'd been somewhat unmanageable until then, but I thank my stars every day for that woman's insight, because music healed my soul. They were amazing people." His expression grew somber. "Both passed last year just after I left to go back to college. I could have stayed where I was with the short amount of time I had left at college, but I wanted a clean break from Atlanta. Too many memories."

Flynn's voice cracked a little at the end, and he turned his head and stared out the kitchen window for few moments, seemingly in deep thought again. We all sat silently until he smiled and looked up. "So glad I did too, because here I am in this awesome family, sharing Thanksgiving with you all."

When he'd opened up to us, I had the urge to hug him. Maybe I'd wanted to hug him for me as well. I couldn't imagine what it would be like to be nineteen and lose the people I loved. *It must have taken a lot for him to expose his soul like that.*

Martin stood up and snapped his laptop closed. "Right. Come on, Flynn, get your coat. We're heading out for the night. I've rounded up some of the guys, and I heard through the grapevine there's a party going down. It'll be good to catch up with everyone, and I can introduce you to a few of my old buddies."

I didn't want him to go out. I wanted him to stay so I could learn more about him.

Flynn looked at Adam, then at me, like he wanted to stay as well. Less than a minute later, he tapped the table, and his wooden chair scraped back slowly on the tile floor as he stood up. A soft smile spread on his lips as he glanced down at me. "Thanks for listening. I guess I'll catch up with you later," he said, and excused himself.

Both Martin and Flynn went to find Kayden and, as usual, Kayden played chauffer. Adam and I curled up and watched an old movie on TV about the world ending yet again. Once it was done, I prepared for bed. Mom and Dad had gone out to visit some neighbors and weren't back by the time Buster was creating havoc at the door, demanding to be let out.

We always went out there with him because we worried a bigger animal would hurt him after dark. I'd already changed into my pajamas, but I still wanted to protect him. It was freezing outside, so I pulled Dad's huge wax-proof jacket off the peg in the utility room to wear. Grabbing Buster's leash just in case, I unlatched the door, and he bounded outside.

Immediately, he headed for the old barn at the back, and I went after him when I noticed the light was on. I figured Kayden had forgotten to turn it off when they left. He'd been working on Susie, as usual, when the boys had gone to find him, and it wouldn't have been the first time he'd left without shutting everything off.

As I neared the barn, I heard Flynn's voice. I couldn't make out what he was saying, but I heard Martin exclaim, "Damn. That was amazing."

I slowed up when I heard a girl giggling, and I was almost visible to them by that time. I peered into the barn, and at first, I couldn't see anyone. Then I saw Flynn. His jeans were around his ankles, and Daisy McGinty, from Martin's high school class, was standing with the foot of one bare leg balanced on the hood of a car Kayden had bought for spare parts. Her other foot was on the ground, her jeans pooled around that ankle.

Staring at Flynn's tight, bare backside was the last thing I'd expected when I'd headed out to the barn. From the angle of my view, I could see one taut butt cheek, but the rest of the view was horrific. My heart felt like it was caught in a vice.

The shock of seeing two people "doing it" was one thing, but the fact it was Flynn with his pants around his ankles, crushed me. I almost turned and ran, but I couldn't turn away. Something rooted me to the spot. Being able to watch him in that situation turned me on.

My panties became notably soaked, and when the night air cooled my heat, I was painfully aware of the lustful effect he'd had on me from that cold, wet patch of material between my legs. Jealousy raged inside me, and my furious reaction appalled me.

Hooking up for ten minutes of pleasure wasn't how a boy should treat a girl. All his talk about how boys should treat me well, and he'd forgotten all his words the moment he'd gone into the barn with Daisy. My feelings were in conflict, everything from lust to hate, anger to excitement, passed through me until there were so many they swept over my mind and body. I was both freaked out and fascinated by what I saw. Then I settled once again on being crushed.

Whatever he was doing to her obviously felt good. Daisy's soft then louder moans and words of encouragement were both needy, urgent, and full of praise. My heart ached at the sight of them together. Flynn's hand moved fast between her legs as he buried his face in the bend of her neck. Watching him do that to her affected me, to the point that everything lower than my belly button pulsed, aching for him to do those things to me. He was pleasuring her in a way I'd only ever imagined.

After a couple of minutes, Daisy's legs buckled and she screamed before she slumped forward and Flynn held her close to his chest. They both chuckled, and Flynn held her head again and kissed her hungrily. The intimacy between them left me feeling abandoned. I had no reason to feel that way. He wasn't mine. Daisy pulled away from him with a smirk on her face and mascara smudged black underneath both eyes. She dropped to her knees, and Flynn turned to her but was now almost directly facing me.

Quietly, I stood watching them. Flynn's butt was no longer visible, but I saw his reaction the instant she must have taken his cock in her hand. His eyes closed and he tilted his head back. I was devastated and desperate. I wanted to be Daisy. I wanted Flynn to want me the way he wanted her, to look at me the way he was looking at her.

I swallowed hard and thought it was never going to happen with me, and that realization crushed me. Daisy sat to the side of his feet on the barn floor, and my breath hitched because her change in position meant I'd been able to see all of him. She began licking his cock, fondling his balls, and stroking his shaft. My view was, unfortunately, perfect.

Turning away from the sight of them, I heard Flynn gasp. I looked back and saw Daisy had taken his dick in her mouth. She was stroking his shaft with one hand and sucking at the same time.

Tears rolled down my cheeks, but I stayed and stared at Flynn's face, his head thrown back facing the barn ceiling, and his eyes closed again. Both of his hands were cradling her head, and his hips were canting back and forth while his cock thrust in and out of her mouth. She gagged a few times but grinned, and time after time, she took him back between her lips. Eventually, Flynn pulled out, and I saw threads of his cum shoot over her hair. I'd never seen anything like that before, and the rawness of what they were doing choked me.

Without a sound, I turned away and picked my steps carefully for the first ten to ensure I didn't make any noise. Then I quietly headed back to the house. Thank God I'd never seen Martin like that; I never heard him or saw Martin again while I'd been at the barn, so I assumed he'd cut out before the freak show began. Buster lay down in his bed as we went inside and I turned the light off. My stomach was upset, and my chest felt tight as I made my way upstairs.

Slipping into bed, I fought back a huge lump I just couldn't swallow down no matter how hard I tried, and I wept silently for having a foolish crush on Flynn.

The next thing I remembered was waking to Buster barking, as the sound of tires crunched on the dirt driveway outside the house. Placing my feet on the floor, I wandered to my small box window in time to see my parents' old Buick disappearing in a cloud of dust.

The memory of Flynn from the previous night came to mind. My stomach lurched and fell, and depression sank in. I'd thought it was stupid to have such strong feelings for someone like him. So, I made up my mind right then to get past those feelings, for the sake of my sanity.

Chapter Six

YOU HAVE NO IDEA

ornflakes and scrambled eggs waited for me as I walked into the kitchen. "There you are, Valerie. I was just about to call for you. Eat up. We've got to make tracks and pick up the stuff on the list Mom left for us to get at the store," Adam said.

"Where is Martin? Isn't he coming today?"

Adam smirked knowingly. "I heard them come home at six this morning. He's probably still asleep. I think he and Flynn made a night of it somewhere."

I sank into my chair at the table. I knew where "somewhere" was, and as I poured cornflakes into a bowl, I still fought to purge the images I'd seen, from my mind. I ate in silence and then went to shower and dress, while Adam got his car ready. Us kids always went to buy all the fruit and vegetables every Thanksgiving week.

Adam chatted excitedly about football, his upcoming graduation, and what he wanted to do after college. I sat listening until he turned to look at me.

"What's wrong, Valerie? You're very quiet. You worried about going back to school?"

"Not in the least. I'm over all that. I just want to keep my head down and get good grades." My answer seemed to satisfy him, and he changed the subject back to his beloved football.

We arrived at the store, and the rest of our errand was uneventful. When we returned home, Martin and Flynn were already up, playing a video game in the living room.

Flynn turned and gave me a broad smile, and my heart flipped over just like all the other times he'd done that. I gave him a tight smile in return and walked to the table. I picked up my tablet and went up to my room.

Opening the Kindle app, I scrolled through the books I'd downloaded and chose a romantic-comedy to read. I needed something to lift my mood, and distract me. Around half an hour later, Martin knocked on my door. "Hey gorgeous, there you are. Did I do something wrong?"

Martin had been home for over thirty-six hours and we'd hardly spoken.

"Of course not. I was just giving you time with your friend," I answered, in as genuine a tone as I could muster.

"Well, thank you, but you don't have to do that. I see him every day at St. Cloud. I don't get to see you there. You're my friend too, Val. Is that what this is— you're avoiding me because I brought a buddy home?"

"You're the one who went out last night. I'm not avoiding you. I'm just giving you … space."

A split second later, Martin whipped my tablet from my hand to get my attention, and plopped down on the mattress beside me. "Bullshit, Beatnik. What's going on? What did I do?"

Tears sprang to my eyes, and a lump grew in my throat again. I tried to move away from him, but he caught my wrist and pulled it back.

"Val. Stop. Don't you dare turn away from me. It's me—Martin, remember? I've known you all your life, and I know when you're not being honest. What's going on in that pretty little head of yours, making you hide away like this?"

Every pent-up emotion spilled from my body and I cried. Martin

39

tugged me tightly to his chest and rubbed my back as he rocked us both back and forth.

"What is it? You can tell me, Val. You can tell me anything. This is you and me. We don't do secrets. Share what's going on. Maybe I can help."

"You can't make me eighteen." I sobbed. I was distressed, and when I heard what I'd said, it sounded like such a stupid thing to say.

"Eighteen? Why the fuck do you need to be eighteen?" His eyes searched mine, and his face scowled. "Is it because of Flynn? What he said the other day when I thought he was hitting on you?"

I considered telling him the truth, but I knew Martin well enough to know that if I answered *yes* to his question, I'd never have seen Flynn again, and I *didn't* want that.

"No. What made you say that?" I said, trying to sound as if I was stunned he should even think such a thing.

"Maybe it's that brotherly thing where I want to punch every guy who looks at you, Val. I spoke to him before we came here. Flynn, I mean. I warned him about you and how attractive you were and told him to be entirely appropriate. He's a great guy, and I don't think he'd make a move on you out of respect for me, but he's a... ladies man."

"Didn't Kayden say you're all like that, Marty?"

Martin smiled and looked sheepish. "He did. And we are—which is why I'm hoping I didn't make a mistake by bringing Flynn here."

"You didn't, okay? It's me. Last night and the night before, you all made a big deal of me being my age. I can't change that about me. It's never been a problem before, but suddenly it is. I've gone from being Valerie—the girl with three amazing brothers who were my friends—to the kid sister who needs three growly bears around to warn all the boys away, like they're all after my cherry."

A growl tore from Martin's throat. "Don't talk like that. You're not that kind of girl, Val. I love that you're young, strong willed, and have a mind that isn't shaped by all those giggling girls you know at school. We've always treated you the same, regardless of your age. I think it's just *this* age. It's hard for us. We're almost all adults, and we're kind of mindful that you are at a sensitive age right now."

His reply didn't make me any happier. It just confirmed that I was always going to be young as far as Flynn was concerned, and that was pure torture to hear.

"I'm sorry, Martin. I don't want to spoil your visit home. I've never really felt this way around you all before. I used to enjoy being the little sister, but I guess I'm outgrowing it."

"Respect is important, Val. No matter how young or old someone is. We've all got to support each other. Look at Flynn. Poor guy doesn't have anyone in the world to care about him. You think he gives a fuck about how old someone is? That worries me about him. He wouldn't hold back because of age. I respect you, and I'm sorry if you felt I put you down by the way I acted yesterday. I know you know right from wrong. I trust your judgment. It's everyone else's that I have issues with."

"Even Flynn?"

"Even Flynn, Val. He's a great guy—one of the best I've ever met. One thing that concerns me about him is I've seen girls go insane for him. He's a chick magnet. I love having him around, but I don't want someone like him for my baby sister."

"Flynn would never look at me like that, Martin. I'm just a kid, and he's a man."

Martin was silent as he stared intensely at my face and then his eyes flitted over it. He smiled a half smile and brushed a strand of hair from my face. "This may be an inappropriate thing for a brother to say, but I'm going to, just this once. I want to let you know why us Darsin men behave the way we do, when it comes to you. You have no idea how beautiful you are, Valerie. I don't think age would ever be a barrier for most men with you. Why do you think Kayden and I want to protect you so much? We've heard comments from buddies, who are no longer part of our lives because they voiced their thoughts about what they'd *do* to you. And Flynn ... there's just under a five-year difference, I think. That's too close in age for me."

Heat stained my cheeks, and Martin looked a little awkward as he stood up from the bed.

"Whatever it takes, I'm here for you Val. We're family. Everyone else is dispensable. Anyone disrespects you, Kayden and I... and Adam for that matter, we've got your back. We're always going to want more for you than the average guy."

Once Martin had said his piece, I wanted to say mine. If we were clearing the air, then I had to be frank with him about what his comments meant to me.

"Martin, how come guys can do what they want when they want, but it's different for a girl? You know I'm turning sixteen Christmas week? Do you all breathe a sigh of relief then? You said I have a mind of my own, but on the other hand, you think my judgment isn't good enough to pick my boyfriend?"

"You picked Bradley, Val."

Throwing Bradley in my face was the last thing I'd expected. It hurt.

"Okay, Martin, this conversation is over." I felt humiliated all over again. I rolled away from him and got out of the bed. Striding over to my bathroom, I stepped inside and banged the door closed.

"Shit! I didn't mean that, honey." Martin's voice was laced with frustration as he rattled the door knob. I sat on the toilet seat and ignored him at first. "Come on, Val. Open the goddamn door."

"Or what, you'll go all caveman and kick it in? Go away, Martin. If your talk was meant to make me feel better, it didn't work."

I turned on the water faucet so I couldn't hear what he said after that. Eventually, he went quiet, and I stripped down and got into the tub. Wetting a washcloth, I covered my face and lay back with the rim of the bathtub under my neck. *Life sucks.*

Almost an hour later, I got out and dried myself. The water was freezing, and skin on my fingers resembled prunes. I didn't want to go back downstairs and face Martin, and that was a first. The gap between us had widened, and I hadn't seen it coming. The thought made me cry all over again.

Mom knocked on the door as I was pulling up my yoga pants. I'd already put my t-shirt on. She hadn't waited for me to answer before she pushed her way into the room. Her expression was sad when she saw mine, and she hugged me.

"This isn't like you at all, Val. What's going on with my baby?"

The word *baby* made me feel even worse, and I shook my head, unable to speak. My throat swelled with emotion, and for the first time in my life, I wished I were anywhere else but home.

"Do you think being at Auntie Joan's for so long has brought your mood down, honey?"

I hadn't thought of that and wondered if it was a possibility. Was it a delayed response to keeping it all together for the time I'd been up in Michigan? "Could be," I squeaked, happy to accept any reason for my misery, other than my feelings for Flynn.

Mom talked me into going down for dinner, and when I arrived in the sitting room, Martin stood up and leaned in to hug me. Placing a kiss on my cheek, he whispered, "Sorry, sweetheart."

I nodded but said nothing. I just wanted to forget our whole conversation from earlier. Flynn looked up with a fleeting wave of concern in his eyes but quickly turned to ask my mom what time my aunt was arriving.

Afterwards, the focus wasn't on me anymore. We sat to eat, and I listened to Flynn tell my dad that his tutors at college didn't think he'd make it as a mentor. One commented that there was too much rock and roll in Flynn for him to succeed in the dull environment of being a classical guitar mentor.

Martin chuckled heartily and told us Flynn had confidence in any situation, except when he had to display his talent.

"I count myself fortunate he lives with me. Every night, without fail, I hear this frantic, full-on flamenco guitar playing, which turns into Led Zeppelin or Metallica tunes after half an hour. He's amazing —but ridiculously awesome. Problem is, he's so shy when it comes to his music, but I think he's got enough talent to rival the best of the best."

Flynn looked suitably mortified that Martin had bragged about his playing abilities. "He's lying, of course. I'm okay. Just not good enough to earn a living at it is all."

I noted Flynn's hands. His fingers gently touched his silverware nervously, then he wrapped them around one of the bulb-shaped glasses my mom used for water. Watching him lift it to his lips, I suddenly became thirsty, and my tongue darted out to wet mine. As I did, he looked over at me and smiled around his glass. *Crap.*

As if on cue, Auntie Joan's headlamps shone through the kitchen window, and Kayden's wooden chair legs scraped back against the tile. "She's here," he announced. Both of my parents and Buster headed straight to the back door to welcome her.

Dad called to the boys to lend a hand, and all three left the table. Flynn almost stood, but Martin told him to stay with me. My cheeks filled with heat at Martin's command, and Flynn stared at me with a puzzled look on his face. When they'd gone outside, Flynn covered my warm hand with his cold one, from holding the drink, and he offered a soft smile.

"I'm really sorry, Val."

Confused, I wondered what he thought he had to be sorry for. He'd been the perfect houseguest, apart from stealing my heart and fucking Daisy McGinty's mouth. But he never knew how I felt or what I'd seen.

"I don't understand," I replied.

"The barn— Daisy. I don't know how much you saw. I feel bad about you seeing that."

My heart skipped a beat as I tried to find something clever to say in response. Something to help me deny I'd witnessed any of what he'd done with her. I couldn't think of anything. I was a bad liar, and my bitter side rose to the fore.

"You knew I was there? Well, you weren't feeling bad enough to stop. Yes, I saw some of it, but I wasn't snooping. Buster just headed for the barn and with the light on I— anyway, it's no big deal, and it's not like I haven't been around stuff before. I have three brothers, after all. Although, I have to admit, I've never seen any of them fuck a girl's mouth before."

"You don't have to remind me of your brothers. It's not like I could fail to notice them. They protect you with everything they have. I'm not your brother, though, Valerie. It had to be different seeing me do those things to her. Were you turned on? Did you feel jealous?"

He was so spot-on! It had turned me on, but the thought of him with another girl had made me want to vomit at the same time. "What do you mean?" I retorted.

"You're almost sixteen, Valerie. You've got raging hormones. I'm not stupid. I know when a girl breaks out in goosebumps, she's responding to my touch. What you probably didn't notice was that when you touched my thigh up there on those bleachers, my skin did the same."

Flynn's eyes darted to the doorway to check that we weren't being overheard. Then he ran his thumb over mine.

"I fucked her mouth because I couldn't have you. Do you know *that*?"

My stomach instantly rolled and knotted at his words. To think for a second that he felt something for me too brought on a sudden head rush, but then again, I wondered if he was just playing with my feelings. I pulled my hand away and placed it on my lap.

"Stop it! Stop toying with me, Flynn. It's a horrible thing to do. Leave me alone."

"Stop? If you weren't Martin's sister and only fifteen, I'd pin you to the fucking wall right here. You're so fucking innocent and hot, you take my breath away."

I'd have given anything for those words to be genuine before I'd seen him with Daisy. I wanted to believe him. In my head, this was where his mouth claimed mine in a scorching-hot kiss and his hand slipped down to caress between *my* legs. My reasoning kicked in, and I thought, *hot men who hit on dull teenagers are plots reserved for the movies.* What Martin told me about Flynn suddenly made sense. Flynn had seducing girls down to a fine art.

"Save your lines for girls like Daisy, Flynn. I'm not interested. Like you said, I'm fifteen. I don't need guys like you to make me feel good about myself. You don't need to pin me to a wall. There are plenty of eighteen-year-old girls, and older, out there you can do that to."

"You're right, you're too young, so have it your way, Valerie—for now ... but if I'm still around when you're older, I may just do that, and if I ever have you..." Flynn stopped talking and stretched up to look out the window. Then he leaned in and spoke in a sexy, hushed tone that sent a shiver down my spine. "I may just die, trying to get enough of that sweet body of yours, pretty girl."

It was my turn to check if anyone was in earshot while my heart hammered in my chest. I was out of my depth, and I had no clue how

45

to respond to a comment like that. Then something he'd said to Adam and my dad came to mind.

"I can see what your tutors at college mean. There's far too much rock star in you to be a contender for anything serious. Leave me alone, Flynn. I'm glad you fucked Daisy and not me. She's more your type. I hear she puts out for anyone. Just hope you both used condoms. There are a lot of serious STD's in the world."

Unable to stem the bitterness from my voice, I'd allowed my passion for Flynn to spill into words. We both knew he shouldn't have spoken to me that way, but the passion in his voice was raw. Like he was getting off on voicing thoughts he knew he'd never get the opportunity to put into action. If I thought he was serious, my newly discovered reckless side may well have given in to him.

The thought shocked me. The angel in me had already preened her wings and was floating off into the distance. No matter how magnetic my feelings were for him, I had to stop wanting someone who I knew without a doubt, had the ability to destroy any idea of the happy life I imagined for myself.

Auntie Joan's voice called out from the doorway, and Flynn straightened up in his chair, his hand back on his glass and a ready smile on his face, as she entered the kitchen. Pushing his chair back with his legs, he stood and wrapped his hand softly around Auntie Joan's offered hand. Flynn was once again the charming young man Martin had brought home for Thanksgiving, outwardly at least.

The rest of the evening was a bit of a blur for me. I sat mulling over everything I'd learned about Flynn, everything he'd ever said to me. Finally I looked at myself and how I had responded.

There was no doubt about it. My feelings were real. I had a crush on Flynn, and he'd made it clear he liked what he saw in me, but he'd told himself I was too young. I consoled myself that it was just as well because, in a few days he'd be gone. And I'd have even more heartache than I felt at that moment. As soon as I could escape the family crowd, I excused myself and went upstairs to my room. I'd never been uncomfortable in my home before Flynn arrived.

I slid between my sheets and my mind whirred relentlessly with thoughts my aching heart absorbed. Maybe Martin was right. He'd warned me about Flynn, and my track record with Bradley had proven I had no idea what I was doing with boys. I decided I'd have to be careful around Flynn until they left to go back to school. Then I'd work out how to get over him. I tossed and turned at that thought, until I exhausted myself and finally fell asleep.

Chapter Seven
SECOND WARNING

The dog scratching at my bedroom door pulled me from sleep. Dawn wasn't even on the horizon as Auntie Joan and Mom spoke to each other on the landing outside my door. It was farcical that they thought they were quiet, because the volume of their speech resembled stage whispers. I'm sure they could have spoken quieter in their normal voices. When they'd reached the kitchen, the sound of metal pots and pans made me feel guilty about lying in bed, when there was so much to do for our Thanksgiving dinner.

I dressed in loose, gray sweat pants and pulled on a white, fitted t-shirt. As I left my room, I got a fright when a hand grabbed my wrist. A second hand went over my mouth and muffled my scream. "Shh, babe," Flynn whispered so close to my ear it made me shiver. I hadn't heard him on the landing. Somehow, I knew it was him. There was something raw in the action of his hand pressed across my mouth. It made my heart rate spike, and ignited passion and desire throughout my body.

His naked chest was so close I could feel his heat. He smelled of shower gel and that musky boy smell, but it was distinct from the scent of my brothers. It was unique to him and so enticing. It made me want to put my face to his skin and inhale his scent deep into my lungs.

A smile curved his mouth in the low light from my room, and I noticed his unshaven jawline when his perfect lips began to move. "Valerie, I'm sorry about yesterday," he whispered softly in a rushed and apologetic tone, as his hand dropped from my mouth to my shoulder. His callused fingertips brushing against my soft skin was like the ignition paper at the end of a firework. It felt precarious, as if the slightest friction was going to set me ablaze.

I pulled my wrist out of his grasp, and he didn't resist. Instead, he held his hands up as if surrendering. Glancing quickly over his shoulder in the direction of my brothers' bedrooms, he looked back and met my gaze again before stepping even closer. His forearm brushed against mine as he spoke in a low murmur. "I had no right to say what I said to you. It was a shitty thing to do." Sincerity shone in his eyes.

"Then why did you say those things to me?" I bit back as my anger rose.

"You got me all frustrated," he said, and shrugged. He reached out and took my hand. I tugged it away from him as fast as he'd touched it.

"So you decided to humiliate me? What did I ever do to you, Flynn?"

"You were watching. All you had to do was step into that barn, and everything would have stopped. I would have stopped, Valerie," he said, shaking his head.

I stared in disbelief at him for a long pause before I closed the gap between us. I controlled my voice to tamp the anger brewing in my belly. My head dipped toward his and, in a low, angry whisper I said, "Oh! So now I'm the reason you fucked Daisy McGinty? It's my fault she was in our barn with her leg perched on Kayden's junk car? You knew what you were doing when you invited her back to our place, so don't go trying to excuse what you did by making this about me. I'm sorry I was there. That wasn't my intention at all. Jesus, I wanted to come back inside and bleach my eyes to get rid of the sight of you both."

"The sight of what, Valerie? Two people consenting to share each other's bodies? Two people having raw pleasure with no bullshit attached? An attractive girl being pleasured by a guy *you* wouldn't mind a little one-on-one with? I saw you. You couldn't tear your eyes away from what was going on."

"Get over yourself, Flynn."

"No, Valerie. You want to be with the adults on this? Own the feelings that go with what you saw."

"I liked you when I first met you. You seemed like a decent guy. After the barn, and then how you spoke to me yesterday, let's just say— I've re-evaluated my opinion. I'm a fifteen-year-old girl, Flynn, and you're a guy who likes to mess around with girls you don't even know. Why would I allow you anywhere near me?"

I stared indignantly. "Do you know the reputation Daisy has? No, probably not, but I do. Why would I ever want anything to do with someone who doesn't care about that? I'd never want you, even if I was ready to go there and lose my virginity. When I am ready to take that step, it sure as hell won't be with someone like you."

Flynn growled, grabbed me by my arm, steering me backward into my room. He swiftly closed the door, and my heart flipped wildly in my chest. I turned, ready to walk away from him, thinking he was making the conversation more private, but that wasn't the case. He suddenly grabbed me by my upper arms, spun me around and pushed me against the door.

He covered my body with his and pressed so hard I struggled to breathe and I should have been worried, but that wasn't what I felt. It was pure lust. It had excited me how he'd grabbed me, and I wanted more. The thrill of his abrupt move had made me wet and I wanted to grab him by the hair and kiss his mouth, despite what I'd just said to him. I didn't. Instead, I goaded him with a smirk.

"Sweet, sweet, Valerie. You're nowhere near ready to handle me. I'll know when you are, and *no one* will know your body like I will."

"What do you mean? The guys I decide to sleep with won't be able to do me the way you could? Newsflash, I've heard plenty of boys talk like you. You're full of yourself." I lifted my hands to his chest and felt his warm skin under them. The smooth, hard lines of his pectorals played into my already-heightened state of arousal, but I pushed him back.

Flynn didn't resist my move. "I'm done with this conversation.

Don't touch me again, and stay away from me while you're here. You may be Martin's guest, but this is my home too."

Most girls would have declared me insane for that move. Flynn had awoken feelings in me before I was ready to act on them. And he'd been pressed hard against me in my bedroom. Thinking what may happen if Martin or my parents found him in my room made me afraid for him. But the way he'd pushed himself at me only made that fear more exciting. My heart pumped so fast I thought I'd pass out.

Stubble brushed my cheek. "One kiss," he whispered gruffly, and licked his lips. Heat radiated from his naked chest through my t-shirt, as he leaned into me again. His scent filled my nostrils. I inhaled it deeply and was immediately seduced by it. I trembled in anticipation. I'd never wanted anyone to kiss me as badly as I wanted Flynn to.

If I'd been stronger, I'd have pushed him away again, but I wanted that kiss desperately. I knew I'd probably regret it afterward, but I wanted it like I'd die if he didn't do it. Flynn's pupils were blown wide as they bore into my eyes and sucked my soul right out of me. When I made no attempt to push him away, his eyes dropped to his thumb as he traced it gently across my mouth. As he licked his bottom lip again, his gaze flicked quickly from my mouth to my eyes. A second later, he pressed his warm, soft lips against mine as his eyes slowly closed.

Heat exploded throughout my body. My heart rate spiked and my knees buckled. My heart pounded all the way to my throat with desire. Instinctively, Flynn tilted his hips, pressing himself harder against my body and firmly to the door. A small groan came from his throat, and I felt his solid bulge against my belly. I'd felt similar before when Bradley had kissed me. Back then, I was embarrassed about it.

Embarrassment wasn't what I felt with Flynn. The passion his action had stirred in me was different. It was only a small kiss. An unexpectedly tender kiss, not what I'd imagined he would do at all.

Without thinking, I placed my hands on his back and trailed them down the smooth hard lines. His hot, silky skin shivered under my touch. Flynn's whole body stiffened, and he stilled before he exhaled a ragged breath and tore his mouth away. He took a big step back. The sudden loss of heat from his touch made my heart sad.

"Don't worry, honey. Your virtue is safe. I won't touch you again until you beg me," he whispered seductively.

Flynn turned me away from the door, opened it slowly, checking the hallway, before he slipped around it and walked away. I didn't even have a chance to respond. I watched him close his door behind him, and I sighed with a heavy sinking feeling in my belly.

Everything about our little encounter had turned me on. My body vibrated from how closely he'd held me and used his body to excite me. I fought to control the effect the smell of his half-naked body had on me. Instead of going downstairs, I closed the door and went over to my bed. I lay there wondering how I was going to get through the rest of the day after that.

I hated *and craved* Flynn. I knew if Martin found out what he'd done, I'd never see him again. There was no way I should have wanted him near me, and then again, there was no way I could have let him walk away, knowing he'd never come back. Understanding the complexity of those feelings, with no prior experience, felt impossible for a girl like me.

By dinner time, I'd avoided him for much of the day, but Thanksgiving wasn't as bad as I'd expected. Flynn was the perfect guest. Polite and charming, he was mindful of our parents, and he'd won Auntie Joan over in a heartbeat.

Just before bedtime, she cornered me in the kitchen. "So, Flynn has a thing for you. How do you feel about that, Valerie?"

My heart stuttered at her comment, and I blushed. *Why would she say that?*

"Sorry, Auntie Joan, but I think you've had too much wine this evening. I've got no idea what you're talking about."

"So, you think I was born yesterday? You think I don't recognize when a boy looks at a girl in a certain way?"

As far as I was concerned, Flynn hadn't looked at me at all. We hadn't conversed with each other, apart from on the landing, but Auntie Joan had been in the kitchen with Mom when that happened. I'd gone to the barn to spend time with Kayden and Adam, and we'd listened to music and talked about people we knew. Martin had stayed in the house with Flynn, and they'd been watching some music documentary on TV while my parents prepped for our Thanksgiving dinner.

"What way?" I said, sounding surprised.

"In a way you must be strong enough to resist, Val. The boy was devouring you with his eyes."

Her comment was so straight talking I almost collapsed on the spot. "Well, now I know you've had too much to drink."

"Valerie that boy has watched every breath you've taken today. His eyes have followed you around the room, and when you left to go to the barn, he almost fell out of the chair, craning his neck to watch you through the window."

"Is that so?" I said as my heart raced, both with delight that he'd done that, but also worry that Martin would suspect he'd been flirting with me.

"It is."

A short silence passed between us.

"He's a college boy, Auntie Joan. They look at all girls' behinds," I said, trying to sound dismissive.

"He's a college boy holding a torch for my favorite niece, honey."

"Your only niece," I corrected her, and smirked.

"Mark my words, Valerie. That boy definitely has a thing for you."

"That boy has a thing for all girls, I'd bet."

"Hmm, you are more astute than I give you credit for. I mean, I'm an old widow, and even I've not been able to stop staring at him. He's a very handsome young man. You haven't looked or talked to him all day, so I'm guessing there's a crush you're trying hard to smooth out in that heart of yours. Am I close?"

She'd read the situation perfectly.

"Enough! Nothing's ever going to happen between Flynn and me, so you're going to have to look to your Harlequin books for a tawdry romance, Auntie Joan."

Leaving the kitchen for my room, I was relieved when I'd made it without another interlude with Flynn. I undressed and got into bed. Lying flat on my back, I stared at the ceiling, feeling less happy about being home.

My thoughts turned to Martin. He was leaving too soon. I hadn't sensed the closeness we'd once shared, and that tore my heart. Tears fell, and I felt so discontent by how the holiday had gone. My emotions had ridden stormy waters since I'd come home and it had left me flat. Eventually, I cried myself to sleep.

Kayden knocked on the door and called out to me to get up. I listened to him walk away, and I rolled to my side, staring at the window. I hadn't really wanted to answer him. Martin was leaving early due to the snowstorm coming on Saturday. I'd heard them taking all their things downstairs.

After a while, the trunk slammed shut with a dull thud, signifying the last time I'd see Martin until Christmas. Almost as important, perhaps the last time I'd see Flynn. I slipped out of bed and padded barefoot to look down at the driveway.

A thick dusting of snow had fallen. Everything looked picturesque outside. Martin's car had been cleared of snow, swipe marks on the roof as far as their arms could reach. The snow on the hood had melted from the engine turning over. Kayden opened the door and poked his head in.

"Ah, you're up. Martin is about ready to leave, Val."

I noticed Martin hadn't come to tell me himself. Digging in my drawer, I pulled on some black yoga pants and a black t-shirt, and found a thick, red sweater on the back of my bedroom chair. I cracked open the door slowly and then headed downstairs.

Martin was leaning on the countertop, cradling a mug of coffee between both hands.

"Oh, you're up. I was going to leave you sleeping; it's still early."

"You were going to leave without saying goodbye?"

Stunned, I stood speechless. I'd have been devastated if Martin had done that. This was the brother who'd been so in tune with me until a couple of days ago, and we'd reached the point where he wasn't even going to say goodbye.

My eyes stared when his words hit me low in my chest. I'd been too choked to say anything else and fought to swallow the emotion. After a few seconds, I set myself up with a cup of coffee to break the hurt and angry thoughts circling in my mind. I'd have preferred not to have seen him, and for that particular conversation to not have taken place between us. Maybe he was right. Maybe I should have stayed in bed and let him go.

Flynn came in the back door, and Martin looked up at him.

"Can you give us a few minutes?" Martin asked Flynn.

Flynn's eyes flicked to me. He hesitated before he nodded. "Sure. I'll be in the car. He turned to leave but glanced back and said, "I need to do this real quick."

Flynn came over to me and took my cup away, placing it on the counter. "It was a real pleasure to meet you, Valerie. Martin had told me his sister was beautiful inside and out. I think he was being modest when he made that statement. I hope we'll meet again sometime in the future."

Leaning forward, Flynn pulled me to his chest and hugged me tightly. His hands gave me an extra squeeze on my back, which I hoped at the time was a secret sign, but for what? I felt by body yield and melt into his arms. He bent and kissed me briefly on my mouth. It was just a peck but enough to leave an imprint on my lips, and his touch embedded in my brain. Without a backwards glance, he left the room as quickly as he'd entered.

Martin came to my side and leaned on the granite countertop. "I'm sorry this holiday has sucked for you, Val. If I'd known bringing Flynn here would have taken so much of my time, I'd have thought twice about it."

"No, you wouldn't have, Martin, you're too nice. It's not his fault; it was probably the fact I'd been living somewhere else as well. It's been... unsettling. He's been fine. I've enjoyed him staying. You can bring him back," I said, trying to sound neutral.

Martin accepted me excusing him, because I think he needed something to console himself with. We never disagreed about anything, so what had happened was a first. When we went outside, all my brothers were together, until my parents and my aunt arrived to say their goodbyes.

Ten minutes later, I was staring at the taillights braking, as Martin rounded the bend in the driveway and he and Flynn headed for the highway. I hugged myself against the biting wind and the cold morning air, and turned with tears welling until they rolled down my face. *Worst Thanksgiving ever.*

I moped around the house all day, following Martin and Flynn's departure. Replays sprang to mind of the conversations between everyone. I'd texted Martin twice that I loved him and couldn't wait to see him at Christmas. I hated how we'd left things between us, and that I wouldn't be able to put it right for weeks. When I went to bed that night, I pulled open my pajama drawer and found a music notation sheet. It had been folded into quarters. Opening it, I saw a scribbled phone number and one line of words.

Call me when you're ready.

Flynn x

My heart soared at those five words. I read it again and thought about the last conversation we'd had. When I'm ready for what— to sleep with him? *HA!* Did he mean when I'd turned eighteen? Did he mean call him when I wanted to see him again, or when I'd lost my virginity? Those five words made the note too ambiguous to know exactly what had been going on in his head when he wrote it.

Martin's words resonated with me about girls going *insane* for Flynn, and I could relate. I'd almost lost *my* mind in the few days he'd been with us. Had he only written the note because there were no other women to give his attention to here? Surely he wouldn't want me once he was back in St. Cloud.

Leaving his number for me like that felt like some kind of test, but I was determined not to play his game. If he wanted to see me, he knew where I lived. We were listed in the phone book, and our name wasn't very common. He'd find us easily enough. I'd been warned off him both by Martin and my aunt already, so there was no way I was chasing after him.

Chapter Eight

INSTANT ROCK STAR

nce Martin had gone back to college, I'd spent a good chunk of each day dreaming about what I would say if Flynn ever called me. I needn't have bothered, because he didn't. What he did do was save me the trauma of rehashing the Bradley stuff. Suddenly, I was bombarded with questions about how I'd met someone as amazing as Flynn, no mention of Bradley.

I was honest and told them he was Martin's roommate at college, and that we weren't together anymore, because of both distance and timing. They knew I wanted to go to college, and if Flynn was in Martin's year, he'd be finishing. That part was true, except we weren't together in the first place.

After the questions died down, life got a little easier, and I was asked out a few times by different boys. I didn't accept, at first, because I still couldn't shake my feelings for Flynn, even though the whole thing was impossible. It seemed my heart wanted Flynn, no matter what my head told it.

~

During the following five weeks, Martin called home weekly as usual, and sent me the occasional text. I'd been dying to ask about Flynn, but Martin never mentioned him, so I was afraid to broach the subject. It drove me crazy that I hadn't heard any news about him.

When Martin called on my sixteenth birthday, I finally found the courage to ask him about Flynn. He mentioned he was flying in for Christmas a few days later, and I braved it by asking if Flynn would be tagging along.

Martin snickered down the line before he said, "Flynn? Nah, we won't see him again, Beatnik. He's loved up and infatuated with some woman. Stupid guy dropped out and is missing his college degree, with only two semesters to go."

My breath caught at the back of my throat, and I stood silently listening in shock. Flynn had only left me the note about a week before he'd found his next victim. I should have known better. It was my sixteenth birthday, and it wasn't lost on me that the day I could legally have sex, was the day I found out Flynn Docherty had only been toying with me. I was heartbroken.

When the call was over, I rushed upstairs to my room, plunged heavily onto my bed, and cried buckets into my pillow. After a while, I opened my drawer and saw the note I'd been treasuring. I stared at it before ripping it into tiny pieces. The guy had played me, and I'd been stupid enough to think he may have meant what he'd said.

Martin came home a few days later and the awkward, distant feelings between us dissipated as soon as he got in the car at the airport. His familiar smile and warm hugs were all I'd needed to perk back up. I hadn't realized how down I'd been about the stuff with Flynn, until Martin made me feel better.

"Here, I should have sent this in the mail for your birthday, but I wanted to see your face when you opened it."

Martin handed me a small box wrapped in golden metallic gift wrap.

I grinned and shook my head. Spending time at home with him was enough present for me. "What are you doing buying me things? You're supposed to be a poor student," I said, and smirked as I eagerly tore the paper from the box. Inside was a beautiful silver bracelet with music symbol charms.

"Oh, it's perfect. I adore it, Martin," I gushed and leaped over the back seat to hug him hard from behind. Kayden was driving, and he scolded me for distracting him.

Martin unclasped the hook and fastened the bracelet on my wrist. I swung it lightly and examined the charms again, paying attention to the detail of each one. It was beautiful, and the thought that Martin had picked it out especially for me, made it even more treasured.

As we rode along, Kayden began quizzing Martin about Flynn. I sat in the back, quietly listening, with my heart thumping in my chest at the mention of his name.

Apparently, Flynn had been seeing a girl on and off at college before he'd come to our place for Thanksgiving. She was really into music, and she sang in some college band. Flynn had been invited to her place the weekend after they'd gone home. Next thing, Martin knew he came back to collect his stuff and told Martin he'd quit college and was moving to California.

"Get this. You know how shy he was about playing his guitar? Well, not now— he's in a band, and some hotshot manager is taking them all the way. I tried to talk him into finishing his degree, but he said it was pointless. When he went home with Iria, the new girlfriend, it turned out her father is a buddy to some record producer and manager in LA. Flynn was offered an audition for some band a record company guru was putting together.

Iria persuaded Flynn to go for it, and once the record producer heard Flynn sing and play the guitar, the guy offered him the lead position."

Martin turned and looked at me, and I tried to maintain a nonchalant expression.

"At first, Flynn refused his offer because of his stage fright, but they've been giving him confidence therapy and, from all accounts, he's doing great. He doesn't contact me directly anymore. I guess he's too busy. But the girl I've been seeing, Jessica, is friends with his girl. The band is called Major ScAlz, so we should watch out for them."

"Is that so?" Kayden asked.

"Yup. Looks like Flynn's gone from being a shy guy to a rock star in a few months. I saw a video of him. Iria sent it to Jessica. I can't believe the difference in him. The band's going to be massively famous."

"Never heard of them," I blurted out in a bitter tone.

"Who? Major ScAlz? Well, you wouldn't have yet, Beatnik. They're still rehearsing. Putting a band together isn't something you get right overnight. It takes a few months of training their voices to blend, and getting to know the timing of all the songs once they learn them."

"Get you, Mr. Expert-on-bands-all-of-a-sudden," I said, my voice dripping with sarcasm.

"Only relaying what I was told, Beatnik. There's no need to be bitchy about it."

"I wasn't being bitchy. I just can't see how someone can go from nothing to everything in one hit. Are you sure they're being honest with you?"

My anger had nothing to do with Flynn's success. It was the fact that he had moved on to a new girl so quickly. Not that I was his girl, or anything.

"Well, we'll find out soon enough. Their first track is being released New Year's week. To be honest with you, Val, I was glad when he took up with Iria. When he was here, I got the vibe that he was about to hit on you. Flynn's definitely one to spread the love around, so I'd questioned myself after his performance with you at Adam's game, whether or not I'd made a mistake bringing him home with me."

"Like I told you at the time, Marty, I was fifteen. So, you needn't have worried on that score." I seethed, thinking back to that moment. I'd been humiliated by the way Martin and Flynn had discussed me, as if I weren't even in the room.

"And now you're sixteen and, thank God, Flynn isn't around anymore. It would have been a different story this time, I think. I know him, and he was really attracted to you."

"And now I'm sixteen? You mean *legal* ... and you think I'd give up my virginity to a guy like Flynn? Really? I think you boys need to start giving me some credit for being my own woman. I'm not stupid, Martin. I learned my lesson with Bradley."

"Val, Flynn popped the cherries of plenty of girls just like you, so I know what I'm talking about."

"Doesn't he sound like a real darling? Like you said, he's not here, so why are we still discussing him?"

Martin apologized and pulled me in for a hug, and our heated moods gradually evened out. That night, everyone went to bed except for the two of us. It felt like old times as we sat across from each other, cross-legged, me on the sofa and him on the floor facing me. Reminiscing about people we knew, places we'd been. Our favorite playlist was on shuffle in the background, and I didn't want the night to end. We were equals again, and I learned a lot about Martin I hadn't known before. By the time we headed upstairs, the gap between us was firmly closed.

Christmas Day was everything it was supposed to be. Full of love and laughter, and to have our whole family together gave me a sense of what was important. I did spare a thought for Flynn that morning, and hoped that wherever he was, he'd been made welcome. I pondered the thought of how awful it would have been not to have my loved ones around me. When I thought of losing people close to me, it was too painful for words.

By evening, we'd all had too much to eat and we'd laughed until we cried, watching a corny old movie on TV. Martin's sudden movements caught my eye, and I watched as he took his phone out of his pocket, checked the screen, and held his phone away from his body. His mouth dropped as he blinked and shook his head.

"Oh. My. God. No way. It looks like Flynn is going to be a real rock star in a few days' time. They are opening at Madison Square Garden for Bon Jovi."

"You're kidding, right?" Kayden's eyes were wide, and he crawled from his position on the floor, nearer to Martin.

"Nope. Look, he just sent this."

Martin turned his phone in Kayden's direction, and I craned my neck to see the screen. Flynn was smiling widely in the picture. Behind him was a massive stage set with a laser image of Jon Bon Jovi's face on a screen in an empty stadium. It looked as if the projected images were being tested before a concert.

Martin's thumbs moved over the keypad in response. Seconds later, another text alert beeped on his cell.

Snickering, Martin turned the cell away from me and read it, biting his bottom lip in concentration. He laughed out loud and then shared it with Kayden, who also burst out laughing.

"Dirty fucker," Kayden muttered, sounding amused.

Shaking his head at Kayden, Martin chuckled. "I told him it'll fall off one day."

Whatever was on the text wasn't shared with me, so I figured it had to be crude. Once again, Flynn had managed to alienate me from my brothers, and he wasn't even in the same place. I stood, picked up some of my presents, and mumbled that I was going to bed. It was only 9:00 P.M., but I had to get away ... from *all* of them.

As I climbed the stairs, tears welled in my eyes. I knew what I felt about Flynn was irrational. He'd messed with my head. The guy had only been at our house for a few days, but the impact he'd had on me was lingering. Moreover, my curiosity about the text message he'd sent, had gotten the better of me.

The following two days were a little strained at times, mainly due to Martin and Kayden talking non-stop about how lucky Flynn was. I'd found myself doing chores around the house, volunteering for anything other than spend time listening to them speculate about Flynn. My anger flared that someone we hardly knew could drive a wedge between us, or maybe my jealousy was responsible for that?

Flynn sent two more texts that were never shared with me. One of them seemed to have annoyed Martin. I watched him read the message and then shove his phone in his pocket and mutter, "In your dreams, Flynn." He never mentioned that one to Kayden, and I wondered if it was personal to Martin. By the time Martin left for college, I was moping again—a lot.

New Year's Day came, and I couldn't prevent myself from Googling Major ScAlz. Their name was connected to the Bon Jovi gig. The site I'd clicked had tons of reviews, and I searched through them like an obsessed fan. One site led to another, and eventually there were mentions of Major ScAlz as the main articles.

One report I found, mentioning Major ScAlz, had over a thousand comments. My eyes bugged out as I scanned down the list and each entrant cited them as, "truly awesome," "magnificent new band," "da bomb," "incredible discovery," "major talent."

Hundreds— mainly posted by female fans — cooed that Flynn was "sex on legs" while others commented that he "oozed pure testosterone." I'd had personal experience of that, and the effect he'd had on me was heady. I pictured him with a guitar, sweat glistening on his skin as he belted out tunes, and I guessed Flynn could have induced an ovary explosion. There were a couple of mentions for Tyler Chisholm, the band's bassist, and one for the drummer, Tommy Alzaci.

Searching YouTube to see what all this "truly awesome magnificence" was about, as soon as I laid eyes on him, I understood. My heart thumped fiercely, as my trembling hand clicked the trackpad on my laptop to start the video clip. I sat back and stared at Flynn on the screen. The effect of the moving images, and the raspy alto tones from the guy who'd only been in my mind for the past six weeks, hit me like a punch in the center of my chest. I fell for him all over again.

I sat enthralled by his performance, and I was confused by how the simple guy who had been at my home was now on my computer, in the form of a rock star. He worked the stage, connecting with his audience, before he sang to the camera, that was obviously meant to be there. Flynn was everything that made the perfect rock star, but the guy I was watching at that time was nothing like the college guy who'd been sitting at our table less than seven weeks prior.

Groomed for stardom, Flynn appeared completely polished in a rugged-rock-star way. He was the ultimate professional on stage, but the flirtatious side of his personality shone though in his performance. He smiled, and I swear it could have melted ice off the frostiest of hearts.

The audience on the video looked completely captivated by him. He was the embodiment of the guy most guys secretly wished they could be, and all the girls wished they could be with. Even more, Flynn wasn't just a good-looking guy who'd been stuck in a manufactured group. He *made* the band. I sat, mesmerized by the complex riffs from his guitar and the rich, raspy tones of his voice. He looked perfectly at home and sounded like he'd been born to be on stage.

More searches revealed thousands of images of Flynn. His perfect smile on those perfect lips that he'd once held to mine. If I'd been more experienced, I'd have made him kiss me properly. It would have been my chance to know what that was like. I'd been wondering what that would be like since we'd met.

I swallowed past the lump in my throat, as tears rolled down my face, because I'd probably never experience that with him. It was too late. He belonged to the public as soon as he'd performed his first gig. For Flynn, life would never be the same, and life would go on for the both of us. *Martin was right. At sixteen, a guy like him would have eaten me alive.*

I closed my laptop while the video still played, and made up my mind the only way to get Flynn out of my head was to date again.

For a few days, I stayed strong on my resolution, but that hadn't stopped me from opening new accounts on Instagram, Twitter, and Facebook. I even set myself up with a fake name to do that, just in case. I didn't want to take a chance on him recognizing me. Flynn usually tweeted early in the evenings, mainly about his songs, band information, and tour dates. But there were some flirtatious tweets, aimed at female fans. Occasionally, he acknowledged a male who gave him a compliment about his musical talent. Otherwise, he focused on how to cultivate female fans.

On the first Tuesday of January, I drove to high school with Kayden by my side. I'd been driving on our land since I turned thirteen, but I had to take a test the following week for my license to drive around on my own. We'd taken Dad's old truck because Kayden wouldn't allow me anywhere near Susie. My need to practice was greater than the embarrassment of turning up in that old thing.

Ziggy Ally came over to me as I closed the door. He shoved his hands in his pockets and watched Kayden drive off. I turned to look at him, and he smiled. I'd always thought he had a great smile.

"Hey, Valerie. Happy New Year." He offered a bashful grin, and it had appealed to me that I'd made him feel awkward.

"Hi, Ziggy. Happy New Year. Did you have a good time on New Year's Eve?"

"Yeah, it was pretty cool. You?"

"Yeah, and no. My brother was home, which was cool, but some other stuff got in the way of me relaxing," I answered honestly.

"Ah. The ex-boyfriend-soon-to-become-superstar thing, huh?"

"Jesus. Is that why you're talking to me, Ziggy?"

"God. No. Well, yes ... it is," he huffed, looking frustrated with himself.

"Look, what I wanted to say ... ask ... I don't care about anything else. I just ... wanted to ask you out. I've wanted to ask you out since eighth grade. Bradley's balls grew faster than mine is all," he said, and smirked.

I laughed and immediately regretted it. Ziggy was serious. That's why he'd been so awkward. It wasn't about Flynn or anything else. It was because he wanted me.

"You want to take me out?"

"I just said so, didn't I?"

"I think so— somewhere in between your reference of one of my ex-boyfriend's being a rock star, and the other having faster-growing balls than yours."

Ziggy chuckled at my summation. "Guess I made a mess of that, huh?"

"Ziggy, as your hit-up line has been the most original I've heard in a long time, I'd love to go on a date with you."

I meant it. He was a really sweet boy. Handsome and athletic, and he had manners.

Ziggy looked bashfully at me and then shoved his hands even further into his pockets as he inhaled sharply. He caught his breath in his mouth before he puffed his lips and let out a slow trail of mist into the cold morning air. "Damn, that wasn't as hard as I'd thought it was going to be. I was prepared to beg," he said with a smirk, glancing over toward the football field.

Ziggy became cuter by the minute. His boyish flirting wasn't even practiced, but it was working on me. The way he kept saying what he was thinking was endearing. And funny.

"So, are you going to stand there and talk me out of this, or do you have a plan for this date you want to take me on?"

"Sure, I have a plan. I have two. Both boring, of course, and corny. Same ol' same ol'. Back of my truck with a picnic basket, drive to a corn field to watch the stars ... until your brothers find us, or if that's too scary, a movie and popcorn is cool. Although, I wondered about having the popcorn because, if we kiss, and there's a bit of—" He started gesturing at my mouth with his finger, grimaced, and shuddered. I giggled.

"So, what you're saying is, you have a plan but no plan? So, what if I have a plan instead? Can you cope with your date leading the way?"

"Hell yes. I read all about female domination. I'm sure I can deal with that, Val."

"I'm going to pretend that didn't just fall out of your mouth, Ziggy, okay?"

"Sure," he said with a wry grin.

Ziggy walked me to class and, during the lecture, he kept stealing glances at me. I became self-conscious that others might have seen him, and I giggled out loud. I was admonished by our teacher, and by the time we broke for lunch, Ziggy was more than ready to pounce.

"So—I'm growing on you, right?"

Slowly, my smile widened at how cute he looked as he sought my approval. "Yup, but don't overdo it."

"Gotcha."

Without another word, he walked away, leaving me standing alone in the middle of the corridor, wondering what I'd said. I giggled, shook my head, and turned to make my way to the lunchroom.

Chapter Nine

SWEET TALKING GUY

Strange, but I'd felt reservations once I'd agreed to date Ziggy. Although, I'd been pleasantly surprised at how attractive he looked standing at my door in his cowboy boots, faded jeans, white vest, red plaid shirt and black leather jacket. I'd only ever seen him in gray baggy sweatshirts, black or blue skinny jeans, and Chucks. The "evening" version of Ziggy looked much older than sixteen and more like an eighteen-year-old. He was taller than most in school—maybe six feet—and he wasn't at all scrawny. He'd filled out, as my mom would say.

Shiny blond hair flopped sexily over his almond-shaped blue eyes, and his smile was open and honest. The kind of smile I knew I could handle. My eyes flicked back to meet his, because they were just so attractive to look at. Everyone in my family had hazel or green eyes, so Ziggy's blue ones seemed to pull me in.

"Alright, I'm ready for this. You want to bring your dad to the door?" I was surprised everyone wasn't already in the yard, vetting him. My mom quizzed me endlessly. "What does his father do for a living? Does his mom work or is she a homemaker? Does he have siblings? If so, what gender?" I felt like I was on an episode of Jeopardy, and she was waiting for me to give her the wrong answer.

I rolled my eyes at Ziggy and was just about to tell him not to be ridiculous, when my dad came up close behind me.

"And you'd be?"

"Ziggy Ally, sir."

"Ziggy? Are your parents David Bowie fans?"

"No, sir. My father's a clinical psychologist. My actual name is Sigmund, after Sigmund Freud, the famous psychologist, sir."

"I see. I can also see why you'd go by Ziggy. I take it you don't have the same level of psychoanalytical bullshit as him?"

My jaw dropped, and I turned sharply and narrowed my eyes at my father's unsavory tone.

"Who, my dad, or Freud?" My dad chuckled heartily before Ziggy continued, "No, sir. That's another reason for preferring Ziggy. People hear my name, and I hear countless references about him and his theories. I mean no one thinks everyone called David can kick a ball like Beckham from the UK, do they? So how come I get the one guy..."

My father held up his hand in silence.

"Point taken. You have my permission to take my daughter out. You be respectful of her virtue. You hear me, boy? And have her back by eleven."

I almost fell to the floor with mortification when my dad said that about my *virtue*. I'd always known I'd been sheltered and because of that, I was limited in my experiences and friends. But what he'd said to Ziggy sounded like something out of an early nineteenth-century cowboy movie.

"Right, Dad, you've had your fun. We're leaving now." I reached out and pulled Ziggy's shirt sleeve, and he followed me down the yard to his truck. Kayden was just leaving the barn, and I heard the heavy pine door bang shut.

"In the truck and drive," I said as Kayden began to walk toward us purposefully.

Ziggy said nothing but climbed in his side and started the engine as I closed the door on my side.

We passed my brother just as he was reaching the edge of the dirt road, so I waved and smiled sweetly, priding myself for handling the situation of Ziggy's first visit quite well.

"So where are we going, princess?"

"Don't call me that. My name is Valerie."

Ziggy fell silent and drove, until we reached the fork in the road signaling east and west.

"So, is this part of the date?"

"What?"

"You— dominating me."

"Domineering, Ziggy. The word is domineering. And I'm not doing that."

"No? So, 'Get in the car and drive' and 'Don't call me princess,' don't sound kinda *domineering* to you?"

I drew a breath to argue, and glanced over at his face. His smirk revealed a dimple in his right cheek, and I knew he was teasing me.

"Oh, you've changed your tune from yes, sir?"

"So, you think I'd have been better saying, 'We're going down by the lake with a blanket, to have some cheese and drink two contraband bottles of beer. Then, when we're done eating and drinking, I'm going to try my hardest not to get a hard-on while looking at your stunning daughter by the moonlight?' Would that have been more appropriate?"

Keeping my laughter in check, I stared straight-faced at Ziggy. "Is that the plan?"

"Do you have a better one? Because right now, Valerie, I'm not even making it to the lake with these feelings stirring in my pants."

I knew what he meant. I'd been full of lust, simply looking at Flynn. The way Ziggy spoke to me made me feel desired, in the same way I had when Flynn pushed me against my bedroom door.

"Do you have some kind of honesty disease or something? I don't know any other boy who would have said something like that to a girl on a first date. In fact, I don't think Bradley ever said anything like that to me—ever. I mean, he tried to..."

"Valerie, let's get this straight. I'm not Bradley. He's a dickhead for what he did to you. His loss is my gain. Not that you're his seconds or anything..."

I started laughing. Ziggy was trying to make me feel better, but his ability to put his foot in his mouth was something of a talent. "So, what am I?" I asked.

"You're a stunningly, gorgeous young lady who's way out of my league. But—for some weird reason, you said yes to a date with me, and here I am. Ta Da! Yours for however long that may be. I'm not like my namesake. I'm not going to try to analyze it; I'm just going to live it for what it is. I never expected you to agree to date me. Not in a million years. And, at some point, your real guy will come and sweep you off your feet, and all I can hope is you remember me with warmth and affection. We're sixteen and I'm not going to pretend this is forever, but we can make this time a good memory, right?"

Ziggy pulled the car over at a spot overlooking the lake. There was frost on the ground, and the trees surrounding the lake had brittle white, bare branches. The leafless wood allowed the fading winter light to show through the trees as the birds fell silent. Dusk was a quiet time, and we sat in silence for a short while. Ziggy's comment was probably the most honest one any man would ever say to me. And it had shocked me that he didn't think he was good enough for me.

"I'd really like that, Ziggy."

Turning toward me, his arm swept along the back of the car seat. His hand curled around my shoulder, and he tugged me closer. My body held no resistance toward his as he pulled me close. Being with him felt natural, and the warmth from his body was comforting.

"Is this okay?" he said, resting his head on mine.

"Sure," I answered, as my body trembled slightly at his touch. A little thrill of excitement ran through my veins for the first time since Flynn. I'd missed the closeness of cuddling with a boy. Bradley and I used to do it all the time, until he started pressuring me for more, so Ziggy's forwardness that night was welcome.

I leaned away from him to look up, and his free hand caught my chin. "Anyone ever tell you, you're all that?"

A smile curved my lips. "Depends what 'all that' is," I countered.

"The perfect girl. How you look, talk, walk, smell."

"You're smelling me?"

"How can I not? You're all around me, Valerie."

"Like a skunk, you mean?"

The rumbly laugh he gave made me smile wider.

"Jesus. No. Valerie, you smell like pears and violets."

"Pears and violets, huh? I must tell my brothers that one. We all use the same generic body wash my mom buys at the store. I wonder if girls tell them the same."

I was still laughing when Ziggy brought his mouth down and pressed a kiss to my lips. When I didn't object, his tongue skimmed the small opening between my lips and probed my mouth, and then he deepened his intentions. He was a great kisser. My heart rate picked up its pace, and small bursts of electrical energy hit zones in my body that had been previously awakened by Flynn.

Ziggy pulled away a little breathless and adjusted himself in his seat. Then in an abrupt motion, he pulled the door handle and jumped down onto the grass. Clearing his throat, he smiled back at me.

"Don't worry, you weren't bad enough to make me run away. I'm just getting some drinks for us. This is thirsty work, and I think we're going to need a bit more practice," he said with a wink, and I shook my head at his words.

Feeling good was something I'd taken for granted most of my life. Incidents in those previous few months had changed that. The tipping point for that had been Bradley's betrayal, but I felt nothing at all for him as soon as I'd met Flynn.

As I sat in the warmth of Ziggy's truck, I knew I was entering a new chapter of my life, and for the first time in a while, I was excited to look forward. Ziggy wasn't Flynn, but he was easy to be around, he said what he meant, and because he was so open, I knew what he was thinking. I figured he'd quite possibly be the person to heal the ache in my heart, left in Flynn's wake.

Three hours later, we'd kissed ourselves drunk. Both of us had rewarded the other with soft sighs and moans to the point where twice, Ziggy popped the door on the truck and jumped out to wander around it, muttering under his breath and adjusting his pants. It had made me chuckle and each time he'd done it, I gave him a little more of my heart.

Dropping me home at 10:45 P.M., Ziggy turned to me, the moonlight shining through the windshield. "I hope your dad doesn't think I brought you back early because you wouldn't put out."

I giggled almost uncontrollably. "How do you know I wouldn't? You didn't try."

Ziggy glanced over with shock on his face. "Sweet Jesus, are you saying..."

I chuckled even more and felt bad for leading him on.

"You're right, I'm not saying," I said, and smiled, and held his hand.

"Figured. I reckon it'll take some fancy talking from a smooth tongue to get into your drawers, Valerie."

I almost choked with laughter and doubled up in his truck, banging my head on the glove compartment. My dad walked out onto the porch before I could respond to Ziggy. He'd jumped out of his side of the truck and ran around the hood to open my door for me. Taking my hand, he helped me down and closed it before looking back with a sheepish look on his face.

Dad called out, "Ten minutes, Valerie. Good job, Ziggy," and entered the house again.

"So, did I blow it? I was doing okay until the *drawers* comment, I think. Too much information, Val?" he asked, cringing as he screwed his eyes tight. A moment later, he peeked out of one eye and held his body in a freeze frame until I smiled and patted his chest.

"Yes, but you can come back. I enjoyed our time tonight; it was nice and easy."

"Yeah, unlike you," he said, and looked horrified with himself.

"I mean you're not ... and you shouldn't be..."

I pulled him in for a hug, and his arms wrapped around me in an instant.

"I know what you meant. I was just teasing you."

"You've been doing that all night, sweet Valerie."

"Don't you ever stop, Ziggy?"

"Stop what?" he said, throwing his arm out like he had no idea.

He leaned in and kissed me softly, and I sagged against the car door. Ziggy, in his quest to keep his lips connected with mine, dropped forward until his hips touched mine. I could feel his hard cock press against my belly, and he moaned at the sudden contact. Breathlessly, I pushed him back, and I could tell we both felt out of our depth.

"Okay, well—goodnight," I mumbled, and ran for the door with my head down. I didn't want to wait around to give him the chance to point out the obvious about what had happened. Once inside, I pressed the door closed and leaned against it with a smile on my face.

After that night, Ziggy became somewhat of a permanent fixture around our place. Mom and Dad really warmed to him. Kayden and Adam watched from a distance at first, but he gradually won them over as well. Part of his success with that was that Ziggy's main hobby was building motorcycles with his dad. Once the boys found out, Kayden and my dad invited him to tinker with some of the projects they'd salvaged from the wrecker's yard.

Our boy-girl dates had turned into a more serious affair, without either of us trying. Naturally, as our relationship and feelings grew, so did our desires. We'd started to mess around a bit, and hit second base more than a few times. At those times, Ziggy had run outside, and I'd watched him drive off into the distance, because our feelings were getting the better of us, and he was trying hard not to overstep the mark ... because of what happened with Bradley. But Ziggy wasn't Bradley, and it was different with him.

If I was honest, I had been struggling not to go further, so I was glad he was trying to keep us on safe ground. Ziggy told me one night he loved me since that first kiss, and I realized my feelings for him had grown into love as well. It was different from what I'd felt with Bradley and Flynn. He felt safe, made me smile, and we were almost inseparable.

The acid test was Martin. He came home for the Easter break, and I'd been nervous because I wanted him to like Ziggy. He had a great heart, and we'd grown close. After spending the first evening home in Ziggy's company, Martin flung himself down beside me after Ziggy had gone home. He placed a beer to his lips, chugged some down, and stared pointedly in my direction.

"Never thought I'd hear myself say this about a guy you were with Valerie, but Ziggy's a good kid. He's good for you, Beatnik. I can tell he makes you happy. And it's good to see you smile again."

Martin's approval was important to me. And to hear him say that he liked my boyfriend, only confirmed that to me.

Chapter Ten

FEELINGS

artin had been gone for eleven weeks since Christmas, yet I felt his presence as soon as he'd walked through the door. Everyone came to life when he was home. Or so it seemed. Mom appeared chirpier; Dad, much more talkative —no, more like argumentative, and it brought a smile to my lips when I saw how easily Martin could rile him when they talked football and cars.

He was home for two and a half weeks before he was headed back to St. Cloud for a few weeks to finish his senior seminar and graduate. When he'd said he was coming back to live at home, I was excited. Something had changed with him, though. For the first time, he'd brought a girl to our home. Jessica, his girlfriend, arrived on the Wednesday after he had, and we all planned a road trip to Las Vegas. I was thrilled when both Ziggy's and my parents agreed Ziggy and I could go with them. It seemed that since I'd found a boy who everyone agreed they liked, the age barrier was no longer an issue hanging over my head.

When we picked Jessica up from the airport, it was strange. I'd met girls Martin had been out with before, but the way he spoke about Jessica was completely different. They'd been seeing each other since the fall semester, but he hadn't mentioned her until he'd been home the Christmas before. I knew as soon as she walked out the door it was her. Martin's whole body language changed, like he was being pulled toward her. He'd shown me pictures of her, and I thought she was pretty, but when I saw her in the flesh, I was bowled over by how incredibly elegant she was.

I smirked and folded my arms as he almost ran to her. His lack of awareness for those around him gave away just how much she meant to him. When he cupped her face, and spoke inches from her mouth, and the way she looked back at him, it told me she was *the one*. Martin offered her slow, tender kisses.

He broke away and pulled his head back to look at her. She returned his stare with a look of adoration. He turned with her in his arms and looked over at me, with a weird expression. I was as if he were trying to tell me what I already knew. He'd love her no matter what anyone else thought.

As it happened, I loved her. Really loved her. She was warm and friendly, funny, and ridiculously intelligent. She was a computer graphics graduate and was currently an intern at MGM studios, training to produce special effects for movies. I can't remember what her exact title was, but it sounded pretty damn cool.

Jess, as she liked to be called, explained she'd already graduated when she started dating my brother. Martin attended a workshop she'd run as a senior the year before. They'd met in a bar again the week he'd gone back to college last year, and they'd been seeing each other ever since. The only downside to Jessica was Iria— Flynn's girl. She was Jess's best friend.

Jess was perfect for Martin, and they seemed made for each other. She was a strong girl and knew what she wanted, and I felt she was good for Martin. Sometimes he liked to get his way a little too much, and I was confident she'd stand up to him. I heard some of her strength the following night when she mentioned Flynn's name, and instantly my legs wouldn't move. I stood between the kitchen and sitting room as she began talking about him to Martin.

"Grr. Flynn makes me so mad! Why the hell does she put up with him?"

"Told you already, Jess, the guy's never gonna change. He's definitely in the right job for his nature. I don't think Flynn has monogamy in his vocabulary, much less in his habits."

"Three separate journalists reported him having sex by a pool with two of the wait staff in Chicago. Three, not just one rogue guy, and Iria would rather believe his bullshit set-up story. His jeans were at his ankles in the picture, for God's sake."

"Give me that cell. I'm tired of listening to you complain about Iria's issues with Flynn. I'm only human. There's only so much rock-star bullshit a guy can take before he's tuckered out."

"Martin, I can't believe you were friends with him. He's nothing like you."

"Nope. Poor, normal, monogamous..."

"You bet, and I'd have you over that shitty-excuse-of-a-guy any day of the week."

"Until he paid you attention. I've seen him. Fuck, I thought *I* had the lines and the moves ... until I met Flynn. He made me look like an amateur, I swear. I saw him turn sweet little girls into rampant, sex-thirsty whores."

Jess snickered. "So, you had the moves, huh?"

"You know what I mean. I was confident with girls. Flynn—he was cocksure. Never saw the guy strike out once. As soon as I brought him here, I regretted it. The way he looked at my little sister, I knew he wanted her. I had it out with him more than once, and in the end, I was taking no chances. I called on my buddies here just to get him away from her. He found a local whore to tap, and I'd done my job in keeping him away from Valerie. Hell, we even left early to go back to college, I was so worried."

I stood frozen, digesting what he'd just told Jess. Martin was the one who had instigated Flynn and Daisy's hook-up. I'd thought Flynn had covered himself well when he was here, so maybe I'd been more naïve than I'd been prepared to admit. Had I known everything I knew about Flynn at the time, I may have reacted differently. If I was honest, I doubted it.

For the previous few months, I'd been unable to get Flynn out of my head. It didn't help that he was everywhere. On TV, the radio; their track had gone to the top of the charts, so it was played on a loop from the local coffee shop to department stores. It had seemed like there was no escaping him. Smooth talking, flirty, and charismatic, he'd made my heart ache as I'd watched him hone his skills in the media limelight.

Jess came to our place a couple of days before Martin turned twenty-one. The day after his birthday, we were leaving for our trip. It was kind of a combined graduation and twenty-first birthday celebration. Martin had made it so awkward that my parents could not refuse to let me go with them. Sure, they protested, but Martin was adept at winning them over. He'd said all he wanted for his birthday was to share his trip with me.

What finally swung it in our favor was Kayden was almost twenty-three, and a responsible adult in my parent's eyes. He swore to protect me with his life, and they reluctantly agreed I could go, as long as I didn't drink. I'd have agreed to have my brows stapled together to go to Las Vegas for a whole weekend with no parents.

Obviously, my brothers played the tough guys and gave Ziggy "the talk" about their sister, and Ziggy didn't say anything to screw up his invitation. I was relieved about that. With four days to go, all any of us could talk about was planning the trip to Sin City.

The night before we were due to leave, Ziggy was very straight-talking. He asked me outright how I felt about Flynn, when he'd caught me watching a video on YouTube. I told him I loved their band's song "Thinking in Black and White". I did still have feelings deep down inside, but I'd explained long ago that there hadn't been anything but role play between us in the bleachers. That wasn't strictly true for his whole visit, but that was nothing important. None of what he'd said was genuine as far as I was concerned.

I was over Flynn. Mostly. I realized I loved Ziggy. He was sweet, affectionate, funny, and kind— and he loved me madly. An honest-to-goodness nice boy. Having him close by made me feel happy, and he thought I was the moon and stars. There was no denying that.

I didn't want to feel anything for Flynn. I'd hardly known him, but it hadn't stopped the clenching that rose in my chest, or the bottom falling out of my belly, whenever I heard his voice or saw him in a live interview on the screen.

Mom rapped on the door. "Valerie, honey. Ziggy's downstairs." I squinted my stinging eyes at my alarm clock. It read 6:21 A.M.

"Are you serious? What is he doing here so early?"

"He said he was too excited to sleep. Seems he was too excited for us to sleep as well."

Both of us burst out laughing.

"Aww, I think it's just so cute. He's a smart boy. He just has a bit of a child inside. Tell you what, Valerie. That boy will never grow old. Even when he's eighty, he'll still have an inner child wiggling his way out."

I knew what she was saying. Some people get old and grumpy. No one could ever have imagined that happening to Ziggy.

Laughter emanated from downstairs as I left my room fully dressed. As I wandered into the kitchen, everyone was already seated at the table with a bowl of cereal and a mug of coffee.

"Jeez, Beatnik. What kept you?"

I wasn't feeling well. Five minutes after Mom left the room, I'd doubled over with stomach cramps.

"Oh God, Valerie, do you feel okay? You don't look good, honey," my mom managed to get out before a wave of nausea swept over me. I spun on my heels and headed in the direction of our downstairs bathroom.

Forty minutes later, I was still vomiting. My legs and body shook violently, with the effort my body made to get rid of the bug plaguing me.

"That's it, we're going nowhere. I'm not taking her out of state while she's barfing her guts up," Martin stated flatly.

My heart sank; I couldn't ruin his birthday. "Go without me."

"Just go, Martin," Mom said, and I was sure she felt relieved I couldn't go with them.

"Not without Valerie. I'm not leaving her behind."

Ziggy spoke up, "You all go. I'll stay with Valerie."

"No, Ziggy! I want you to go. Please..." I stated weakly. I just wanted everyone to leave me to my misery.

After a lot of persuading, Martin, Jess, Ziggy, Kayden, and Adam finally set off for Las Vegas without me. It was the right decision. I cried, hurt because I was missing out, but I was too ill to do anything about it. Dad pacified me with the promise of an airline ticket if I recovered quickly. Mom gave me a drink to replace the salts in my body, and settled me in bed when I'd finally stopped vomiting.

Ziggy sent me a text.

Ziggy: This sux balls.

Me: I know, but I want you to have a good time.

Ziggy: How do I do that when you're not here?

Me: If I'm better tomorrow, Dad says he'll fly me out there.

Ziggy: Your dad wouldn't buy you a ticket if he knew what I was thinking.

Me: What are you thinking?

Ziggy: Me and you, tucked up in bed with little to no clothes. Scratch that — definitely no clothes. Cuddling skin to skin.

An unyielding ache resonated in my loins, as I thought about his words for a minute. Did I want *that*? I'd been booked in a room alone. Ziggy had been booked in a separate room. Martin had wanted Adam and Ziggy to share. Adam protested by saying, "It's Vegas, Martin. No."

Me: Sounds like I need to get well quickly.

Ziggy: I was expecting a text slap for that.

Me: At one time, maybe, but that's before I loved you.

Ziggy: Big grin. So, I'm still growing on you, huh?

Me: Totally.

Ziggy: So, if I learn some fancy talking, will I get in your drawers?

Me: Ziggy, the only way into my drawers is a secret.

Ziggy: Victoria's secret? I'll call and ask her what it is.

I smirked. Even in our texts, he managed to raise a smile from me while I was sick in bed.

Me: You're a tonic, you know that?

Ziggy: Yup, and you're my gin. Haven't felt sober since the day you agreed to go out with me.

Me: Have you always been this cute?

Ziggy: Wait until you see me with no clothes. Cute doesn't begin to cut it.

Me: LOL Is that your best line for displaying yourself naked to me?

Ziggy: You don't need lines with a body like mine. Been honed on the best prime beef and mashed potatoes the good ol' US of A has to offer.

Me: There you go killing my mood by mentioning food again.

Ziggy: Sorry, honey. You just make me so hungry sometimes. I can't help it.

Me: Me too, except when I'm sick.

Ziggy: Go to sleep. Text you when we arrive. Love you. Be well so you can come here. The hotel has great sheets - 500 thread I read.

Me: LOL You really are a dork. Night, Ziggy. xox

Ziggy: Valerie, I love you. Please get better. I'm lonely. You need to be here. I'm stuck in a car full of old people.

That made me giggle. He was only a year younger than Adam.

Me: I'll try. Night. X

When he didn't reply, I placed the cell back on my bedside table and sighed deeply. I was starting to feel better. The sickness had stopped, so I figured going to sleep was the best cure option I had. Drifting off, I heard my text alert again and checked the ID. It was Ziggy again.

Ziggy: One day, Valerie Darsin, I'm going to marry you. I take back all that junk I said about not analyzing us at sixteen. If you've kept me this long, I figure I must be doing something right. Love you x

I shook my head but felt thrilled that Ziggy loved me enough to rethink his original statement, and I adored his spontaneous nature for sharing it with me. I was thinking about that when I slipped off to sleep.

I woke in the darkness of my room and checked the time. It was only 5:47 in the morning, and I was starving. I slipped my feet to the floor and pulled on a bathrobe, before heading to the kitchen. Dad was already there, reading a newspaper.

"Hey, honey, how are you feeling?"

I thought for a second. "Good as new, I think. I'm hungry."

Dad smiled and shook his paper out. "So, that 'good as new' is going to cost the price of an airplane ticket, I take it?" I grinned but felt a little guilty that he'd be more out of pocket to fund my trip.

"Sorry."

"Don't be. You're my baby girl. If I didn't spend the family inheritance on you, life wouldn't be worth it. Your brothers have more than their fair share." My father pushed his chair back. "Get your tablet and find the numbers for the airlines."

Twenty minutes later, I was booked on an evening flight to Vegas, and I texted Ziggy the news.

Me: I'm coming. Flight won't be in until nine tonight, but at least I'm coming.

Ziggy: Yay. You said you were coming twice in that text. <raising my eyebrows> Pity you'll miss the trip to the Canyon. Still, at least you'll be here just after we get back.

Me: It's not a bunch of rocks I'm coming to see.

Ziggy: So, I'm a better attraction than the Grand Canyon?

Me: Well, of course.

Ziggy: Aww, I think I love you a little bit more now.

Me: Go do your thing. I'm nervous for tonight.

Ziggy: Ah, you mean my body—the naked thing? I'd be nervous too.

Me: Why would you be nervous?

Ziggy: I've seen my body. I'm hot. You may faint.

Me: LOL I'll be too busy laughing.

Ziggy: Nothing down there to laugh about, and it can all be yours. Just say the word.

Me: The word?

Ziggy: WOW.

I giggled loudly, and my dad raised his eyebrow, so I contained my smile.

Me: *shake my head* Okay, dork, catch you later. Mwah x

Ziggy: You already caught me. Love you.

I stood, clutching my cell to my chest, and smiled. Our text exchange had made me even more excited, and a little apprehensive about what would happen between us in Las Vegas. I wasn't sure we'd go all the way, but I felt ready for more than we'd experimented with already.

The feelings I had building inside for Ziggy made my heart flutter. I knew those yearnings weren't much different from his. All I had to do was ensure what I did was at my pace. Ziggy was a patient person so far, and I trusted he'd never ask me to do anything I wasn't ready for.

Chapter Eleven

EXCITED

ime passed slowly, way too slowly. Every time I stared at the clock on the kitchen wall, it seemed stuck. Nails painted, hair brushed for the hundredth time, lips glossed, I hadn't stopped fidgeting. Buster was whimpering to go out, so I took the leash, like always, and opened the door. A lump caught in my throat at the beautiful scenery around our place. We were so lucky to have all of that to look at in springtime, and I hoped I'd never take it for granted.

My excitement was difficult to contain. Four more hours and I'd be on a plane to join Ziggy, my brothers, and Jess. Even the Iowa weather cooperated that day. Snow was on the ground, but the sunshine gave the land a brilliance you'd only find on the cover of a glossy brochure.

Walking with Buster settled my nerves and gave me time to think about what I'd like from the few days away with Ziggy, but in the end, I figured if the time was right, I'd know it. The dog and I managed twenty minutes of outdoor play before he began to head back to the kitchen door. Turning the handle, I opened it, and the heat from inside was stifling.

Mom and Dad were in the sitting room, so I kicked off my boots and wandered in. The atmosphere was tense as I watched them glued to the T.V.

"How terrible, what a tragedy," Mom said.

"It's horrifying. See, that's why I don't like the kids going off without us. I know they have to grow up but…"

"What's wrong?" I asked, alarmed, as I glanced from them to the large screen.

"Some kids are missing from a white-water rafting trip in the Grand Canyon. Promise me you won't go there, Valerie."

I stared at the TV screen and saw divers and rescue workers along the river bank. A police helicopter hovered overhead, and an Air Ambulance One sat on the ground, with rangers and other officials milling around at the river bank.

"I won't. Anyway, I've missed the trip to the Canyon. They were going today."

I'd only finished talking when the TV station cut their repeated footage to interview a bystander who'd seen the boat capsize, and had caught the accident on his cellphone camera. The middle-aged guy looked grief-stricken. He glanced nervously at the camera, and then his eyes dropped toward the interviewer's mike.

"Ladies and gentlemen, this is Scott Rochford ,who witnessed the scene earlier and called 911 at the time. Thank you for speaking to us about this dreadful event unfolding before us. Mr. Rochford, can you tell our viewers what you saw, and explain the direction for us so we have a clearer picture of what happened?"

Dad rose from his seat and folded his arms, still watching the TV. What I'd said had registered with him, and his head suddenly snapped in my direction.

"Today? They were going to the Canyon today? Jesus. God. No," he said loudly, as he made his way to the kitchen.

"Yeah, but they were going on a helicopter ride, I think."

"Good. I mean, I'd have hated the boys to have seen any of this live," he expressed, sounding relieved. His hands rested on the counter top, and he continued to watch the TV again.

Meanwhile, the guy being interviewed was pointing out directions, and the interviewer cut back to the studio.

"Sorry, Mr. Rochford, I'm hearing from the studio we have your exclusive footage ready for our viewers, so let's take a look. Please excuse the quality of the filming. I repeat, this is amateur footage from the scene earlier taken by our witness on his cell as the tragedy unfolded."

Immediately, the feed of his video filled the screen. The quality wasn't great, like they'd said, but it was good enough for us to see the bright-blue inflatable boat that bounced in the foamy water. Seven people in life jackets clung to ropes attached to the boat. Two waved directly at the person filming, but before we could get a good look at them, it flipped over. But not quick enough for us not to recognize Jess's crazy luminous, self-knit berry and her red and white love heart jeans.

My dad flopped heavily into the chair, with a stunned expression, while Mom stood, wringing her hands, her eyes staring hauntingly into mine.

Hoping to breaking the tension, I grabbed my cell. "It's not them. Let me call Ziggy."

I pressed speed dial while Dad rose from his chair again, and grappled for his phone that was buried under newspapers on the table.

"Calling Kayden," a female voice sliced through the room.

"It went to voicemail," Dad said, stone-faced.

"Calling Ziggy," another female voice proclaimed.

Ziggy's cheerful voice answered, "Hi, if you're getting this, you're not getting me. I mean, you will eventually, I'm just not taking your call right now. Probably because I'm doing something better than talking on the phone. Leave a message. If I like you, I'll call you back when I'm bored. If you don't hear from me well, that'll probably be because I don't."

Meeting my father's gaze again, I hung up and tried not to sound as worried as I was.

"That would be normal if they were in an environment where they can't hear. Like a bar or a loud shopping area? Maybe they're on silent? Maybe they just haven't seen we've called yet."

My stomach had sunk to the floor. Blood rushed into my ears and the sound deafened me, drowning out my ability to think straight as my heart rate became erratic with panic. The uncertainty of my brothers' and Ziggy's whereabouts was beginning to take hold, and I tried not to alarm my parents any more than they were already. The panic was rising from deep inside, and I fought with everything I had not to lose control. Being hysterical wasn't going to give me information.

I called Martin. It went straight to voicemail. It didn't ring like the other two. *Is he on the phone?* "Martin, it's me."

Dad stood and flung out his hand in my direction.

"Give me that."

"It's voicemail, Dad. He's not there." I continued to leave a message, "Martin there's been an accident in the Grand Canyon. We know you were all going there today. Please call us as soon as you get this and let us know you're okay. See you later. Love You."

Dread and anguish had replaced my excitement about Las Vegas. My adrenaline was still running, but the feelings I had were completely opposite to those before I went to walk Buster.

Dad slapped his hands hard on the granite countertop, his arms shaking, as tears began to roll down his face. At first, I thought he'd snapped, and the pressure of waiting had become too much. I was about to go over and reassure him about everyone, but I noticed him staring out the window. My eyes followed his gaze and it was when I saw the Sheriff's car coming toward the house that the significance of what I was watching, hit me.

Pained, blood-curdling screams shook me from a daze. Scanning the room, both my parents were standing and crying, as their horrified faces stared back at me. An arm curled around my shoulder, and I turned my head to the left to see who it belonged to. A female who had entered the house with the sheriff stared with the same kind of pained look on her face the sheriff was wearing. Then, at some point, I realized the horrible wailing I'd heard, came from me.

Something snapped inside of me, and I recoiled from her touch. I tore myself away from her, as her hands reached out and tried to grab hold of me again. I couldn't breathe and threw the kitchen door open because I needed air.

Panic gripped my body and almost suffocated me. I heaved, but my lungs wouldn't expand. Pins and needles riddled my body from the lack of oxygen, and my heart was unable to pump fast enough.

A lightheaded feeling washed over me and I ran for the door. I had to get away. As I ran out, cold air seared into my throat and down to my lungs. The heady rush made me feel even dizzier, and the sunny landscape blinded me. Wailing rang in my ears, and suddenly I saw white light as I felt myself fall, and blackness descended.

Vomit covered my clothing as I came around. I'd fainted, and I was sitting up, supported by my dad and the stranger the Sheriff had brought with him. At first, the memory of being sick the day before came to mind, and I wondered if I'd had a relapse, then fear hit my nerves as I remembered my father's face immediately before the sheriff arrived. A tight fist squeezed my heart and once again, I struggled for breath.

Dad's tear-stained face came into focus as he knelt before me, sitting back on his haunches, looking helpless.

"Baby, you have to be strong. We don't know much yet, but we know Kayden and Jess are safe. Kayden managed to grab an overhanging tree branch. They've been flown to the hospital in Las Vegas. Adam, Martin, Ziggy... we can only hope they're somewhere downstream. That's the hope we've got to hang on to for now."

Fear and despair made my frame rigid. Foggy thoughts of the scene of the rubber boat capsizing left me distraught. I began to bargain with God for their safe return, and then screamed my pleas loudly into the open air around me as I looked to the heavens. "Please God, please, please don't take them." Mom was standing in the driveway, sobbing quietly and hugging herself, and I saw Auntie Joan's car arrive. She only lived ten minutes away from us by then.

After a while, I was persuaded to go back inside, was cleaned up, and a new t-shirt slipped over my head. I sat hugging myself, rocking in the chair, staring at the TV for God alone knows how long. News feed after news feed gave the same information over and over until I screamed at the TV to tell me something I didn't already know.

At some point, I went back to check my phone, and my heart leaped in my chest when I saw a new text from Ziggy. Quickly keying in the password, my eyes scanned the page.

Ziggy: Eek this river seems a little rough. I think this is to going to be a rocky ride. I'm pooping my pants and trying to look brave for your brothers. Wish you were here. See you soon, I love you.

If my heart ached before, I felt it crack at his message. I glanced up when two couples, who were neighbors and good friends of ours, turned up at the house. Sheriff Alex, had called them to support us. Four more people stood helplessly in our living room. I thought their presence was confusing, because they couldn't bring my brothers back.

An hour later, Dad was leaving with Dan and Stewart, our neighbors, to fly to Las Vegas. My pleas to go with them were dismissed when I was told Mom needed me at home. I needed them there with me, and when they left me stuck at home in Iowa, it made me feel helpless.

Sheriff Metcalf had someone go over to Ziggy's house, and his dad was meeting mine at the airport. The Sheriff drove off with my dad and the others. The rest of us sat glued to the TV, waiting for news after they'd gone. Two hours after they left, the rescue team found the first body, and even though I'd feared the worse and hoped for the best, I passed out again.

All of us women sat sobbing, even Debbie, because I guess what was going on was too much for her. She had no training in that kind of event; she'd been an acquaintance of my dad's through having her car serviced at the workshop is all. She'd come with her husband in case there was something she could do for us. Auntie Joan stood, strode over, and picked up the TV remote. She pointed it at the TV and the room fell silent. Turning, she headed toward the kitchen and started making more coffee.

"Valerie, you can make yourself useful and stack these cups in the dishwasher."

I'd seen this side of Auntie Joan before. She went into her practical mode because she couldn't be anything else. Without speaking, I complied with her demand and watched her take out more cups, pouring fresh coffee into them lined up on the black counter-top.

Retreating to the other side of the sitting room by the window, I stared out at the fading light, waves of grief hitting me with each new agonizing thought I pushed away. Six anguish-filled hours later, the phone rang. Auntie Joan stood, smoothed her hands down her skirt, and glanced over at me. She looked dismayed. I watched her swallow with difficulty and make her way over to the phone.

With every passing hour of no news, I feared the phone would ring. When it did, my instinct was to run. I couldn't. My mom was in the room. They may have been my brothers and boyfriend, but they were her children. Every ring was like a death knell, one closer to news I prayed not to hear, as I watched Auntie Joan nervously walk over to answer it.

Lifting the receiver, I noticed my aunt's hand shake as she held the phone to her ear. "Hello. Yes, it's me."

When she said that, I knew it was my dad on the phone. I held my breath as I watched her listen, and saw her hand cover her mouth and her eyes slowly close. For the longest time, she didn't move. After what seemed like forever, she shook her head and said, "I can't. Please..."

Another minute passed, and I wanted to scream. Then. I heard her murmur, "Okay." Her voice was barely audible.

The phone beeped, and my dad's voice came over the speaker on the phone.

"Marian? Valerie? Can you hear me?"

I sat motionless but glanced at my mom. She whispered, "I wish I couldn't."

Dad's voice sounded like he was trying to fight his emotions. His gruff, husky tone broke as he said, "I wish I had better news."

"Say it. Just say it, Gordon." My mom was trying to help him completely in that heart-stopping moment together.

"They found them, all three. All dead. Marian, they're gone. Ziggy, our beautiful boys..."

Mom and I started screaming, "No!" Auntie Joan took the phone back, and it beeped again. She was talking quickly, shielding the receiver to stem the tide of grief from my dad. Then she put the phone down.

Mom sat, rocking herself the same way I had been doing for hours, but sobbing, loudly.

"My beautiful babies. How cruel. Three beautiful boys, and now I only have one."

I ran and hugged her, but she shoved me away violently as she stood and headed for the outside door, just like I had done. I recognized the signs; she felt like she was suffocating. I did too. Running after her, my aunt reached her first. She was halfway down the driveway, screaming.

We caught her as she fell to her knees. Weak and worn from the trauma, she allowed us to lead her back toward the house. Our two neighbors stood helplessly by the door. Mrs. Metcalf told Auntie Joan she'd called the doctor as we passed her, while each of us was holding my mom upright. I didn't understand why Esther had done that at first, then it dawned on me that we needed help with the news we'd just received.

Twenty long, harrowing minutes later, Dr. Harding—the same doctor who had brought each one of us kids into the world, came and sedated my mom and me. I lay down on the couch and felt detached as my drug-induced calm descended. My thoughts became nothing, and I eventually fell asleep.

Chapter Twelve

NO HOPE

*R*olling over, I woke with a start, and I almost fell off the couch. Then, in the split second between waking and remembering what happened, I'd felt at peace. Then it was like the sky fell, when the horrible nightmare we were in came back. I sat bolt upright, my legs still stretched out in front of me.

"Martin?" I called out.

Auntie Joan appeared at my side and knelt to comfort me. "Ah, Valerie, you're awake, honey. Let me get you some coffee."

I stared blankly at my aunt walking away. I didn't want coffee. I wanted everyone to come home. Another huge wave of anguish and sorrow washed over me, and I cried again. I'd woken up to a living nightmare, and my split-second reaction had been to pray that my family's ordeal was a horrible mistake. Not that I wished it on another family. I just wanted it never to have happened at all.

The shrill ring of the house phone made me jump. My aunt hurried to answer, and listened before she handed it to Debbie. The Sheriff had more news. I rose swiftly to my feet and started crying again. I moved close to the countertop and asked what was happening. I already knew the outcome. All I needed to know now was when Kayden could come home with my dad.

Arthur, my dad's mechanic, arrived at the house and explained that Dad had sent him to pick my mom up and take her to Las Vegas. I screamed profanities and banged every door in the house, furious that my dad wasn't sending for me. I was family. His only daughter, and he left me alone in Iowa while he and my mom dealt with all the officials, and supported Kayden and Jess. Auntie Joan was left to support me. I'd had the feeling of being left out before, but this time, it made me livid.

Screaming uncontrollably, my irrational side took over, and I ordered everyone out of the house and told them to go home. When they protested, I became hysterical. Eventually, they left. My auntie and I stood inside the kitchen, watching Debbie climb into the Sheriff's car as he came to take her home. I was so eaten up with rage I couldn't think straight, and when she tried to pull me into a hug, I took my anger out on her as well.

"Don't. Don't fucking touch me. Don't try to comfort me when my own family has abandoned me."

"I *am* family, Valerie," she chided, with a hurt look in her eyes.

"Well, I don't fucking want you. I want Martin and Adam ... and Ziggy." I sobbed, heartbroken.

Tears rolled down her face at my brutal onslaught. She'd recently lost the person closest to her as well, I rationalized. Then I remembered Uncle Terry was older; Martin and Adam had their whole lives ahead of them, and they were snuffed out just like that.

My body was wracked with grief. An uncomfortable ache made my stomach feel like a deflated balloon, shriveled and hollow inside, just like my heart. My life was over. I didn't want to live in this world if they weren't in it with me. I stomped to the bathroom and flung open the cabinet, but all I found was Advil and a packet of acid-reducing pills.

Auntie Joan made me take more meds the doctor left, and within the hour, I was spaced out again, feeling numb. And when I let my mind go to the fact that Martin, Adam, and Ziggy were dead ... I felt nothing.

Feeling hopeless and helpless when the drugs wore off, I had nothing to console myself with. Every so often, my mind would kick in, and I'd start to bargain with fate. It was like, okay, there's this problem, and if I looked hard enough, I'd work out the solution. Except with this particular problem, the only solution I could come up with was for me to go the same way they had gone.

I didn't want to live. Not without all of us being together. My normal life was so far removed from the tragedy I faced. I couldn't imagine a time when the gaping hole left by the loss of my brothers would ever shrink to a manageable level.

Somehow, I found myself in bed, and my emotions started to leak back into my bloodstream, and once there, they coursed through my veins and consumed me again. The tide of grief rushed in, and it drowned my heart. I sobbed again and again, my breath hitching repeatedly, and my chest tightened repeatedly until I had no more tears and I fell unconscious, exhausted from bargaining with God, and fearing the future.

Trucks? I woke to the sound of a loud diesel engine idling outside. My head felt muggy and heavy. The fuzzy, screwed-up thoughts inside my head were a chaotic mess. I was nauseous and thirsty. As soon as I moved, my body ached. Rolling off the bed, I made my way to the bathroom and barely reached the toilet bowl as my stomach lurched.

Voices on the landing made me freeze for a second before the wave of nausea came crashing in again, and I dry heaved over the bowl. The voices drew nearer, but I couldn't move. I sat back on my haunches just long enough to hear my aunt say, "Stay here, I'll see if she's awake."

Instantly, the bathroom was bathed in bright light, and my aunt crouched down beside me. She started to cry at the sight of me, and began rubbing my back. When I looked at her, she looked like I felt. Wrecked.

"That friend of Martin's is outside, Valerie. I told him we weren't taking guests, but he insists on seeing you."

I dry heaved and sat back on my legs again, wiping my mouth with yet more toilet tissue.

"What friend?"

"You know, the one from Thanksgiving. Flynn."

My heart almost stopped. *Flynn's here?* My stomach tightened. I was confused that he'd turned up at the door. Especially with what had happened to Martin. *Does he know?* I didn't feel strong enough to tell him if not. I was struggling to accept it, so the thought of voicing the words to Flynn was hard because it would make it all too real.

Seeing him at my weakest and knowing how bad my heart felt before, when he'd crashed in and walked out of my life, there was no way on God's earth I was letting Flynn Docherty within spitting distance of me.

"Tell him to go away. I don't want to see him. We have enough to deal with, without some egotistical rock star bringing attention to our door. Get him out of here, Auntie Joan. I don't want to see him."

"I think he's come a long way, Valerie."

"I don't give a shit how far he's come. Flynn Docherty doesn't get to waltz in here and play on our grief."

She stood, leaned over the bath, and began to run water into the tub. "Are you sure? I mean, if he goes away now and you change your mind, it doesn't look like you'll be able to just pick up the phone. He's got a bus out there with his face on the side. I think he's come straight from work, Valerie."

From where? What is she talking about? "Get rid of him. I don't want to see him. I don't want to talk about Martin and Adam. I don't want to be the one to tell him that news. Tell him to go away. He's not welcome here." I sobbed again and doubled over in pain.

"Okay, just stop. Calm down. It's okay, honey. No one is going to make you do anything right now, except maybe me. Get in the tub. You need to get clean. You've been sick, and you have to clean up; it's in your hair."

Tears rolled down my face as she helped me strip and I sat in the tub. Devoid of modesty or shame. It wasn't a time for being embarrassed. I was so tired and worn down with the most unimaginable grief, I hardly knew what I was doing.

Auntie Joan stayed with me and washed my hair. She was so gentle and caring, and her kindness was almost too much for me, when I remembered what I'd said to her before.

"Sorry about earlier—"

"Stop. I know. You don't have to tell me, Valerie. Life isn't fair. You were angry, and I know that was your hurt talking. I'll go and tell him you're not accepting visitors right now."

That earned a smile from me because I was buck naked, sitting in the bath with the stench of puke still fresh in the air. Of course, I wasn't up for having company. She stepped outside and softly closed the door. I heard muffled voices. Flynn's tone sounded pleading and urgent, but a few minutes later, I heard the front door close and the pneumatic release of his bus door closing.

I lay back and rinsed the sponge down my body. The distraction of Flynn in our house had made me even more confused and hurt. I finished washing and stepped out, pulling my bathrobe from the door, and wrapping it tightly around me. I padded back into the bedroom and wandered over to the window. I wasn't impressed with what I saw.

A huge fancy touring bus with black metallic paint and a purple and white sash running down the side, with Flynn and three other guys' faces on it, was sitting in our driveway. *He can stay there for all I care.* He'd never really kept in touch with Martin when he left college, except for that time at Christmas, so I figured he hadn't been a true friend to him. Martin collected people. He made friends like no one else I'd ever met. He always used to say, "You can't have too many friends."

I pulled on some sweatpants and a hoodie, and slowly made my way downstairs. Auntie Joan was sitting, staring at the fireplace when I entered the room.

"I'm not hungry, but maybe I should try some dry toast or something."

She turned to look at me and smiled. "Sure, I think that would be a wise move, honey."

She stood and looked out the window. "Flynn's bus is still out there, Valerie. Are you sure you don't want to talk to him?"

"No. He's nothing. Martin was a good friend to him, and he walked away. I'm not letting him have that luxury twice."

"Valerie, we all do things in our lives that we regret later or wish we'd handled differently. When you've been around as long as I have, you'll learn that in life."

"I don't want to be around that long, not without my brothers and Ziggy," I answered angrily.

Auntie Joan nodded as her eyes softened. "Valerie, it's a terrible,

terrible tragedy ... for all of us. I understand how you feel right now, but your life *will* go on. You'll find your new normal, just like I'm trying to find mine, and now that the boys... What I'm saying is, it's not easy, it's never easy. But you will find your smile again in time."

Banging the knife on the countertop, I turned, furious at her comment. "I don't want my fucking smile. I want my brothers back."

Auntie Joan looked helplessly at me. A loud knock tamped my anger toward her and my focus turned in the direction of the door. "Flynn Docherty, if that's you, go the fuck away. You're not welcome."

Buster stood and began barking at the door. I huffed loudly, exasperated that Flynn wouldn't leave. I grabbed the door handle and threw the heavy door open wide until it banged against the wall. The sight of him took my breath away. He looked stunning as always, but his face bore the same tear-stained, haunted look my mom had worn before she left for Las Vegas.

Without a word, he stepped forward and pulled me tightly to his chest. My heart cracked, and my throat constricted with emotions too powerful to place. Flynn's warm body leaned into mine. I eventually responded by sagging into the physical comfort he offered. I hadn't been able to accept anyone touching me until Flynn held me in his arms.

I vaguely heard Auntie Joan take Buster's leash and call him out the door. Then it closed softly, and we were alone.

Once again, I began to sob loudly. Flynn's shoulders shook as he pulled me tighter against him. His breathing became uneven and I realized he was crying as well. I pushed him back and stared up at him.

"I can't bear this. I don't want to need you to do this," I said as I rubbed my forehead across his chest when I shook my head.

"Sweet, Valerie. There is nowhere else I could be right now. Martin had such a big heart, and I know how much he meant to you. If being here helps you in some small way, then it's the least I can do. He was an amazing person. I just didn't know what I'd lost until I didn't have him around anymore."

Flynn was silent for a couple of seconds, and I heard him swallow. "Once I'd moved, I figured I'd blown it with him. I mean, I just upped and left, but that's been my problem all my life. Someone gets too close, and I need to let them go before they let me down and leave me. That way I can cope, and I know exactly where I stand."

"Martin wasn't like that, Flynn, once you were his friend you were there for life." I began crying again and my face was still close to Flynn's chest. He smelled of Flynn. His strong hands splayed protectively over my back, holding me tightly in place.

"We'll get through this, Valerie. We'll help each other."

I placed my hand on his chest and pushed him away. "No. Martin didn't want you near me. He told me all about you and how you are with girls."

"I know. That's one of the reasons I went with Iria. I had to put you in my past. He hated that I liked you, and with your age... We had a huge argument about you. Did he tell you?"

"He told me you had words."

Flynn laughed. "Words? Jesus, Valerie, he told me he'd cut my dick off if I went anywhere near you. It was out of respect for him I stayed away after we'd left. I figured with the number I'd left, if you were interested in me, you'd have called. You didn't."

"You played with me. Martin told me you went with that girl a few days after you left here. You saw a young, impressionable girl, and you toyed with my feelings. I hate you for that."

"Good, keep it that way. I'm not good for you, Valerie, but that may not stop me from wanting you. You're sweet sixteen, and fooling around with you would be a terrible idea."

"See? You're doing it again. Don't mess with my mind, Flynn. There's nothing left to mess with. There's nothing you could say or do now that would make me want to be romantically involved with you. Out. Now. I want you out of here."

"Don't worry, I'm going, but I'll be in the driveway. I'm not going anywhere. I'm here for as long as you need me. I can do that much for Martin, at least."

Chapter Thirteen

VISITORS

*S*lamming the door behind Flynn, I stood, shaking, with my hands on my hips. *How dare he show up here and do that to me!* I banged and crashed my way around the kitchen in frustration, too mad to cry anymore. I began making the toast I didn't want to eat, but knew I had to if my stomach was going to feel any better. The toaster popped just as Auntie Joan opened the kitchen door.

"This Iowa weather ... I can't figure it out; one day it's sunny, the next it's frosty out there again."

We heard the bus engine start and rev up outside. It began to pull away. "I think Flynn's leaving, Valerie."

"Good. At least he took my advice," I said, but my heart felt heavy. I was hurt he hadn't stayed and fought for me, despite what I'd said. I didn't know what I wanted at that point. The pain of losing my brothers and Ziggy was incredibly hard to bear. All my defenses were completely broken down. I was heartbroken. Flynn skipping out again was no more than I'd expected. There were too many overwhelming thoughts to think about, without him confusing me further, but I was still inconsolable after he left. God alone knows how long I sat, staring at the wall between crying bouts.

Streaks of light started to come through the plantation shutters in the kitchen, and I realized Auntie Joan and I had sat there all night. We hadn't spoken much. Our minds were locked in the grief we both felt. I glanced at the kitchen door, and the thought of Martin and Adam never walking through it again set off another bout of crying. Auntie Joan joined in, but I wasn't sure we were crying for the same people. She had new people to grieve for, and she hadn't had a chance to grieve properly for her husband.

Hearing the sound of a car coming up the driveway, I pushed up off my chair to look out the window. It was two of Martin's friends from high school, Matthew and Ryan. They'd always been close, and Martin had invited them along on the trip with us. Neither could come, due to work commitments.

Auntie Joan opened the door, and two ashen faces stared in at us. Ryan let his tears run down his face unashamed while Matthew choked back tears and cleared his throat. "We had to come..."

"Come inside," I said in a small voice.

Ryan swept past Auntie Joan and hugged me tightly.

"I'm so sorry, Valerie. They were..." His voice broke, and he cried openly into my shoulder.

I found myself rubbing his back, comforting him, when it was *my* loss. Then I realized they weren't exclusively my losses. Lots of people loved Martin and Adam. Lots of people loved Ziggy.

The boys were a welcome distraction for us, as it turned out. After paying their respects, they talked with affection about funny things that had happened in the past, and in a strange way, it brought me closer to my brothers. Having people around who knew them and remembered stories from their childhood, was comforting. We laughed and cried together, and by the time they left, I had a sense of Martin and Adam near me again, even though that wasn't possible. All I truly had were memories.

Another vehicle came up the driveway, just after the boys left. It was loud and heavy. Auntie Joan poked her head up and peeked through the blinds. "Who's this? It's a huge recreational vehicle." The RV ground to a halt across from the house, but no one got out of it.

My aunt pulled on some boots and called Buster from his basket.

Grabbing Dad's wax-proof jacket she headed out to see who it was. I watched from the window as she walked over to the door and knocked.

When the door swung open, Flynn stood in the doorway, and adrenaline flooded my body. *He came back!* My mind was in disarray at the emotions running through it, but I know I felt elated and relieved that he hadn't just disappeared again. I watched them talking, then Auntie Joan stepped back as he went inside and pulled the door closed. She turned and headed back toward the house.

Cold morning air wafted into the kitchen when she opened the door, and she bustled around, taking her things off again.

"His bus had to go. His band tour is finished, so the bus had to go back because it's used for other bands, apparently. He rented that RV. There's some guy in there with him, and Flynn said he's got no commitments for at least two weeks." Her face softened as she read my confused expression.

"He's here for you if you want to talk, Valerie, but he says he's here for all the family and is ready to do whatever needs to be done. He told me he'll make the arrangements for whatever we need."

Mr. Big Shot Rock Star. After our previous conversation, I wondered if his guilt had brought him back. From everything Martin had said, I'd thought of Flynn as a self-centered person. As far as I knew, he'd always taken what he wanted from people, when he wanted. Once I had that thought, I wondered if he had some ulterior motive for coming. If so, I had to figure out what it was.

Sometime around one in the morning, I headed upstairs. Mom and Dad hadn't called, and I was feeling angry and deserted by them. It felt like an afterthought to them, even though deep down I knew that that wasn't true. None of us were thinking straight; none of us knew what to do. None of us were coping with the impact the boys' deaths were having on us.

~

Sleep didn't come easy that night, and knowing Flynn was sleeping a few feet from the house was even more unsettling. Buster began to whimper at my door, so I rolled out of bed and pulled on my robe. I padded downstairs and into the kitchen. Opening the door, I saw Flynn standing outside his RV, the inside light shining out into the darkness and casting a long shadow of him in my direction. He was talking on his phone. It was the dead of night and he was out there in the dark, talking on his phone.

Buster barked and ran over to him, and my heart ached in my chest. The last thing I wanted was another angry conversation with Flynn. He glanced up and pulled his phone from his ear. He held it mid-air and stared over at me. Placing the phone back to his ear, I heard, "I'll call you back," before he ended his call and shoved his cell into his left jacket pocket. Flynn stalked toward me, and I was rooted to the spot. I was tired and angry and sad. There was no fight left in me that night.

"Hey, babe. How are you holding up?" His voice was soft, and he made no attempt to touch me. I noted how hard he was pushing his hands deeper into his jeans pockets, and wondered if it was because he knew I'd erupt if he had reached out for me.

I hugged myself because the sympathy in his voice drew me toward him. One sentence and I wanted him to hold me again. I wasn't sure if that was because I just needed someone to hold me, or because I needed him. Tears sprang to my eyes again. It took nothing to set me off on another wave of sorrow. Instantly, his arms curled around my back, hugging me tightly, and he cried with me again. At that point, I realized Martin's death had truly affected him.

There were no words to describe how I was feeling. I needed what Flynn offered me, even though I knew Martin would have hated what we were doing. I began to shake violently in shock again, and he wrapped his arm around me.

"Come on babe, let's get you inside," Flynn coaxed softly.

"I can't..."

"It's okay, Lee's inside. We won't be alone. It's too cold out here for you. Come inside."

Reluctantly, I climbed the stairs and entered the cabin of the RV. A spacious seating area with two plush, soft velvet sofas made the space comfortable.

"Sit. Let me get you a hot drink."

Flynn strode over to a small kitchen area and lifted the coffee pot sitting on the hot plate.

"No cream, right?"

I was surprised he'd remembered such a small thing about me after six months.

Flynn handed me the mug of steaming hot coffee, and I cupped my hands around it.

"Ziggy was my boyfriend," I whispered, and started to cry again.

"The other kid with them? Shit, Valerie. I'm so sorry, sweetheart."

"I was flying to meet them. I should have been there. I should have been in that boat with them," I said, sobbing between shaky breaths.

Flynn huffed loudly and leaned forward on the sofa opposite me. "I'll thank God every day you weren't, babe."

"And what do I get to thank God for? You?"

"Maybe one day you will," he said, smiling softly, and his eyes held my gaze.

"More like I'd be thanking the devil for bringing you back here."

Flynn exhaled heavily, stood up, and ran his hands through his hair, looking helpless again. Suddenly the space inside the RV felt cramped.

"I know what you said about Martin, but I think he'd like that I came back to take care of you."

My eyes ticked over Flynn. Even in my grief, I couldn't fail to notice how stunningly handsome a man he was. The boy in him had gone. He seemed more mature, even though it had only been six months since we'd met.

"I doubt that. Both he and Auntie Joan warned me off you."

"Well, all I can say is, they both knew what it was like to lust after someone. Trust me. once you've felt it, you recognize it in others."

My eyes roamed the inside of the RV because I had no idea what to say to that. I'd felt excited when he'd pushed me into my room that one time, but I despised the effect he'd had, because I felt the situation was hopeless. I thought about how he'd kissed me, stopping short of a proper passionate kiss. *Why had he stopped? Was it because he saw me as a child? Was it because of Martin, like he said? Or had he been tormenting me for the sake of it?*

"So, you came back because I'm sixteen, and you see me as some kind of challenge now?"

His expression was angry. "Is that what you think? God, no, Valerie. I'm here because I care about you. I'm here because I loved Martin like a brother. I'm also here because I feel if there is anything I can do to ease everyone's grief, no matter how little that may be, then it's the only place I want to be." The tone of his voice was angry, and I knew I'd offended him.

"And what about what *we* want? What about what *I* want?"

"What do you want, Valerie?"

"I wanted you to leave, and here you are, still here." I gestured weakly with my hand toward him.

"That was your hurt talking, babe. If I'd shown my face and disappeared again, you'd have been even more upset. Am I right?"

He was. I was venting at him because I wanted him there, but at the same time I didn't want to want him. Ultimately, I was just so heartbroken and angry. I sat, staring up at him again, and tried to think while my eyes searched his face. Stubble had grown on his chin since he'd arrived last night, and this made his appearance more rugged. Instead of looking disheveled, it had only made him even better looking. He stood and peeled his jacket off his shoulders, folded the front of it together, and draped it over the arm of his sofa. His right arm was covered in an intricate tattoo, a new addition to his previously smooth, tanned skin I'd remembered.

"What do you want, Flynn?"

"Honestly? You, Valerie, but... I know that's a bad idea, and the timing couldn't be shittier to say it to you. Besides that, I want to help you all get through this horrible, horrible thing."

"It's not a 'thing,' Flynn. It's my brothers. They died. My boyfriend *died*."

I sat, tortured with the reality of that again, and burst into tears again.

"I was getting close to sleeping with Ziggy. I loved him. Still love him."

Flynn couldn't stem the growl that tore from his throat, but he said nothing.

"This is where you growl and tell me you're glad I didn't; that I should save myself for someone like you?"

"Nope. Never me. I'd hate to be your first. It hurts, and I never want you to hurt again."

"Is that right?"

"Yes, it is. You want to know how I feel about you, Val?"

"Not if you're about to bullshit me. I'm all bull-shitted out right now, if it's all the same to you."

"No bull, just straight talking, you think you can handle that?"

"I'm not a child, Flynn. Stop talking to me like I am one."

"Okay, first. I want you. Fuck … I want you so fucking badly. I've said it before. I've never wanted any woman as much as I want you, but you're barely legal and innocent as hell. I'll respect your wishes. The first move would have to be entirely yours."

"You kissed me before. So, I guess you already made the first move."

"Hardly. Do you know how damned hard it was to walk away from you? Touching your lips like that left a stain on mine. I think, had it been another time and place, that encounter wouldn't have ended anywhere near as composed as I left it."

"Me being fifteen wouldn't have stopped you?"

"That's why I said another time. Your age and my friendship with Martin were the only things that saved you. If it hadn't been for those two things, I may have acted differently."

"But now you're a big-shot rock star, and those barriers are gone. You can have any girl you want, right?"

Flynn snickered and looked down at his Chuck's before meeting my gaze again. "So the stories go."

"What does that mean?"

"You shouldn't believe everything you read in the papers."

"And what should I believe? Are you saying you were set up in Los Angeles by the pool? From the pictures in the papers, your jeans were at your ankles. How did you spin that one to your girl?"

"What can I say? I'd tried repeatedly to end things with her after a couple of months together, but she wouldn't let me go."

"So you publicly humiliated her instead?"

"Nope. She already knew how I felt, and if you must know, I was just honest-to-God blind drunk. I had no idea how I even got to that pool, let alone the aware of the stuff that was going on."

"That says it all. You're not capable of thinking of others. I'd never want to be with someone like that. Ziggy ... he adored me. He would have loved me my whole life if I'd let him."

My eyes filled to the brim with tears and rolled down my cheeks. This time, it was for Ziggy. For *what could have been* that was ripped right out from under me. Mixed emotions made my head swim as I sat in his RV. The sad, lost feelings from knowing I'd never see Ziggy again, sadness that we'd never experienced a more intimate connection, and the pure frustration because I had thoughts connected to lust.

Pushing myself from the sofa, I made my way to the door. "I'm going back inside, Flynn. Do what you want about staying here. Nothing I say will make any difference to a guy like you anyway. You'll always try to get your way, but you're wasting your time with me."

I pulled on the latch and the door sprung open.

"Valerie?"

I stopped and turned to look in his direction. Flynn stood up and walked over to where I was standing. "I mean it. I want to help. Despite what you think, I loved Martin. I want to honor his death."

We stared silently at each other for about a minute. Neither of us blinked. I slowly nodded my acceptance that he thought he was doing the right thing. I jumped down onto the driveway and called out to Buster. We headed inside and, once Buster was settled in bed, I went back to mine. My last thought that night was it had been more than a day since Adam, Martin, and Ziggy had drawn their last breath, and then I cried some more.

Chapter Fourteen

YOU HAVE TO EAT

*B*rilliant sunshine streamed in through the window. I hadn't bothered to close the shutters when I went to bed. When the house phone rang, my aunt clomped her way downstairs to answer. There was a phone in my parents' bedroom and in Kayden's. I wasn't sure why she'd gone all the way downstairs to answer.

Slipping out from between the sheets, I padded through to my bathroom. I felt like a mess, and what I saw staring back at me was basically how I felt—disastrous. Staring blankly at the mirror, there was not a thought in my head, other than one that kept circling in my brain like a needle stuck in the same groove: *How do I live without them?*

"Can you come and speak with your father, Valerie?" Auntie Joan called up to me.

Spinning away from the mirror, I hurriedly ran to my parents' room and lifted the receiver of the phone.

"Hello? Dad? How's Kayden doing? When are you coming home?" My voice quivered on the last sentence, and I tried to swallow back the emotions I was feeling, but it was too late. I sobbed into the phone for my dad to come back. His response was gentle but firm.

"Valerie. We're all struggling with being apart. Your mom and I are doing our best. We hope to be home tomorrow or the next day." A long pause filled the airwaves between us.

"Dad?"

He continued, "There has to be a medical examination of the boys. We know it was an accident, but they were young men, and a cause of death has to be recorded."

My father's voice wavered like he was going to cry, and he cleared his throat. "Kayden will be in the hospital for another day, at least. You'll have to be patient because we refuse to come home until we can bring all our boys home."

Of course, he was right. He couldn't fly back just because I needed him. Detaching myself from the grief helped me to see it from my parents' perspectives. Somewhat comforted by the way he said, "all our boys," I accepted that he should stay in Las Vegas and do what was necessary before he came home.

"Flynn called me, Valerie. He seems like a good boy. He's there for you and Joan. Take care of yourself for us. Eat and sleep; it's important. You may feel you won't cope with this, Valerie. But you will. It takes a long time when you lose someone you love, but you'll learn to live with it."

My dad's words sounded so callous. Normally, he'd always tried to smooth the waters for me, against anything that wasn't palatable. When he spoke to me like that, I realized I was no longer his baby. I had to grow up quickly.

Placing the receiver back on the cradle, I wandered back to my room. As I passed my brothers' rooms, my fingers trailed across their wooden doors, and my heart silently screamed *WHY?* I couldn't bring myself to open their doors and step inside. I took a deep breath and walked more purposefully into my room and closed the door. Auntie Joan had left meds on my nightstand when I was on the phone. I swallowed them without hesitation.

Sedated, washed and dressed, I made my way downstairs and once again, Buster jumped and fussed to be let out. Without thinking, I opened the door, and Flynn jumped out of the RV and immediately headed toward me.

"Did you sleep, babe?"

"Some."

"Have you eaten? You—your aunt? Either of you eaten?"

I shrugged. The last thing I'd thought about was food.

"Come inside. Lee's making some scrambled eggs and bacon. You need to eat."

Too tired to argue, I trudged inside and sat heavily on the sofa. Flynn sat next to me, lifted my hand, and laced his fingers in mine. His touch felt warm, safe, and intimate.

"I'm here, Valerie," he murmured softly, squeezing his fingers around mine.

I didn't feel emotional. Drugs can do that. I was numb and calm.

Lee was introduced to me as Flynn's assistant. I studied him while he moved around the tiny kitchen area. He was built like a Sherman Tank.

"Is he your bodyguard?"

"I prefer *close protector*."

"Whatever, he takes punches that are meant for you," I said, sounding mean.

"Valerie, he's never been punched on my behalf. Have you, Lee?"

"Nah, no one is jealous enough to punch this dude," he chuckled, and glanced at Flynn.

Flynn smirked knowingly. "Jealous no, mad ... maybe. I wouldn't put it past Valerie to swing a punch at some point. She sure as hell gets mad enough sometimes."

"I'd have to feel something for you. I don't."

"Well, Valerie. I don't think that's strictly true, but I'm not going to push that button right now. We need to focus on helping you get your strength back, babe."

Lee placed three plates of food on the table and motioned for me to sit. "Eat. I hate seeing food go to waste," he said, making brief eye contact.

Flynn stood up, tugging at my hand, and I realized his fingers were still threaded between mine. I started to pull it away, and his fingers tightened.

"Don't. Come over and sit."

Without speaking, I stood, stepped over, and slid into the chair at the table by the window. Flynn sat next to me, never breaking his grasp on my hand.

"Can I have my hand back to eat, or are you going to feed me?"

He dropped my hand and picked up his fork. "So, after this, I think we should take a walk. This place is huge. I'd like you to show it to me."

Flynn stuffed some eggs into his mouth and glanced in Lee's direction.

Lee glanced out the window. "More visitors."

Doors banged. I counted four of them. There were four people outside. Flynn looked over at me. "Stay there. I'll get rid of them."

Pushing the door open, he jumped down and closed it behind him. Lee looked straight at me. "That guy is golden. You can abuse him all you want, but since he heard the news about your brother, his only thoughts have been about him and y'all. He made the bus driver come straight here, and he paid for the rest of the band to go to a hotel, and their flights home. Six hours straight it took him to get here when he saw what happened on TV."

My eyes held his, and we sat silently for what seemed like eternity, neither of us backing down with our gazes, until I eventually spoke again. "Really?"

"Uh, huh. Now I know you feel like your heart's being ripped out of your chest. It's your kin n' all, but that fella over there, who's got your back, has no one. You'd do well to remember that. What you're going through? He's got first-hand knowledge of that. So, even though this is none of my business, I'm making it mine. You might want to cut him some slack for the kindness he's showing right now."

Grief wasn't exclusive. Lee was right. I'd had no idea what Flynn had been through or what had shaped him to be the way he was. Inhaling deeply, I held it for a second and then let my breath out in as a controlled fashion as I could manage.

"You're right. I'm being a bitch, but you don't know the whole story."

"You, the girl in the barn, the way he almost took you even though you were underage? That story?"

I swallowed awkwardly and coughed, stunned that Flynn would tell anyone what happened with me. It left me wondering if perhaps I'd meant more to him after all. The click of the latch halted our conversation, and Flynn came back inside.

"Elsie Hammond, she went to school with Martin? It was her and her family."

I nodded. Elsie and Martin were boyfriend and girlfriend for almost two years, on and off. Neither of them could admit they still liked each other after they split up. Martin would have been pleased she showed up.

"Finished?" Flynn gestured his head at my plate. "Don't worry, they said they wouldn't tell anyone I was here."

I nodded, and Lee took it away.

"Let's get Buster and head out."

Flynn reached out his hand, and I took it. It was a small gesture on my part to let him know I appreciated his support. He tugged me out of the seat and led me outside. We walked to the house, and I grabbed the leash from behind the door. I called for Buster but then remembered I'd let him out already. I opened the door and called his name, and he came running from the back of the house.

Flynn and I started walking, and our conversation covered everything from us growing up in the house as kids, the games we played, the music we listened to, and eventually the subject turned to me meeting Ziggy.

A lump formed in my throat and my chest tightened when I spoke about him. The meds were wearing off. I had no awkward feelings about telling Flynn how Ziggy made me feel. That boy had given me some of the best emotions I'd ever had. He walked in silence beside me, allowing me to tell him as much about Ziggy as I could cope with. I was thankful for his quiet presence; having someone to listen was invaluable.

Most people don't want to ask anything or talk about the deceased when someone has died, for fear of upsetting the survivors. Nothing can upset us more than losing our loved ones in the first place. If it had been the one thing I had learned from my time with Auntie Joan, it was that talking about the dead to the people closest to them, seemed to bring the kind of comfort sympathy cards and tea couldn't reach.

Glancing at his watch, Flynn continued to listen, but steered us in the direction of the house again. We'd started the walk together in an awkward, side-by-side kind of way. Each of us keeping our distance from the other, by the time we headed back, Flynn's arm was around my shoulder and I was hugging his waistline. At some point, I don't remember exactly when, he'd stepped closer and offered his arm to me. I accepted his offer of comfort, without question.

Seeing another car in the drive, Flynn directed me straight to his RV again, opened the door, and stepped inside with me. Lee was watching TV and straightened up in the chair.

"More visitors, Valerie. There's been a steady stream since you've been gone. That's the fourth car since you left. Joan took them inside the house," Lee explained.

The sound of car doors closing was quickly followed by my aunt knocking on the RV door. Lee opened the door, and my aunt explained they were taking her into town with them for a while. Flynn had stayed out of sight that time. She asked me to stay with Flynn and Lee while it was daylight, just in case more people turn up. No one but Flynn ever came to our place in the dark, unless they were invited.

Standing, I shook my head. "Thanks for today, Flynn, but, no Auntie Joan. I'm going inside now. I won't answer the door if they come."

"You're not staying alone, Valerie. I promised your dad."

"Fine. Then you can come and sit in the house. I'm not spending my time in a caravan thing when the house is right over there."

"It's not a caravan," Flynn said indignantly.

"Sorry, RV, motor home, whatever. I need to go home."

Flynn stood and took my hand. "Fine, then we'll go back."

My emotions were running high again. The meds weren't doing their job anymore. I stood and meekly followed him back to the house. Once inside, I was at a loss for what to do with myself.

We sat in silence for about twenty minutes when Flynn asked, "Have you gone into their rooms yet?"

My head snapped up in his direction and tears sprang to my eyes. "No," I whispered, feeling dismayed at the thought of facing that.

"It helps. Want to go up there?"

I shook my head as panic gripped my chest.

"Trust me, Valerie. It helps. The longer you avoid it, the more of a barrier it becomes."

"And you became an expert on this stuff, when exactly?"

"When I was eleven. A lot younger than you are now."

Our eyes met, and I saw the flicker of pain and honesty he bore in them as he stared intensely into mine.

"What happened?"

"My dad killed my brother and my mom."

My heart stuttered because I hadn't expected what he said.

"Oh. My. God. Flynn. I had no idea."

The horror of him being a young boy who had lived with that burden shook me to my core. Not only had he experienced separation and loss, he had been willing to suffer the grief and all its devastating feelings to come back to offer comfort to us in our time of need.

"It isn't widely known, Valerie. My dad didn't mean it. I mean, he meant to hurt us. He did that a lot. He just threw two unlucky punches —one at my mom's temple, and the other at my brother's throat when he went to help her. He wiped out half of my family in one violent span of madness. He was drunk. Thankfully, I don't remember it at all. The memory has been blocked from my mind since the night it happened."

Less than a heartbeat later, I flung my arms around him in a tight hug. Flynn immediately reciprocated in the same way. We clung to each other desperately in our joint sorrow. It hadn't occurred to me, until Lee spoke earlier, that Flynn really understood what I was going through. When he leaned back, I saw the pained look in his eyes. There was no doubt he knew what I was going through. I buried my face in the crook of his neck, as a wave of sadness washed over me. Tears pooled in my eyes and spilled over yet again.

Flynn pushed me away and stood up. He took my hand and started leading me toward the stairs. "You need to do this, Valerie. Trust me."

I tried hard to pull my hand away. "No."

Flynn grabbed me by the waist, and the fear of what he wanted me to do made me panic., "Look at me, Valerie. Have I helped you get through the day so far?"

"Yes, but..."

"Then trust me to get you through the rest of it."

With a heart full of dread and my stomach in knots, I let Flynn lead me upstairs. We stopped outside Adam's door. Flynn reached out and turned the handle. The door opened, and the first thing I saw was Adam's prized possession—his signed, framed Wez Welker number eighty-three jersey hanging on his wall. Next to it was a cabinet where he shelved his football trophies.

My dad made the cabinet when Adam won his third one when he was seven years old. That's when we knew he was going to be a football star. He'd have been a huge celebrity football player in time. Everyone who knew Adam said so.

My eyes continued to scan the room and rested on his bed. My breath caught in my throat because the room smelled of Adam. My throat closed with emotion when I pictured him lying there asleep, in my mind's eye. His room was neat, just like Adam. He was always organized. I closed the door and breathed a heavy sigh of grief, as more tears rolled down my face.

Flynn squeezed my hand and leaned closer, brushing my tears with the fingertips of his other hand. "You're doing great, Valerie," he cooed softly ,and began tugging me toward Martin's door. I initially struggled and tried to flee. He pulled me in for a tight hug and rubbed my back again. My heart felt as if it would break if he opened Martin's door.

"You can do this, babe. Martin wouldn't want you to be afraid of him or anything about him."

He was right, of course. Flynn turned the handle and opened the door. He pulled me inside before I could think too much about it. Martin's familiar smell filled my lungs and I inhaled it deeply. It was like he was there. My eyes darted around the room, and I saw the large mirror he'd bought at a yard sale. He said it made him feel like there was more space in his room.

He'd pinned his favorite pictures of all his family and friends down both sides of the mirror. I wandered closer to look at them. Nearly all the photos had one of us siblings with him. Kayden and Martin, Adam and Martin, the whole family. Martin and me. I ran my fingertips lightly across the pictures, and fresh tears welled in my eyes until the pictures blurred.

Another caught my eye just as I was turning away. I stopped and picked it off. Holding it close I stared at Adam, Kayden, Flynn, and me. *The night of the game.* I hadn't even seen the picture before. We were at the edge of the field when the game finished, the day I met Flynn. It looked like an intimate pose, with Flynn's arm resting on the bottom of my back. Martin must have taken it with his phone.

Turning, I held the photo out to Flynn. His fingertips plucked it from mine. I walked over and sat on his bed, smoothing the cover reverently under my hand. I picked up his pillow and held it close to my face, and felt his presence when I closed my eyes. I imagined he was there with me, and I inhaled his scent deeply before reality crept back into my heart and I sobbed into his pillow.

After a couple of minutes, Flynn took the pillow from me and placed it gently back at the headboard. Scooping me up in his arms, he carried me out the door and down the hall. Opening the door to my room, he carefully laid me down on my bed. The mattress dipped as he sat beside me and stroked my hair, and spoke in a soft tone, "Good girl. I know that was hard, but those rooms hold no fear for you now."

Air passed between us as I felt him move away. I clutched tightly at his hand and pulled him back toward me. "Hold me. Please stay. I don't want to be alone."

"Valerie, I don't—"

"Please... I need..." I buried my face in my hands and wailed loudly.

Flynn climbed onto the bed and lay down behind me. His arm swept under my neck, while his other one pulled me tightly against him. I felt him exhale heavily into my hair before he placed a tender kiss on the top of my head. I felt centered, briefly, by his action. It was like he'd somehow absorbed some of my pain.

"It's okay. I've got you, Valerie. Try to sleep, babe."

I was too tired to think about him in any way other than as someone who'd helped me through that day. For the first time since we'd heard the news, I slept without having to be chemically induced.

Chapter Fifteen

AIRPORT RUN

*B*uster's claws scratched at my bedroom door. I rolled over in bed, feeling drained. Flynn had obviously left me sometime in the night, because the rest of my queen bed was cold. I was still dressed in my clothes from the previous day. Dragging myself to the bathroom, I turned on the shower and water sprayed in a fast flow from the showerhead.

Undressing, I noted we were day-three post the accident that changed all our lives, and I needed my family desperately. I showered and dressed in some skinny jeans and a white sweater, then headed to the kitchen. Auntie Joan was emptying the dishwasher and stopped when she saw me.

"Morning, honey. How are you doing?"

"I'm doing," was my flat reply.

"I know ... me too," she said, and gave me a small smile and a hug. "I heard Flynn leave earlier. Did he stay the night with you?"

"He took me into Adam's and Martin's rooms last night. I was upset so he..."

I didn't know how to say it, but she finished it for me.

"He stayed with you. He's a good boy, Valerie. I think I made an error in my judgment on that one. The way he looks at you..."

"He can look all he wants, Aunt Joan, he's a friend. Nothing more. I don't want us to be anything else. I don't know what the hell I want anymore."

Two sharp knocks interrupted us. She shot me a glance and went to open the door. Flynn stood there with his hands on the doorframe.

"Lee made breakfast. Both of you beautiful ladies are invited. He made tons, so I'm not taking no for an answer."

Flynn pushed into the kitchen and slipped his hand into mine. "I can see an excuse brewing in that gorgeous head of yours. You have to eat." Without protest, I allowed him to lead me from the kitchen, across the driveway. We were almost there when the house phone rang. Auntie Joan told us to go ahead, and she'd catch up, so we continued without her.

Lee had made another hearty breakfast. I wasn't hungry but forced down some scrambled eggs, toast, and coffee. My aunt arrived, gave me a tight smile, and sat down quietly beside me.

"They're coming home today, sweetheart."

Flynn glanced at me, then at my aunt, and reached out and held my hand over the table. "I know. I was waiting for us to finish breakfast before I said anything. Do you want me to take you to the airport to meet the plane?" Auntie Joan shook her head. "I don't think I could cope with that heartbreaking sight."

I swallowed noisily at the thought of a funeral- type cavalcade of cars, and the mental image almost choked me. "Will they be in caskets?" I heard myself ask in a small voice.

"Of course. They may be transported to the funeral home in a black van, though. You want me to find out those arrangements?" Flynn asked.

I nodded. I could cope with a black van, not if it was in funeral hearses with us traveling behind them. The memorial was going to be bad enough, and I knew I couldn't have faced the heartache twice.

Flynn stood and went outside. I assumed it was to make that call. He didn't come back for a while. I wondered what was keeping him and realized how quickly I'd come to rely on him for comfort. Maybe because my parents weren't around.

A seven-seater SUV drove up the driveway, and I leaned over to look out the window. I saw a balding man get out, and he and Flynn walked around the car. They were examining the paintwork. I'd seen Kayden do that kind of inspection a million times with his pride and joy, Susie.

Reaching into the back seat, the man pulled out a clipboard and handed it to Flynn. As Flynn signed it, another car drove up. The guy who had brought the car, got in with the driver. I watched as they drove away, while Flynn walked over to us.

Banging the side of the RV, he gave a tight smile. "Okay, we can't drive around in this all the time. I've arranged a car for us. Anything you need, let me know."

"You could have had my car," Aunt Joan offered.

"Not enough room for everyone, Joan, and anyway, have you seen me drive? You wouldn't let me near your car. Actually, I'm fine with driving. It's parking the damn things that I don't quite hit the mark with."

Lee smirked. "He's not wrong. Why do you think I'm here?"

The rest of the morning was full of anticipation and anguish, and I started to think about seeing my dead brothers, and possibly, Ziggy. I was terrified, yet the worst had already happened. Flynn never tried to comfort me when I cried, and I was pleased about that. I'd felt it was okay to cry around him. He even encouraged it.

At around a quarter to three, we set off for the airport, with Lee in the back. Watching Auntie Joan at the door, I knew the next time I saw her and the house, my life would never be the same. It was already changed forever. And even though I'd known about the boys and grieved for them, the reality of them being back in Iowa, and putting them *to rest*, sat heavily on my chest. I had no idea how I was going to get through it, and I was genuinely thankful for Flynn.

"Why are you doing this? Why would you come here and put yourself in such a horrible situation?"

"Because I wanted to be here for you. Because I thought it was necessary, and mainly because I care what happens to you and your family. I loved Martin."

I accepted his reasons and sat quietly staring out of the window, until Flynn reached over and took my hand in his. Something warm happened to me inside when he did. I felt oddly protected by his little gesture. My gaze dropped to stare at my little pale hand in his big tanned one, and his thumb had begun to stroke the back of it. "Terrible situation, babe."

"It's not a situation, it's a condition," I retorted.

"How so?"

"This is akin to a lifelong chronic disease. Something I'm going to have to learn to live with."

"Huh," Flynn huffed, "True."

"Well, I'm not going to fucking college now, that's for sure," I cussed, not even recognizing myself.

"What do you mean? Of course, you're going to college. Your life continues," Flynn said.

"No point."

"Why the hell not?"

"Martin did all that studying, and Adam ... all those hours of training to get to the top of his game, for what? They died. How do I know that's not going to happen to me? How do I know studying for all those years would be worth it? No one can guarantee I'd get to use what I learned."

Flynn's head snapped around, his eyes piercing mine, and said with conviction, "Nothing is going to happen to you, Valerie."

"Yeah? Like nothing could happen to my brothers. We're all invincible until it affects us, right Flynn? Well, hello! It happened. My fucking bright, drop-dead-gorgeous, talented brothers... It happened to them, so don't bullshit me."

Flynn just looked at me and shook his head. I took that as dissension, but who knew with Flynn?

We drove on in silence. When we arrived at the airport, Flynn swung the car into the short-term parking lot and did a bad job of parking. I could have parked better. "Okay, babe. I know you aren't ready for this. No one ever is. Breathe in and out, and put one foot in front of the other. If you feel dizzy, sit down on the floor. Last thing you need is an injury if you pass out. I'm with you all the way on this, Valerie. It's just another hurdle to make it over, okay?"

Flynn had stopped treating me with kid gloves and started to instruct me on how to deal with the gruesome task ahead. Hence, his reference to a *situation*. I could relate to that term when I thought about it like that.

Taking my hand, he confidently weaved through passengers in the airport terminal building behind Lee, and for the first time, I realized who I was with. He was risking so much being there, but more importantly, I didn't want my brothers' homecoming to be turned into a spectacle. Just as that thought entered my mind, Flynn was suddenly recognized. Screaming hordes of girls had just finished at the check-in desk and were running toward us. It was apparent Flynn being there had made their day.

"Please ladies, not today. I'm here on very personal business," he pleaded with gravity in his voice that asked them not to intrude.

"Who's the bitch?" One of them shouted.

Lee held them back, and Flynn waved over security. "I have a situation here." That made me smile, despite the circumstances. He seemed to like that word.

Security ushered us in the direction of the VIP arrivals lounge, because of the circumstances, then had one of the airline staff talk to us. They knew who Flynn was, and when he explained why we were there, a woman directed us to a room with frosted glass at the back of a walled-off area.

"Please wait here, Mr. Docherty."

Flynn pulled me to his chest and hugged me tightly, rubbing my back in a soothing gesture. "Sorry about that. Occupational hazard."

Once again, we stood in silence, and it struck me that we could both have comfortable periods like that without feeling the need to talk just for the sake of it.

Swing doors swished softly open on the other side of the room, and I saw Mom, Dad, and Kayden walk through. My heart broke in two for the second time that week at the sight of my one surviving brother.

I ran and threw my arms around him. He looked broken, pale, and full of grief like the rest of us, but as soon as I'd touched him, he dissolved into a teary mess. He clung to me so tightly he was hurting me. I couldn't breathe. Flynn must have seen my distress and was beside me immediately, pulling him off me.

"Dude, you're hurting her," he growled.

Kayden didn't release the hold he had on me, and Flynn put his hand on Kayden's shoulder. "Kayden ease up, dude, she's in pain."

Kayden's arms dropped to his sides, his eyes connecting with mine, and he stood, crying openly in the middle of the room before his legs buckled.

"Fuck," Flynn cussed as he and Lee grabbed Kayden under his arms and held him up. They dragged him over to a row of blue seats, and sat him down.

"It's okay, buddy. You're back now. We're going to get you home, okay?"

Mom and Dad stood, hanging on to each other, and I wondered where everyone else was. Then it dawned on me. This was the rest of us. We'd always have two people missing.

The way Flynn took charge was impressive. He had a real, no-nonsense approach, and we'd been fortunate that he'd been there for us. As a family, we'd always been very capable, but we were divided that day, and we all needed direction.

All my fears about seeing the boys were for nothing. We were informed they were in closed caskets and had been transferred to the funeral home directly from the plane. Initially, I was upset by that. Eventually, we arrived home and Auntie Joan had made a buffet-style dinner, even though she knew none of us would do anything more than pick at any food. Flynn and Lee insisted we try to eat.

Kayden hadn't spoken at all and sat staring out the window. My mom put him to bed after dinner and both of my parents, and Auntie Joan, discussed the funeral arrangements with Flynn. When I was asked to perform a eulogy for my brothers, I choked. How could I stand in front of all their friends and reminisce fondly? My heart felt like a pile of wet splinters inside my chest, and my stomach rolled every time I thought about them. I told them I wasn't strong enough to do it.

Flynn suggested I write something and he'd present it for me. I liked that idea, at first, but penning my thoughts about my brothers placed me in an emotional shredder. By 1:00 A.M., I'd written something that had barely begun to do them justice.

I handed the notebook to Flynn to read what I'd written and realized it was late, but I didn't want to go to bed. After a few minutes, Flynn closed the notebook and nodded at the stairs, almost as if he'd read my mind. "Come on. Bed. It's going to be a long day tomorrow."

I pulled myself up from my chair at the kitchen table, and it was the first time I'd noticed the cards and flowers surrounding us. There was a hefty pile on the kitchen counter when I passed to go to the stairs. Seeing all the people our tragedy had affected made me feel even more bereft as I continued to the stairs.

"Please come with me," I pleaded quietly to Flynn, as my foot touched the bottom step.

"I don't think that's—"

"I need you to sleep beside me. I can't face being alone tonight. Please, Flynn..."

His eyes darted up the stairs and then back to mine. He let out a long breath and swallowed. Then he slowly nodded and took my hand. He allowed me to guide him upstairs to my room. Once there, I brushed my teeth and changed into a tank top and pajama bottoms in the bathroom, and then slid between the sheets. Flynn took off his jacket and hoodie, and toed off his shoes. He climbed on beside me and, once again, spooned with me, holding me tightly, like he had the night before.

I felt safe with Flynn around. I wasn't happy, but I was ... comfortable. With him next to me, I lay quietly, thinking and crying, until I finally fell asleep. That day he'd made me feel ... protected.

I stirred in the night and felt a vice-like grip on my breast. Then I realized Flynn's palm was cupping it. My heart sped up as my head did a mental checklist, and then denial crept over me.

I was certain Flynn would never have taken advantage of me at a time like that. I'd reasoned it was purely accidental and tried to roll away from him. Flynn's grip tightened and he nudged himself closer, and I felt his bulge press against my body. Sometime in the night, Flynn had worked his way underneath my comforter. He moaned against my back, then his face nuzzled into my neck, giving me shivers down my spine.

Swallowing hard, I tried to move again, and Flynn stirred, his tongue darting out to lick my skin and he bit down on my neck. "Fly-nn?" His body stiffened, then his hand swept away from me as he jerked back to make space. "Shit. I'm so sorry. I had no idea I was doing that, Valerie."

"I figured," I said flatly. My heart thumped wildly in my chest. In my weakened emotional state, his touch had excited me, and I had no place feeling like that with everything else going on.

"What does that mean?"

"Well, you wouldn't do that."

"You don't know me at all. In another situation, if it wasn't you. I so would have."

"If it wasn't me?"

"I told you. I'm no good for you. I'm fighting with all I am not to corrupt that sweet little mind and body of yours."

I lay and thought about his words. My brothers were dead. I was sure my brothers had been with girls, but Ziggy was a virgin when he died. We never really talked about sex much, but he'd told me that much. I was sad he'd never gotten to experience such pleasure in his short life on earth.

I knew was becoming more interested about what sex was like, and with everything that had happened, I saw no point in waiting any more. My brothers' protection weakened my ability to cope in real life situations like the one I'd run away from, and I'd learned through my brothers' deaths the world was full of mess and destruction.

"What if I wanted you to?"

"Valerie, I'm going to do my utmost to pretend I didn't just hear that. Now go back to sleep." Flynn turned over and faced the opposite direction, but continued to lie beside me. I cried softly at his rejection, but he never turned to comfort me. Eventually, I fell asleep again.

122

Chapter Sixteen

FACING FACTS

*L*oud knocking woke me. I rose onto my elbows and turned with a start, initially worried that Flynn was still in the room. He'd slipped out, just like the night before. "Yeah?"

My dad slowly opened the door.

"We're going to the funeral home, Valerie. The caskets are closed. You won't be able to see Martin or Adam. It's better you remember them the way they were, honey. The funeral is tomorrow. We've spoken to Ziggy's parents and decided to have a joint service; we thought it would be less harrowing for all of us than to have two. Most of the arrangements were made when we were in Las Vegas."

Those words twisted my gut, and I wondered, *Where was I in that* **we***?* On top of that, the hurt I felt about not having one last moment with either of my brothers tore me to pieces. The lack of consideration by anyone for my feelings in all of this seemed mind-blowing.

"It's better that we do this quickly. The longer Flynn is here, the more chance it will turn into a circus. We don't want that kind of attention. It's been bad enough that the press has been relentless in their pursuit of a bigger story."

"So, we're burying my brothers to Flynn Docherty's tune? We hardly know the guy."

Dad sat on my bed and took my hand. "I'm sorry you've had to weather this on your own, Valerie. It's not how I'd have wanted this. God, what I'd give for this not to have happened. But it has. We've been dictated to by the other agencies involved, so we've had to allow them to do their jobs so we could bring the boys home. Now that they're here, we have to lay them to rest. Delaying the inevitable would only be more painful for all. Flynn is only a small part of the equation."

"And where is Jess? She was supposed to love Martin. I haven't heard a word about her. Didn't she care, after all?"

"Like I said, it's been tough on all of us, Valerie. Everyone grieves differently. She's coming to the funeral, but she needed time to come to terms with the accident. Just like Kayden."

With those words, Dad became lost in his thoughts, then he stood and left the room.

Twenty minutes later, I was dressed and downstairs. Mom and Dad left with Auntie Joan. Flynn assured him he'd watch over my brother. I was so angry with my parents because they seemed so distant and I really needed my family. Kayden was still in bed and refused to get up, so I took a page out of Flynn's book and went to talk to him.

Pushing his door open, I saw him curled up, facing away from me.

"Hey," I said in a soft voice. When he didn't respond, I tried again. "Kayden? Please, talk to me."

"How can I face you? I let you down. I let you all down."

I shook my head, not understanding what he meant. "How did you let me down?"

"They were my kid brothers. I should have been looking out for them. They died because I never let that fucking branch go to go with them."

"Stop it right now," I screamed, "I won't have that talk. Get out of that fucking bed. You are all I have left. I don't want to start regretting that it was you who God chose to save. Get up."

Kayden rolled over. "You'd rather have had Martin, wouldn't you?"

"Stop it. How can you say that? Get up."

Kayden rolled back and stared at the wall. "No. I wish it was me instead of them," he grumbled, and his voice cracked.

I flung back his door, barged out into the hallway, and banged the door behind me. Stomping down the hall, my rage had gotten the better of me. Fury rose from deep inside me. I spun on my heel and went back and threw the door open again.

"Fuck you, Kayden, you selfish prick. I need you too," I said, my voice filled with venom. I strode over to his dresser. There was no way I could allow him to blame himself. I picked up some of the collectible model cars he'd had since he was a small boy, and threw them at him, one by one. I'd expected that to have some impact, but he still didn't move.

Flynn came running in the door, grabbed my hand, and stopped me from throwing another.

"This is fucking unbearable. I can't stand it anymore," I screamed hysterically.

"Come on, I think you've explained to Kayden how much you need him right now. Dude, your sister is hurting as much as you are. Kayden, I know this is tough, but try to get your ass out of that bed and help me support her."

Flynn led me from the room, sobbing, and closed the door. Taking hold of my shoulders, he softly said, "Look at me." I turned and glanced up at him. The tear tracks on my face must have been a familiar sight by then.

"Breathe, Valerie. You just did Kayden a huge favor. That's shock talking and thinking for him. I read about this, and I suffered just like Kayden is. It's called survivor's syndrome. He's lying there feeling guilty because he survived and your brothers didn't. He'll think about what we said and come down in his own time."

After his intervention, Flynn kept me occupied by honing the wording of the eulogy for the service. I was thankful for his help because he seemed to be the only person who wanted to include me, and he wasn't even family. His encouragement and guidance amazed me. I was happy he provoked my thoughts, which helped me say some of the important things my brothers had impressed upon me during their young lives.

Kayden finally made an appearance just after my parents came back from the funeral home. I could see he was struggling with what to do, and that he was lost, even in his home. I reached out and took him by the hand, and as soon as his hand was in mine, his fingers clamped tightly around it. His grip felt desperate, and I'll never forget the haunted look he gave me. Once I sat him on the sofa, I leaned in and placed my head on his chest. His arms circled my body, and we sat there hugging for most of the day.

Even as we sat, the constant stream of visitors didn't let up. Many were kind and brought flowers, potted plants, casseroles, and enough pies to start a small bakery. People shared in our sorrow, and that seemed to help my parents. Kayden and I were irritated and restless when they came, because we just wanted to be left alone. Flynn was conspicuous by his absence until my aunt explained he was giving us space. He never came around for the rest of that day.

⁓

Dressed in black, we were all in somber moods, as would be expected for the funeral. Everyone looked immaculate in suits and heels that morning. Flynn knocked on the door just before the cars arrived to take us to the service. He looked like some businessman in his black designer suit and crisp white shirt. Dad nodded a sort of *thank you for coming* to Flynn. My father was supporting Mom, who wasn't coping at all, and Kayden was being managed by Auntie Joan.

I realized I'd been waiting for Flynn. I needed him. He was almost a stranger by all accounts, apart from that one visit as Martin's friend, yet he was the only person to step up to the plate for me when I needed someone the most. School friends had called, but I felt it was more for information than to offer any real support. Having Flynn with me, who instinctively knew what I needed, was an epic relief and reassurance.

My father had chosen the pallbearers. All of Martin's friends were there for him. Kayden was head pallbearer for Adam, and my dad had Matthew and Ryan lead Martin's. Ziggy had his dad, uncles, and some family friends. When I saw the three silver caskets all in a row at the church alter, I didn't even feel my legs buckle.

Thankfully, Flynn caught my fall as I sobbed uncontrollably into his chest. I wished and wished for it all to be a horrible dream, but it wasn't. It was real. Parts of my heart were in each of those caskets, and the rest was in tatters inside me.

The service was beautiful and ugly at the same time. Everything was too perfect and pristine for my brothers, when their lives had been organized chaos. I glanced around the church and saw faces we'd all grown up with, and eventually my eyes settled on Jess. Pale and gaunt, her eyes darted nervously around the church. I recognized the signs; she was struggling to hold it together.

I'd been angry about Jess. Why her? What made her so special over the other three people who were so important to me, that she got to survive? As soon as I saw how grief-stricken she was, all those feelings dissolved. All I felt was pity when I hugged her. She'd lost Martin too, and she was probably the one person in the room who knew how I felt, in the sense she had lost a love before it had really flourished.

After deciding I owed it to Martin and Adam to say my piece at the funeral, I stood and tried my best through rolling tears and shaky breaths. When it became overwhelming, Flynn appeared by my side. He held my hand in support to help me finish what I wanted to say.

At one point, he had to take over, continuing to read when I couldn't finish a particularly emotional memory I wanted to share. He even read the part I'd written for Ziggy, about our young love that was untapped and full of hope when he'd left that day.

~

Flynn gave his eulogy and sang a song he'd written especially for the family. It was an amazing gesture, and it touched the hearts of everyone present. He told me later that his record company was going to release it in the boys' memories with all proceeds going to bereavement counseling for anyone who knew them. I was choked with emotion by his thoughtfulness, and it would ensure the boys would not be forgotten.

Once the family had paid their respects and our part of the memorial was over, Ziggy's family paid their tributes to him, and I cried when most of them mentioned his affection for me, saying, "He was the happiest boy alive because Valerie was his girl."

How we all got through that heartbreaking morning in church, I had no idea. When it was done and we'd gone to the graveside, I felt totally wiped out from crying. When we got back to the house for the wake, I couldn't go inside and face all the people telling me they were sorry for my loss.

In all honesty, I'd become immune to those words. I didn't want people to be sorry. I wanted someone to do something ... anything to make what happened a sick joke, and for my brothers to walk through our door again. When I refused to go inside, Flynn took me with him, and I spent most of the rest of the day in the RV parked in our driveway.

The house was awash with friends and acquaintances of the boys, and I didn't want to face them anymore. I was angry they all got to live when my brothers were gone.

The service was done, and my brothers were laid to rest, and I just wanted to be left alone. At times during the day, I had found it hard to breathe. The suffocating feelings of distress and sorrow overwhelmed me so many times. Flynn was there for me, telling me to breathe, encouraging me to get through it. Everyone in town was respectful of the fact that, although Flynn was a major celebrity, he was grieving as well. I was thankful for their common decency toward him.

Once cocooned in the privacy of Flynn's mobile accommodation, he flopped down and lifted his feet up on the sofa, and stretched out. I sat in much the same position, but on the sofa on the opposite side of the RV. We started chatting, and eventually we reminisced about the boys. He talked about Martin at college, and I filled him in on various adventures we'd all had together as a family. I'd been doing well until he said something that triggered a complete breakdown.

"Come here," he said, his arms outstretched. He didn't have to say it twice. I leaped onto the sofa beside him and snuggled in at the back, resting my head on his chest. Flynn inhaled deeply and stroked my hair.

"I wish I could take all your hurt away, Valerie."

My throat burned with fresh tears that I couldn't stem, and I gave in to them yet again. I wondered for the first time how I was going to get by once Flynn had gone. The thought triggered a tight knot in my stomach, and my heart jolted. I was headed for even more sadness.

Somehow Flynn had wormed his way back into my affections, despite all the grief I was suffering. It made me cry harder. He probably thought it was more of the same grief, but that time it was because I'd be saying another goodbye. To him.

"It's okay, babe. Look at it this way. The worst has already happened. That may sound like an outlandish thing to say, but it has. Everything else from today can only go upward."

I pulled my head back from his chest and looked up at him and thought that was a callous remark; then I wondered how I could possibly let him go. Flynn's eyes dropped to my lips and, for a second, I thought he was going to kiss me. Instead, he placed his hand on the back of my head and pushed it back to his chest.

"Just rest," he ordered, and let out a shaky, barely controlled breath. I wondered if he was exasperated with me. I knew my behavior had been erratic. I still hadn't made sense of anything I'd been through during those previous four days, or was it five? Even that was a blur.

Lying, listening to his strong, steady heartbeat was soothing. The regular rhythm lulled me until I fell asleep. Flynn woke me by changing positions so that he lay facing me. I lifted my head, confused about where I was for a second, and my eyes stared straight into his.

"Sorry, my ass was numb," he said with a smile, and his hand squeezed my hip. I'd been cradled in his arms while I lay sleeping, and he didn't seem in a hurry for me to leave them.

"Has any man told you how beautiful you look when you're asleep, or do I get a 'first' with you?"

"No man has ever seen me sleep, apart from my brothers and my dad."

"Then it's my pleasure. Valerie, you're beautiful when you are sleeping, babe. Your face is like an angel's. Perfect dark eyelashes rest on your beautiful pale skin and your rose-colored lips... The combination is breathtaking."

I continued to watch his face and saw nothing loaded behind his comment. He was telling me honestly how he felt.

"Thank you, but that's only outer beauty. I think a good heart is more important."

"Indeed, and you have both, Valerie, you are doubly blessed."

As he offered a slow smile, I found a small one forming on my own face. It felt wrong to smile on such a day, but I knew Martin, Adam, and Ziggy wouldn't want me to cry for the rest of my life.

Flynn held my face in his hand, and I leaned into it and inhaled a shaky breath. "Thank you," I whispered.

"For?" he asked softly.

"Being here."

"Least I could do."

His warm hand stayed on my face, his thumb strummed over my cheek. Something shifted between us and his eyes filled with lust.

"God, Valerie. What you do to me."

"What is it I do?"

"You make me want what I have no business to."

"Meaning?"

"It doesn't matter."

"It does to me."

Flynn's gaze dropped from my eyes to my lips. He licked his, pulling his bottom one into his mouth, and bit down on it.

"You are so fucking tempting."

"Kiss me," I whispered. My heart drummed in my chest with anticipation. I yearned for his soft lips that had teased mine six months previously.

Flynn skimmed his hand from my hip to my head and guided my face toward his. I saw his Adam's apple bob in his neck, and I glanced back into his eyes. His pupils were huge as he pressed his lips to mine, and without hesitation, my tongue darted out to taste him. I traced the seam of his mouth, and he took me by surprise when he kissed me back, with fierce intention. His tongue thrust quickly into my mouth as he pressed my head closer, deepening the kiss.

Electricity coursed through my body. A soft moan left my mouth and I was lost. As our tongues lashed against the other, the sensation was thrilling. Tiny explosions, like mini fireworks, burst all over my body, and I ached for him to lay his hands on me.

My hand found his hair and I grasped desperately at a fistful, tugging it tightly. Flynn groaned and swiftly changed my position, lying me down on the sofa and pressing his hard body on top of mine. His hand wandered down the side of my hair to my neck and then cupped my breast, squeezing it tightly.

Breathless and full of want, I wriggled underneath him, enjoying the hard bulge that had settled between my legs. The feelings he awakened in me were on another level; everything from excited and needy, to exhilarating and electrifying. New feelings that were much removed from the sorrow I'd been feeling. As lust overtook me. I placed my hands on Flynn's behind and pulled him hard against me. Flynn ground his erection over my mound, and we both moaned loudly.

Suddenly, Flynn tore himself away from me, and the feeling of loss was back instantly.

"Fuck." He pulled off me and stood up, shakily running his fingers through his hair. He had a shocked expression.

"Fuck, Fuck. Fuck. Damn, that shouldn't have happened," he barked, pacing around the RV, running his hands through his hair.

He stared at me for a long minute, and the conflict he was feeling was clear on his face. "Get up and go home," he said, unable to keep his frustration out of his voice.

"Why? What's wrong with me?"

"Jesus, Valerie. Nothing is wrong with you. I refuse to take advantage of you. That should never have happened. Get the fuck home."

"You're not taking advantage. I want this."

"No, you don't. I don't. I can't."

"Why not? I'm sixteen."

"Exactly. You need to go home. Forget we did that."

"I liked it."

"So did I, God help me, so did I. *Like* doesn't even begin to describe how I felt, but I'm not going to take advantage. Get your shoes on and go home."

"No. Will you stop treating me like a child."

"Valerie, I'm trying to fight with all I have to do the right thing for you. Please don't argue, just go."

When I still hadn't moved, he shouted in frustration, "Get. Your. Fucking. Shoes. On."

Lee opened the door to the RV. "Everything okay, boss?"

"Make sure she gets back to the house," Flynn barked before he went into his bedroom and slammed the door shut.

"Coward," I called after him.

"You heard the boss. Shoes, Valerie, or am I carrying you across to your house?"

I slipped my feet angrily into my shoes and stormed out of the RV and across to the kitchen door. When I turned to look, the RV door was closed. I went inside and slammed the door; my heart was hurt and I hated my life.

Nothing seemed as easy as it had before my brothers died. I undressed and climbed into bed. My heart felt like it was aching in my chest, and I had no idea how I was supposed to continue, but I was drained and numb, so sleep came easier that night.

Chapter Seventeen

DISRESPECT

My first thought the following morning was that I couldn't be hard on Flynn for thinking he had done the right thing. He'd been trying to respect my emotional state, and I think I'd have regretted anything we did because I was grief-stricken. I knew he'd assume I hadn't been thinking straight the day before, but he was wrong.

I knew exactly what I was doing in his RV. Flynn had told me to call him when I was ready, and I felt I was. Despite missing Ziggy, Flynn was stirring feelings in me. Maybe my feelings weren't rational at all. My boyfriend hadn't been dead a week, and I'd kissed another boy. What did that say about me? Maybe Flynn was right, and I didn't know what I wanted.

I decided to act maturely about what happened and go to talk to him about it. That decision made, I showered and dressed, then looked out the window to check on his RV before going downstairs. It was gone. Panic tightened my chest. I hadn't heard the engine start. My first thought was, *Where has he gone*, and my second was, *When would he be back?*

I raced downstairs and found my parents sitting at the kitchen table.

"Did Flynn say when he'd be back?" I asked, my voice a bit panicked.

"He's gone, sweetheart. He said he had to get back to his work."

Without shame, I threw myself self onto the sofa and began to cry. "He can't have left without saying goodbye." *Could he?*

Mom gave me a weak smile. "He said he'd rather we didn't wake you when I offered."

"He did what? Did he leave a number?" My mind was frantic that he'd just ducked out like that.

"There was no message for you, Valerie."

"So, he left deliberately without seeing me?"

"He felt it would be kinder if you didn't have to deal with that."

"I suppose Martin, Adam, and Ziggy felt the same, right?"

Dad stood up and tried to put his arm around me. I shrugged him off and moved away from him. "Don't start trying to comfort me now. Neither of you have been here for me in all of this. Flynn was the only one who showed any recognition that I'd lost my Martin and Adam, or even Ziggy.

"Seriously, this has to stop, Valerie. We're all hurting. You don't own the rights for being angry. You have to find something to help you contain these outbursts."

"Fuck you. You left me here alone. You had each other; I had no one. Then, the one person who did get what I was feeling just screwed up by abandoning me again. I'll be as angry as I have to be until I feel something normal in this whole fucked-up life I've fallen into."

I knew they thought Auntie Joan was enough and would have been supportive had Flynn not taken over. I was just being irrational.

Dad slapped my arm hard. "Don't you dare swear in front of your mom and me again. I won't have you disrespect us like this. Auntie Joan and Flynn made sure you were well taken care of for us."

"Fuck you and your *disrespect*. I'm so fucking angry at the world right now, and my words are all I have to express myself with. I'm stifled and hurt, angry doesn't even cut it. I'm beyond livid at what God has given us."

Mom stared blankly in my direction. She hadn't spoken since my outburst. She stood and hugged herself.

"Valerie Darsin, I did not bring you up to bad-mouth either of us in this way. I know you're hurting, as we all are. Flynn didn't desert you, but he's a busy man with a life of his own. It's *our* job to take care of you, not his. The fact that he came here for you and all of us says a lot about that boy. You should be grateful," my mom said to me, her voice shaking with anger of her own.

"Oh, so you remember what your job is now? Pity I had to wait until you buried them for you to remember I was still here."

Neither of my parents responded, and there was no point in arguing. They could spin Flynn's leaving whichever way they wanted. Flynn and I were the only ones who'd ever know my true feelings about him and what had happened between us.

I realized I didn't have any way of contacting him. "Can I have his number? I want to call him."

Dad shook his head and glanced at my mom. "Flynn thinks it would be best for you if you didn't call him. I think he wants you to move forward now that we've laid your brothers to rest. You're just a girl, Valerie, and he's a famous young man who's still establishing himself as a musician with his band."

When my father told me Flynn had asked him not to share his phone number, it was like a knife in my gut. I wasn't sure how much more I could take. Losing my brothers brought Flynn back to me, but as soon as I'd thrown myself at him, he'd packed up and headed out. I felt ashamed, embarrassed, and devastated that he'd flat out rejected me after I'd put myself on the line.

"A girl? After what we've been through? I'm sorry if I sound selfish, but do you even realize what I've been through this past few months? Have you any idea? I was with Bradley for over a year, and he cheated on me and walked away because I was trying to do the right thing. Heidi, my best friend for nine years, betrayed me with him. Two major changes, two layers of hurt, separation, and loss in one hit. Uncle Terry dying was another one. Watching Auntie Joan grieving, another layer of hurt. The deaths of the boys ... my brothers who had been in my life for relatively more of it than in yours. Think about it. How old are you? They were there for some of your life, but for the *whole* of mine. Ziggy was my boyfriend. I loved him too, and Flynn... I feel guilty about losing Ziggy, but I have feelings for Flynn. I don't know what they are, but I felt safe when he was with me."

Everyone sat silently, absorbing my rant, so I continued to express my feelings. "I'm *not* an innocent girl anymore. I lost that the day the boys died. There's no way I'm going back to school. What good did it do for those boys? Study hard; keep your head down. Martin could have lived a bigger life than the one he had if he'd ignored trying to do what everyone else told him. I'll home school again— get my diploma, but I am *not* sitting in a class full of people I don't like for another year. I only have one year left after the next semester, anyway. I promise I'll take it seriously, but I'm going to live life the way I want now, instead of the way everyone else tells me I can."

My father shook his head in protest. "You'll never be able to do photography the way you want without a college degree."

"Pfft, this is the age of the internet, Dad. I'll do online courses for photography and digital imagery, and I'll learn more at my own pace. I'm sure I'll find some freelance work, and I'll fund myself with baby portraits and kindergarten shoots until I learn my craft."

The uproar about my suggestion continued, but the rebel in me was born. They were drained with grief and had misplaced guilt about letting the boys take the trip in the first place. So, it was probably part due to their need to keep me close that they agreed I could stay home, provided I kept my grades up. I wondered if they thought I'd fail and see the error of my ways by the end of summer, because the deal was, I had to prove I could pay for, and pass, my classes by then. Otherwise, I had to go back to school.

It didn't resolve any of the stuff with Flynn. I was as mad as hell that he'd swept in and out of my life again. I sat watching late night TV, too angry to sleep. I reflected on how amazing Flynn had been when I needed him, and then he'd let me down by running again. I was beyond wild that he kissed me, and then left before giving me the opportunity to discuss it with him.

A break in the program I'd been watching gave me the excuse to grab a bottle of water from the fridge. I found my dad's phone lying on the countertop and I scrolled through and found Flynn's cell phone number.

My hand shook as I copied his number from one phone to the other. I placed the cell back where I'd found it and went back through to the family room. I sat down and quickly fired off a text I knew would bring a reaction.

Me: Where did you run away to, douchebag? Such a coward. I'll find a real man to teach me about my body.

A short time later a text came back.

Flynn: How did U get this number?

Me: It wasn't exactly rocket science.

Flynn: Forget about me, Val.

Me: You are a douchebag for running out.

Flynn: What happened ... I can't let that happen again. I'm no good for you.

Me: Y don't you let me be the judge of that?

Flynn: U think U R hurting now? I'd let you down and destroy U.

Me: You already did.

Flynn: Find a nice guy. You deserve the best.

Me: Fuck you, Flynn Docherty. I'm not stupid. I know when I'm being brushed aside.

Flynn: U R sixteen and we just don't fit, Val. The way I live is no way for someone like you. U'd get hurt.

Me: I already hurt. I wish I'd never met you.

If he responded, I never saw it. I spun around, and in my temper, I threw my cell at the window. It bounced off the wooden plantation shutters and smashed on the floor. "Asshole," I screamed. Kayden came downstairs and sat beside me. It was the most animated I'd seen him since the accident. He wrapped his arms around me and restrained me before I had the chance to do anything else.

"Don't tell me, let me guess. Flynn, right?"

Reluctantly, I nodded, my emotions bringing tears to my eyes. Kayden closed his eyes briefly, as if seeing me hurt was too much for him.

"I'm glad he's gone. Martin was right. The guy had eyes for you."

"*Eyes* for me? What the fuck does that even mean, Kayden."

"You know, the way a guy looks at a girl when he wants to get into her panties."

"You mean he was eye fucking me? I've heard you say that plenty of times. Why can't any of you just speak normally around me? I'm sixteen, Kayd, not twelve."

"You're my sister, Val, it's different."

"So, it's okay to talk about boning someone else's sister and shit like that, but not say it about your own?"

"Don't talk that way. You're better than that."

I knew my behavior was vile towards Kayden, but all I wanted was to be treated like an adult. The innocent version of me left the day my brothers died. Ziggy, I couldn't even think about; I loved and missed him, but I'd lived my whole life with my brothers, and they dominated my thoughts. Maybe that's why I kissed Flynn, to leave Ziggy's memories behind me. If that sounded harsh, it was because my life had been tipped upside down, and that turned me inside out. None of my thoughts were coherent anymore.

Spring break ended the following week, and I didn't return to school. After another five weeks of home study and my mid-term grades hadn't suffered, my knowledge of digital imagery and photography had grown substantially with the extra study I'd added to my current coursework.

Kayden and I took car rides in the countryside, where I snapped photos to build different portfolios like nature and landscapes, famous sites, and inanimate objects. The photos were a collection for my end-of-year assignment. When my dad saw them, he had to admit I was growing into a talented and professional photographer. I'd passed four exams and my online tutor Edgar said I had a natural eye for framing the perfect picture.

My artistic nature helped me cope with the loss of my brothers. We'd had various hurdles to conquer during our period of adjustment. Adam's birthday was three weeks after he died, and Kayden's was right before my finals. Adam's friends turned up at the house, and there were almost fifty of us who had an impromptu barbecue in the backyard. We lit lanterns and hung them all over the trees, and sat out under the stars all night with a small fire pit. It was a vigil and felt just right for what would have been his eighteenth birthday.

I'm not sure why, but I'd somehow expected Flynn to call that day, and when he didn't, I think that was the point I shut him out. I had to move forward and try to forget about him.

Sean and Daryl Langley, two of Martin's friends, turned up at the house. Sean had always been a sweet guy, and he came over often to hang out with Martin. We got to talking, and I found I had more in common with Daryl. He'd just finished a graphics and digital images course at college and did some work for an agency that bought photographs and then licensed them. He explained that they sold pictures to the public under license, then the person purchasing had the right to use the pictures. The company got paid commission by the owner of the picture. It seemed easy.

By the following weekend, he'd come to our house several times and sat at our dining room table, helping me upload photos I'd chosen, to their online stock albums. That afternoon, Kayden wandered in through the dining room, then the glass doors to the family room. Flopping down on the oversized sofa, he turned on the TV and switched on MTV. Flynn's band was on the screen, and my world crashed to a halt. I hadn't seen much about him since the day he'd left.

I'd avoided the radio most of the time because Major ScAlz' music seemed to be constantly seeping into my veins via the airwaves. I hadn't watched TV because I'd been so wrapped up in my homework and online studies; there just hadn't been time. When I heard his low, rich, distinctive timbre as he sang, my heart almost stopped. I instantly turned to look at the screen and stood slowly, completely enthralled by the sight of him. My eyes were still glued to the television long after their spot had finished.

"Want to talk about it?"

Daryl's head nodded toward the screen, alluding to my connection to Flynn. Everyone had seen him when he'd accompanied me on the day of the funeral. Most knew about the time he'd sat and cuddled with me on the bleachers. And now, Flynn was big news. Even more so in our little town.

"There's nothing to talk about, Daryl. It was all bullshit. Flynn never had a thing for me, and we never dated," I commented, and Kayden turned his head and smirked. Daryl hadn't seen him.

"Well, that's a relief. I mean, how does a guy compete with that?"

I smirked at Daryl. "You want to compete? Or do you mean in general."

"Listen, I know it's not really the time, I mean, Ziggy..."

"Ziggy's dead. I'm sixteen. I'm not over him, but I need to move past that. Or else I keep pining for someone who'll never come back into my life again, no matter how much I wish for that," I said, sounding both harsh and sad.

"And Flynn? You pining for him?"

"No, he's an asshole. A self-centered asshole."

"A rich, hot, and talented celebrity asshole," Daryl corrected.

"Whatever."

"So, does that mean you'd consider going on a date with me?"

Daryl was the same age as Flynn. He was in Martin's class at school, yet he had no hang-ups about asking me out. He was a good-looking guy with brown hair and had this hot, brooding look about him. He was built more like a hot ranchman than a computer geek, had a bright future, and I liked how easy things were between us.

"Well, I think it's only fair I tell you ... my heart is still healing, and Ziggy will always have a piece of it ... but I'd love to go to a movie or something with you." Daryl smiled, nodded his understanding, pleased with my response.

I knew I had to try to put all the hurt behind me and not let it consume me. Being strong and determined was the best strategy I had to cope with all I had faced. I'd felt if I gave it my best shot, I was bound to find harmony at some point. With all that in mind, I'd agreed to a date with Daryl. My stomach had tightened considerably when I saw Flynn on TV, but he'd already made it clear we were never going to get off the ground.

～

Nine weeks after Flynn left, and ten since Ziggy died, I went out on a casual date with one of Martin's friends. I'd known Daryl since I was five. He moved to our town with his brother and parents when his dad became manager of our local bank. Laid back and reserved, Daryl had his share of interest from girls in high school. He didn't seem the type who wanted anything serious, so it made sense for us to hang out together. Although I'd seen him around Martin, he wasn't a regular at our house; it was more Sean, his brother, who I knew through his friendship with Adam.

During our date, I wasn't prepared for him to act like the perfect gentleman, opening doors and pulling chairs out, but Daryl had the same manners I'd experienced with Ziggy. It was one of the things I'd found attractive ... in them both.

All evening, I noticed Daryl was being careful with his body space. He hadn't touched me, and he'd paid for everything, from the movie to pizza afterward, despite my protests. When he drove me home, I wasn't prepared when he made his move on me in the car. I just didn't expect anything from him after our evening.

As I said goodnight, I was about to reach for the handle to open the car door when he leaned over and turned my face toward him by my chin. His eyes twinkled in the darkness, as the light from above our kitchen door reflected in them. He leaned forward and dipped his head, then he kissed me hungrily.

The thrill of his sudden unexpected move, and the level of skill he used when he kissed me, left me breathless. My spine tingled as goosebumps spread across my skin from his touch. The groan he expelled, along with my awakened feelings, told me I'd definitely be seeing Daryl again.

That night when I went to bed, I remembered feeling that my evening with Daryl had lifted my mood, and that at some point, I may learn to live again. Looking back, it was probably the turning point for me.

Life slowly crept into a new kind of normal for my family, and there were days when we cried, days we were sad, and days where we raised a few smiles. We dealt with each significant day, like birthdays and other milestones, one by one, and got by, day by day.

My anger subsided, and I realized what a brat I'd been during those dark days. Then again, everyone reacts to grief differently, and being young, I'd viewed the whole horrible event from a very personal perspective. Gradually, we learned to live without Martin and Adam, and life settled into a new kind or normal, just like Aunt Joan said it would.

At first, I felt guilty for having fun again, but after a while, I realized that the last thing Martin, Adam—or Ziggy, for that matter—would want is for my life to be consumed with the sadness of their passing.

I threw myself into photography as a way of escaping my grief. Kayden returned to work and, with the help of his friends, started to live again. My parents supported each other, and they also had some brilliantly sympathetic friends who helped them cope. As a family, we were fractured, but we had somehow found solace in our combined grief, and our lives moved slowly forward.

TWO YEARS LATER

Chapter Eighteen

LIFE THROUGH A LENS

"*I*'m so proud of you, Valerie. I can't describe how in awe I am of all you've achieved during the past two years," Dad said with a smile.

Dad and Kayden had converted a small store downtown into my new commercial space. Daryl's support in helping me start my online photography business had been invaluable. I'd had a steady income from some of the most popular shots, and with some bigger sales from the exclusively licensed pictures.

Over the two previous years, I'd bought the best camera equipment I could find, as well as some sophisticated editing software. Along the way, I'd picked up proper studio lighting and cheap photographic backdrops on eBay. By the time my new venture had branched out, I had projection equipment, and was doing video advertising for local companies.

The more projects I took on, the more excited I'd become. The quality and standard of my work grew with every new facet of work I produced. I could see my growth. With the studio in place, I'd posted audition opportunities on the local college ad board for potential new faces, and thirty-eight applicants from the art department applied to model for me. I hired an office manager to oversee appointments, deal with inquiries, and catalog my work. I was eighteen and legally responsible for everything I did at work, and I finally felt like I'd grown into my own skin.

Auditioning models was fun. I ended up choosing eight—four males and four females. They all agreed to meet for a couples shoot. I knew I didn't want them to be portrait shots but more situational, so I'd gathered as many props as I could think of to use.

Guitars, mic stands, and mics from our old karaoke machine, cowboy boots, a couple of cowgirl skirts, a saddle, and chaps from when Adam was in a play, football gear and various other bits and pieces filled my studio. Fashionable clothing and strange attire were also in my collection, courtesy of Goodwill. My models had been chosen for their different looks: dark, blonde, petite, tall, pale with dark hair, ripped, and tattooed. My idea was to get as many different looks as I could in one session.

Nine hours after the first shoot, I'd taken over seven hundred frames, including colored, black and white, tinted, and raw frames. For the first couple of hours, we'd all been self-conscious and giggling, but by the end of the shoot, we were more professional and technical in our collective thoughts, to capture the best shots. Most of the students were older than me, but they weren't bothered by the age difference, and all of them were impressed by everything I'd achieved.

Sharing the best pictures with Daryl was exciting, and there were three he thought were exceptional. One was of me I'd taken with a timer. I sat cross-legged, playing my guitar on the wooden floor of my bedroom, and my long, dark hair looked wild. I looked much cooler than I felt in real life. Daryl kept going back to it and, although it was a great picture, I'd not been able to see what the fuss was about.

When Kayden saw it, he kept that picture aside when he'd looked at them and asked if he could have it. I gave it to him because it wasn't even a proper shot. I'd been messing around with a new lens and had taken it to gauge the images I might have expected from it.

After we'd reviewed the photos and selected the best, I began editing to perfect them. I eventually uploaded almost two hundred of those pictures. Another fifty-three were licensed through another site. From that point on in my career, I'd never looked back.

I thought back to the day Dad took me into town to meet with his accountant when I had just turned seventeen, and my business was growing. Technically, my dad was in charge until I turned eighteen, so his signature was all over my work. He never interfered with what I was doing, just gently advised, and encouraged me.

I had a line of credit and cards in the company name, and I just used it when I needed to. If I wanted to purchase something high-end, he'd discuss it with me first. When I needed new equipment, or went on location to shoot, he'd been supportive. In truth, I'd had no need to use either for much.

By my eighteenth birthday, I had over ninety-three thousand dollars profit in my account, and what had started out as a fun little hobby had grown into a substantial small business. I'd been determined not to take a salary until I turned eighteen, preferring to invest a regular sum of money back into better software and equipment. A month after my birthday, my photographic studio in town opened.

I'd also survived two Thanksgiving anniversaries without the boys, which were dark days. The memory of their loss still brought me to tears, but Daryl had been by my side, which helped a lot. Flynn never called again, and the first year I cursed him for that, but by the second year, I was more resigned.

I'd grown from a naïve girl to a shrewd and tough young woman. I was a lot tougher and much less innocent. Looking back, I was glad Flynn had done what he had because I was happy with Daryl. He was normal and fun to be around, and incredibly supportive of my business. He gave me space to do my own thing, and his life seemed to center around mine.

Auntie Joan had been right. Life had gone on, despite the loss of my brothers, and I'd found my new *normal*. I still missed Martin and Adam dreadfully. Ziggy and my brothers would always hold a little piece of my heart.

Kayden was doing much better, although he was still in counseling. He'd met a girl named Amber at work, while visiting the service department of a well-known car company. I always smiled when I listened to them talk, because they talked about everything from how long parts took between ordering to delivery, to the best lubricant for specific engines. Not really the kind of conversation others can join in, but they seemed perfectly happy.

My mom seemed to have lost her soul with the deaths of her boys. She wasn't interested in much, and even though she was around me daily in body, her mind wasn't focused in the here and now. She grieved deeply and poured over pictures and albums, arranging and rearranging them. Counseling had brought her so far, but she had a long road ahead to heal and find some kind of resolution regarding their deaths.

Daryl respected the fact that I hadn't been ready to sleep with him, and although I had strong feelings for him and we messed around a lot, we'd stopped short of having sex. Daryl was heavy into the church and advocated abstinence as part of his faith.

One thing my business had taught me was that it was better not to rush into things. Concentrating ninety percent of my time with building my clientele and strategy meant there was very little time for an intimate relationship anyway. Plus, Daryl was out of town two nights a week, dealing with clients as part of his own career progression, reducing our opportunities to make unchangeable mistakes with each other.

As part of my self-development, I attended conferences given by some of the big media and technology corporations. And, on one occasion, I flew to Chicago for a two-day conference that was held jointly by social media giants and one of the world's leading camera producers. It was mainly about using technology in the best way possible without compromising ownership, and protecting copyright.

I was a little nervous because it was my first big event I'd attended solo, and it had given me such a buzz to feel so independent. The conference center was massive, and to be there with so many like-minded people was inspiring. During the lunch break the first day, I bumped into someone familiar.

"Howard, right?"

"Oh, wow, Valerie, isn't it?"

Howard was one of Daryl's buddies from work. I'd seen him at the holiday cookout their company had the previous summer.

"That's right. What are you doing here?" I asked.

"Oh, I'm not officially here. I'm on vacation from work, and as this is my passion as well as my work, I thought I'd kill two birds with one stone by doing some architectural shots, and check out the conference at the same time."

"How long are you here for?"

"I head back Monday."

As it turned out, we'd been booked on the same flight home, and both of us had Monday to kill before our 9:00 P.M. flight. Like me, he'd been traveling alone so when he suggested dinner, I agreed.

During dinner, the bottom fell out of my world again. Part way through the conversation, I sensed he didn't like Daryl much. We'd been talking about his work, and I had pointed out that Daryl had mentioned how he hated traveling and the fact that he'd had to keep going out of town a couple of times a week. Howard challenged my statement before he realized Daryl and I were still together.

Instant shock registered in his expression, and he stammered almost uncontrollably. I could see his embarrassment of having put his foot in his mouth. He'd almost rose from his chair because he was so uncomfortable. Once he realized I'd caught on to his denial about Daryl, he did the decent thing and shared that, as far as he knew, Daryl had a Hispanic girlfriend named Maria who lived just over the state line in Minnesota.

Howard told me Daryl still arrived at work in Iowa Monday through Friday, so it was clear Daryl had been cheating on me. When I calculated the start of his trips, it had been about seven months previously. Around the time, I'd done one of my first photo shoots. I'd been so busy digitally enhancing and perfecting my portfolio, I hadn't noticed the connection between that and Daryl's work schedule changing.

After a few minutes, the delayed shock set in and, although Howard was still talking, I couldn't hear anything he was saying. Blood rushed through my ears as my heart almost burst out of my chest with fury at Daryl's betrayal. I stood from the table and excused myself, but I hadn't made it out of the restaurant before tears streamed unchecked down my face.

Abandoning Howard, I went to my hotel room and sat on the end of the bed, staring at my reflection in the dressing table mirror. I briefly wondered if Howard had gone straight for his cell to warn Daryl what I'd found out when I'd left the table. I didn't care. Daryl was gone, as far as I was concerned. I called my mom. We'd not been close since Martin and Adam's death, but I needed her to be my mom at that moment.

When I told her, she was fuming, and I hadn't heard that level of passion from her for the longest time. I asked her not to say anything to Daryl, and told her I was flying home a day early. I wanted the certificate of attendance from that conference, but what I'd learned was much more valuable and important than anything to do with my work. It was strange because, instead of focusing on Daryl cheating on me, I was more interested in nailing the lying bastard for putting me through such humiliation again.

I packed before I went to bed that night and rescheduled my flight for one that departed at 8:15 the following morning. I'd hardly slept and, by the time I'd arrived at the airport, I was spoiling for a fight through lack of sleep and the anticipation of confronting Daryl.

Arriving at North East Iowa Airport, I saw Kayden waiting for me. He smiled softly, but his facial expression changed to worry the closer I came to him.

"Sorry, Valerie. Mom told me about Daryl. I want to cut the fucker's dick off. Why would anyone do that to you?"

"Probably because he isn't doing anything else with me, Kayd. What the fuck is wrong with me?"

"What do you mean?"

"I mean Daryl didn't push to sleep with me, but I know now that's because he was with someone else."

"So, you two haven't..."

Kayden's face flushed, and I shook my head, too ticked off to care.

"Flynn disappeared when I wanted him and now this..."

"Flynn came on to you?"

"A little when he came home with Martin, but it wasn't really a big deal. Last time, I almost threw myself at him, and he left the next day before I'd gotten out of bed."

"You know he's still in touch with Dad, right?"

How many more things don't I know about? It seemed as if all the men in my life were either running away from me, lying, or dying. Once Kayden told me about Dad and Flynn, my heart pounded in my chest. Flynn had only been in my life for about nine days in total. Daryl had been with me for over two years.

Even when Howard told me the news about Daryl, it should have devastated me. But, I hadn't reacted with the same level of emotion I had after I'd heard about Flynn. My focus instantly shifted to the guy who crushed my heart and stomped on it. Or so it had seemed when I was sixteen, anyway.

"I do now. Seems I'm surrounded by devious men."

"I'm not devious, Valerie. I've never lied to you."

"Present company excluded, Kayden, but what is it about me that makes guys freak out? I don't know anyone else who got treated as if they're fragile flowers, like everyone does with me. Every guy I've ever liked has gone to another girl for sex."

"I think that's because any guy who has you ... you know, in that way, will want to keep you. If they can't do what it takes to make that happen, or they don't think they're good enough, then they'd probably back off."

"How the hell would you know that, Kayd?"

"Martin." The sound of Kayden mentioning Martin made my stomach tighten.

"What does Martin have to do with anything?"

"Just something he said to his friend Glenn once."

"So?"

"He said something like, 'No one fucks my sister unless it's forever. She's not the type of girl to give herself to just anyone, so back off. It's going to take the best of the best to satisfy her and capture her heart. Anyone who does and doesn't take care of it, I'll personally kill with my bare hands,' or words to that effect."

"Martin said that?"

"He did. And he was right. Those guys—Brad, Daryl, and Flynn ... they know they aren't faithful, so they won't ruin you for someone else."

"Bullshit. You make me sound like fucking Rapunzel."

"And that's exactly what I said to Martin at the time. Our brother was fiercely protective of you, Valerie. He hated that Flynn had a thing for you, but personally having been around him, I reckon he's a pretty stand-up guy, and not the same guy he was around Martin. The way he came at a moment's notice for us ... for you, speaks volumes about the man's integrity."

Kayden's remarks about Martin being wrong hurt, because it felt like he was being disloyal, and I hated anyone saying something about him that made him less than perfect. However, since his death, I'd been able to see how his behavior may have scared his friends from acting naturally around me.

Chapter Nineteen

STILL THE SMART ASS

*O*nce I was on home ground, it made me more determined to get even with Daryl. There was no use yelling at him or accusing him. He'd only deny it. I also knew he would try to weasel out of the entire thing. I'd gotten a vibe that Howard didn't like Daryl, and I knew Daryl well enough to accuse me of taking someone else's word over his. Plus, I had no physical proof.

There were two things I wanted at that moment: To get even with Daryl, and to hear Flynn's voice. I was nervous, but he'd once told me to call him when I was ready. I wasn't quite sure what he'd meant by that when I was sixteen. However, two years later, when I looked back, I knew he'd been right. I was totally immature and there was no way I'd have been able to deal with a guy like him.

A lot had happened since I'd last seen him, and I bore no resemblance to the naïve, innocent girl I once was. I'd built a flourishing business and was much wiser to that girl he met back then. I felt if he came, Flynn would meet a young, self-assured woman. Whether he'd respond or not would be his call.

As far as he was concerned, I obviously hadn't moved on from him much, when the first thing I'd wanted, when Kayden told me about Dad having his number, was to hear his voice. I knew Flynn would never be able to forget me; we both had Martin's memory, and he was there for me during those dark days. Two years was a long time, though, and I figured Flynn would probably have shelved the memory of me as a horrible chapter in his life that he was glad to put behind him.

Surely, he'd have contacted me at some point if that hadn't been the case? Even with that thought, as soon as we were home, I challenged my dad about keeping his calls from Flynn secret, and when he looked sheepish and pursed his lips together, I lost it.

"Dad. Flynn's number, now!"

He opened his mouth to protest, but Kayden cut him off before he lied to me. "I told her you were still in touch."

Dad's brow furrowed and he shook his head at Kayden, frustrated that he'd shared that information with me. "He doesn't want you to call him, Valerie. I don't even know where he is. All I know is he calls from time to time, asks how your mom and I are doing, and he follows the progress of your career. Kayden talks to him occasionally as well."

I glared at Kayden because he'd purposely omitted that little nugget of information.

"Is that right? So, everyone *loves* Flynn, but don't tell Valerie? Since when did we become a family who keeps secrets, because I don't recall ever getting that memo? And where's your loyalty?"

Both my dad and Kayden looked sheepishly at me again. "Number, please?" I said, holding my hand out and waving my fingers in a "gimme" gesture for the phone.

Dad sighed and sat down, pushing his hair back with both hands. "It's the same number as before."

"He told me he was changing it the last time I spoke to him."

"Well, what he told you and what he did don't appear to be the same thing."

"You mean his number has been on my cell phone this whole time and I never knew it?" I said, fishing in my oversized bag for my cell. I pulled it out and scrolled through the numbers saved to my sim card, and wondered why I hadn't ever called or deleted the number. Even after I'd destroyed my phone, when I got my new one, his number was still there. I'd seen it a thousand times when I'd been scrolling through to find a contact, yet even though I thought he'd changed it, I had left it untouched between the "E's" and "G's." He was the only "F" listed.

My initial reaction was to call him, but I decided against it because he'd avoided me for all that time, so I'd figured he'd let the call go to voicemail. I texted him instead.

Me: Rock star asshole, help me. I need you.

My fingers had worked so quickly, I'd fired off the text before my brain computed what I'd written.

Immediately, my cell rang.

"I'm impressed you know your name," I drawled sarcastically, as my heart raced, and my body vibrated with delight. Flynn was on the other side of the line and we were communicating again.

"What's up?" Hearing his voice made me weak in my knees.

"Two years and your first words to me are, 'What's up?'"

"And yours were 'I'm impressed,' so that got my attention."

"Still the smart ass." I couldn't help the smile that lifted the corners of my mouth.

"Still the prissy little girl."

I tensed in defense and straightened my stance. "Don't fucking call me that. Where are you?"

"Chicago. Why?"

I exhaled heavily. He was too far away for what I had in mind.

"Same ol' same ol'. I've discovered my faithful boyfriend is not so faithful. I was hoping for a rerun of the infamous stunt we pulled in the bleachers."

"On my way." Flynn hung up and I laughed to myself. He'd always had a sense of humor, I smiled, even though my heart felt instantly heavy because I knew he hadn't meant it. *Had I really expected him to?*

I tapped the phone to my chin, waiting for him to call me back. When he didn't, I called him. As soon as he answered, I could tell he was on the move. Checking my watch, I figured he'd be on his way to one of his concerts or another engagement. Flynn's band had been heavily in demand for the past couple of years. Although I had made a point of not following him closely, I'd heard enough to know that he was becoming a worldwide household name. I was surprised he was even in the USA when I'd called him.

"Valerie, it's dangerous to talk on a cell phone and drive. I can't do both. Can this wait until I get there?" My heart skipped a beat and continued to stutter in my chest for rhythm, even though I still thought he was teasing me.

"Seriously? Like... you're coming all the way from Chicago?" My heart pounded in my chest as an adrenaline dump hit me. I shook at the thought that he'd dropped everything at my silly request, but when he confirmed he was on his way, I almost fell over.

"Yeah. I have five days free, and I was craving a good road trip. I figured it was about time I paid your family a visit. It's long overdue. I had to be sure you were strong enough to be around me," he said, with a smile in his voice.

Was I? Knowing he was actually coming, and just hearing his voice, caused my girly muscles to clench with desire. I'd been stupid to call him, because within two minutes of talking to him, he was beginning to melt my heart again.

My eyes closed with a visual flashback of our kiss as I listened to his soft, low voice. The affect it had on me was like thick syrup drizzling all over me. He only had to speak to stir up feelings I had fought hard to leave behind.

"Fuck you, Flynn. Get the fuck over yourself." I had sounded aggressive, but inside my belly was doing flip-flops with excitement.

Flynn chuckled, and it turned into a belly laugh. "Damn, you've developed one helluva potty mouth, Valerie Darsin. It's making me hard."

His dirty comment stirred the memory of his erect cock pressing against me when he'd pushed me against my door that first time we'd met.

"Yeah, yeah, and you're such a comedian and just as irritating as you've always been. But since you are coming to help me, I'll try to be nice."

"Don't. I love this bitchy new version of Valerie with the dirty mouth."

"That's the only place you'll see my dirty mouth, because it certainly won't be on you," I responded, forgetting where I was. My jaw dropped in a silent scream as I turned to see my dad's scowling face. I was about to correct what I said when Flynn interjected again.

"Okay, sassy Val, I have to go. I've got to keep my eyes on the road. It's raining ice, and I'm trying to concentrate. You don't want me arriving in a casket, now do you?"

The phone line between us fell silent until Flynn cursed angrily.

"Fuck, babe, I wasn't thinking when I said that." I heard the sincerity and hurt in his voice at his thoughtless comment.

"I know. Take your time. Be safe. I'd hate anything to happen to you," I responded. My stomach suddenly knotted with a horrible thought that he might have an accident on my account. A dreadful feeling hung over me as we hung up. I turned to my parents and Kayden.

"Sorry. That's not who I am," I said, pointing at my cell. "Flynn just tends to bring out the devil in me. He's coming because I asked him for help. If Daryl calls, please stall him. He's not expecting to see me until Tuesday, so I'm hoping his colleague Howard doesn't catch up with him before I do."

"I hope you know what you're doing, Valerie. I think Flynn still holds a torch for you," Mom said.

Kayden smiled at me and stood to place his hand on my shoulder. "You need to give Flynn a break, Valerie. He's always tried to do the right thing by you. Jeez, think about it. You call him after two years, and he drops everything to come straight here because you yell, 'Help'? That doesn't say he's still holding a torch for you, it's more like a bonfire. The guy is a huge rock star, did you forget? How many rock stars would do that for a woman? They use and abuse them, normally, from what I hear."

"Nah, I think Flynn still has a lot of guilt about Martin, Kayden. That's why he's making an appearance. It makes him feel better." I picked up my suitcase and computer bag and headed for the stairs, looking unaffected. Inside I was excited at the thought Kayden had put in my head. "I'm not sure when he'll be here, but he may need somewhere to sleep tomorrow. Can he use Auntie Joan's room?"

Mom looked up from her e-reader again and nodded. "Sure. The room is clean and the bed is made. Of course, he can stay. That boy is like family now after what he did for us. I just worry about how you'll deal with him."

I realized I hadn't been as private with my feelings as I'd thought the last time he'd been around. "I'm not sixteen any more, Mom," was my only reply.

Reaching the top of the stairs, my belly was fluttered with excitement, and the adrenaline rush Kayden's words had given me had already affected my heart rate. I had just hours to prepare, and wondered if I'd be able to keep my emotions in check after all this time.

After two years of dating Daryl, I should have been heartbroken, but his betrayal and my belly anger toward him about his cheating, overrode any feelings I had for him. I should have been distraught, yet I was fueled by the prospect of getting even. Even with all those thoughts going through my mind, seeing Flynn was the most dominant thought stirring my emotions.

~

Gravel crunching on the driveway outside signaled his arrival. I'd been too excited to sleep. I flung back the covers and ran to the window and stood, silently hugging myself, as I watched the door of the black BMW sedan open. Flynn's tall, familiar frame appeared in the darkness.

The security light had gone on by the kitchen door, and I caught my first glimpse of him. I saw him clearly and took a second to remember the last time I had seen him. I gasped when he unexpectedly glanced in the direction of my bedroom window, his face bathed in the light from above the door. A smile played on his lips right before he walked toward the door, and it stole my breath from me.

The time was 1:20 A.M. From Chicago to where we lived was a good four-and-a-half-hour drive and he'd made great time. I checked my hair in the mirror and pulled the elastic from the end of the braid I'd tied it into before I went to bed. Shaking my hair loose, I let it cascade down my back as I quickly made my way downstairs.

My heart beat erratically, and I fought the nerves that fluttered in my belly as I stood gathering my thoughts for a second. When I opened the door, Lee was standing beside Flynn as a reminder that Flynn was a famous rock star. His breath caught in his throat as he stared appreciatively at me.

"Holy Fuck, Valerie. You look absolutely beautiful, babe," he exclaimed excitedly, as his eyes ticked over my body. I noticed his pupils had dilated widely as he looked me over, which made me smile.

One short sentence of approval from his mouth had my heart and body on fire. He pushed his way forward into the kitchen, placing a small black leather bag on the countertop.

"Come here," he said, as he opened his arms wide to hug me. I hesitated because I knew as soon as he touched me, my heart would ache for him all over again. Everything I'd told myself about being over him, suddenly confirmed as me kidding myself. Avoiding him, I rounded the countertop and began making coffee. Lee chuckled at me blowing him off, while Flynn snickered and smirked back at him.

"Well, that's not much of a welcome, considering you need my help. What's the deal?"

I stared pointedly at Lee as he sat down at the kitchen table and tried to look disinterested. His eyes wandered around the room as he pretended he wasn't listening.

"Lee, upstairs, second door on the right. That's Auntie Joan's room. You can sleep there."

Lee smirked. "Are you offering me your aunt?"

"Don't be smart, Lee," I grated.

Lee glanced at Flynn. "You want me to go to bed?"

"She does, Lee, but not with her or her aunt. Am I right?" The smile in the tone of his smart-ass answer irked me.

"Is everything a joke to you?"

Lee shuffled past Flynn and headed for the stairs. "See you in the morning boss. Good luck," he mumbled sarcastically as his eyes fleetingly met mine.

Once he'd gone, Flynn came around the countertop to where I was standing. Suddenly, the space instantly seemed smaller.

He turned and rolled his hip on the countertop, leaning against it.

Folding his arms, he looked directly at me and the effect left me breathless.

"Slow down with the hostility, babe. It doesn't suit you. So, what's this emergency?"

"Daryl."

"The boyfriend?"

"Soon to be ex-boyfriend."

"He's growing on me. Go on, what's the deal?"

I explained what Howard had told me, minus the part about us never sleeping together, and Flynn sat quietly until I was done.

"Damn. Did you get tested?"

I was speechless at his initial reaction. Of all the things he could have said, that was probably the last thing I expected. "I'm clean, Flynn."

Flynn's head reeled back from the neck at my statement, his body tensing momentarily. He stared in thought for a few seconds and then took a sharp breath.

"You sound confident about that. So how do you want to play this?"

"I want Daryl to get the most unexpected 'fuck-you-Daryl-look-at-me' surprise I can manage."

"So, you want you and I to fuck him together, right?" he said as he gave me a secret smile.

I smiled back at his suggestive question. "Flynn, that sounds like a very loaded question coming from a rock star."

Flynn chuckled. "Damn, Valerie, you've changed a lot, babe."

"How so?"

"You're mouth now matches your looks. You look great by the way... No, you look fucking breathtakingly beautiful, actually."

I bunched my brow, unsure what that answer even meant, but pleased he had complimented me on how I looked.

"I mean, you are gorgeous ... stunning ... sexy-as-fuck. I only need to look at you and my dick's rock solid. That hasn't happened to me with any other woman on the planet. Your mouth ... the way you used to speak ... it always seemed way too pure for that body. I'd never have crossed the line with that girl. Now, the confident and ballsy woman you've grown into is a game changer."

Coughing, I caught my heart in my mouth as it attempted to leap from my body at his statement. Flynn was an expert in seduction, and expressing he liked the changes in me had me doing a happy dance inside.

"Uh huh," I stated sarcastically, as if his bullshit hadn't touched me, but I continued my fight to swallow my heart back down into my chest, as it stuttered trying to find a regular rhythm. If we'd been in an ideal world where inhibitions, consciences, and reputations weren't invented, I'd have somehow wrapped my legs around his waist as he leaned back against that countertop. Daryl had never gotten that kind of reaction from me, even during our hottest interludes.

Flynn rolled his hips and looked at his feet. The fluidity of his movement drew my eyes to his crotch, and they settled on the bulge in his pants. I swallowed audibly when I saw he was aroused, and once again my heart leaped into my throat with wanton desire and the need to touch him.

"Alright. I'm here. What is it you want me to do?"

My face flushed, and I suddenly felt like I was fifteen again.

"I want him to see us together."

"Like in a coffee shop?" He smirked, goading me to say exactly what I wanted.

"No, I want him to turn up here and see me in a compromising position with you."

"Valerie, how do we do that when you wouldn't even let me hug you just now?"

I felt my face redden and forced myself to make eye contact with him. "That's not true. I was just busy welcoming you and making coffee."

Flynn snickered, pushed off the countertop, and put his hands out toward me. "Then I'll take that hug now; it's long overdue."

Before I could think, he moved forward swiftly and wrapped his arms tightly around me. His touch instantly ignited a fizzing cascade of sensation throughout my body. His head fell forward, and he nestled his face into the curve of my neck. Initially, my frame stiffened, but a second later, I found all our curves molding together to fit me to his position.

161

A large, warm hand centered at the base of my spine, and a shiver ran down it. The way he inhaled heavily against my skin gave me another buzz of electricity before he dragged his nose the length of it, until his mouth was level with my ear. I was instantly aroused. My arms slid around his waist because I could no longer fight the urge to touch him.

"Damn, babe, you smell so good. My pretty little schoolgirl has turned into a stunningly beautiful woman." He whispered huskily before his breath blew softly into my ear. His seductive move and the moisture from his breath spiked my desire further. Burning with sensation, I sagged further against him, both of us swaying slightly on our feet.

I swallowed with difficulty, because his hand was caressing my neck as he inhaled deeply again. His warm lips brushed the same spot and he pulled out of our embrace. Extending his arms, he pushed me away and stood silently, with a soul-searching look on his face.

Shaking his head, his arms dropped as he turned and paced the kitchen space, and when there wasn't enough room to do that, he rounded the kitchen counter and paced into the wider dining area.

"It's been over two and a half years since the first time I saw you, and you're still in here, Valerie," he said, pointing at his forehead. "How the fuck did you do that?" he asked with his arms stretched on either side of him as he stared at me, appearing confused.

I crossed my arms over my body, conscious of the fact that I'd responded to his touch. My veins were on fire with the electrical pulses still running through me. He glanced at my rock-hard nipples, poking through the thin tank top I'd been sleeping in. I was still reeling from the after effects of his hug as I tried hard to pull myself together, and responded with as little emotion as possible.

"You were the one who ran away, Flynn. I've always been here. I may have been young, but you can't say I didn't own my feelings the last time we saw each other."

"Valerie, you were grieving the loss of your brothers and boyfriend. I had no right kissing you in the first place. That was a shitty thing I did. Yeah, I ran because if I hadn't, I'd have hurt you. How do you think I felt? Have you ever once tried to see things from my perspective? Val, I was a guy with a new career that pulled me in all kinds of directions, traveling the world, and meeting all kinds of new situations. Temptations? Fuck, Valerie. I'm human. How would you have felt to have read online that I'd fucked a couple of girls in a bar, or seen me with women draped all over me, or any of the other shit I've done?"

Searching his face, I knew I'd have been devastated. He'd done what he thought was the best thing for me at the time. And he was right, it would have killed me. I'd willingly admit I was emotionally wrung out after the boys' deaths, and although Flynn leaving like that devastated me, the way he'd explained it made sense. He made me hate him because anger and hate were easier to deal with than heartache.

At that moment, I finally accepted that everyone was right. Flynn had walked away to save me further hurt if I'd come to rely on him, and if he'd somehow let me down. All the time I'd been mad at him, all he'd been doing was protecting me, from myself.

Chapter Twenty

ABSURDITY

*A*ll my anger had been for nothing. Flynn had done what was necessary because he couldn't see any other way. "I guess I owe you an apology."

"I'm sorry if I hurt you, Valerie, but I couldn't act on what I was feeling in that RV. You were vulnerable and too young. My head was up my ass for a long time after I left that day. I felt like crap for leaving you like that, but I had to think of the consequences and impact of what had happened between us. I would have felt responsible for you Valerie, and I wasn't in a position to take that on."

"Well, it looks like we've moved past all that now. I'm all grown up and deeply involved in my growing business, and you're a big-shot rock star. I'm glad to see you, though, Flynn. Thank you for answering my distress call. I didn't know who else to trust with my dilemma."

"I can't believe you've done what you have with your business. You've grown up fast, and what a beautiful woman you've become, babe. From the first time I set eyes on you, I knew you were different. The past couple of years have only enhanced your beauty. And I'm glad you felt you could still trust me. That's quite a novelty in my line of work."

My cheeks heated at his comment. I smirked at the absurdity of

Flynn Docherty, lead singer of Major ScAlz, a huge rock band, standing in my kitchen paying me compliments on how I looked, and agreeing to be my fake boyfriend. Again. Beautiful women from all over the world threw themselves at him every day of the week.

Glancing at the clock, I frowned. "It's almost 2:00 A.M. We should go to bed." Lee had taken my aunt's bedroom. "Shit, you'd better take my bed. I'll sleep down here on the couch. I was going to put you in Auntie Joan's room."

"Yeah, like I'm gonna let that happen? I've never thrown a chick from her bed so I can sleep there. Nope, not my style."

"You're not staying in Martin's or Adam's rooms. Mom has kept them..."

He held his hands up. "Wouldn't dream of that either. I'm too big for the sofa, so I guess we're just going to have to squeeze into your bed, babe. Unless you don't trust me to keep my hands to myself."

Once Flynn threw down the challenge, I was damned if I was going to back down. "I trust you. I'm going up to get into bed."

Ascending the stairs with him behind me, I was consciously trying not to wiggle my ass. I didn't want to risk sending him a message that I'd make the same mistake twice. Nor did I want to give him the idea I was coming on to him.

Once we were in the bedroom, there was an awkward moment before Flynn went into the bathroom. I quickly slipped between the sheets but, when I heard the shower running, my heart rate raced inside my chest. I knew he had to be naked, and only about six feet from my bed. The only thing that separated us was a thinly tiled wall. I began imagining him washing himself, working up a lather with the body wash before soap suds cascaded down the hard lines of his belly. The thought made me wet down below, and I berated myself for that reaction. I turned on my side, facing away from the bathroom, and punched the pillow as I tried to ignore my body's reaction to the mere thought of him, naked.

I heard the shower turn off, and a few minutes later, the light switch clicked. The dull light from the bathroom went out. I pretended to be asleep. Flynn slid under the covers and, when his foot touched mine, I moved it and found more exposed skin on his leg. His arm slid down the side of me, and he rested it on my hip. Instantly, my heart started another workout and pumped faster than my body could match.

Goosebumps popped up all over where we were touching, and a rush of saliva formed in my mouth at the mere fact that he was in my bed. I tried so hard not to swallow. Flynn edged nearer, inhaled deeply, and controlled his breath as he exhaled slowly. I felt his hot breath on my shoulder, and swallowed anyway. He sighed again before he rolled over in the opposite direction.

I lay quiet, trying to get my heart back in check. When I'd heard his soft, deep, even breathing, I knew he'd fallen asleep.

Slowly, I changed my position and turned to face Flynn's back. Heat radiated from it, and his manly scent filled my nostrils. He was right there in front of me. The man who had captured my heart when I was fifteen. It didn't seem to matter that I'd loved Ziggy or Daryl, because I'd loved him first. I'd read somewhere that you never forget your first love. It's a love that cuts into your heart and marks your soul. No matter what comes after, the memory of that love continues to ooze from the wound. That part I could definitely vouch for.

Nothing could have prevented me from snuggling closer. All I had to do was pretend to be asleep. Flynn couldn't blame me for doing what I wasn't aware of, so I rolled into him and snaked my hand around his waist. Soft, warm skin stretched over hard lines, and my forefinger tracked his six-pack. I nudged the waistband of his boxer shorts, brushing the head of his cock through them by accident, and he stretched out and rolled back slightly toward me. A soft groan left his lips, and I froze, my heart beating erratically as if it had been hit by a bolt of lightning.

Once I'd ensured he was still asleep, I adjusted myself as one would in sleep and, this time, rested my hand on the hardness of his pecs. Flynn was solid, hard muscle, and I was desperate to explore him more. I dipped my head until my face was buried into his side, and the touch of his arm against it was exquisite. Flynn rolled over in his sleep, scooped me into his side, and his big hand slid down and cupped my behind. I froze again.

It was torture lying in his arms and not being able to kiss him. His chest rose and fell against my cheek, while my level of arousal was beyond anything I'd ever felt before. Swiftly, Flynn rolled me on top of him, and I felt his hard cock beneath me.

Before I could move away, his fingers curled around my hips as he adjusted me over him. My head was above his heart, and I could hear the strong beat in his chest. Again, his breath wafted over me. He swallowed and cleared his throat.

I wanted to kiss him so badly, but I was determined not to go there because I thought he'd break my heart, so I tried to move away. Without warning, his hand moved from my hip to my hair and began to massage my scalp at the back of my head. "Are you awake?" I whispered nervously, and felt embarrassed I was lying on top of him in the first place.

"No," he whispered back gruffly.

I giggled and tried to roll off him, but he held me firmly on top of him.

"I need to lie down," I stated.

"You are—on me. Shh, let me finish this dream first," he pleaded.

"What dream?"

"The one where I grind myself against you, and then kiss you like you need it to breathe."

That's exactly how I felt. Like I needed that kiss to breathe. I smiled. "And that would be a good dream?"

"Fuck yeah. It would be an awesome dream, babe," he husked, and pulled me tighter against his body. His back bowed off the mattress for greater friction, like our contact wasn't enough.

I stared hungrily at his mouth as his eyes watched me intensely. "We don't really want to go there, do we?" I questioned, even though I *so* did.

"I do—desperately. But... that wouldn't be a great idea because a kiss wouldn't be enough this time."

Every muscle in my body pulsed with need as my desire soaked my shorts. As if I needed physical evidence of how he affected me. Instinctively, I lifted my head and pressed a soft kiss to his neck. I was rewarded with a long groan as he dug his fingertips into my flesh through my pajamas. Pressing me closer against his erection, he ground his hard cock against me and growled deeply.

"Sweet Jesus, two years away and still... what you do to me, girl," he declared in a deliciously sexy tone.

I pressed a soft kiss to his lips and couldn't resist dipping my head and tracing the vein in his neck with my tongue. Without warning, he instantly flipped me onto my back, surrounded me with his body, and cradled my head between his arms. His hands held my head in place at the top.

"Are you prick-teasing me, Valerie?"

"I hope so. I've waited a long time for my revenge for when you ran out on me."

Flynn snickered and, although I couldn't see him in the dark, I could feel his mouth only a few inches from mine.

"Fuck, babe. I don't want to do this, but if I don't, I think I might die. You understand?"

"I do," I stated honestly. Every fiber in my body was alert and screaming for him to do it. Hovering over no man's land was agonizing.

A smooth thumb scored across my lips, and I heard Flynn take in a deep, shaky breath.

"Fuck it," he muttered before his mouth crashed down on mine. Sparks flew in all directions inside me as his tongue swept into my mouth. It was instant rapture. He shifted his weight and lay on top of me again, increasing the pressure between us so his cock thrust between my legs. Flynn scooped his hands under me, one at my back - one at my butt, and he rolled me on top of him again.

Tightening his arms around my body, he pulled me harder against him still. I felt like he was trying to climb inside me. I moaned softly, and this seemed to spur him on because he ground more urgently against me.

Breaking the kiss, we both panted breathlessly, and he rolled us to the side, releasing his grip. He shifted his body away from mine and the loss of heat I felt was instant.

"Fuck," he hissed again. "Jesus Christ. When I kiss you ... it makes me feel so high, but we need to stop right now, or we will be fucking."

I'd wanted to tell him not to stop, but he already had. It hurt that the passion between us hadn't been enough to swallow whatever was holding him back, and I wanted his need to be as big as mine. I wasn't going to beg him, so I rolled away from him onto my other side again. Tears threatened to fall, but I was determined not to cry this time.

Flynn kept his distance on the bed and didn't speak to me after that, so my wildly beating heart eventually calmed. I think I fell asleep before he did, because the last thing I remember was him sweeping his hand through his hair for the hundredth time and sighing loudly.

Buster barked, and I heard someone walking down the hallway. Dad's heavy footsteps came near the door, and then got further away as he went downstairs. Flynn's arm was across my belly, splayed protectively. His thick cock was long and hard against the crease of my butt, and he was pressed tightly against me. He stirred, and I lay quiet and still as he pressed his lips lightly on the back of my neck and eased me closer. I was tired of playing games. He wanted me and I wanted him, no matter what the consequences were later.

"I wanted that kiss last night. In fact, I wanted more," I stated, my heart speeding up at the bravery of my confession.

"Me too, babe, but I won't start something I can't finish."

"What do you mean?"

"I can't fool around and not have a release. I'm way past that these days."

My face heated at his blunt disclosure. How could he know there may not be more? I'd fooled around with Daryl to the point where he'd jerked himself off afterward. I knew I was way behind my peers as far as sex was concerned, but my upbringing and Daryl's laughable abstinence accounted for that.

"Who says you won't finish?" My heart thumped wildly, and the vein in my neck was pulsing quickly at the thought of a home run with Flynn.

"I'm not fucking you here in your bed, Val. If things go badly, then you're stuck with me right here. I won't do that to you."

Wiggling free, I sat up and turned my head to face him. "Jeez, Flynn, you're supposed to be a fucking rock star, and you're trying to talk me out of something you've shown no sign of getting from me in the first place."

Flynn pulled me down on the bed to face him, and he kissed me hard. His lips were bruising mine as his tongue explored my mouth deeply. I almost lost my mind at how raw and carnal it felt, and tremors within my body made me feel like I was going to explode. "More," tore from my throat.

Breaking the kiss, he turned me away from him and slid his hand around my belly again. Nuzzling the back of my neck brought on a fresh wave of goosebumps. His hand slid down the soft skin of my belly and breached my pajama shorts. When his movement was restricted, he hurriedly tugged them down, tapping my hip in silent communication for me to lift myself to free them. He used his foot to push them down my legs, and I pulled them free.

Sweeping my long hair aside, he peppered kisses around the nape of my neck and over one shoulder. I almost lost my mind with desire. His hand slid down again, and this time his fingertips reached inside my panties. I moaned loudly.

"Shh," he whispered, as a long middle finger traced the seam of my wet center. He growled and pulled his hand away, then lifted it to my mouth. Sliding his glistening finger along my bottom lip, he whispered, "Taste yourself."

Slowly, I licked his finger and he pushed it into my mouth. "Suck it," he commanded. I did as he told me and more fluid wept from between my legs. Once again, his hand slipped down to my seam as he turned my head and kissed the taste of me off my lips, but this time, he slid his knee between my legs and spread mine widely at the top. His finger found my clit and he rubbed soft circles until I thought I would lose my mind. Adjusting, I felt his hard length align with the seam of my butt, and he began to rock his hips against me. The friction made me wetter, and my legs spread wider, almost involuntarily that time.

With his free hand, Flynn scooped my hair into a ponytail and yanked it backward, extending my neck. "Kiss me," he demanded.

His soft lips met mine in a gentle, tentative kiss at first, until his tongue thrust deeply inside my mouth. His finger slipped down and dipped inside me as his mouth tore from my mouth and bit my shoulder. A loud moan escaped my lips and Flynn's mouth was back on me, stifling the sounds he was bringing out.

His fingers pinched and rubbed at my clit and began to work faster. My whole body fizzed with sensation as it began to tingle at my core. My skin erupted in goosebumps, while my legs widened as I began to lose myself in the extreme pleasure of his touch.

When he slipped his free hand to the side of my neck and pulled me tighter, his hand cupped my breast through my tank top. He squeezed it tight and suddenly my brain felt light as flashing lights burst repeatedly behind my eyelids as I came. The force of my release was euphoric. His mouth covered mine again, swallowing my screams as he took me through the aftershocks of my orgasm.

Flynn continued to grind against me and held me tight through the aftershocks, and when I finished, my panties were drenched, as was my backside from the sticky fluid leaking from him. I turned to look at him, and he had his cock in his hand, fisting himself slowly.

I'd seen Daryl's cock before, but it was nothing like Flynn's. Hard and long, the fat mushroom head and veiny appearance of it kind of scared me. It was much bigger than Daryl's. Prettier too, I thought.

I reached out to touch him and his hand fell away, leaving it free for me to hold. I wrapped my fingers around it, and he hissed loudly as it bobbed under my touch. There was strength in his solid cock. Even without ever having sex, I somehow knew he'd be a strong lover. I'd held Daryl before, so I knew what to do to make Flynn feel good.

"Fuck, I never expected this when I woke up this morning." His voice was thick with lust as he grinned widely.

"Me neither," I agreed, and smirked down at him.

"You are so fucking hot, babe. Everything about you... mmm... just like that. Incredible. This feels so good," he murmured softly.

Continuing to groan and moan his way toward his release, he suddenly wrapped his fingers around mine and began to yank his cock up and down, much harder and faster. I felt his balls pull up tight to the bottom of his shaft, and watched as long ribbons of cum shot out of his crown. Flynn cupped his hand in front of it to keep it from landing on my comforter.

He continued to tug himself for another few strokes, then his head fell back into the pillow and his body, that had been stiff and jerky only moments before, went limp. Flynn growled sexily and turned to me, with a look in his eyes I couldn't read.

"Damn you, Valerie Darsin. What are you doing to me?" he asked seriously.

I had no idea what to say to that, so I slipped off the end of the bed and went to get a washcloth, suddenly a little embarrassed at what had just happened. I ran the cloth under the warm tap and then took it, along with a dry towel, back to Flynn. We cleaned up in silence. I was surprised afterward, because he gestured for me to lie down beside him and tucked me into his side.

"Give me five minutes to recover. Then we need to get up," he said. He kissed my head and closed his eyes, sighing deeply. I closed my eyes and listened once again to his steady beating heart.

Chapter Twenty-One

MAKING MY OWN IMPRESSION

*S*liding out of bed, I snuck over to my bottom drawer. I quietly pulled out some clothes and underwear, and tiptoed into the bathroom. I opted to birdbath in the sink with a washcloth because I didn't want to wake Flynn. I then dressed and glanced back out at the bed. Flynn was asleep on his side. I stared at his tattoo and noticed a new addition to the previous one. R.I.P. was written at the top, and I knew it was in memory of my brothers.

My heart leaped at the sight of him still there. Then it squeezed against my chest as I recalled how he'd touched me. My body immediately trembled at the memory, and I almost tripped walking to my bedroom door.

Tearing my eyes away from him, I smiled slowly, bit my lip, and gently opened the door. When I went downstairs, Buster was pacing around the kitchen, ready to go outside. No one else was around, so I took the dog for a walk to clear my head. I had to figure out what my next move was going to be.

I'd been so tempted to wake Flynn, but I had to make sense of what we'd done. I'd also hoped to avoid having to explain to my parents what he'd been doing in my bedroom. *Good luck with that, Valerie.* If I am honest, I'd been confused, and a little embarrassed to face him because he was a rock star, and what we'd done was probably nowhere near what he was used to while sharing a bed with a woman.

When I'd texted him, it was more of a knee-jerk reaction, and after he said he was coming over, I figured he'd give Daryl a show before he took off again. Then my heart sunk because I had the thought he probably still would. Once I'd looked at the practicalities of the situation for Flynn and me, that's pretty much our history.

Concluding that the best plan would be to act as normal as possible around him, I called on the services of two of my best models to help me out. Their images were the most popular, and they were very much in demand.

Although I'd had good sales from separate shots, my highest earning pictures came from them working as a couple. They were a dream to work with. Both agreed to the impromptu shoot, and I arranged it at the studio for 1:30 P.M. It was time to show Flynn I was a shrewd and talented businesswoman; the girl was gone.

By the time I came back from walking Buster, Flynn was downstairs eating breakfast. Lee and my mom were talking about Lee's job and what it entailed, and my dad was reading the paper. Flynn's eyes caught mine, and he held my gaze. He gave me a kind of wounded look, probably because I left him alone that morning after what we did together.

At that point, I wanted to throw my arms around him and kiss him, but there was no way I'd have shown my hand like that with him. If he rejected me again afterward, I knew I would be distraught.

"I'm going to use today to catch some images if you don't mind, Flynn. I've arranged for a couple of models to come down to the studio. Daryl won't be around until tomorrow, unless he gets wind that I know what he's done. Are you staying here, or do you want to come?"

Flynn rose from the table and smiled. "I gotta see this. Are they nudie pictures you're taking?"

My father smirked and shook his paper, trying to pretend he hadn't heard him.

"Well, not initially. I think they'll do lingerie shots until they warm up, but after that, yes. You can expect to see lots of crawling around, straddling and rolling around naked on the floor, against the wall, legs wrapped around the guy's waist, multi-positions on the bed, her on top, him on top..."

My father shook the paper, dropped it to the table, and appeared shocked.

"Sounds X-rated to me. Are you licensed to do that kind of thing in this state?" Dad asked, sounding alarmed.

Flynn chuckled. "She's teasing you. Can you imagine Valerie telling a guy to take his jeans off? She'd die first."

Jutting out my jaw, I placed my hand on his hip and grinned. "Take your jeans off, Flynn."

Flynn lifted his eyebrow suggestively, and my heart raced at his sexy response to my challenge. I gestured at myself by sweeping my hand down the front of me, and cocked an eyebrow at him. "Do I look dead to you?"

My dad stood, scraping his chair back. "You, young lady, have developed a very smart mouth. I suggest you stop trying to speed up that inheritance by trying to give me a heart attack."

Both Flynn and I chuckled as I wandered over and hugged my father. "Sorry, Dad, that was just too tempting. I saw you trying to pretend you weren't listening."

Leaving them laughing, I'd gone to my home studio to pack a few different cameras I had brought home from a location shoot. Once I was ready to leave, I called for Flynn to join me, and headed out to the car.

"Valerie, I have to say, you're smokin' hot when you're ticked, babe. I might need to rile you now and again just to see that."

"I wasn't ticked, just putting everyone in their place. You're not dealing with a little girl now, Flynn, so try not to treat me like one anymore, okay?"

I knew I sounded a little prissy, but I wanted him to see another side to me. No, I wanted him to take me seriously. He grinned and, as I pushed the key into the ignition, I stopped to take in how handsome he was. With his dark brown hair, dark lashes, and vibrant green eyes, and his perfectly plump, dark red lips; he was stunning. His smile lit up a room.

As a photographer, I was used to looking for striking features.

Flynn was someone who pulled your eyes to him and held them there. He said I'd changed in the two and some change years, but Flynn had too. He was drop-dead gorgeous and full of animal magnetism and charm. That may have sounded like an over-the-top description, but in reality, it was an understatement.

Entering my studio, I ran around turning the electric heaters on. The minimal furniture made the studio hard to keep warm. There were two beds; one plain box set, and the second an antique brass bed.

There were also two sofas; one in white leather, the other cream velvet. And a chaise lounge. I'd always used different throws to create varied effects, and I had rolls of material in every shade from red to black, in silk, satin, and sheers. What I didn't have, I enhanced with Photoshop.

Suggesting to Flynn that he might like to sit on one of two large accent chairs I kept over by the back wall, he nodded and walked over while I continued to set up. My models wouldn't be able to see him properly there. It was a semi-dark corner. As he went over and sat down, Evette, the first model, arrived.

I commissioned Evette for lots of work. Her pale alabaster skin and heavenly, light-blue eyes gave her the most striking appearance. Her irises had a thick black rim, and her eyes were framed with naturally dark lashes and eyebrows. She had ash blonde hair, and the whole way she was put together with her petite features and beautifully shaped mouth, made her a great subject. The camera loved her. She had several tattoos on her body. One was script on her left side. It was a poem.

Entering me from the dark
Your touch sears my heart
Igniting embers from a spark
You brand my soul forever.

On her right hip, there was intricate artwork that looked like a thin piece of lace with a padlock, and on her left thigh, the same lacework as on her hip, that looked like a fancy garter. The black ink on her pale skin was most effective. All her tattoos suited her body perfectly. Evette was a vision. I'd found her mesmerizing to look at when she auditioned. I glanced over at Flynn and saw him cross his leg at the knee and lean back, watching us intently, and I wondered what he was thinking.

The door opened again and Elias, my male subject, wandered in looking all windswept and very handsome. He was a mature Swedish student, studying politics. With his tall, blonde, rugged appearance, most would have thought he was into sports or something artsy.

"Hello beautiful, Miss Valerie," he cooed. He swept his arms around me in a hug and squeezed tight. Flynn cleared his throat, and when I looked over, I saw him drop his foot that was resting on his knee, and he sat up straight in the chair.

Initially, I'd thought he was getting ready to be introduced, but the vibe I got was that he wasn't happy. My heart raced for a second when I thought he hadn't liked Elias doing that with me. I dismissed that and thought he was probably just restless, bored already.

"Okay, what is our scene?" Evette enquired, taking her butt-long hair out of its bun, and shaking it sexily down her back. My eyes flicked to Flynn, but he showed little reaction to her. I'd found that strange, considering how amazing she looked.

Once I'd explained to them I'd had been thinking romance books - mature content romance books - and chose their attire, they began to pose for the cameras. Evette wasn't ashamed to flounce around in lingerie, and from how Elias behaved around her, it was clear he'd handled more than a few beautiful women.

After an hour, the couple had really gotten into the shoot and was striking some pretty raunchy poses, and although I'd been reserved around Flynn, this was my job. There was no room for awkwardness. If I expected my models to relax, they had to be confident in my ability.

Flynn had been sitting in the only shadowy area of the studio, and although both models knew someone else was there, they had no idea who was watching them. They'd dealt with that exact scenario before, when a couple of movie producers had been looking for extras for a sex-club scene in a movie being shot locally.

After another hour, I felt my models were tiring, so I called an end to the shoot and thanked them for their efforts. I had around four hundred good digital images to sift through and refine from our work today.

Evette stood and discarded the bra of the lingerie set. She wandered over to her bag, pulled out a black camisole top, fed her arms into the spaghetti straps, and slipped it over her head.

Bending at the waist, she dipped into her bag again and found some leggings. Oozing sex appeal as she fed her long slim legs into those, she slipped her arms into a red, oversized wool cardigan. Once again, she bent at the waist and swept her long hair forward. Bunching it together, she straightened again and twirled it into a top knot.

Elias had stopped changing to watch her, enthralled by her fluid movements. When she was done, he shook his head and smiled to himself in appreciation. Both left at the same time, and Flynn, who had been observing, cleared his throat and stood up.

"Jesus. You do *that* for a living? I'd *never* have figured you doing something like this. I'm in the wrong job. Fuck! My dick almost broke in my pants. That was like live porn, but hotter." Flynn's pupils were blown big with desire, and his voice sounded like he had gravel in his throat. The photo shoot had made him horny.

"It's art, Flynn. Capturing images helps sell ideas and makes things come to life."

"You're not fucking joking. What was going on in that bed was porn without dicks and pussies. Prick teasing at its very best. It certainly brought my dick to life," he said with a chuckle, and stared at the bed, shaking his head.

I pretended to ignore his crude outburst and started packing up, grinning when I turned my back to him. Flynn wandered over to the bed and began fingering some of the props, and I heard him chuckle.

Without warning, he unbuttoned his jeans, pulled them to his ankles, and stepped out. He wasn't wearing boxers. I was a little shocked and excited at what he'd done, but continued to store my equipment. Reaching over, he grabbed a handful of material from his t-shirt and pulled it over his head. The way he did that turned me on, and my panties were ruined again.

Standing naked, he climbed onto the brass bed after he picked up a pair of handcuffs. He had his back to me, and my heart fluttered when my eyes roamed over his strong muscular back and the view of his perfect, delectable butt.

He lifted the cuffs with one finger and swung them around, before clamping one around his left wrist, and the other to the headboard railing. Flynn lay totally exposed and propped himself up on a pillow. Watching him like that almost made me drool. He was such an incredibly sexy, good-looking man. Bunching the white satin sheet, he dragged it over his cock and posed seductively, giving me a naughty smirk. "Come on, a Flynn Docherty exclusive shoot."

"I'm not taking pictures of you like that," I said, and giggled.

"Why not? Better still, put the timer thingy on and climb in beside me."

"In your dreams."

"There you go! Pretend we're dreaming like last night, better still, like this morning." he goaded, and my heart crashed against my breastbone at the instant memory.

"You don't have it in you, do you, babe? See? This is why you and I would never work. This kind of spontaneity embarrasses you."

"It does? Nothing much embarrasses me these days." *Apart from when I'm around you.*

"No? Then why are you not taking me up on my challenge? I dare you, babe."

I hesitated for a second before I went over to my tripods and began setting them up with cameras to prove a point. Butterflies flew wildly in my belly. I set five cameras at different angles around the bed and attached cameras, all with different lenses from fisheye, prime, wide-angle, telephoto, and a macro lens, which is designed to pick up the minute detail. Then I turned to face him.

Flynn lay cuffed to the bed, watching me intensely, and I had the feeling he was waiting for me to bolt. The smirk he wore was his insurance to stop me from doing that, no matter how hard I'd found climbing on that bed. Focusing on my equipment centered me, as I told myself repeatedly it was *just another shoot*, trying to convince myself I could show him I wasn't afraid of his dare.

My gaze caught Flynn's chest as I lined up the shot through the one camera. My heart leaped at the sight of him again. I stayed there a few seconds longer than was necessary, and shook slightly when I wondered what would happen once the shutters started to click.

All the cameras were primed to take shots on repeat, three-second delayed settings, and when I'd finished, I had nothing else to stall with. Turning toward him, I snapped the button on my jeans.

Flynn's eyes fell to my hands, while I kept my eyes focused on his. I slid the pants down my legs and stepped out of them. He shifted slightly on the bed and continued to watch me in silence. The atmosphere between us was tense. I folded my arms across my body and grabbed the hem of my t-shirt. I swept it over my head, grabbing the chance to swallow hard as I tried to keep my composure.

My eyes flicked to Flynn, and he shifted on the bed again and ran his tongue over his lips, as his free hand rested over his cock on top of the sheet. Turning away, I chucked my clothes out of the shot. Wandering slowly around the bed, I started each camera as I went.

Click...click...click...click...click. All five shutters started to capture the action. I reached the bottom of the bed on the right-hand side. Flynn's left hand was cuffed, his arm hung loosely above his head.

Kneeling on the bed, I stretched my arms above my head, and Flynn groaned loudly. Reaching for my hair tie, I let my hair down and shook it out slowly. It trailed over my back as I arched my neck. I was trying to think about what I was doing, from a technical aspect, and what kind of shots I'd taken during previous sessions. But it was Flynn and me, and that was a struggle. I leaned over and picked up a soft, black leather flogger and my excitement grew. Elias had contributed that prop to my repertoire. I'd been shocked when he'd enlightened me about the world of BDSM.

Flynn grinned, but I saw his Adam's apple bob in his throat. His mouth had gone dry. His eyes had taken the glassy look of lust, and I played up on his cues. They almost popped out of his head when I straddled his legs, wearing my black lacy boy shorts and black see-through bra.

After a second or two of observing me, the fingers of his free hand grabbed my butt. He sunk them into my plump, firm flesh, released, and smoothed his palm over it. Then, he slipped his fingers inside the lace and gripped me much firmer than before.

I traced the flogger down his chest, and the satin sheet covering him tented. The sight of his arousal caused a good kind of ache in me.

His breaths became shallower and faster as I continued to tease him with the thin strips of leather. I crawled up to him and sat directly on his leg. His arm flopped out to the side, allowing me complete control.

Continuing his sweet torture, I dragged my fingertips down his body, but the feel of his warm, hard flesh had started to turn me on. Without warning, his hand grabbed a fistful of hair as he pulled me down on top of him. Electricity coursed through my body in reaction. His mouth took mine in a punishing kiss, his tongue probing roughly and deep inside. I groaned loudly as flames of passion ignited. I was desperate for more.

He pulled my head back by the hair and smiled when I looked into his eyes. He continued to control me with one hand, somehow managing to edge himself off the bed, and swung my body to face him sideways in front of him. Eye to eye, we stared in a connection that took my breath away. Even I could interpret the look of pure want. Flynn placed his mouth on my warm belly and peppered light kisses down toward my mound as he remained partly restrained, still cuffed to the bed.

Watching his eyes hold my gaze as his mouth wreaked havoc with my senses, was incredible. Desire ripped through my body under his watchful stare, and I found myself arching up off the bed, making his fragile contact more solid. Continuing lower, he knelt on the floor and began to trace his hot, wet tongue leisurely up my thighs as the elbow of his free hand spread my knees. He then gripped my hand tightly, pushing me into the bed. "I want to taste you, Valerie. Stop the cameras," he murmured softly.

Shaking my head, I smiled. The entire time my cameras were snapping photos, they were giving me my chance to explore Flynn without this going too far, unless it was what I wanted. I was in control. Flynn knew about all aspects of security in his rock-star world, and I felt he'd never have taken a chance at being caught having sex on camera. I thought he'd have stopped before it had gotten this far, but I'd been wrong about that.

Flynn lay over me. Grinding his length right between my legs, gyrating his hips while his tongue assaulted my mouth. He groaned, and the vibration made my emotions run riot. As I became more uninhibited, I wrapped my legs tightly around his waist. I'd begun to synchronize my movements with his, completely caught up in the passion of our heated connection.

"Fucking incredible," he muttered, and then grunted as he thrust his cock against me again. He dragged his mouth away from me, and his lust-filled eyes almost stopped my heart.

"Stop the cameras and give me the key to this fucking thing," he said, rattling the cuff against the metal bar. I began to move, and he thought I was granting his plea, but once I'd worked free, I knelt on the bed and was the same height as him.

Reaching out, I took his cock in my hand. It felt thick, satiny smooth and warm, but solid. Flynn's cock pulsed in my hand. I dipped my face toward him and buried it in his neck. His skin reacted in a rash of goosebumps, while I peppered it with small kisses. I wanted to mark him, and bit gently on his shoulder when my desire flared. I felt pre-cum leak onto my fingers, and pulled back grinning naughtily when I saw the shock on his face.

"Now, what's got you all worked up? This will teach you to challenge me, hot-shot rock star. You want more? You better be serious about that, because no one plays with my feelings anymore, understand? I'm turning the cameras off, and I'll give you the keys. The next move is crucial, Flynn. The only guarantee is there will be no second chances this time. You play with my feelings, I'll take your heart and feed it to Buster. Are we clear? How's that for spontaneity, Mr. Docherty?"

Inside, my stomach was curled in a ball. Flynn had captured my heart years ago, but I knew that if I was going to keep him, I'd have to have more than one trick up my sleeve. As I waited for his reaction, I held my breath.

Chapter Twenty-Two

UNCUFFED

Seconds passed while Flynn stared at me, stunned as he digested what I'd said to him. I was still kneeling on the bed, and he was still standing in front of me, naked as the day he was born, but way more appealing than any baby I'd ever seen. My heart pounded in my chest, and I knew I probably looked a lot more confident than I felt inside.

When he still hadn't responded, I exhaled slowly and shifted to sit on my butt with my legs to the side. I eased myself away from him and, once I had some distance, I rolled off the mattress and stood up on the other side of the bed. The cameras had stopped. I'd known their batteries wouldn't last much more than twenty minutes. I'd used most of the cameras during my shoot with Evette and Elias.

I wandered over and grabbed my jeans, trying to look casual. I pulled them on and slipped into my t-shirt. Flynn stilled, silently watching me, and I thought he was having second thoughts about what we'd done.

"Don't worry, Flynn. You're off the hook. These shots are safe. I'll delete them, and that was fun ... but I wouldn't dream of fucking a guy like you. Messing around like this is one thing, but I don't do groupie hook-ups."

"Take off the cuff."

"I will in a minute. Let me finish this first." I had started putting the cameras back in their cases.

"Valerie, come here and take the fucking cuff off."

When he swore, I felt his anger. It radiated off him. His tone added tension to the already-tense atmosphere between us.

I glanced at him and smirked. "And that's definitely the way to make me respond to your demand. Those PR guys need to send you on a 'Powers of Persuasion' course, or 'Diplomacy for Dummies'— that may work."

"Take the fucking cuff off now, Valerie."

"Anyone ever tell you, you're hot when you're ticked?" I said, throwing his words back at him. I placed the last camera in the case while I gawked at his naked body. I'd never been able to look at a naked man in the flesh before, without it being work. It may sound strange, but I'd never seen Daryl fully naked. I'd seen all of him just ... not altogether. And my brothers didn't count.

Walking over to the props table, I lifted the key to the cuffs and wandered around to Flynn's side of the bed.

"Dumb move, cuffing yourself out of reach of the keys, huh?" I giggled as I chided him.

Flynn smirked wryly and shook his head. "Oh, dear God, Valerie. What the fuck are you doing to me?"

"I'm un-cuffing you. Isn't that what you wanted?" I said in my best seductive tone. Placing the key in the cuff, I unlocked it. Flynn took his wrist and rubbed the red mark on it. I continued taking the cuff off the metal bar of the headboard and dropped them onto the bed.

In the blink of an eye, Flynn grabbed the cuffs and snapped one on my left wrist. He caught me by the waist from behind and carried me up toward the top of the bed and cuffed the other end to the head-board again. I yelped loudly as he lifted me up and dropped my body a little roughly onto the mattress.

"You want to play, huh? Think you're smart leaving me with my dick hanging out while you get off on watching me?"

"I was only teasing."

Flynn smirked. "Is that what this whole thing was about, today? Bring Flynn here to watch two hot people simulate fucking on a bed? Giving me a boner that ached so fucking much that the thought passed through my mind to take my dick out and toss one off, fuck the consequences?"

Hard and primed, Flynn was frustrated, testosterone oozing from his pores. Lust clouded his eyes, and the way they raked over my fully-clothed body made me wish I hadn't dressed.

"I don't know what your intention was when you brought me here, but we're here. Alone. You're lying there staring up at me with those innocent eyes and a body made for sin. You look as hot as hell lying there, but you'd look ten times hotter without these."

Flynn's hands skimmed the waistband of my jeans, his fingers curling under the material. The rough pads of his callused fingertips brushed the warm skin on my belly, and I shuddered. Goosebumps changed my smooth skin and Flynn's eyes focused on them on my belly. A smile curved his lips.

Popping the button open, he wasted no time in stripping the jeans from my body. He threw them recklessly to the floor as his hungry eyes concentrated on the hem of my t-shirt before they quickly flicked up to mine. I swallowed quietly as he began to push the soft cotton material up my body. He then hooked his fingers under my bra as he pushed it up as well.

Flynn stepped back to look at me. I was a disheveled hot mess and half undressed. My hair was strewn loosely across the sheet and Flynn looked like he was embroiled in an internal struggle as he stood over me.

Hearing his breath when it caught in his throat was the sexiest thing I'd ever encountered. It made my body hum in anticipation of his touch. "I need to take these off," he husked, his voice laced with frustration and lust as he tugged at my garments.

My heart began to pound as his hand slipped under my head. He pulled and tugged the t-shirt until it was hanging down my arm that was cuffed to the bed. Heat radiated from between my legs, and I was so excited I thought I might faint. Reaching forward, his face was inches from mine as he unclipped the hooks on my bra, then shoved it down the same arm to join my t-shirt.

Standing back to study his handiwork, his eyes became darker with every second he perused my body. He shook his head again. "You know you have a perfect body, right? Your tits are more than a handful, your curves have the perfect amount of flesh for gripping, and your ass is so deliciously plump and firm I just want to sink my teeth into it. I want to mark you so badly. The way your waist dips at both sides here..." His fingers skimmed down my sides from my ribs to my hips, and my body vibrated in response. Flynn shook his head.

"You're so responsive to my touch, and when I look at you it does crazy things to me."

I lay there speechless, but my heart was flipping continuously with each compliment, and I kept thinking, *This is it. Flynn is finally going to rock my world after all this time. Is this what I want? Would I be happy for this one time? No.*

"It's only a body, Flynn. Anyone can fuck someone and enjoy their body. Everyone is capable of turning someone on. It's fucking with your mind that's more difficult. That's what I want. Someone who wants all of me, not just my body."

"You've changed, babe. You're all I imagined you'd be one day when I met that fifteen-year-old girl, but I have to admit that, although I'd seen most of this in you then, you're even better than I'd imagined."

"How so?"

"You don't need me."

"That's true," I lied, feeling that I'd never needed him more since we'd crossed the line that morning, because the line had been drawn in the sand and we'd jumped right over it.

"I mean, look at you, babe," he said, his eyes feasting on my body all over again. "You're fucking perfect. Smart, sexy, sassy, independent. I see you, and I want to fuck you into next week ... not just for your body, but for all those reasons."

A lump formed in my throat because this was Flynn Docherty saying this to me. My Flynn, and I was struggling to breathe with his declaration.

Without another word, he took my other hand and placed it

together with the one already above my head. The backs of his finger-tips skimmed down both of my arms, and he cupped my breasts in his hands. His thick cock stood solid and proud. It twitched as his eyes connected with his thoughts, and his arousal increased. Flynn spread his legs to stand wider. Bending forward, his cock brushed against my knee when he did. It left a small trail of pre-cum in its wake.

His mouth engulfed my right breast. "Mmm," he murmured plea-surably. His appreciative sound and vibration he made registered at my core. I moaned, and my breast fell from his mouth with a small pop as his mouth trailed up to my neck. Soft sucks and licks brushed up my neck to my chin as he showered me with small kisses.

Lifting his head, his tongue trailed along the seam of my mouth before he thrust it inside to meet my own tongue. Flynn kissed me with a depth of passion I had no idea existed. Moans rolled from his mouth and mine as we began to lose ourselves to the moment.

Making his way down my body again, his warm hands skated over my skin, and every nerve ending sprang to life. When I checked his reaction, he looked at my face every now and again for my response to his touch. Then he continued to work down to my panty line.

My body became so attuned and responsive as his hands explored me. Inside, my brain was in meltdown from his expert touch, and I wondered if I was about to lose my virginity, and if I did, would it have any effect on how he treated me afterwards?

Slipping his thumbs into my lacy boy shorts at both hips, he eased them gently over my hips and pulled them down as I fought to keep eye contact with him. Smiling warmly in reassurance, I tried to mimic his smile back, but inside I was scared I was out of my depth.

My mound was shaved smooth. Even though I know Flynn already knew this because he'd touched me there the previous night, and that morning. All the models I worked with always talked about why they did it. Once I'd tried it, I'd never looked back.

Flynn stood at the side of the bed, glanced down, and his eyes darkened when they settled on my center. His tongue slipped out as he wet his lips and dropped to his knees before me. My body vibrated, trembling in anticipation of what he was going to do. I'd never had oral sex before. Of course, I'd known about it, even witnessed him and

Daisy, but with Daryl's fake religious abstinence, the most he had done was jerk off or rubbed my clit. What Flynn was doing was leading me into my personal unchartered territory. I was apprehensive, but excited.

He pressed his closed lips against my mound and I bucked off the bed. I was so sensitive—no one had ever kissed me there before. He buried his nose and inhaled my essence. My initial reaction was to clamp my thighs closed on his head.

He chuckled and glanced up at me. "Did I tickle you?"

I nodded my head and stared down at him. Emotions ran riot inside me, and I thought my heart was going to burst out of my chest with excitement. At the same time, my throat attempted to close, because I worried Flynn was about to discover I was still a virgin at any second, and reject me when I really wanted to be with him.

Grabbing my thighs, Flynn pushed them apart like the wings of a butterfly and stroked his forefinger the length of my wet sheath. He lifted me off the bed to his lips and lapped at my swollen, sensitive flesh with his tongue. My breath hitched when I saw him do that. He glanced up at me and smiled slowly. "You know how long I've wanted this? How long I've imagined you like this? It definitely pays to be a patient man."

Dipping his head, he ran his tongue the length of my seam, and I thought my head was going to explode at the sensation. Desire coursed through my veins and, after several gentle strokes the full length of me, and up the crease of my butt with his tongue, I almost lost my mind. My body arched off the bed because the sensation was so hard to manage. "Oh. My. God," I exclaimed.

"You're so sensitive ... so fucking responsive," he stated, and grinned wickedly at me before gripping me tighter. He smiled seductively again and then began his onslaught of rapture on my body. Lapping at my little bundle of nerves, he sucked it both hard and softly until I tried to wriggle away.

Flynn pinned me down, his strong arms clamping tighter around my thighs to keep me right where he wanted me. Within a few minutes of his punishing pleasure, my mind went into meltdown on his tongue. My legs and my belly shook as I fell over the edge and into paradise, screaming so loudly that Flynn brought his head to my mouth and kissed me, to absorb the sound and quiet my body.

Afterward, he stood, stroking his cock totally unashamed, and I was a bit afraid of what was next.

"Got any condoms here?"

"No. This isn't *that* kind of a studio, Flynn."

"I wasn't implying it was. I just wondered if you had any lying around."

"I never brought Daryl here."

Daryl drew a line, and he never wanted to be present when I captured photos for my business, so he never came to one of my shoots. I didn't want Flynn to know about my inexperience, so I sat up and wrapped my fingers around his cock. It was warm and solid in my grasp. I dragged my thumb across the mushroom head, and Flynn hissed.

"Fuuuckkk." A long groan of satisfaction left his mouth as his eyes closed.

I'd never performed oral sex, but from what I'd heard, I just had to take him in my mouth, bob up and down, and suck. I surprised myself because it really turned me on, and I wanted to do it. I wanted to show him I wasn't afraid of him, or sex, if the circumstances were right. With Flynn, everything felt right.

My nerves were creating another colony of butterflies in my chest and stomach, and my heart raced at the thought of what I was about to do, but this was maybe my one chance with Flynn, and wasn't letting it pass without my best efforts.

I glanced up at Flynn, and the look of expectancy on his face said it all. I think he may possibly have killed me if I'd lost courage, so I swallowed past the lump of nerves caught in my throat and took his cock in my mouth. The warm silky skin pushed back and forth as I sucked and pulled it. My tongue swirled around the head and down his shaft as I explored the sensation of it.

I liked it. Despite some initial doubts about pleasuring a man in this way, it was a total turn on to see Flynn become dependent on me for his pleasure. He groaned and hissed, and every sound he emitted was a reward for the effort I'd put in.

None of what I was doing was easy with one hand cuffed to the bed. Flynn's hips started to thrust forward, and I was no longer in charge. Chasing his orgasm, he rocked in and out, fucking my mouth faster and faster. I gagged, and he pulled out for a second to check I was okay, and then resumed taking his pleasure from my mouth.

When I released my grip on his shaft, Flynn immediately took over stroking himself, but still rocked into my mouth. I cupped his balls, and they were hard, and when I did that, I felt them draw up tightly against the base of his cock.

"I'm about to come," he said, pulling out.

As soon as he cleared my mouth, three long ribbons of cum shot out of his cock and landed on my neck and breasts. He continued to stroke himself through the aftershocks, his body jerking repeatedly, before he leaned forward and collapsed beside me.

He lay silently with his eyes closed for a minute before turning to face me. I was wiping my front on the sheet, and he rose and un-cuffed me. I turned on my side to face him. One elbow propped my head up, and I stared at his beautiful, peaceful face. He stared back at me, his eyes clear and vibrant after his release. He closed his eyes slowly as his chest rose and fell, while his body quieted again.

"I've come twice in less than ten hours, and I've still not fucked you, babe. Are you trying to torture me? You need to leave a stash of condoms in a place like this. If that's how you make me feel messing around, I'm gonna blow my load as soon as I get inside you," he muttered softly.

Sitting up, I climbed off the bed and cleaned up the best I could with the guest towels from the restroom. I began to dress without speaking. Flynn followed suit and then I pulled the wet, tangled sheet off the bed and stuffed it in my oversized bag.

On the drive back to the house, Flynn sat quietly, but he had the biggest smirk on his face. It began to irritate me and I became self-conscious about my inexperience. I began to think he'd somehow worked out that I was a virgin.

"Alright, what's so amusing?"

"A flogger and handcuffs? Fuck, Valerie. That's so hot. I never figured you'd even know about sex toys. I just never imagined you as kinky. Then again, they always say it's the quiet ones you have to look out for. You're just full of surprises," he said, and chuckled heartily.

"There's a lot you don't know about me," I responded, and wondered how quickly he'd back off once he found out the truth about me.

Chapter Twenty-Three

COMPLICATED

*B*uster barked loudly as he ran after my car when I pulled up our driveway. Flynn's phone rang, and he glanced at the incoming caller's ID before his eyes flicked to mine. I watched him as he quickly declined the call, but not before I saw Iria's name light up on the screen.

Suddenly my stomach felt like I'd swallowed some lead. I'd been so selfish. I hadn't heard her name mentioned in a while in the media. It hadn't even occurred to me that Flynn may still be with her.

"Did you just cheat on Iria with me?"

Flynn chewed his lip, drew in a deep breath, and exhaled heavily. "No. We're not together."

"So why is she calling you?"

Who am I to him anyway? I've no right to question him. I'd called him. I'd been the one to turn into him in bed. What Flynn did was really none of my business. "Sorry, I shouldn't have behaved like that. It's none of my business who you are with."

Flynn put his hand on my arm, turned and looked directly at me. His face softened. "I'm not with her, okay?" His voice sounded like he was trying to convince me.

Suddenly, I was embarrassed with how I'd reacted and wondered why it hadn't even occurred to me that he'd be in a relationship? The guy was smoking-hot property. I turned off the engine and grabbed my bag from the back seat.

"Seriously, it's fine, Flynn. Who you see has nothing to do with me. You're your own man."

"What the fuck does that mean?"

I pulled on the handle and got out the car without answering him. Taking my camera cases from the trunk, I locked it and headed toward the kitchen. When he didn't follow me, I looked back saw he was still seated in the car, holding his cell to his ear.

Tears clouded my vision as I rushed upstairs and grabbed some of the extra camera batteries I'd had on charge. Slipping out the glass slider in the dining room with my equipment, I headed to the make-shift studio Dad and Kayden had made me.

I was thankful I still did my editing, developing, and printing work at home. It gave me the ideal excuse to make some space from him, especially when I knew my temper had flared. Whatever happened in my personal life had to be put aside. I still had work to do. So, I did my best to concentrate with a heavy heart. I'd been a fool to fall for Flynn again.

Almost three hours later, there was a soft tapping noise on the wooden door. I had taken all the stills and backed them up to my cloud drive and had begun working through the first SD card of pictures. It had to be Flynn; the rest of my family just walked in. My heart reacted before I even opened the door. He stood with his hands in his pockets and an apologetic expression on his face.

"Is it a good time to talk? I can explain."

"You don't have to. It's my fault. I should never have started ... *that* between us."

He looked at his feet and turned them outward, showing the soles of his bare feet. He snickered. "Alright, you shouldn't have, but I guess it was half and half."

"You should have told me Iria was around when I texted."

"Iria and me ... we're not ... it's complicated."

Turning away from him, I wandered around my desk and tried outwardly to appear unaffected, "Like I said, Flynn, nothing to do with me. Apart from the fact that you fooled around with me. That makes me feel kinda dirty now."

"You were kinda dirty. Fucking hot and dirty," he said with a smirk, looking at me from under his lashes. I noticed his cheeks became a little flushed, like he was thinking about what we'd done.

"Go home, Flynn. I should never have asked you to come here. It was immature of me. I'll deal with Daryl on my own."

"Like hell, I'll go home. You don't get to run hot and cold with me like that, Valerie. You called me here for one thing, and it led to another. You messed around with me, got me all riled up, and now that you've had your fun it's 'Thanks, Flynn, but no thanks?' I told you Iria and I... It's complicated. I'm not with her."

"Does she know that?"

Biting his lip, he stood facing me, but hadn't answered. I stared back in defiance, and when there was no movement on either side, I spoke again, "Look, Flynn, I don't really have time for this. I work for myself. Time is money. I have to get these finished, and the longer we stand here, the later I'll get to bed tonight. I'm sorry I made that call to you. You were right. I'm not ready for you. I'll never be ready for you. Not in this lifetime, anyway." I was shocked at how bitchy I sounded when I was jealous.

Flynn stepped outside and began to walk away. As I was closing the door, he started walking back toward me and began to talk, but I continued to shut the door, leaving him talking to himself. All the special feelings we'd had together felt tainted, and I tried to dismiss any silly notions I'd had about being with him.

Struggling through my tears, I continued to try to perfect my shots. I gave up after a few minutes and turned my camera and desktop off. Laying my head on my desk, I fought back my tears and swallowed roughly past the lump in my throat. Packing up, I figured it was no use staying there, and I'd thought, given his track record, Flynn would probably have left by then. Once I ensured everything was in order, I turned out the lights, locked the door, and headed back to the house.

As I neared the kitchen door, I saw Flynn's outline standing under the light, and as I got closer, I heard him speaking on his cell phone.

"Give him a hug from me. Yep, I'll be back the day after tomorrow, hon. No problem. See you around four."

Pretending not to notice him, I had almost made it to the door when he quickly placed himself between me and the doorframe.

"You ready to listen to reason now, Valerie?"

"I'm tired. I'm going to bed."

"Fine. We'll talk there."

"No way. You're not sleeping in my room."

"Where the fuck am I supposed to sleep? I guess I'll have to bunk down in Martin's..."

"Don't you fucking dare taunt me with that again," I said, as he slanted his head at me and raised a brow at my outburst.

"Fine. Whatever," I said, throwing my hands up in surrender. I wondered why my parents hadn't picked up on where Flynn had slept the night before, but neither of them had mentioned it. I had no intention of sleeping beside him again.

After we'd gone upstairs, Flynn hadn't allowed any awkwardness to develop. He headed straight to the bathroom, closing the door. The shower started, and the dull whir of the fan in there seemed deafening as I tried to think of how to play my next move. I decided I'd keep my mind on Daryl, and on giving him a taste of his own medicine. I hoped after that was accomplished, Flynn would leave.

Inside, my stomach was in turmoil, my heart felt torn, and a crushed feeling was back in my chest. I had no idea how I was going to get through the night without crying. He'd warned me he wasn't good for me, and I had begun to think he was right about that too.

I was really upset with Flynn and had intended to sleep on the floor. I went to grab an extra comforter and pillow, as my head and my heart fought about how I felt him. He'd been in my heart since the day I'd met him, and the last time I'd seen him, he'd taken a toll on it. This time, the scar he'd made there had burst open. When the time came for him to leave again, nothing short of amputation was going to get him out of my system this time. Martin was right—I had poor judgment when it came to men.

Spreading the comforter on the floor, I was in the process of pulling out some pajamas when I heard the shower turn off. My mind went back to Iria again. Although I'd done my best not to follow his press, everything I had ever read said Flynn had been unfaithful to her. I'd known that, and it never once popped into my head that they may have still been together. *Am I completely stupid?* I'd seen Flynn mentioned a few times in the news at various events, but I hadn't seen him linked to Iria for a while.

Cracking open the door, Flynn came back into view, wearing only a towel. My mind went back to the first time I saw him like that, and my face flushed. Glancing at his firm body, I noted the towel hung low on his waist, and the fresh smell of his clean body filled my nostrils when he passed by me to leave his clothes on the chair. I scooted to my feet and quickly made for the bathroom. I stayed there for twenty-five minutes, showering, in the hope that he would have fallen asleep by the time I stepped back into my room. No such luck.

He was lying down on the makeshift bed on his side, perched up on his elbow staring directly at me.

"You smell good enough to eat," he said, smirking, as his eyes followed me all the way to my bed. I never replied, and slid between the sheets with my heart thumping hard in my chest. I'd barely turned the lamp off when my throat constricted as I swallowed down the emotional tidal wave that tried to rise from my chest.

"So, are you not talking to me?"

When I didn't reply, he spoke again, "I'm just going to get the silent treatment? No adult conversation about this?"

"There's nothing to discuss, Flynn. I guess I got a little carried away with you today. It must have been a rebound thing from Daryl," I suggested, knowing full well that wasn't the case.

"Well, if that's the case, I'd be happy to be your rebound, go-to fuck buddy anytime."

The harshness in his tone tore another strip off my heart. I knew he was angry. *Wasn't that what I'd wanted to achieve by that remark?* Tears sprang to my eyes and I blinked rapidly, trying to stop them from rolling down my face. Flynn didn't deserve my tears. Not when he'd played with my heart with such disregard.

"Fuck you, Flynn," I spat.

"I wish you would, babe. It might relieve some of the tension that has you wound up so tight."

"I won't be fucking you, and you won't be fucking me," I declared. My tone sounded high-pitched and cutting.

"Nope. I won't. Not unless you beg, remember?" he chuckled, goading me further.

I rolled away from him and felt so frustrated that I feared I'd burst a blood vessel. I decided not to dignify him with an answer. After about ten minutes, Flynn blew out a long deep breath. "I'm sorry, babe. I've created this situation all by myself."

"Created what? Being a man-whore?" My response was so rapid I'd forgotten I'd decided to ignore him.

"I'm not a man-whore. That may have been true to some extent when I first met Martin, but not anymore. Sure, I slept with more than a few girls in college, but I've had six women in three years. Six and a half, if we count what we've been doing. That may be a lot by your standards, but not many compared to the constant opportunities I have."

"Still, five and a half too many. Poor Iria."

"What? I'm almost twenty-four, Valerie. I'm male, and I like sex. And yeah, poor Iria is right," he said in a sad tone.

"That's rich coming from you. You're the one causing her heartache, Flynn."

"And that judgmental issue you have needs addressing," he spat back.

I heard him moving around in the dark, and then felt the bed dip as he sat on the edge of it. "The call from her threw me today," he said.

"Yeah, right under a truck. At what point were you going to discuss her still being in the picture, Flynn?"

"I wasn't going to discuss her. Do you want to hear what I have to say or not?"

"Go on, give it your best shot, but I don't see what difference it'll make. Like I said, it's none of my business."

"Like hell, it isn't. We've got this chemistry going on that makes me want to fuck you or kill you. A fiery burn that seems to be ingrained in me since the day I set eyes on you. I wanted to hold you, and when that wasn't enough, I had to taste you, and that still wasn't enough. But you know what? I wished to God you'd had condoms in that studio today because we'd probably still be in there right now, and Iria's call wouldn't have mattered."

"Well, I suppose I have to be thankful for small miracles."

"Nothing small about me, babe. You had me right there in your hand," he said with a smirk.

When I didn't respond, he reached out and touched my feet through the covers. I pulled my legs away. "Don't touch me."

"I didn't hear you complaining when I touched you earlier."

I lay in the dark, shaking my head, infuriated at him for trying to make light of this situation with his cocksure attitude.

"Alright. I don't have to tell you this, but you mean a lot to me, Valerie. I care about you, so here's the truth about Iria and me. I bagged her a few times before we started hanging out in a more connected way. She came on to me again at a party the weekend after we went back to college after Thanksgiving. Martin and I argued non-stop about how I'd behaved around you. He knew I was becoming a little... obsessed with you. I kept asking him questions I thought were safe ones, but he was already suspicious that I'd set my sights on you."

He snickered and stood quiet, staring at me. *He was becoming obsessed with me?* My heart sped up as he continued talking.

"Your brother became fierce about keeping me from you... and he was right. My behavior before I met you was shameful. I had no respect for women, and the women I slept with never had respect for me. All they wanted was a quick fuck, or to marry me. Nothing in between. All I wanted was to fuck them."

Clearing his throat, he continued, "Iria seemed like a cool chick at first, but then she was full-on from the moment she took me home to her place. At first, I was happy to have someone who loved me ... who wanted to help me. Then she wanted to own me, and that wasn't okay. Before I knew what had happened, I'd become entrenched because Bernie, my manager, was a close friend of her father's. It's driving me crazy how they all want a piece of me. I was grateful for the opportunity to be in a band, and for the confidence training, but the other stuff..."

Shifting on the bed, I waited for Flynn to continue. His constant change in position told me he wasn't comfortable about what he'd wanted to share.

"Iria began to get jealous and accused me of sleeping with every woman I came in contact with. I'd smile at someone in the grocery store, and no matter what age these women were, according to her, I was flirting.

Iria's the kind of girl who could start a fight in an empty house. I tried to understand her perspective, and I knew that I'd probably have felt insecure if it had been the other way around, but there was no reasoning with her. After a few months and just as the band was becoming known, I tried to break up with her. I just couldn't take it anymore. The girl she was when I met her was nowhere in sight. When I told her we were done, she took it badly, even though she knew the relationship wasn't repairable."

"What about the girls at the swimming pool?" I blurted out, and could have kicked myself for letting on I'd been reading about him.

Flynn chuckled in the dark. "Yeah that was all me. I was high. Someone coaxed me to try some shit they had... Never again. That was a one-time deal. I was bombed, and those girls..."

"Those girls what?" I probed.

"I fucked one, and the other gave me oral. Happy now?"

I wasn't. "It has nothing to do with me."

"Like hell it doesn't. All I've wanted, all this time, was to see you again. I can still remember how tight and heavy my heart was when I left that morning after the funeral. We had unfinished business. It's still unfinished as far as I'm concerned."

"It's finished now," I said.

"Valerie, it's never going to be finished between us."

My heart flipped over in my chest, but I couldn't see any way forward. I knew I wanted to be with him, but apart from Iria, I had my business, and Flynn was living a nomadic lifestyle. I wasn't sure where I'd fit in.

Chapter Twenty-Four

GETTING EVEN

*L*ying in the dark with a famous rock star sitting at my feet wasn't something that happened every day. Flynn had just told me he had serious feelings for me, and I'd been trying to figure out what to do with that information. He'd opened up and tried to explain why Iria was still in the picture. My body ignored that, and desire instantly overcame me. I wanted him to hold me.

"Like I said, Iria's a really needy person. I thought she was cool when I met her, but she's focused on marrying a famous rock star. I don't think it's me she wants. I think she sees me as an easy target. My problem is, she isn't well. She knows exactly how I feel, and has for two months since I set things straight with her, but there is stuff that stops me from walking away from her right now."

"Sounds to me like you want to have some fun with me and keep a girl waiting in the wings."

"Valerie, I know how it sounds, but trust me, I can't just walk away from her yet."

"And that sounds like a line out of a million movies about a guy cheating on his woman."

The mattress dipped in as he stood and paced around the room again. "Fuck! That's not it. This is probably why I didn't want to talk about her in the car. There's no easy way forward with this shit. Martin was right. Run, Valerie. I'm only going to hurt you."

What was I supposed to say to that? "I should never have asked you to come."

"I'm so fucking glad you did. I wouldn't have changed the past twenty-four hours for anything. Being with you has been beyond my expectations. I might be living a certain lifestyle where sex, booze, and rock 'n roll are supposed to be an everyday occurrence, but what happened in that studio ... and with you here? That was far better than anything my sick head could have conjured up. It was teasing, so fucking sexy, and I get a boner just thinking about it. And I have fun with you, more than I've had in the past couple of years."

My core tightened when he said that with so much passion, despite my anger and hurt. "What are you doing here? What are *we* doing? Why did you *really* come when I called? One minute you're all over me, and the next you're telling me to run. You're the one in *my* bedroom. You're the one giving me mixed messages."

Flynn crawled up beside me and lay down, snuggling up behind me, before draping his arm over my hip. My body stiffened again, but my heart responded one beat later by doubling its pace. My mind told me to shove him away, but my heart thrummed with excitement, so my doubts ebbed away and were replaced by contentment when he held me. I wanted him to make everything okay, and my body ached for the closeness we'd shared earlier in the day.

"We're doing what we wanted to do years ago. We met too soon, Valerie, that's all."

"So, we both felt what? Instant lust for each other? Is that what this is?"

I swallowed noisily, and another wave of emotion gripped my throat. *If it hadn't been for Martin, we wouldn't have met at all.* Sometimes I wondered what Martin's and Adam's lives had been for. Martin brought Flynn to me, and Adam had brought him closer when he played that football game. It made me wonder if the purpose of my brothers' lives was to shape *my* destiny. I hated that thought, because if they had been born, and died, for my sake, that would have been harder to live with. I decided it was an irrational thought brought on by my emotional state.

"I don't think it's just lust, Valerie. And I don't want to be with Iria. I want to be with you, babe. You need to know that by now. I thought I'd get past you, but I can't. I've never been able to get you out of my head, and we hadn't done anything more intimate than that kiss."

Hearing him say what I wanted to hear left me speechless. Butterflies took flight and attempted to soar out of me. I'd known what *I* felt, and I knew he wanted me in a sexual way, because all I'd heard was about lust and longing, nothing about what he was going to do about it. Then again, he'd driven across states after all this time to be with me as soon as I'd called him.

"Listen, Valerie, you may as well know all of it. I'd probably have been back for you long before now if it wasn't for Iria."

My breath caught in my throat at his admission. I forced it out. I wasn't sure what to believe anymore. The warnings from Martin, who knew him far better than me, rang in my ears. I couldn't reconcile everything I'd been told by him because Flynn had done nothing but be there for me when I needed him. A familiar, helpless feeling washed over me again. My recovery from the death of my brothers had been a hard battle. I'd been determined to do that, and worked hard to be strong and independent. Most of the time I coped well, but sometimes it was overwhelming. That day was one of those times. Flynn was shaking the protective barriers I'd put in place since my brothers died.

If it wasn't for Iria? An age-old excuse for forbidden love. So, what was he saying? Was I supposed to have the scraps of time he could spare when he wasn't with her? He's not with her, but she's there? None of it was making sense. Flynn was a rock star with a life that had no stability, and I worried he was on the verge of dragging me into something I wasn't sure I'd be able to live with.

"Want me to be completely honest? I hate my life. All I want is to play music, settle down after a while ... but mostly, I want to be happy," he said as he squeezed me closer to him, and my body steeled again.

"My management team tells me I'm supposed to settle for one out of three, but I'm greedy, Valerie. I want it all—music, you, and to live happily ever after."

He was quiet in thought for a few seconds.

"In an ideal world, I'd sweep you off your feet and love you so hard you'd never doubt me. But I know that's not possible. Not for the foreseeable future, at least."

My heart soared and immediately felt crushed during that statement. I was furious he'd said something like that and then disappointed me.

I turned to face him. "What the fuck are you talking about? Are you trying to mess with my head? You have a girlfriend, and you're laying your cards on the table about wanting me? Lying here on my bed with me?"

I struggled to get up, but he pulled me tightly to him and breathed heavily, disturbing my hair.

"Stop, Valerie. Don't, babe. Listen. She's ill, Valerie. Iria is sick. So, I guess I'm stuck. That makes me sound really shitty, right? She's not well and I don't want her. I don't even know how I got here. Everything was okay until I tried to back off and she wouldn't let me go. I know that makes me sound pathetic and weak, and I don't expect you to understand, but my management and PR team aren't the best. For almost two years, I've been in this hell. I can't help that I don't love her. It isn't possible to love someone on purpose, it just ... happens. It happened to me with you."

Blood rushed in my ears, and I waited for him to say, *"But we can't do this,"* or something to that effect. When I didn't respond, he shifted on the bed uncomfortably.

"Don't you have anything to say to what I just told you?"

"Not really, apart from you already having a girl, so it's not my place to make your relationship with Iria more ... *complicated* by discussing how that makes me feel."

"Jess, her friend, told me she's sick, tore me a new one when I tried to break up with Iria."

When he mentioned Jess's name, I pulled out of his hold and sat up quickly in the dark.

"Martin's Jess?"

"Yeah, the day after I was caught with those girls by the pool, she called me. I'd already told Iria we were through. Let's see, it was a day or two before the accident, I think. I don't remember exactly. She was pissed at me, but I told her I could never give my heart to her because I was pretty sure I'd already lost it to someone else."

Did he mean me?

"The relationship between Iria and me has been a bone of contention for my band since before our first album was released. Everyone knew I didn't want to be with her, but they felt she'd given me my start with the band, and wanted me to stay with her.

Any bad press about dumping the person who made you famous was bad form when we were just starting out. I was thankful for what she did, but I just couldn't make myself love her. I'd even spoken to Bernie, my manager, and the other guys in the band about walking away from her, but they, and the PR guys, told me I had to stick with it, at least until they could figure a way out. We were too new for any controversy."

"I may have understood that in the beginning, but after all this time? Shitty PR guys you have, Flynn. Don't they specialize in damage control? And where's your self-respect in all of that? Is being famous more important than being happy?"

Flynn got up and flicked the light on. "You may as well know everything. Then you can make your mind up with all the information, instead of second guessing me." He stared pointedly for a minute, then started to pace again.

"First, the band... For the first time since my mom and brother died, I felt a part of something. Iria had a miscarriage five weeks after we got together. I swear it wasn't mine. She told me she was nine weeks along when she met me. I supported her through that, but I saw how manipulative she was, and I didn't want to be with someone who could hide something that big to get what she wanted. I wasn't in love with her, and I tried to back off then."

"Flynn, you had no problem walking away from me, so why not her?"

"She started behaving like a loose cannon and fired warning shots about discrediting me before the band had even gotten off the ground. Bernie came down heavily on me and told me I had to keep her happy, for the band's sake. I know I should have stood up to them, but I was thinking of all the guys in the band and the effort they'd all put into it."

I understood how that could have affected them when they were getting started, but that was well over two years ago.

"And then, when Jess told me Iria's sick... Can you imagine what the press would do to me? Rough kid from the care system meets rich debutant, knocks her up, then deserts her when she's got a life-threatening disease?"

"What's wrong with her?"

"Some chronic lung disorder or something. Idiopathic Pulmonary Fibrosis. It doesn't get better."

"So, what you're saying is you want to be with me, but we have to wait until she dies? Meanwhile, you live your life alongside her, and what? Once in a while, she gets a pity fuck to keep her quiet?"

"No. I haven't slept with her since I told her we were quits. She just won't go away, and I'm... stuck ... in this shitty situation."

"You and your *situations*. You're not in a situation, you're dealing with a condition—one that will never go away. You have to face it head on. If you really don't love her, it's not fair to drag it out. I know that sounds harsh, but I know better than anyone that life is short. If you are serious, then you have to understand what's happening here is emotional blackmail at its best. You're a rock star, Flynn. Fuck your PR guys, your band, and your manager. You get one life. You may lose some fans, but your true fans will say, 'So what, he's a rock star. What did we expect?' "

He snickered and sat down to face me, looking straight into my eyes. A small smile curved his mouth as he reached out and took my hands in his. "And what do you think?"

"Me? I think if you were serious about me, you'd grow a bigger pair of balls and deal with her. And then ... if you can show me you really want me, I might be able to think about where we go from there. It's the most I can tell you right now. I'd need time to think about it."

Flynn chuckled. "I'm so glad I never crossed the line with you when you were younger. You have grown in so many ways, babe. I remember saying you weren't ready for me. I think that may have been the other way around."

"Flynn, I can't guarantee we'd work. I have my work here, and you'd be on the road. And I think you know I'd never put up with anyone cheating on me. The insecurities of your job might make me walk away."

"I'd never cheat on you, babe. It's not who I am. What I did with those girls was a one-time thing. I was out of my mind on drugs, and I'd already told Iria we were through. I'm more scared of you coping with my lifestyle."

"Are you sure I'm not just forbidden fruit? Someone you crushed on because it wasn't appropriate?"

"You're fucking kidding, right? All that shit about love at first sight? Well, I have news for you, it isn't total shit after all." He squeezed my hands. "It's real. It happened to me—with you. You are the love of my life. My heart knows that. Know how? Thousands of girls have come on to me in the past couple of years. I've had insane offers. A girl fell to her knees in an elevator once and begged me to let her blow me. I'm not saying this to upset you. What I'm saying is, despite all those women, you have never gone away. It's been *you* since the day we met."

Closing the space between us, I pressed a kiss to his lips. Flynn's hands dropped mine, and they found my head on both sides. Pulling me forward, he deepened the kiss. We poured every ounce of passion we had into it. When he pulled back, he'd left me breathless. He reached for my tank top and yanked it over my head. My whole body was tight, buzzing with electrical currents in every vein. Excitement and lust boiled up from my belly, and his touch left me dizzy.

Flynn stood and yanked his boxers down and then threw back the comforter and slid in beside me. His hand slipped down my naked front and into my pajama pants and panties, until his warm palm cupped my wet mound in a possessive hold.

"Take them off, babe," he gently murmured as he kissed my neck. He set me on fire with his mouth, and I squirmed with delight on the bed. I felt like my heart was going to explode in my chest with his constant stroking, his kisses, and my anxiety over my inexperience.

Flynn's need became more urgent, and he yanked at the waistband of my pajamas. "Come on, babe. Take these off."

Nervously, I slipped them over my butt, and he was there helping me out of them. He dropped them to the floor and knelt back on his haunches on the bed. Hooking his fingers into the waistband of my panties at both hips, he glanced at the door.

"You did lock the door, right?" he said, and chuckled.

When I nodded, his fingers gained tension on the material. Leaning forward, he placed a small kiss on my lower belly as he moved down my body.

"You are so fucking beautiful, Valerie." His fingers tugged at the waistband and he pulled my panties down in a painfully slow movement, like he was unveiling me.

Flynn bunched the panties in his hands and brought them to his nose, inhaling deeply. I blushed, embarrassed about that. "Fuck, babe. You smell delicious. I'm so fucking turned on by you."

"A handcuff turns you on, Flynn," I teased, to cover my awkwardness.

"True," he said, and chuckled, cradling both my ankles in his hands.

He ran his palms slowly up both of my legs from my outer ankles to my hips. When he looked up, his studious expression softened as he flashed a sexy smile at me. I'd heard about the look of love, and that was definitely what I read on his face. Flynn Docherty wasn't lying; he loved me.

Something shifted inside of me, and all my fears slid from my mind. My emotions were centered on the one thought I felt to be true. I was meant to be with him. As soon as I reconciled myself with that reality, another thought immediately followed. Being in love with someone like him wasn't going to be easy.

"What's up? What are you thinking?"

"Am I making a decision that's going to hurt me badly in the future?"

"Fuck no, babe. If you're with me, that's it. No matter what I do, or who I'm with, I'll always come home to you at the end of the day."

I stared at his face and knew he meant every word. But words are easy. Living up to those words would take strength and commitment. I knew I had that, but Flynn, I wasn't so sure about.

Chapter Twenty-Five

TAKING A CHANCE

*S*oft palms swept over my skin again as Flynn slid them up the insides of my legs. My body was alight, every cell positively charged and fizzing under his skillful caresses. Stopping short of my entrance, he swept them out over the front of my thighs, and rounded my hips to slide them under my butt. Lifting me off the bed, he pulled my nub to his mouth and kissed it gently before dropping me back to the bed.

I watched as his lust-darkened eyes explored my curves. The tactile scrutiny that followed his gaze charged the trail in its wake with a buzz of anticipation. I'd never been so exposed to anyone before, and that somehow felt right.

Brushing his hands up my body, he cupped my breasts in both hands and squeezed them gently. "Fuck, you're beautiful," he said in a husky voice, as his eyes drew a line up from them to my face. "I can't believe we're doing this after all this time."

I flushed with pleasure and quietly looked back at him, and his smile made my heart squeeze with excitement to have him worship me slowly like that.

As he continued to touch me, he slid off the end of the bed onto his knees and pulled me down toward him, spreading my legs widely.

Watching the lust in his eyes when he looked between them made my hollow core tighten with desire. His fingers traced the outer lips, and my body hummed with pleasure under his gentle touch.

Flynn licked his lips, and my butt shifted in his hands. Glancing up, he smirked in his sexy way again and squeezed my butt as his mouth edged downward, while his eyes stared intensely into mine.

One long lick at my seam and I arched off the bed. The sensation was exquisite. He continued, and I relaxed into his rhythm until his hot tongue darted and pushed its way inside me. It lathed around and, as he tasted more, he hummed with satisfaction. His lips and mouth covered my entire girly area, and he sucked me hard. More juice leaked from my core as he stirred heightened arousal from it.

Flynn's tongue found and probed my entrance and then licked its way up to my clit. Two soft strokes were following by rapid licks. His punishing pace made my shoulders sink into the mattress as I bowed up to meet his mouth. I moaned loudly in rapturous delight.

Drawing back to look up at me, Flynn whispered, "Shh, babe, you're going to have everyone banging on the door."

A finger traced my folds and circled my cave as he slid it inside to the first knuckle. I tensed, and he pulled back again. "Fuck, babe, you're so tight in there. Did I hurt you? My cock is aching to be where my finger is, but I want to take my time with you."

My mouth was dry as I was swept away with all the new feelings I was experiencing. I was a little scared about having sex, but it felt right with Flynn. I had no reservations about going all the way, I just didn't want it to hurt. His finger probed deeper, and he swirled it around. "Jeez, babe, relax. You're so closed and tense."

I lay there, wondering what to say to him, and how he'd respond. He'd once said to me he never wanted to be my first. I was so glad he was. Once we were in the moment, I knew I'd never really wanted to do it with anyone else. Even though, with Ziggy and Daryl, there were times when I'd thought I had.

After a minute or two, I relaxed, and his finger felt good gliding in and out as his tongue continued to pleasure me. I moaned when he withdrew a finger and pushed another in and I yelped at the sudden stretch and burn. My fingers grabbed a handful of his hair and yanked it tightly.

Flynn pulled back again. "Jeez, Valerie, you're tight as hell down here," he said, his fingers still inside me. He dipped forward and began sucking my clit again, and I felt more fluid ooze from my center. "Damn, you're so wet but so tight. I'm scared to take you."

I was scared as well, and if that was my opportunity to tell him I'd never gone that far before, I missed it. He withdrew his hand and kissed his way up my belly, and then lay on top of me. My hands instantly wrapped around his back, and I traced my fingers over the muscular contours and hard lines there. Flynn's mouth took mine, kissing me so passionately I moaned into it.

When he broke the kiss, he buried his face in the curve of my neck, and I felt his lips flatten in smile against my skin. His body vibrated with need, and the wet tip of his hard cock settled once again at my entrance.

"Fuck, this isn't easy. I'm trying to be controlled, but my body is screaming to fuck you." His breathing became labored as his right hand dug into the flesh on my upper left arm. The lust in his voice intensified my longing. Pulling back to face me, his hips arched, and once again his cock nudged at my wet entrance. Electrical pulses shot through my body at the thought he may try to enter me. My pulse soared with excitement, but I was a little scared at the same time.

"We should have talked about this before we got to this point, but do you have any condoms here?"

I shook my head. I didn't have any, anywhere. Kayden probably had some. I'd had no idea where that particular thought came from. As if I'd ask him.

"I'm clean, I tested two weeks ago, and I've never been bareback before. Do you trust me?"

Bareback? No condom? Is that what it means? Do I trust him? Can I believe he's been careful? What if I get pregnant? That would be my luck. "I'm not on any birth control."

"Neither am I," Flynn teased. "Well fuck," he hissed more seriously, and pushed himself off the bed. He ran his hands through his hair, thinking, and began dressing.

"Where are you going?"

"Where do you think? I'm going to ask Lee if he has any."

I was mortified. "You can't go to Lee. He'll know what we're doing. You're not a very seasoned rock star, are you? I thought you'd have some stapled to the inside of your jacket for events like these."

Glancing at me with a serious, frustrated expression he huffed, "Valerie, if I was the kind of guy who fucked all the groupies who offered, then yeah, I would. But I told you, I'm not interested in doing this with anyone but you."

He pulled his t-shirt over his head and buttoned up his jeans. "Back in a minute."

Once he'd left the room, the reality of what was happening set in, and I wondered if I was emotionally ready for being with Flynn Docherty. I'd dreamed about him since I was fifteen, and he was about to take my virginity. That was a huge thing to come to terms with.

A pang of guilt hit me, and I wondered if I should come clean with him about it being my first time. Then I remembered him saying he'd never take me in my bed if it was my first time, and the thought that he wouldn't do it because of that distressed me.

My mind flicked through so many things in the span of a few seconds, and I pondered if it was Lee's job to keep condoms for Flynn. I pushed that thought away, because despite everything, I could never imagine feeling the same depth of feelings I had for Flynn, with anyone else.

Two minutes later, Flynn slid around the door and locked it again. "Bingo!" He smirked and waved a red strip of four condoms in front of me. He tossed them on the bed and stripped his clothes off. Climbing into the bed, he swept his arms around me and smiled down at me again. "In the future, I'm stocking these everywhere we go. My balls are blue with me running around like a sixteen-year-old trying to get my rocks off."

I smiled up at him but felt the moment was gone. We'd been so heated before, and I thought we wouldn't be able to recapture that passion.

"So, Valerie Darsin, love of my life. Where were we?"

Love of my life? My heart stuttered at his statement, and I tried to act normal while I absorbed his declaration. "I think you were playing bingo."

"Hmm." He chuckled.

Suddenly, he grabbed my hips and flipped me on my back, sweeping over me. He caged me in with his limbs against the mattress. Flynn pushed his groin into mine and ground his erect cock into my pubic bone. "Fuck. See what you do to me, babe? All fucking day I've been like this. Your body is torturing me. I'm so hard for you."

Looking down at his solid, thick cock, I understood exactly what he meant. My body and mind were battered from all the teasing, and I had no real clue about sex.

Five minutes later, I was moaning softly under his touch again, as the dizzying, crazy sensations he pulled from my body were nothing short of the sweetest torture to my inexperienced, emotional self. His fingers slid the length of my crease and back, until his thumb found my clit and drew small circles on my bundle of nerves until my mind fell apart at the seams. I began to make soft, mewling noises, and Flynn covered my mouth with his, absorbing the sounds of ecstasy.

I was spent after that. It had been a long emotional day, but Flynn wasn't anywhere near done. His hand fished around above the comforter until he found the condoms. He tore one from the foil strip before chucking the rest on the floor. Ripping the packet, he took the little latex wrap and rolled it all the way down to his root. He looked huge, and I almost crawled off the bed, feeling scared about him trying to put all of that inside my body.

Smiling, he crawled over me and I felt his cock rest at my entrance, followed by one hand. "You're soaking wet for me."

His face nestled into the crease of my neck and he sucked my skin gently. Goosebumps erupted the length of my body, and a shiver ran down to the base of my spine from the excitement that had taken over my thought functions. He chuckled and moved up onto his arms before taking a breast in his mouth. "Mmm," he murmured, and the vibration centered in my core. Squirming under him, my legs relaxed wider, and I lifted my knees. Flynn nudged closer.

"You are the most beautiful woman I've ever known, you know that?"

"And flattery will get you anywhere."

"I was hoping you'd say that, because there is this little place I've never been before," he flirted, smiling playfully as he held my gaze.

Swallowing, I cleared my throat and stared back at his lust-filled, cloudy eyes. I couldn't think. The green hue was dwarfed by his huge pupils. I shivered as soon as his hand skimmed my belly when he positioned himself at my entrance. He nudged forward a tiny bit, and it stung. A course of adrenaline rushed through me. His cock wasn't small, and as soon as he started to enter me, I'd felt it stretch and burn.

My body tensed with the pain and he stopped, immediately pulling his cock out.

"I thought you wanted this. Why are you tensing up?"

"I do. It's just..."

"It's just that you want to tease me some more? Let me tell you, babe, I am strung out with all the cock-teasing." He stared into my eyes and his expression suddenly became one of shock as he realized why I wasn't being very spontaneous.

"Shit! You weren't going to tell me this is your first time?"

Emotion closed my throat, and I couldn't answer him because if I tried, I would have cried.

"You've had a boyfriend all this time, and you've never—what the fuck is he? A monk? How could he touch you and not want to fuck you?"

Tears welled in my eyes, and I swallowed hard to keep them at bay.

"Oh, no, hey ... don't. Please don't cry. I'm sorry. I'm stunned," he said softly.

"Can you just do it? I want you to do it," I whispered, with almost a plea in my voice as I tried to hold his gaze.

"I'll hurt you," he said, his lips forming a line and giving his face a tense expression.

"Physically, yes. But if you don't, I'll be emotionally hurt. That takes longer to heal. I already know that."

He studied my face, and then stared into my eyes. It was unnerving. I'll never forget that look, because I knew he felt the significance of the connection between us. I wondered what he was thinking, as my heart ached for him to have the courage to keep going.

Flynn crawled down the bed again and flipped me over him, turning me away from him. Pulling my butt down, he began licking my lady lips slowly, giving me a tender kiss. I lay in a sixty-nine position with my head down on his legs, and got lost in the sensation. Once again, my body began to vibrate with anticipation, and after a few minutes, what he was doing was no longer enough. As if he sensed this, he readjusted me on my back and crawled toward me, spreading my legs with his knees.

"This is going to hurt a little, babe. I'm sorry." The pained look on his face made my heart quicken, because I knew it was the point of no return.

Nudging forward, his arms cocooned my head, and he dipped his forehead to mine.

"I can't believe I get to be your first."

"I'm glad it's you," I said, smiling weakly as my heart hammered inside my chest.

"If it's too much, tell me, and I'll stop. If you tell me to get out, we're done for now. I'm not doing this twice; I'd hurt you more that way." The serious look on his face scared me even more.

I nodded, and Flynn inched forward. "Fuck, you're so tight," he muttered, his eyes never leaving mine.

Inch by inch he pushed into me, and I lay silently biting my lip. It hurt. Every squeak I made, he countered it with a kiss. "That's it, baby, relax for me."

Suddenly, I felt as if something tore inside and his cock glided in up to its root. I cried out because of the stretching, burning sensation, and Flynn covered my mouth with his hand.

"Shh, babe," he said. He stilled, cupping my mouth. His eyes searched my face and his brow furrowed.

"I'm sorry, babe. I never wanted to hurt you," he said, shifting a little inside.

I winced, and he kissed my forehead as worry became etched in his eyes "Does it always hurt?"

"Fuck no, maybe the first few times it might, until you get used to my size, but after that—I'm going to ride you so fucking hard, Valerie, because I don't want you to ever forget who you're with."

"Isn't that supposed to be my line? You're the rock star, after all," I teased.

"Babe, I could watch your body beneath me all day long. We all have to be fans of someone."

The pain in my lower area had eased, and he drew back a little and sank back into me. "How's that? Is it okay?"

"Bearable," I said, and smiled. It burned like hell, but I didn't want him to stop.

Flynn took my mouth in a kiss and stuck his tongue deep inside. I moaned, and he rocked gently against me again. After a couple of minutes, I found myself arching back into him. "Good girl, now you're feeling it," he smiled as he glanced at me quickly, and kissed me again. His hands began to roam over my body, and he moved a little more freely inside. It still felt tight, but the burn had gone. Every thrust made my inner lips pulse, and he hissed with each one.

"Valerie, I love you, but I don't think I'm gonna last much longer. I'm sorry," he ground out as he tried to control his urge to go faster.

I wasn't sure what he meant, but his voice sounded urgent. His butt reared back more, and he rocked in longer thrusts, his face an inch from mine as our foreheads pressed firmly together. Beads of sweat formed on his forehead from the effort of trying to control himself.

"You are the most beautiful woman in the world, you know that?"

I smiled because I believed he meant that, even though I'd heard a man was capable of saying anything to a woman to get her to do this. "And you're the most beautiful man. I love you, Flynn Docherty," I countered, raking my nails firmly down his back. As I confessed what was in my heart, his body went rigid, jerked above me, and I felt his cock pulse inside. Flynn's mouth took mine in a possessive kiss. Even through his orgasm, he responded to my declaration.

I held him through his aftershocks, then slowly he eased out of me and rolled onto his back. He pulled the condom off and tied the end. Then he leaned over and placed it carefully on his boxers. Lying back down, his chest heaved as his body quieted and he pulled me into his side.

"Say that again," Flynn panted.

"About you being beautiful?" I teased.

"No, the other thing."

"I love you?"

Flynn squeezed me into his body. "Yeah, that."

"I love you, Flynn. I've loved you since I was fifteen," I stated honestly.

"And I've loved you since then as well, Valerie. You stole my heart the first time I touched you that night in the bleachers."

Flynn kissed me tenderly, and when we broke the kiss, we lay staring into one another's eyes.

"You know we're going to be dealing with a whole heap of shit if we do this?"

"Flynn, I've had the shittiest things in the world happen to me so far in my life. How much worse can it be?"

He gripped my hip and squeezed. "True, but babe, you're going to have to be tough and ride it out with me. You'll hear a ton of shit about me. If it's true, I'll be honest with you; if I tell you it's not, you have to trust me. Think you can you do that?"

"Not blindly, but I'll try. I'll say this, though, Flynn. Cheat on me once and we're done."

Flynn stared into my eyes and his softened as he brushed some strands of hair from my face and smiled. "Fair enough. I'm confident I'd never cheat on you. It's never going to happen. I love you too much for that, babe."

As I lay wrapped in his arms, I prayed that what he was feeling would stay at the forefront of his mind to keep him strong in the future. He'd said it himself; in his line of work, there were too many temptations. I knew it would have to be my life that changed to prevent our relationship from becoming a car wreck like other celebrities. I wasn't even nineteen, so I wasn't confident I had what it took to do that.

Chapter Twenty-Six

CHICAGO

A few minutes later, Flynn kissed the top of my head and pulled away. I felt the loss of his heat from my body immediately. He sat, swinging his feet to the floor and stood, picked up the condom, and wandered into the bathroom.

My heart sank to my stomach because I thought I'd been so poor at sex. I heard the water running and knew he was cleaning up. He came back with a washcloth and towel and pulled back the cover. Blood was streaked at the top of my thighs, and there was a small amount on the sheet.

"Let me get you cleaned up, babe," he said, his voice full of concern as he started to spread my legs. I winced, then felt pathetic for doing so.

"Fuck, you want me to get you some Advil or something? I'm sorry I hurt you, Valerie."

Feeling embarrassed, I tried to take the cloth to clean myself, but he insisted on trying to make me as comfortable as he could. Ten minutes later, he fitted me snugly into his side again, and we settled down in the darkness. I felt cared for and happy once I was cuddled back between the sheets in his arms again.

"Sorry," I offered.

"For what?"

"Not being good at sex," I stated.

"You think I was the first time? Hell, I shot my load inside a minute I was so excited," he said with a chuckle.

"It takes a little time, babe. And we'll have that. I want you to come with me, Valerie. I know you have your life here, but I hope we can work something out. If you do come with me, I have to warn you, life with me will be so different from anything you've been used to. It'll be so fucking hard at times. Are you sure you want to put yourself in that position?"

I worried that he was having second thoughts. "Do you want me to be in that position?"

"To witness all the shit that goes with what I do? No, I don't. If you mean, do I want you with me all the time? Nothing would please me more. I'm not easy to live with at times, especially when I'm with the band. I don't get along with a couple of them. They like to stir up trouble for me, feeding the press with garbage about my life."

"Let's get through tomorrow. The good thing is, I'm a fast learner. There is a lot we have to discuss before I start running away with you," I stated flatly.

I curled further into him and ran my fingertip lightly across his hard belly. Flynn bucked. "Fuck. Don't do that. I'm hypersensitive. I want you again, but I know you're sore. Get some rest, babe," he said, squeezing me tightly before he relaxed his arms again. I was just about asleep when I heard him whisper, "I love you, Valerie."

A smile stretched my lips in satisfaction. A short while later, I heard his steady deep breaths, and not long after that, I sagged into his side and gave his chest a small kiss. Then sleep took me.

Rolling over in bed, I grimaced. Between my legs hurt, and my bed was empty. I sat with a start, and listened to hear if Flynn was in the bathroom, but instinctively I knew he wasn't.

I eased myself out of bed and went to pee. It hurt to even walk. Turning on the faucet in the tub, I opened the bathroom cabinet in search of some painkillers. Every movement I made seemed to jar under my legs. My poor sensitive spot stung, but I still felt happy inside. If I had to have the pain, then I was glad it was Flynn who had taken me.

After my bath, I dressed, and the pain relief had begun to work so I could at least walk; the ache between my legs was much more tolerable. When I went into the kitchen, it was empty, except for Flynn, who was on the phone.

"Alright, I'll be back by nine tonight. I know I was supposed to call you, but I had an emergency I had to take care of," he said, running his hand through his hair. Glancing up, he smirked and stood in front of me. Waving his forefinger at me, he mouthed "emergency," then winked playfully. He ended his call and wandered over to the kitchen area, where I began to fill the coffee pot.

Flynn slid his arms around my waist from behind and laid his chin on my shoulder. His hot breath tickled my neck. Despite the pain, my center instinctively arched toward him. His woodsy, musky smell and expert touch reignited the embers that still burned deep within me from the day before. I put the pot down and turned into his arms. His hand immediately slid to cup my butt, and he pulled me flush against him, rubbing his hard bulge into my belly with a slow smile.

"How are you feeling?"

"I'm doing okay; I'm more interested in how you're feeling." I giggled and was rewarded with a wicked grin.

"Hard and horny at the sight of you, babe. I've been talking *him* down all morning, watching you sleep in that bed. That's why I came down here. He wanted to jump you, but I knew you would be sensitive today."

Smiling again, I stretched on tiptoes to kiss his mouth. It was supposed to be a peck on the lips, but Flynn had other ideas. His large hands cupped the sides of my face, and he stared into my eyes. His were glassy and half closed, his pupils blown with desire. The way he looked at me told me everything he said the night before was true. I felt that look; it touched my soul. My heart stuttered inside as he stole my breath with the next kiss that followed.

Lee cracked open the kitchen door, and I broke the kiss. I stepped away from Flynn slightly as I'd thought it might be one of my parents.

"Looks like the welcome-home party is about to get started.

There's a guy out front who asked me, 'Who the fuck are you?' My guess is that would be Daryl?" he said, and chuckled.

I stared at Flynn, and he pulled me in for a tight hug. "Go to your studio, Valerie. I'll bring him up there. Then follow my lead. This is where he gets the rock-star experience," he said with a big, wicked smile. I froze for a second and when I didn't move, Flynn waved his hands to shoo me out the door. "Go. I'm so looking forward to this."

I turned and opened the glass slider, let myself out, and ran toward the studio. Quickly firing up my laptop, I sat, clicking past each frame I'd taken on the SD card. When the ones of Evette and Elias ran out, the ones of Flynn and I started to flip by. The first few were me climbing on the bed, but they got progressively raunchier. A certain one made me catch my breath. The angle of the camera had caught Flynn staring up at me, and I've never seen raw sexual need pour from a picture as the look on his face did in that frame.

The studio door opened, and Daryl burst in, followed by Flynn, who casually closed the door and leaned against the wall. A shadow passed by the window and I knew Lee was outside, and that he would have been inside in a heartbeat if we needed him.

"When the fuck did he get here?" Daryl asked angrily.

"Hey, Daryl, did you miss me?"

"Of course, I did. I asked you a question."

"The day before yesterday," I said, turning to Flynn. "That was when you got here, isn't it? It's been so busy it feels more like a week."

"So, you got back when? I thought you were coming home last night. Why the fuck didn't you call me? Did he pick you up from the airport?"

I smirked at Flynn and he raised his brow in question. "Don't…"

I held my hand up to Flynn and said, "I got this."

"I found out everything I needed to know the first day of the meeting, Daryl. I never called because I knew you weren't expecting me home. I used that time to work and hang out with Flynn."

"So the rock star turns up, and you suddenly forget about me?"

"Kind of. I mean, I called him, so it was only right we spent some time catching up."

"Well, now that he's caught up to date, he knows you're taken, right?" He snarled and glanced angrily at Flynn.

"Hmm, I do," Flynn replied. An amused smile played on his lips when his eyes met mine.

"What the fuck's the deal, Val?" Daryl asked in his barking voice again.

"The deal is, there is no deal between us, Daryl."

"What are you talking about?" he asked, looking confused.

"You were right when you said she was taken, Daryl. Valerie's *mine*," Flynn stated with authority.

"You've been cheating on me— with him? All this time, I've treasured you. I've never pressured you because I thought we were waiting."

"No, Daryl, you were making *me* wait. What were you thinking? I know about your woman in Minnesota, by the way."

Daryl stopped moving. "What? What the fuck are you talking about?"

"Don't insult her intelligence. Listen, I don't know why you never had sex with Valerie, but I guess you had your reasons. I have to thank you for saving that gift for me," Flynn goaded.

Daryl chuckled and shook his head. "Yeah, I know about the shit you two pulled on the bleachers that night, but you're not dealing with a bunch of fifteen and sixteen-year-olds now. I call bullshit on you two sleeping together. I've been with Valerie since she was sixteen, and when she comes to her senses and realizes I've been faithful, all this shit will go away. *You'll* go away again, Mr. Rock Star, and one day I'll ask her to marry me. We've abstained because my princess is going to be a virgin when I take her to my bed on our wedding night."

Watching Daryl lying made me wonder if I really knew him at all. I should have been heartbroken, but I had no feelings at all for him. I wasn't even angry at him, or sorry. Not since Flynn arrived.

"Oops," Flynn commented. I almost laughed when he said that, and he raised his eyebrows in surprise, "You failed to mention that last night, Valerie. Naughty girl." Flynn began chuckling,

Daryl banged on the table. "Alright, you sick fuck. I've had about all I can take from you and your fucking games. Valerie, you know I'd never cheat on you, and I'm surprised you've taken things this far. Call off the dogs and send them home. I'm tired of this. I can't believe you'd let him pretend you'd slept with him either," Daryl said angrily.

"Oh, there wasn't much sleeping, Daryl. How are you, by the way, babe? Still sore?"

I blushed but I knew why Flynn said that.

It was Daryl's chance to laugh. "Now you're really trying to fuck with me," he said moving closer to Flynn.

"I wouldn't fuck you, Daryl. You're not my type. Besides, Valerie and I are into monogamy," Flynn goaded.

"Maybe you'll want to check some of these out and see if you still don't believe him." I opened the laptop, and turned it around to face Daryl. Flynn moved slightly behind him, and I saw by the way his pupils dilated and he grinned widely as he looked at the pictures, he loved them. His eyes flicked to mine and creased at the corners as his smile reached them.

Before he could say anything, Daryl snapped the laptop closed and took a swing at Flynn, but missed. Flynn chuckled. "Oh, you want to hit me now, huh? See her?" Flynn pointed at me. "She's mine. I've come back to claim her," he stated decisively.

Daryl turned to stare at me. Anger radiated from his body as he rolled his shoulders. "You're wrong. You need to live with that, Valerie. I never cheated on you, but I guess you're nothing but a dirty little groupie, after all. He'll tire of you. Wait and see, and don't come back looking for sympathy. And you'll be sorry, because there is no other girl, you were *it* for me."

"Lee, bring your ass in here," Flynn shouted. Lee cracked the door open and came over to the desk.

"No girl, huh? Lee? Do you have something you want to share with Daryl here? Seems like the guy has a terrible memory about the woman he's involved with."

Lee pulled out his phone and swiped it. He shared a picture of a petite Hispanic woman and Daryl walking into a restaurant. Daryl had his arm around her, and she was glancing up at him with an adoring look on her face. He turned the phone to point the picture toward Daryl. "It's not what it looks like..." he protested.

"It never is, Daryl," Lee muttered back sarcastically. "I have more if you want them. One of you arriving at her home with her. Another one leaving this morning in the same clothes..."

Daryl knocked the phone out of Lee's hand, and it skimmed across the wooden floor.

"I think, unless Daryl has anything more to contribute, we're about done here, babe. I need to fly to Chicago later, so I guess we'll have to cut this short. You've got packing to do."

Daryl strode toward the door and turned to face me. "I'm telling you, Valerie, he's going to fuck you over, and when he hurts you..."

"If he ever does, *you* are the last person I'd come to for a shoulder, Daryl. Good luck with your life. It seems like you're going to need it."

Without another word, he slammed the door as he left. Lee, Flynn, and I stood silently in the studio for a moment. Flynn reached over and disconnected the laptop and placed it under his arm. "Alright, now that *fuckwad* is dealt with. Grab the charger for this, Lee. I think what's in here is the in-flight entertainment. I'll leave the car here and have it driven or shipped back. Charter a flight to leave at four. I have a meeting at nine o'clock downtown."

Turning to face me, Flynn lifted his brow and exhaled deeply. "I never even got the chance to ask you, will you come with me?"

I'd thought he was joking about me going with him. I had my studios and appointments I'd committed to. My independence was important to me. It wasn't as important as Flynn, though. My heart began to race, and those tight feelings rose in my belly. *What if I do this, and he lets me down? What if I can't stand the pace? What if he breaks my heart?* Even with all the questions and doubts I had, I knew I wanted him badly, so I went with my gut.

"I'll come, Flynn, but only for a few days. My business is here, and I've made commitments. I need to see those through. I won't add anything new to my schedule for a while, and we'll see how it goes. This is so new... I don't want to be left with my heart broken and my business in ruins."

"Well, fuck, that shows a lot of faith in me, babe. I told you the road was going to be rocky, and there'll be a few humps along the way. It's up to you to hang tough with me. You think you can do that? I really want you with me, babe."

My split-second decision was that I wanted to try. I'd die if I didn't give it my best shot.

Chapter Twenty-Seven

CONCERNS

No one seemed surprised when I told my family I was going to Chicago with Flynn, but my father was my strongest objector. I understood his fears; I was only one of two children he had left, but I couldn't live life in a bubble. Flynn again declared his feelings for me and promised my parents he'd keep me safe and treasure me. He was adamant about that.

"She's eighteen, Flynn. I don't want my daughter around that sick, corrupt lifestyle you live."

"Neither do I, sir, but we love each other. If you let her come with me, I promise you with my life, I'll do my best to protect her. She's it for me. I have loved her since the first day I saw her. You know that. How many conversations have we had where I've expressed my feelings for her? She's smart, strong, and she's much different than the girl she was a couple of years ago. I'm different too. What you read in the papers? It's not who I am anymore. I'm in love with Valerie, and she loves me. We'll ride all the waves that come, and I'll make sure that I'm always there for her."

I stared adoringly at Flynn, proud and touched by his conversation with my dad, and more than a little surprised that he'd already shared his feelings with my dad before he shared them with me.

The only thing my mom asked was if I'd thought about what I was doing. I'd done nothing but think about it from the moment he'd asked me to go. I'd been expecting more resistance, but after Flynn's speech, my dad agreed with a look of resignation on his face, and he said that he knew I'd be okay. When I asked what changed his mind, he said, "God's got my quota of children. I don't reckon he'll take another." It hurt my heart that my dad could be so blunt.

I had lived for the previous two years in a house full of broken people. The pain of losing my brothers was excruciating, and I'd felt abandoned when my brothers died and my parents went to face the horrible sight of their demise. I believe that whole experience made me the person I became—strong and independent, and a little selfish. For some reason, I felt like I was abandoning them because leaving the place full of memories meant I was moving on, and they were stuck with the past all around them.

Kayden was the one who took me aside to have a quiet word.

"Valerie, you sure you're happy about this?"

"I am."

"Then I'm happy for you. I know Martin would have had something to say about this, but I hope *my* judgment is good. Flynn seems to really care about you. You'll need to keep your head straight stepping into his world, honey. Stay clear of anything that's going to make your body or your mind sick. And don't believe everything you hear. Always question if something is too good, or too bad, to accept as fact."

I'd thought that was Kayden's way of saying don't take drugs and watch out for sharks. Neither had any place in my life. Flynn had said he'd taken some drugs at the beginning but that it had been a one-time thing. Since he'd been with me, I hadn't seen any evidence of drugs. In fact, apart from that first time he came home with Martin, I hadn't seen him drink alcohol either.

I pulled Flynn aside for another conversation about drinking and drugs, and he'd told me that since that day at the pool, he hadn't touched drugs. It had been a one-off experience, and he was happy not to repeat it. As for alcohol, he could take or leave it, but he did drink socially. At eighteen, it still wasn't legal for me.

Less than four hours later, we were in the air, cruising at 29,000 feet in a small chartered plane, heading for Chicago, and I was as nervous as hell. My last plane trip, I was due to take a flight the day of the accident. I sat, reflecting on some memories of my brothers, and I had to fight back tears, because the last time I'd even been in an airport was the day they came home.

It was my first time on an airplane, and the ride was bumpy. Flynn was great, keeping me calm, distracting me with kisses and talking about the band and Bernie, his manager. He filled me in on their personalities and the issues they had. It was the first time I'd heard him talk freely about them in depth.

Chicago was Flynn's base and his home, and from the instant we landed, his cell rang repeatedly. I commented on that, and he said he'd had it switched off most of the time he'd been with me. Callers were making up for that fact as we left the airport. Each time it rang, he'd take his cell out, reject the call, and put it back in his pocket.

I began to wonder if it was the same person or different people. I wondered each time if it was Iria. The thought of dealing with that obstacle to get to happier times made my chest tight.

Flynn seemed genuinely excited to take me home, but I was nervous about going to his house. It was different being on my home ground, to stepping into his world. I'd been through a lot, and I'd grown up quickly since the boys died, but suddenly I felt my age.

Everyone appeared so sophisticated, and I felt a little awkward and shy by the time his management's car service dropped us back at his house. One thing I'd promised myself before I stepped off the plane was that I was determined to appear confident and secure to everyone, even if I didn't always feel it.

Lee pointed his phone at the solid metal gates and pressed the security code to open the solid, twelve-feet-tall black steel gates that protected Flynn from his fans. The noise they made when they clunked back heavily made me understand the risk he took coming to see me. We were lucky enough to have the anonymity my parents' place offered.

I expected a house behind the gates, but instead there was a long, tree-lined gravel driveway for about half a mile before the road curved and dipped to another, which led up a hill to a large, white board-clad house. His place was stunning. Everything about it had been considered in great detail.

Immaculate lawns bordered by rugged rock gardens, with cherry trees either side, flanked a large, wide flagstone driveway leading to the house itself. Huge willow trees swayed gently along either side of the house, creating a feeling of privacy. The massive wrap-around veranda framed both sides at the front leading up to the grand, centrally positioned oak double doors. Symmetry was obviously important to the person who'd designed the house and the surrounding area; the effect was breathtaking.

Lee opened the front car door and jumped out, then he ran around the trunk to open Flynn's door. Flynn slid out of the seat and grabbed my hand. "Come on, Valerie. We're home."

His use of *we* made my heart flutter. I hadn't agreed I was staying long-term, and everything seemed to be moving at a pace I wasn't sure I could manage. A security guard in uniform appeared at the side of the lawn a few hundred yards away, and again my concerns about the security needed to keep Flynn safe, played on my mind. He followed my gaze and put his arm around me.

"Don't worry about that. No one has ever tried to come over the walls. It's just Bernie's way of showing me he loves me," he said, and snickered.

Lee was already inside the house, and when I heard him talking, I realized someone else was there. Taking my hand, Flynn pulled me through the den. It had the biggest, white leather, sectional sofa I'd ever seen. A tall bank of windows adorned one wall, with expensive sheers covering the whole way across them.

Adjacent to the den was a simple music room. We passed a few guitars and a baby grand piano. It linked the den and the kitchen. A small, blonde female was cooking, and when she saw Flynn, she dropped her bowl, wiped her hands on her jeans, and ran to hug him. Instant embarrassment flushed my cheeks, and I wasn't prepared for how jealous it made me. "Niamh, this is Valerie. The love of my life."

Niamh eyed me from head to toe, smiled widely, and stepped forward to hug me. "So, when did your short-sightedness start to be a problem," she joked, "I'd imagined this ugly bugger would have struggled for a woman to love him for the rest of his life."

Flynn chuckled and stepped forward, tugged me away from Niamh, and wrapped his arms around me. "I've been waiting a few years for this one," he stated, without a hint of humor in his voice.

"Well, thank goodness she agreed to come with you then, or we'd all have suffered. We know what it's like having to live with that grumpy fucker you have hidden right now."

Dipping his head, Flynn kissed me, and Niamh went back to cooking dinner. I felt a little embarrassed about that, but then again, he was a rock star. He didn't care who was looking at him, and his confidence gave me the confidence to accept his ways.

After eating a succulent dinner of Beef Wellington, mashed sweet potatoes, and asparagus, Niamh was clearing away dishes when Flynn's cell rang. Flynn glanced at his phone and sighed. "Excuse me, I have to take this one... Hey, Bernie," I heard him say, before he made his way back out of the kitchen toward the den.

Niamh smiled. "You look good on him," she said, and continued to empty the plates and stack the dishwasher. At first, I thought she meant I was eye candy for the press, but when I realized it was just her way of saying she approved, I relaxed. I loved Niamh from our first conversation.

While Flynn was on the phone, she told me she'd worked for Flynn since he'd bought the house the year before. His management had advertised with an agency for a housekeeper, and they had rejected her application because she was an Irish immigrant with a five-year-old boy. His management security couldn't check her background details enough for an interview.

Flynn being of Irish ancestry had heard how his grandparents had struggled to get a foothold in their newly adopted country when they arrived in America. He put his foot down because he, more than anyone, knew how difficult life was when you were different, so he'd dismissed the rest of the applicants as unsuitable and hired her, without an interview.

A soft tap on the glass slider distracted Niamh. "Oh, here's my little son," she said, bustling to the door and drying her hands on her jeans. A small, dark-haired boy of around six threw himself at her.

"Mommy, I had a great time at Toby's house. Can he come over next week?" Niamh brushed his hair from his forehead and crouched down beside him. "I don't think we can do next week, Teague. Flynn's home."

Teague's eyes lit up. "He is? Can I go see him, please Mommy?"

"Not right now, baby, he's working. Maybe tomorrow, okay?"

Teague appeared dejected. "Alright," he said, accepting his mom's explanation.

Niamh slipped on a wool jacket and flicked her hair out of the collar. "Teague, this is Flynn's special friend, Valerie. She's going to be staying here with Flynn."

Teague's eyes lit up and formed wide saucers. "Wow, are you having sleepovers with him?"

Niamh chuckled and rubbed his head. "Something like that, baby," she said, winking at me. "I live in the gate house down the hill at the back. There's a second entrance to this place there. If I leave this way, can you lock the door behind me?"

I nodded, and she left, closing the door. I turned the lock and then felt a little awkward because Flynn still hadn't returned. As he'd left the room, I didn't want to walk in on his call. I poured a cup of coffee and sat, hugging it at the table. I'd barely sat down when he came back. "Niamh gone already?"

I nodded. "I met her son Teague. He's excited I'm having a sleep-over with you."

Flynn grinned, and a smile lit up his face. Widening his eyes, he said, "Fuck. *He's* excited? I'm almost coming in my pants at the thought of having you here at my beck and call."

He came around the table and took the cup out of my hand. "You haven't even been upstairs yet. We should probably freshen up and get ready. I've got a band meeting at nine tonight. Pick your outfit carefully; you're about to enter the zoo," he said.

Flynn took my hand and pulled me out through the kitchen and into a large marble hallway. A staircase swept around from the bottom to the top floor, and a wrought-iron banister ran the length of the upstairs landing.

We ascended the stairs and, on reaching the landing, Flynn gave me a whirlwind tour without opening the doors. Nodding left and right, he familiarized me to the layout. "Guest room, bathroom, guest room, study, another bathroom, my office, my library, and this..." he threw open the double doors at the end of the corridor, "Is my love pad," he said, chuckling.

It was masculine and very *Flynn*. Cool vintage gray and white lines, plain gray curtains and black furniture. White sheets and a cool gray, luxury silk comforter covered the massive bed. "It's custom made for orgies."

My head snapped round from looking at the bed to face him, my eyes bored holes into him. Raucous laughter erupted from his throat. "Fuck, Valerie, I'm joking. I get restless after gigs. I kept falling out of the bed, so I had a bigger one made. I only got it three weeks ago, and I can't wait to break it in with you." His eyes heavy with lust as he scooped me off the floor and threw me down on the bed. He threw himself next to me and lifted me into his arms.

Pulling his head back to make eye contact, he groaned and ground against me. "Last thing I want to do is to work tonight. As soon as we're done, we're out of there, okay?" I nodded, and he kissed hungrily. Then he broke the kiss, leaving me gasping for air.

"Go freshen up. I'm not coming into that bathroom with you. We'll never get out of here if I do, and I want to take my time with you in my big bed when we get home."

Thirty-five minutes later, I'd showered and dried my hair, then stood staring at my suitcase, wondering what one wore to a band meeting. I found some gray skinny jeans and a dark red form-fitting t-shirt.

When I looked in the full-length mirror, my heart sank. A plain-looking little girl stared back at me. I pulled out some black stiletto boots and took a heavy silver metal belt from a mini-dress I'd packed last minute. I added that to hang over my hips. Better, but I needed more. I didn't wear a lot of make-up, just a little mascara, and red lipstick on occasion. I made my eyes up heavily with kohl eyeliner, and I penciled in my eyebrows slightly.

Staring in the mirror, I decided to go all out with what I had, so I used the eyeliner pencil around my eyes, drawing them out slightly at each corner. I applied my lipstick and a little blusher, then teased my hair in a few places to make it a bit wilder. I stepped back again to see the effect, just as Flynn walked back through from the bathroom, still wearing a towel. He stopped and stared at me as shock registered on his face.

When he didn't speak, I did, "Sorry, I'll take it off, give me ten minutes."

"Oh no, you fucking won't. Valerie, I never thought it possible, but you look so fucking hot. I mean even hotter, and I never thought that possible."

His towel was tenting, and I chuckled. "I just realized I don't have the wardrobe to be a rock star's girlfriend."

"You look fucking perfect. Damn. You didn't have to think about what to wear, Valerie. A paper bag would look good on you. However, if it makes you feel more confident to dress like you're sin in heels, I'll never be the one to tell you, no, as long as it's all for me."

While Flynn was getting dressed, he kept glancing over at me and swearing under his breath. He pulled on some clean jeans and a plain white t-shirt, took a brown leather jacket out of his wardrobe, and closed the door. He slapped on a splash of cologne, and he ran his fingers through his hair. Bending, he pulled on some Chucks. Once he finished primping, he came over and wrapped his arms around my waist.

"No matter what, I love you. They may say hurtful or bitchy things about us, to you, or things about you. We ride it out; it'll die down eventually when they know you're not going away. You got this?"

I swallowed hard because, as he said that, I'd realized my reality wasn't going to be hugs and puppies. I was entering a cutthroat environment where the norm was to shock and gain reactions. I reconciled myself with my history, and nothing much scared me when I'd had that thought.

"Oh, I got this. No worries, Flynn. As long as you're one hundred percent sure, because once I'm out there, it's you and me. Together, we'll be a tough shell to crack."

Bending toward me, he kissed my neck and turned me in the direction of the door. Walking with his arm around me, he glanced at me and chuckled. "Good girl. That's my Valerie. They're going to be pissed about Iria, and creaming their pants at the sight of you," he said, almost to himself, and chuckled again.

Chapter Twenty-Eight

LEGAL

$\mathcal{B}$utterflies weren't what I felt as we entered Bernie's place; it was straight-up nerves. Security was nearly as tight as it was at Flynn's place. His house was superbly positioned by the lake.

Fall in Chicago was a riot of color. Flynn took my hand and slid along the seat of yet another company car, and he pulled me out beside him. "No matter what they say, babe, remember you're here because I love you. Tyler's probably going to shit a brick when he sees you. You are just his type."

I swallowed back my fears and stared into his eyes. Flynn leaned toward me and kissed me softly on the mouth, and squeezed my hand. Every time he tried to reassure me, I became more concerned at what was waiting for me inside Bernie's house.

"Let's get it over with," he said, tugging me to him.

Flynn pushed the main door open and strode confidently down the hallway. I cursed my boots and the tick-tack noise the heels made against Bernie's ceramic-tiled floor. I remember wanting the hallway to be twice as long, because I had no idea what I was about to face.

Six people sat in the room, but one stood out like a sore thumb. Iria. She was sitting with another woman a few years older than her. Tommy Alzaci, their drummer, turned his head, objectified me and grinned. I recognized each of the band members from their videos. "Whoa, if Flynn has to leave the party, he brings the party back with him."

Iria stood up and stared at us. She looked irate as she began to walk toward Flynn with a frown on her face. She was stunningly beautiful, but her face had an ugly expression. Before she reached us, Tyler Chisholm stood up and adjusted his jeans at the waist.

"What the fuck are you doing, dude? We agreed, no groupies in our homes."

Flynn ignored him completely, as Iria had stopped in front of me. She stared me down before exhaling and turning to face Flynn. "I'm tired of this shit, Flynn. Poor girl, what did you promise her?" Looking at me again, she asked, "Did he tell you, you were the love of his life? He said that to me. Tells me that all the time, and now, I get this shit."

Wandering around the sofa, she looked back at me, gestured her hand up, and drew it the length of me. "Call her a cab. If I were you, I'd run sweetheart. He's never going to leave me."

I'd seen pictures of her with Flynn before, so I knew who she was. She wasn't even kind enough to introduce herself. I hated her on sight.

Clinging to my hand, Flynn squeezed it gently in reassurance. My heart thumped in my chest, and for a couple of minutes, I'd almost done what she'd told me. He *had* used those very words, "love of my life." How could she know that unless it was true? And if it was, could I trust him?

Bernie swiveled in his chair and glanced fleetingly at me before turning to Flynn.

"Errol, what the fuck are you playing at? You disappear without a word and bring back a kid who looks barely legal. She is legal, isn't she?"

Tyler stood and wandered over to a crystal decanter and poured himself a tumbler of amber liquid. He threw it down his throat and gasped, pulling a face. It was likely bourbon or whiskey, from the smell on his breath when he came closer.

"Fucking beautiful, I'll give you that. No wonder you didn't want to leave her. I'm calling second dibs. I don't mind leftovers when they're as gorgeous as her," he said as he leered at me and grinned, like what he said may actually happen. I didn't wait for Flynn to speak in my defense because I felt if he fought my battle at that point, it would be a daily occurrence.

"Wow, guys. Thank you for the welcome. I'm humbled. Flynn told me what a great bunch you all were. I see what he means now," I drawled sarcastically.

Turning to face Iria, I smirked. "Thanks for warming Flynn up for me, honey, but your days are numbered I guess because, yes, Flynn told me I was the love of his life. Guess he thought you were until he met me."

Tommy chuckled. "Fuck she's hot and ballsy. I'm getting a hard-on just watching this."

Flynn grinned at Tommy. "She's definitely the one. I'm so fucking head-over-heels in love with her."

I smirked at Bernie. "To answer your question, Bernie, I am legal. Flynn waited a long time to make sure of that. And Tyler, I wouldn't pour water on you if your pants were on fire. Which, judging by that little speech you just gave, may end up your reality if you go around fucking other people's sloppy seconds."

I'd had no idea where the last line I told Tyler came from; I think I had heard it in a movie once.

Bernie started laughing, and the guy I'd seen playing rhythm guitar in the band, and who's name had never really stuck, stood up and offered a hand to me.

"Craig Southers, darlin', best-looking guy in the band. Nice to meet you. Flynn, I'm happy for you, dude. You're a beautiful lady, Valerie."

Flynn slipped an arm around my shoulder. "I've been in love with Valerie for a long time. I can't tell you all how happy I am that she's finally in my life for good." He turned and addressed his ex-girlfriend. "Iria, I have no wish to hurt you, but I've been telling you how I felt all this time. Maybe you'll realize I'm not in your future."

Iria shook her head and wandered over to the sofa where the other girl was sitting, and flopped down heavily beside her. "Like hell, you're not. I haven't wasted all this time waiting for you to come to your senses about us, for you to blow me off now. You think I'm going to disappear because she's here?" she said, tipping her chin in my direction. "Bernie, if he doesn't get rid of her, I think this is one for the press?"

Looking up at me with a smug expression, she asked, "Did he tell you I was pregnant?"

"Of course, he did. And you were already when you two got together. We have no secrets from each other," I stated, hoping that was the case.

Tyler walked over to the decanter again and poured himself a generous measure. "Well, fuck, Iria, I've listened to this blackmailing shit since a few months after Major ScAlz was formed. You fuck with my career and it hurts the band, I'll fuck you, and it won't be pleasurable."

Craig slapped his knees and stood up. "Guess we're all going to have a period of adjustment. Iria, go to the press. The public fucking loves Flynn. You think you'll come out of this looking pure? He might keep his mouth shut about the way you've constantly threatened the band with this shit, but I won't. I'm fucking bored with it, and *you* now, so do your worst. We're a rock band, and I think we're established enough now to weather the storm. You never know, it might bring more fans. Flynn's reputation has been boring lately. A newer, younger, hotter girlfriend may just spice it up a bit for them."

Bernie turned to look at Flynn. "You're a selfish prick. Don't you think about anyone but yourself?"

Flynn looked at me, smiled calmly, and looked Bernie square in the eye. "Seems like that's all I've done for over two years now. Val and me —we're fucking doing this. You don't like it, fire me. I'd be happy to walk away. Valerie means that much to me."

Flynn stepped forward and wrapped his arms around me. He placed his forehead intimately on mine, as if we were the only people in the room, and whispered, "You okay? You did great, babe." I smiled at him and nodded. Then he took a sharp breath, stepped back, and turned to face his bandmates.

"So, what's this urgent meeting about? Or are you going to allow Iria to dictate that as well?"

Upon hearing her name, Iria stood and looked at her friend, but she stayed seated and shrugged her shoulders. "Fuck you, too," she screamed. Turning to Flynn, she warned, "Alright, you asked for it. Let's see how your precious little jailbait girlfriend story plays out in the press." Turning to me, she smirked. "What are you smiling about? You haven't heard the last of this either," she warned.

Alarm registered on Flynn's face as he glanced at me. "Did you forget that Jess was Martin's girl? I know all about you hitting on this teeny bopper when she was a sophomore," Iria said, delivering what she thought was the death knell for Flynn.

"He didn't hit on me. My brother Martin may be dead, but Kayden is very much alive, and he will attest to that. What Martin may have told Jess, and what actually happened, are not the same thing. Go for it. All I'll be able to tell the press is you are a jealous, rejected woman, and I feel sorry for you."

I could see the guys in the band staring at Flynn, because the last thing any of them could deal with was Flynn being accused of having sex with an underage girl. Tommy glanced up at Iria with intent in his eyes.

"Do that and I'll personally hunt you the fuck down. I'll see your chronic lung condition suddenly becomes imminently fucking acute when I choke you with my bare hands."

Iria stared open-mouthed, in shock that no one targeted Flynn. "Fuck all of you," she spat, and stomped out the door. When we heard the main house door slam, Bernie turned to Flynn and shook his head. "What a cluster-fuck. Give me your word you never fucked her before she was legal."

"He never touched me like that until a few days ago," I replied, and felt myself flush. I glanced at Flynn, and his eyes immediately softened, like he was sorry I'd been put in that position.

"Sure she's ready for this?" he asked, nodding at me, but didn't allow Flynn an answer. "I damn well hope so because if that bitch opens her mouth, she's going to try to destroy you and the band."

Craig stood and walked over to Flynn and embraced him in a manly hug. "Don't worry, Flynn, I got your back. I've seen how she's manipulated you and how you've tolerated her for the sake of the band. These two fuckers?" he waved his finger between Tommy and Tyler, "They'll get your back too if they don't want to go back to playing in deadbeat bars, because unlike them, I know where the talent in this band lies."

Flynn took my hand and pulled me around to sit on the sofa beside him. "I never got with Valerie to piss anyone off. I've loved her since she was fifteen. The first time I saw her, I knew I had to stay away because of the feelings she stirred inside me. I never touched her other than an innocent peck on the lips. I'd never have taken advantage of her that way."

Flynn flashed me a warm smile and looked back at Bernie. "She was a few weeks away from her sixteenth birthday, and had my visit been a few weeks later, I may well have had a whole different life. I got with Iria to help me forget Valerie, but as you can see, it didn't work. I stayed away from Val to do the right thing by her brother, and her at the time, but when she called me a few days ago, I couldn't stay away any longer."

Bernie nodded his head. "But fuck, Flynn, look how young she is. She's gonna be eaten alive by the press. This isn't good for the band's image."

Flynn was about to speak, and I put my hand up. "*She* has a name, Bernie. It's Valerie, and why are you talking about me like I'm not here? Let me tell you something about being young. I've been around boys my whole life. I know how they think ... mainly with their cocks, and I'm not a fool. My brothers died around two and a half years ago. Two brothers—one accident. Who came to me in my time of grief? He did." I pointed at Flynn and placed my hand on his knee.

"I had all these feelings for him, but he left me because he wanted to do the right thing. I know that now, but at the time I hated him. There's strength in hate. It brings determination and drive. I believe it's because of Flynn I've got my own business. I know reputations can make or break business ventures. Believe me when I tell you I'm a business woman. I'm more than capable of dealing with people in your line of work, especially if they are narrow-minded like all of you. None of you intimidate or scare me, and despite how I look, I'm no pushover."

Flynn turned and grinned widely, with pride in his eyes for me having put them in their place. "You tell 'em, babe. People need to think twice before they fuck with you."

Bernie snickered and mimicked, "Business woman," widening his eyes and mocking me to the rest of the band. Tommy and Tyler chuckled, so I put them in their place.

"Tell me, Bernie, I know it's Flynn who writes the music and lyrics for Major ScAlz. If he walked tomorrow, what income would you have from your investment in them?" When he said nothing, I continued.

"My line of business is digital photography, mainly some video trailer work and a few other small irons in the fire. I've been building my business since around the time your band hit the airwaves. The difference between you and me is that my business will continue to make me money no matter what. I know how to promote and market. The pictures I've taken bring regular income with each download. If I never took another picture, I'd still make money. I'm eighteen, but many people have lived and died and not had the life experience I'm bringing into my relationship with Flynn."

Flynn hugged me and stroked my hair, then turned back to the guys. "This lady is financially independent and has talent in her own right. More importantly, she's everything to me. So, you know how we began, and how we feel. Valerie is it for me, guys. Take her or leave me. I know she'd never come between the band, and up til now, I've always done my job, and ignored all the shit that comes along with working with you guys. But, if any of you try to come between us, I'll fuck you up so badly you'll wish you were dead. Understand?"

Tyler sat and ran his arm across the back of the chair opposite us. "So, is she gonna be in on everything, or does she become a stay-at-home kinda relationship?"

"Oh, she's with me all the way. Val has a business, and I think, given time, we could use her in our crew, but that would be her call. Like Bernie said, she's a young woman, but she has a mind of her own. I want her to do what makes her happy, but I want her with me."

Bernie raised an eyebrow. "What exactly does running your business entail?"

"Like I said, I'm a photographer."

"So, you take pictures? Of what? Portraits and stuff?"

Flynn snickered and bumped my shoulder. "Nah, I watched a session, and Valerie is one talented woman. It's ... art. The images on her laptop are some of the hottest I've ever seen. People pay a small fortune for her stock pictures, and much more for tailor-made shoots. Maybe we'll share them with you sometime."

I felt my face redden, and I mumbled, "Not if you want to keep your balls, Flynn Docherty."

Flynn and the rest of the band chuckled, and he moved the conversation forward. "So, what's the urgent meeting about? It can't be that much of an emergency when we've spent nearly an hour talking about my love life."

"The guys already know, but I couldn't get a hold of you. The new tour starts October sixth. Stateside for four weeks and Europe for three weeks, back-to-back dates. Organize your shit. Rehearsals start tomorrow at ten sharp." Bernie sounded very authoritative, and I noted that no one questioned him. Once they had all aired their individual gripes and demands, the meeting was over.

Strangely enough, there was no interaction between the band members afterward. Tommy stood and gestured at the girl sitting on the far sofa. "Come on, babe, I need to get out of here."

Bernie nodded at her in acknowledgment as she was leaving. "Take care of him, Clemi, no heavy shit this week. He's on the road next week. Keep him clean. He's gotta be race-ready for the tour."

The undertone in Bernie's voice made Tommy growl, and he'd strode toward the door. "Fuck you, Bernie, that was twice, and over a year ago. I'm clean these days. Let's get the fuck out of here, Clemi. See you guys at ten tomorrow," he said flatly.

Chapter Twenty-Nine

OLD MOVIE STAR

*L*eaving Bernie's house was a relief. I drew in a deep lungful of air. Once I'd witnessed the hostility from the interactions between the band members, it was clear a couple of them were jealous of Flynn. At least I knew who his ally was. Craig seemed to have his back and had been the most open to him being happy. Tommy was hard to get a handle on, but Bernie and Tyler were definitely on my "watch list."

When I saw how they aired their differences, I had a better idea of the issues I would likely face. Tyler was a meddler. I could see him creating havoc for us, given the right circumstances. Tommy was weak. Bernie was difficult to assess because he should have been trying to keep Flynn happy, but that didn't come across at all, and I knew he didn't want me around.

Flynn's band had firm dates, and we'd been driven back to Flynn's place. I wondered why the guy with the SUV was at Flynn's beck and call, then remembered that his car was being shipped back from my parent's place. Something Bernie said came back to me.

"He called you Errol?"

Flynn shook his head. "Yeah, he thinks it's funny to call me after the old movie actor, Errol Flynn."

I smirked, and he smiled back, rolling his eyes, and turned to look ahead. His face changed, and I followed his gaze to see what was wrong. News must have gotten out that Flynn was in town, because when we'd arrived at the entrance in front of his house, there were a few dozen girls around my age, waiting. Some had stuck love notes for him on the solid, high, black-enamel painted gates.

When I saw how desperate some of the girls were, it highlighted the temptations open to Flynn. It made be a bit nervous. I didn't get much time to dwell on my feelings, because a few began to bang on the window, and my heart almost stopped in fear. Although the SUV we were in had black-out windows, it was terrifying. I felt worried for all of us, but mostly for Flynn. I was certain if they'd managed to get into the car, they'd have pulled him apart.

One love-crazed fan stood in front of the gates, looking slightly dazed, until she suddenly slapped her hands on the hood and began screaming hysterically about how much she loved Flynn. Another climbed on the car and pushed her face hard up against the window, cupping her eyes with her hands as she tried to catch a glimpse of him. The driver of the car cursed and tried to wave at her through the window to get off.

Initially, I thought Lee was going to get out and move her, but he shifted in his seat and pulled out his cell instead. I wondered if he was calling the police, but when whoever it was picked up, he simply said, "Top gate."

Less than a minute later, a navy blue Land Rover turned up, and two huge, menacing-looking guys jumped out. One ran around the back and pulled a German shepherd dog out of the back door of the vehicle. The presence of the dog made them effective in moving the fans back to a safe distance. They kept them there with the dog's help, as it barked and bounced, straining viciously against the leash. As soon as it was safe enough, Lee opened the gate and we drove through. The gates closed firmly behind us, and I sighed with relief.

When the car reached Flynn's front door, Lee and the driver got out. Flynn and I were left behind. The doors of the car locked with us still inside, and they walked in the direction of the house. Staring out the window, I'd been about to ask Flynn what they were doing, when he offered an explanation. "They're just checking around the house before we go inside, babe, not that anyone will be there. It's just the routine they've developed to ensure I'm never put at any unnecessary risk."

I nodded, wondering what a *necessary risk* was, but felt uneasy that being with Flynn meant being dependent on other people to keep us safe. Lee reappeared and walked briskly in our direction, pointing the automatic-locking key fob at the door.

"Clear," he declared, his voice muted by the window as the doors clicked open. Flynn slid along the seat, and I quietly followed. It was only when I was finally inside the house that I released the heavy breath that had been almost bursting my lungs. "Jeez, that was a little intense," I stated. Well, that was an understatement.

"You'll get used to it, babe. It's only a couple of minutes every now and then. They don't mean me harm, and for the majority of them, if I pretended to take them up on some of the crazy offers they call out to me, they'd faint or die of embarrassment," he said, making light of the tense situation we'd just experienced.

Lee reappeared from upstairs. "All clear on the top deck, boss. I'll make myself scarce," he informed us. Lee wandered over to a box by the front door. He flipped it open and keyed in a sequence of numbers, closed the door, and lifted a hand farewell before heading down a corridor off the hallway.

"You'll hear a series of beeps around eight in the morning. Don't be worried, Valerie. That'll only be Niamh. If you hear the alarm at any other time, there's a panic room at the back of my bathroom."

I became apprehensive by all the talk about security. *A panic room?* It also made me realize the risks Flynn had taken when he dropped everything the second I had called him. He hadn't given his safety a moment's thought, apart from his comments about focusing on the road to come to me.

Flynn wandered into the kitchen and I followed behind him. He pulled the fridge door open and retrieved something that looked like small meat pies and some plastic containers.

"Hungry? I'm just going to put these in the oven for ten minutes.

Niamh makes amazing Chinese dim sum. Grab some plates from that cabinet over there and some silverware from that drawer."

As I followed his lead, I'd marveled at how at ease he was with *us*. On one hand, we hardly knew each other. He'd lived in a world I had very little idea about, yet I felt Flynn knew me better than anyone else ever had. He'd seen something in me that had held his attention. That was a difficult concept to manage in my head.

Millions of women idolized Flynn the rock star, and I struggled to understand what his fascination was with me. I was Valerie, the little country girl who wasn't very worldly. Yet he'd picked me, with all my baggage.

From my point of view, Flynn was the only man who had struck me from the moment I'd met him. He'd been there at the most difficult times in my young life. I believed I had faced the most horrid experiences life could throw at me. So, as scared as I was, I was prepared to take risks that would have petrified most other girls.

Strong hands wrapped around my waist as I stood with the plates. I placed them on the countertop, just as Flynn's arms tightened and pulled me back against him. I leaned back, trusting him to take my weight, as his mouth dipped to the crook of my neck. His hands and mouth touched me, and my heart rate spiked. Excitement flooded my body. When his lips met with my skin, another rash of goose bumps ensued. He pressed his hand on my belly, pulled me back, and my lower back hit his hard bulge.

A growl of arousal tore from his throat and he whispered, "You're like a drug, babe. I'm having a helluva hard time controlling myself around you."

I turned and slid my hands around his waist, then slipped them under the hem of his t-shirt. Skimming my palms over his soft, warm, silky skin made him shiver. Goosebumps covered his skin, and he moaned into my neck.

His warm mouth came close to my ear again, and his voice sounded thick with lust. "I'm glad you were a virgin, Valerie. It's made me take a look at myself. Going slowly feels torturous right now, but the anticipation of the fun we're going to have when you're comfortable with sex is going to be off the charts. I can't wait to teach you."

I pushed away from him, and our eyes met. Wanton desire reflected in the smoldering look he gave me. His dilated pupils stared intently into mine, and my heart fluttered. I'd had no doubt in that moment that this man was serious about me.

"What if we do this, and you get bored with me?" I asked with genuine concern.

Reaching down, Flynn took my hand and placed it over his heart.

"Feel that? It runs about twenty beats faster every time you're near me. And it's done that since the first time I met you. That's true chemistry, Valerie. Nothing else has ever given me that kind of rush. You're putting my normal heart rate out of whack. Being on stage in front of thousands of people is the only other thing that's ever come close to that kind of rush."

Flynn went over to the oven and turned the heat off. Opening the door, he took the hot snacks and placed them on the plate, poured the sauces down each side, and placed the tray in the sink. "Suddenly, I'm not hungry," he said with a smirk. He leaned in and kissed me lightly on the lips, as he pushed the plate away and lifted me onto the counter.

My heart fluttered with excitement when he pushed my legs apart and nestled himself between them. "Actually, strike that. I'm starving, but not for food," he said huskily, his voice thick with frustration and need.

Excitement at his loaded statement made me wet. My loins ached for his touch. I grabbed his shoulders to pull his upper body closer. Flynn's big hands gripped tightly on my upper arms as he pushed me down on the countertop.

The plate of food went crashing to the floor, but it appeared to have barely registered with him, he was so focused on feeling more of me against him. My fingers curled around his hair, and I grabbed it tight, pulling his face even closer to mine. He broke the kiss and growled again, straightening up and taking me with him.

He slid his hands under my butt and pulled me flush against him, wrapping my legs around his waist. I was pressed firmly against him. He grew harder against me, and I instantly curled my arms around his shoulders and leaned down to kiss his warm neck.

Once again, his intoxicating scent filled my nostrils. I buried my face in his neck and inhaled deeply as he carried me upstairs. I couldn't believe everything that was happening was real. Flynn Docherty had come to my rescue when I'd called, and what had followed with us was way beyond my expectations.

Reaching his bedroom, Flynn flicked on the light and strode over to the bed. His hands gripped my hips and kneaded my flesh with urgency.

"We've got too many clothes on. Get them off, babe. I gotta get naked with you."

I glanced at him and smiled speechlessly. His expression was serious, his eyelids heavy with lust.

Flynn slid me down the front of his body to place my feet on the floor beside the bed, and I felt every inch of his thick, hard cock through the rough material of his jeans. It was then I recognized how empty I was without him inside.

When I reached the floor, his hand wound around my hair, and he pulled my mouth roughly against his. His tongue sought mine and tangled around it, and when he broke the kiss, he stepped away and muttered, "Fuck, sooo fucking sexy. You are the most beautiful woman I've ever been with, Valerie."

He stood, drinking me in. His chest rose and fell as his ragged breaths became shallow and labored. I had no idea how I could have that effect on him. "I doubt that, Flynn, but you're definitely the most beautiful man I've ever been with."

He chuckled as he unbuckled his belt, the buckle clinking gently with the movement of it falling open. "As I'm the only man you've ever been with, I'm going to have to work to keep that title. The competition out there is fierce for a girl like you," he stated, as he started to push his jeans over his hips.

Hearing his flattery and the way he never took his eyes off me while I'd begun to undress, swelled my confidence, but my eighteen-year-old mind felt a bit scared that being in a relationship with someone like Flynn could end as quickly as we'd started.

He stepped out of his jeans and tugged his t-shirt over his head, throwing them onto a pile on the floor. He kicked them out of his way.

I'd only gotten as far as taking my t-shirt off when he swiped my hands away, too impatient to wait for me and the pace I was setting.

"Let me do it," he said with a renewed urgency. His eye raked over my bra-clad breasts as his hands slid to my jeans' button. Unfastening them, he quickly tugged them down my legs and pushed me urgently back onto the bed. Excitement burst through me. The speed and the slightly rough way he handled me took me by surprise.

"Fuck, Valerie." His raspy tone sounded almost as if he were in pain. He focused completely on my skin as his hands gently trailed down from my shoulders to my breasts. Flynn pushed my legs wide and crawled between them until he'd covered my body with his. His cock felt rock solid, the tip damp against my belly. He took hold of my wrists that were already placed above my head.

"You know I can't wait until you're ready for me. I'm going to ride you for hours."

I chuckled. "Yeah? And then what?"

"Then, I'm going to lick you until every fucking nerve in your body tingles at my touch. I'll bring you to the point of orgasm, but I won't take you over the edge. It's called edging. I can't wait to watch you in that state."

"Sounds like torture," I said with a sexy smirk. "Well, for you maybe. For me - I'll be so fucking wired - knowing I can capture your whole body like that. Watching you buzz in anticipation until I want you to come. It will be awesome to watch you like that, and when you do come, you'll feel like your brain is at the point of melting."

"So, you want to control me?"

"Fuck no, Valerie. I want to *own* you. Mark you. Brand you, ruin you for anyone else. Just thinking about all the things I want to do to you, *with* you, to give you pleasure, sets me on fire. There's a riot going on in my mind because of the chemistry I feel with you. Your innocence is like having a blank canvas to work with. I'm not trying to control you, Valerie. I'm trying hard to control myself."

Flynn swallowed hard, and as his gaze grew intense. I had no doubt he meant every word.

"What happens when you've done all of that? What happens once you've ruined me? What am I to expect after that happens?"

"You'll never be able to accept anything less than us, babe. That's what I want to achieve."

"Sounds good, but what happens if things go bad between us, Flynn?"

"That's never going to happen."

Joy bubbled up from my belly and circled my heart. I knew I was already in love with Flynn. I was thrilled at his words, but I was young, and I worried his band and his lifestyle might make that a reality.

There was no time to dwell on that because my body came alive in his hands again. I was carried along a wave of ecstasy, as his mouth and hands pleasured every inch of my body. Soft, feathery kisses and more possessive, hungry ones gave me an array of feelings I could never have imagined possible until that night.

One hand pinned my wrists to the mattress while the fingers of another sifted through my long hair before he twisted it into his fist. Applying just enough tension, he spiked excitement in me that left me breathless. I was on the verge of begging for more. Flynn was a good teacher, and I was already becoming a willing student.

Chapter Thirty

BURN

A stretch of silence passed between us as I stared up at Flynn's handsome face. A lump formed in my throat when I thought about how much progress we'd made since the first time I'd set eyes on him. What we'd just shared was intense, now magnified by our lack of words.

Lying naked together stripped everything away, not just our clothing. The man with the beautiful face had a beautiful heart as well, and he cared about me. To think that someone like him dropped everything and came running for me when I asked, made me feel giddy. I was in Flynn's bed, not because he was a rock star and it was his right of passage, but because he wanted *me* to be with him.

Flynn gave me a slow smile and licked his lips before kissing me softly again. His mouth trailed from mine, down my neck, then over my breasts as my body quivered and hummed against his palms and lips. When he reached my mound, he stretched my legs one at a time, kissing from my insteps to my calves, then behind my knees, before bending them and pushing them widely apart. My body quaked in anticipation.

Within seconds, his mouth worked with a hunger and passion that had me catching my breath. My chest rose and fell in ever increasing shallow breaths until his tongue flicked, sucked, poked, and pleasured my sensitive skin. My body wound tight as I peaked, and I anticipated my release. Lifting my hips off the bed, I tried to get more contact. Flynn held himself short of delivering the right amount of pressure to push me over the edge. He stopped what he was doing and lifted his head. I grunted my disapproval, and he chuckled. His lack of pressure had been deliberate.

"Now you know how it feels. Not nice being teased to the point of explosion without the detonation, is it?"

"Please, Flynn," I pleaded. Instead of laughing again, I watched the smile fall from his face, and a dark, carnal expression took over. He turned and stretched over to his bedside cabinet. "Ahh, I think I'll be nice since you begged so sweetly."

Initially, I looked puzzled and then realized I had *begged him* to let me come. Flynn took a condom out of the bedside drawer and expertly pulled it up over the wide head of his cock. Two fingers of his left hand skimmed the length of my crease and began to play around my entrance. His thumb found my clit and he started to massage it while he teased and stretched me with his fingers. He kissed me, and I could taste myself on his lips. I moaned softly into his mouth.

Breaking the kiss, Flynn pulled himself onto his knees in front of me. Taking my legs, he pulled me up over his thighs. He stroked my wetness with his cock, and I became more aroused by his touch. I wriggled closer.

"Fuck, I have to have you, babe. I can't wait any longer." I muttered something about being gentle with me, and he chuckled. "Damn, Valerie, I'm trying. I'd have fucked you twice since we got home if I wasn't focusing on going *slow*," he husked playfully. His tone was heavy with desire. Suddenly, he was all over me, placing his forehead on mine. His body steeled, and I knew he was about to enter me.

"Watch me, Valerie. Don't close your eyes. I want to see you when I take you. I want you to see how you affect me when our bodies become one." My heart squeezed, because I felt no man would say that to a woman unless he was truly giving himself to her, emotionally and physically, not just having sex with her.

Eyeing each other with an intensity that gave significance to what we were to each other, he began to push forward and tried to ease himself inside. The same burning sensation I'd had the day before, flooded my body. Every inch of his cock he added, stretched my inner walls beyond what I'd thought was their limit. After a few steady thrusts, he sank deep to his root and a cry tore from my throat at the initial discomfort I endured.

Flynn stilled his hips and stroked my hair, soothing me as his arms cocooned my head. Placing his forehead on mine, I felt his ragged breath as he fought for control. His eyes softened when his face filled with concern. "I'm so sorry, baby. Once we get past this, it'll feel so good you'll forget everything except the thrill of what I'm doing to you," he whispered encouragingly.

Gently his hips began a slow, rocking motion. It was only a tiny movement inside my tight space but, with each stroke, I felt the pain lessen. "God, I love you so fucking much, Valerie," he whispered softly, as he peppered small kisses over my face.

When I winced a few times, he stopped. When he kissed my pain away, his care and patience made everything better. I began to absorb what he was doing and after a short time, I relaxed and it began to feel great. My hips moved involuntarily to match Flynn's and minutes after that, he was moving freely within me. The uncomfortable feeling from before was forgotten.

Pain gave way to pleasure and my mind gradually drifted away and stopped thinking, and I began to ... feel. This man was reading my body, responding to the sounds I made, and I lost myself to the sensation of Flynn making love to me.

A few more minutes and I knew I was going to come. My legs began to shake as his pace accelerated, and I could barely concentrate on the sensations invading my body. My sounds became soft moans of pleasure, and my core tightened as my inner walls clamped down around him. "Holy fuck, Valerie."

Bright white lights burst into vivid colors behind my eyelids as a feeling of euphoria washed over me and began to sweep me away. Flynn's breathing became hurried as he whispered, "Open your eyes, Valerie. Let me see you."

Forcing my eyes open, I found his intense gaze focused on mine. A smile spread across his stunning face. "So, beautiful," he murmured, as he continued to gently rock me through the aftershocks of my orgasm. Before long, he had worked up my desire again, and he began to fuck me, again. At first, it was steady, then it became coarser, more carnal and urgent. Flynn was soon thrusting longer and deeper as raw passion and tension consumed his frame.

"This feels so fucking good. You're gripping me perfectly, babe." The effect of Flynn's punishing pace felt like heaven as he gave into satisfying his needs. A few strokes later, and without warning, I started to come. At the same time, he tensed and went rigid as his own release erupted inside the condom. His cock pulsed as I milked the last of his come. Flynn growled and buried his face in my neck. His breathing was ragged as his body shook on top of me.

Seconds later, he lifted his head and I noted his forehead beaded with sweat. He rolled over like dead weight onto the other side of the mattress and grabbed my waist tightly, pulling my body into his.

"Holy fuck, Val. You're going to kill me. I normally last a lot longer than this, but your body gets me riled up in minutes." He moved away and removed the condom, wrapping it in tissue from the bedside table. I rolled over to face him. I still ached, but it wasn't nearly as intense as the day before. I draped my leg over his hip, and he cradled my foot in his hand. "I love you, Flynn," I stated. When he looked down at me, his bright, peaceful eyes creased at the corners as his smile reached them.

"We've waited a long time to say that to each other, yeah?" his words were like a match being struck across my chest. A wave of emotion ran through me again, and tears sprang to my eyes. One fell, and he quickly caught it on his lips. "Don't cry, babe, we're gonna be fine. Whatever happens, remember, I love you. You do that, and no one can touch us. No matter what shit they say. You want to hear the truth about any situation, I swear I'll be honest with you. Even if it isn't what you want to hear. I promise you."

Flynn hugged me to his chest. His smell, touch, and the feel of him brought me peace. The sound of his strong beating heart consumed me, and even though there should have been many hesitations for me to accept what he said to me, I believed in him.

I don't remember falling asleep, but like Flynn had warned me, I woke to the sound of the house alarm. Flynn mumbled something and rolled over, his arm scooping my body into his. Instantly, his long, erect cock was hard against the crease of my butt and lower back.

"That's a great cock rest you've got there," I commented. He chuckled as his length sat cradled between my cheeks. I giggled, and he pressed himself closer. My entire body shivered and I wiggled backward.

"Fuck, Valerie, I can't get enough of you," he exclaimed. Then his desire took over and he pulled me over him and made love to me again.

An hour later, he was kissing my face. I passed out after the vigorous workout he'd given me. I'd come three times that morning, and I was wrecked. I could have stayed in bed all day after that, but Flynn was set on taking me with him to watch the band rehearse.

Once I started moving, I was excited about that, and twenty-five minutes after rolling out of bed, we were showered and dressed. Lee was waiting in the kitchen. As soon as Niamh saw us, she whipped up scrambled eggs and toast within minutes.

A car arrived and took us to his rehearsal, and at 10:04 we walked into the studio at Bernie's place.

"You're late," Bernie barked.

"I'm here," Flynn countered. Both were Alphas in their environment, even if Flynn didn't really demonstrate that. He was measured and calculating, but not in a bad way.

The rest of the band members were still tuning their instruments, and I'd seen no reason for Bernie's curt greeting. Flynn wandered over and picked up a black and silver guitar and began to tune it. In less than a minute, he stopped and wandered over to a small fridge that contained water and sodas, and Tommy joined him.

"No wonder you're late. I wouldn't have turned up if I'd had that to play with," he said, cocking his head in my direction and leering again.

Flynn's expression turned angry. "That's my girl you're talking about. Show her some fucking respect, dude." Flynn slammed the fridge door closed and walked back to the mic. "Apologize or we're not fucking staying." He swigged some water from the bottle and laid it down beside the metal stand.

Tommy raised an eyebrow and shrugged. "Sorry, Valerie," he said in a singsong voice.

"Thinking in Black and White," Flynn stated, without acknowledging the rest of the guys.

Craig's foot tapped on a metal peddle on the floor and struck the first chord. Flynn joined in, playing the intro to the song. A loud, complex guitar riff filled the room and resonated in my chest. My heartbeat soared with excitement when I heard the full effect of their music live in a relatively small space for the first time. It was ten times better than seeing them perform on TV.

Flynn began to sing and time stood still. I feasted my attention on the face of the man I loved and enjoyed this side of his talent. I'd never seen him play live before. I felt behind me for the chair, unable to take my eyes off him. He captivated me from the first line. I had a good idea what his professors meant once I'd heard him. He was an incredible musician and singer, and they were right—he was a rock star. His voice made the hair on the back of my neck stand up while his music touched something deep inside.

I'd never been to a live gig before, and I only realized while he was playing how far he'd come. He'd progressed from someone who was afraid to share his talent with a few friends, to someone who confidently stood up in front of thousands and entertained them for hours.

That change had happened for him in the space of a few months. Two years later, he was a worldwide phenomenon, and yet, my crush had somehow managed to stay grounded, despite what the media reported.

After a while, the photographer in me began to look at them from an image perspective. They were all very handsome men. Even so, Flynn's fabulous appearance made the rest of them look kind of ordinary. The way he dressed, moved, and sounded was completely enthralling. I wished I'd had one of my cameras with me to capture the scene in front of me. A few minutes later, that thought was forgotten as my mind became consumed by their music. I didn't see anyone else except Flynn.

Watching his movements, I eventually focused on his eyes and saw he was staring straight at me. Every word he was singing seemed directed at me. Listening to the words of the song I'd heard hundreds of times before on the radio, it seemed completely different with him right there, ten feet away.

The rock composition sounded kind of chaotic. It was about a guy who couldn't have what he wanted, and he felt he was making do with less in life. It wasn't until the last line before the bridge that it dawned on me ... the song may have been about us.

I've been thinking in black and white
Since I had to walk away
Color faded from my soul that night
Everything from then has been gray
And babe it's been shredding at my heart
Every day that we've been apart,
So young, too pure 'n I've settled for dreaming in color.

If you saw me, would you know me? Would you even wanna?
If you could would you trust me, would you touch me? Would you
even wanna?
And if you smiled and I smiled back at the start
Would you let me take your heart and make it mine?

My heart raced. I'd heard that song hundreds of times but never once connected the words in the way I did in that moment. Not only had Flynn been thinking about me all this time, he'd been writing about his feelings and sharing them with the world. My heart flipped over when I stared back at him. He smiled shyly when he saw tears roll down my face, and I smiled back adoringly when I made the connection.

I became overwhelmed with emotion, my throat burned as I swallowed harshly and suddenly I understood how hard it had been for Flynn to walk away from me that day.

Two hours later, I'd witnessed many heated arguments and minor disagreements about set order, arrangements, and anything Tyler could find to challenge, really. His presence in the group was the most fractious, and I found myself becoming annoyed at his constant snide remarks, especially toward Flynn. I was impressed with Flynn's quick and clever responses to Tyler, because all he achieved with each dumb remark was to make himself look stupid, childish, or envious of Flynn's position in the group.

At one point, I tried to sympathize with him, thinking it must be difficult to be as talented as he was and not be the center of attention. However, after the fourth ridiculous comment, I'd been completely turned off from offering any kind thoughts toward the man.

By the time they finished rehearsal, I was a total fan of the band and their music, but not of the people in the band. Tommy was smart-mouthed and crude, Tyler behaved like a jealous brat, and Bernie just seemed to tolerate Flynn. Craig was quiet and seemed easy going. Apart from Flynn, he was the only one I felt comfortable with.

Placing his guitar on the stand, Flynn strode toward me, grinning. "All set, babe? Let me get you out of here. The air's stale," he commented. Tyler and Bernie were standing over at the opposite side of the room. Tyler called out, "Don't be late Wednesday. Set your alarm earlier if you have to tap that before you get here."

Flynn's expression turned stormy in a flash. His brow furrowed as his shoulders rose as he strode aggressively across the room. "You want to keep that smart mouth from being busted, I suggest you apologize to my girl."

It was the second time Flynn had challenged them about me, and I could defend myself. I made a note to talk to him.

Bernie snickered. "You should remember what I told you in the beginning, Flynn. Women don't come between band members, no matter how good the pussy is."

Pushing his chest into Bernie, Flynn backed him against the wall. "Is that right? How fucking dare you two talk like that in front of Valerie. That's my girlfriend you're both referring to, not some piece of fresh meat Tyler or Tommy has collected along the way. Half of our fucking album has been inspired by that girl over there. You've become rich because of my feelings for her. So watch your fucking mouth, and apologize right now, or I'm not fucking coming at all on Wednesday."

Watching Flynn lash out at them made my stomach turn. I'd never seen him so mad. The fact that he'd defended me and put his band member and manager in their place made me scared for him. I was worried how they'd respond.

Craig stepped up beside Flynn and shook his head at Bernie. "You really are a shitty manager, you know that? When are you gonna learn that this fucker here isn't the band," he said, gesturing at Tyler. "Tyler, you really need to go to a rehab clinic, and while you're at it, get that fucking attitude adjusted because if you don't, you'll be the death of Major ScAlz. I have no idea why Flynn puts up with the shit he takes from all of you, but I'm saying it now. Apologize to Valerie. She's making our main dude happy. She's doing your fucking job for you, Bernie."

Bernie glanced over at me and back at Flynn. "Fuck. Sorry, Valerie. Happy now?" he said insincerely to Flynn and me.

Turning away from Bernie, Flynn gestured me over to him with his open hand. "Come on, Valerie, let's get the fuck out of here."

As I came alongside him, Flynn turned to Bernie. "Friday. I'm not coming back until you apologize properly, and Val and I aren't open for apologies until Thursday," he growled. Looking down at me, Flynn smiled. "Looks like we have a couple of days to sort out some of those appointments of yours, Valerie."

Chapter Thirty-One

SCANDAL

*T*rue to his word, Flynn made the band wait until Friday before showing his face for rehearsals. Bernie tried everything, from threatening, to pleading with him to show his face at the scheduled time. He didn't. Instead, he chartered a plane. We flew to my parents' home so I could deal with some business. It was weird, the big rock star coming with me to help me with my work issues.

I rearranged what I could and passed some other work to a guy I knew a couple of towns away, who worked in a similar style to me. I'd already decided I'd probably try to do some shots on tour while Flynn rehearsed in various cities. All I had to do was contact some model agencies and rent studio space or locations.

By Thursday night, I was on my way back to Chicago with him. My parents had been quite vocal about me going on tour with a band. The fact it was Flynn's hadn't seemed to make much difference. "Alcohol, drugs, and debauchery aren't what I want for my daughter's life," my dad had told Flynn.

Somehow Flynn had remained calm and talked my parents into letting me go. We were out the door before they'd had too much longer to think about it. Not that it would have made much difference.

Once I'd made my mind up about something, it was difficult to persuade me otherwise. But they already knew that.

Touching down in Chicago late that night, Flynn's cell rang as soon as he switched it on. His band's PR team warned him Iria had called in the big guns and had kept her word about going to the press. She'd spun a story so sensational that most of the tabloid newspapers around the world were leading with it. Everyone had been calling the PR team while we were in the air, for comment. When Flynn hadn't been readily available, their stock response had been, "No comment."

Flynn's face was tight as he listened to the feedback, his eyes darting back and forth between me and Lee, who checked his own phone when he sensed something was wrong. Lee found the story they were running online and read it to us.

"Bullshit. Get my legal team," he hissed and punched the seat of the car in frustration. It made me jump, and Flynn pulled me to his chest and kissed my head. "Sorry, babe. I'll fix this, don't worry."

Why was it whenever someone said that to me, I worried?

"They're already on it, boss. I've got an email about it here. I can't take you home. The paps are fucking everywhere. Found a couple of them in the grounds near Niamh's place, they said."

When I heard the paparazzi were hounding us, it worried me even more.

"Shit, get Niamh and Teague out of there for a while."

"Already done, boss. Hired a place for them next to mine, doing stuff as we speak," he said, continuing to study his cell.

"I'm taking you to my place in Lincoln Park. No one knows I have it. It's in my sister's name, an investment I started for her a while back, for her to take over when she becomes an adult," Lee commented.

Forty minutes later, we passed Lake Michigan on our way to our hideout, until Flynn had time to digest the story. Lee drove us to an underground garage and ensured we weren't seen entering the apartment.

The spacious, two-bedroom apartment with polished wooden floors was a beautiful living area. Apart from the living room, there was a kitchen, bedroom, and bathroom downstairs, and a metal spiral staircase leading up to a mezzanine bedroom upstairs. It was adequate, but a world away from the luxurious surroundings Flynn was accustomed to. Lee threw the keys on the table. It was only then I realized it was his intention to stay with us.

For over an hour, I sat, listening to Flynn argue his point of view to his lawyers. He told them he wasn't going to feed into Iria's mental state with denials about anything. His direction to his legal team and PR guy Logan, was to ask the press to prove he was the father of Iria's miscarried baby, or to retract their statement and apologize. He said if they hadn't done so in the following twenty-four hours, he'd instructed his lawyers to sue every one of those who hadn't, for libel.

It was a long night of forced and tensed words as, one by one, the band members called Flynn. Bernie was the last. The phone call between Flynn and him got so heated I jumped at the tone Flynn used with him. It was clear Bernie was not going to support us through the lies Iria had told, and he was more interested in self-preservation. He commented on the phone that he was being tainted by Flynn's reputation because he'd been the one to give the spot in the band to Flynn in the first place.

"Don't be so fucking ridiculous," Flynn spat, "We told you how it was. You'd rather distance yourself from me and let a jealous and deceitful woman, your friend's daughter I might add, control my life than stick up for the truth? What does her dad have over you, Bernie?" When he didn't answer, Flynn lost it. "Well, fuck you, Bernie. As soon as the dust settles on this, I think we need to be parting ways. I'd rather be a fucking wedding singer than make you another dime."

Tyler was a total jerk and implied that Flynn was no better than a child molester, which had Flynn almost out the door to find him, his rage was so out of control. It was a living nightmare, and the more I heard, the worse I felt for Flynn.

A few hours later, I slipped into the bathroom, unable to keep my emotions in check any longer. Tears ran freely down my face as I tried to comprehend why this was happening when I felt at my happiest. I sobbed quietly into a towel, because I felt partly responsible for the position Flynn was in, but I didn't want him to hear me.

I must have been in the bathroom too long because Flynn came looking for me. When he saw how upset I was, he pulled me close to him. Cradling my head in his hands, he wiped my tears away with his thumbs, his eyes pained at the distress I was in.

"Hey, babe, please don't cry."

I sniffed and glanced up at his beautiful face. He looked so worried.

"I hate that she's doing this to you. To us. Maybe it's payback for having those kinds of thoughts about you when you were so young."

"I was the young one. My thoughts about you were the same. So maybe I was giving you signals without knowing. Maybe it was my fault you felt those things."

"Stop it, Valerie. You weren't that young. And for all your inno-cence, you were mature around boys, from growing up with your brothers. It was a few weeks from your sixteenth birthday, for God's sake. Iria just didn't want to accept that I wasn't interested in her. I tried to love her, and I thought I did at one point, but it was a fast-burning infatuation. Probably rebound feelings after meeting you. Once I got to know her, there was nothing in here and I ended it," Flynn said, pointing at his chest.

It had been difficult to hear him talk about his feelings for Iria. Jealousy gripped my heart and squeezed it like a vice.

"Listen, I'm not standing for this. I have no idea what she thought this would do for her. We've got to face this head on. Hold our heads up, Valerie. I think we should just go right back at her with this. What do you think? Can you cope with riding this out?"

I was scared but he was right. Hiding away and not commenting only made him look guilty, and we both knew he wasn't.

When the lawyers were informed of Flynn's intentions, they tried to prevent him from going public. He and I argued that there was no need for us to hide, as Flynn was innocent. Once the lawyers knew they weren't going to change his mind, a draft was started of the state-ment we wanted to share with the public.

Flynn was very open about his feelings when he'd met me and the circumstances around that, and stated categorically that no inappro-priate behavior had taken place between us. The first time our rela-tionship had moved onto an adult theme had only been days before, when he'd come to see me this last visit. I called my parents and told them what was happening.

I'd felt mortified that they had to be told we were in a sexual relationship. My mom surprised me by telling me she was shocked that Flynn was my first, as she'd thought Daryl and I had been sexually active. Flynn chuckled at her description.

The lawyers sent Iria warnings that Flynn was going to sue. Meanwhile, Craig had already broken his silence about Iria, calling her a liar. He told the press she'd been emotionally blackmailing Flynn and the band for a long time with these lies. He outright blamed Bernie for being unable to act in the best interests of Flynn, and stated that he was behind Flynn and me one hundred percent.

Interestingly enough, Tommy hadn't commented, and that made me wonder if he was waiting to see what side of the fence he should jump on. When I said that to Flynn, he said I was far smarter than any of them knew. Flynn joked that when the incident had blown over, maybe I should be his manager. Even with everything going on, he'd managed to make me laugh.

When we drove back to his place, the young fangirls had gone, and now there were TV trucks, hundreds of cameras, and the local sheriff and state police had put up barriers to keep the road clear on the way to Flynn's house. We passed them at the top of the road, and Lee drove for another two miles before we arrived at the back gate. There were still news crews and paparazzi, but nowhere near the level that were at the front of the house.

My heart was in my mouth and I felt like I was going to throw up. Every part of my body was tense, but Flynn sat relaxed in the back seat of the SUV with me, and squeezed my hand. "You okay?"

I nodded, and his serious expression softened. His mouth lifted into a small smile. "I guess today's the day we make it official we're a couple, huh?" he teased.

"You sure you don't want to change your mind?" I asked with a little more seriousness than he was probably expecting.

"Never, Valerie. Don't worry, babe, give this a week, and all this shit in the newspapers will go away. It may take some people a lot longer to fully accept we're together, but eventually, they'll leave us alone. Well, they'll leave me alone, but they'll start asking what the fuck you see in me," he said, and smirked.

Once inside, Flynn took the stairs two at a time to his office. By the time I caught up with him, he was reading a fax. "Listen to this," he said.

"I'm saddened today to have been informed that Iria Santos, my ex-girlfriend, has publicly shown a weaker side to her character. By trying to discredit my new partner Valerie Dansin, and me, she has demonstrated that she has no respect for our previous relationship or my privacy and current relationship with Valerie. Although I don't feel I should have to explain how I know Valarie, I will. Valerie and I have known each other since she was fifteen, five weeks away from her sixteenth birthday, in fact. Valerie was my friend and the sister of my late friend Martin Dansin. Valerie and I have had a long history, as I supported her during the past few years at key times in her life. However, we have only recently reconnected after more than two years, and have become romantically involved. Sometimes one or another partner has difficulty in accepting when a relationship ends. Ms. Santos was indeed having this particular issue long before Valerie and I were connected in any way other than platonic. Still, it is sad for me to realize that someone who'd helped me at the start of my career should wish to spread malicious lies to discredit everything I've worked for since. I'd like to address the issue of paternity on the ill-fated pregnancy Ms. Santos has chosen to discuss. Ms. Santos neglected to divulge, in her carefully worded statement, that the child she miscarried while we were in a relationship, was not mine. I should perhaps clarify that the pregnancy which she had chosen to share with the world was, in fact, from a previous relationship. I had no part in the conception of the miscarried child. What Ms. Santos would have you believe, and what is factual, are poles apart. This is the only statement I will make on this subject, and I will not answer any questions on this matter in the future, because to do so would imply some credibility to the lies Ms. Santos has shared, and indeed, the media has chosen to publish. I have asked for a retraction of these untruths from all parties within the next twenty-four hours. Failure to do this will result in legal action toward any media outlet which has aired these falsehoods. Thank you for your attention."

Once the statement from Flynn went public, there was a flurry of

PR statements issued regarding our wish for privacy, and for the following twenty-four hours, Flynn and his legal team followed the news carefully.

Retractions came thick and fast, but one newspaper seemed to think there was no smoke without fire, and went to my hometown. Heidi, Coleen, and a few others from my high-school days were interviewed, and it felt for a while, our stunt on the bleachers was going to come back and haunt us.

Those interviews could have been damaging for Flynn, except they went to interview Daryl, who stated that I'd cheated on him with Flynn a few days before, which was technically correct because he'd had no idea I'd broken up with him until the following day.

The saving grace for Flynn, when he'd been challenged on our relationship, was when Daisy McGinty came forward and told the press I couldn't have slept with Flynn that week because he'd been with her. The weirdest thought entered my head, and I was suddenly thankful to my late brother for arranging that night out with Flynn to keep him away from me. His protective gesture toward me had given Flynn the perfect cover.

By the time Flynn and I had been together for four whole days, we'd weathered our first official public crisis.

Craig arrived the evening of the final retraction to see Flynn, and I liked his girlfriend Simone straight away. She told me she'd never liked Iria and had often argued with her. Several times, she'd tried to warn her about her hanging on to a relationship that was purely one-sided. Craig said it was the reason Simone had stopped going over to hang out with the band, and stated that he'd also be avoiding them as much as possible.

Flynn turned to Craig and slapped his hand on his back. "We need to have a serious talk, buddy." From the tone of his voice, I knew what he was going to say wasn't good.

"I'm leaving the band," Flynn stated flatly. My jaw almost hit the table.

Craig's eyes flicked to Simone and back to Flynn. "I figured that may happen. You only get one life, dude. I don't blame you. Bernie isn't good for you. If you leave the band, he'll be gutted because, without you, there is no band."

Flynn sat silently for a minute and looked at his bandmate. The expression on Flynn's face told me his decision hadn't been taken lightly. I could tell they cared about each other. Craig looked physically shocked as his reality sank in. He was a good guitar player, but the band wasn't a band without Flynn.

"Don't worry, Craig, where I go you'll go, if you want to, that is?"

Relief washed over Craig's face, and he almost jumped to hug his band brother. "Jesus, you had me going there. Whatever and whenever, I'm with you," he confirmed.

"We're committed to the tour, so we'll see it through, not a word. Understand?"

Craig nodded, and Simone's face brightened. "Thank God, Flynn. You've made my day. I fucking hate those people. We can do the next few months. It was the next few years we were worried about. Craig even talked about walking away. He wouldn't have left you there to deal with them alone, though."

Flynn smiled and hugged her. "And likewise, I'd never have done that to him."

Flynn pulled me tight to his chest. "Just a few more months and we'll be clear of all of them, Valerie. You and Simone just have to stick together and support each other, and when the tour is done, we're all gone, okay?" he asked, rubbing my back.

After Flynn had faced his difficult situation with an amazing amount of dignity, and the humility he'd shown toward Craig, I'd have followed him anywhere.

Chapter Thirty-Two

FIRST CONCERT

The following morning, and for the rest of the rehearsal sessions afterwards, Flynn and Craig had done everything by the book. Both arrived with minutes to spare for practice. They left no time for talking, and barely interacted with the other band members, or their manager.

The promoters took over the organization for the tour, so most of the liaison was through them. Exactly a week after Iria's story broke, I climbed on the tour bus with Flynn, Craig, and Simone for my first tour experience. I was nervous as hell because I knew it wasn't going to be easy living with a bunch of people I hardly knew. And then there were the other guys in the band to deal with.

Or avoid, as it were.

Flynn had insisted we had a bus of our own, and paid for it out of his own pocket from the tour. Craig wasn't as wealthy as Flynn. I was surprised by that, because even although they were in the same band, Flynn earned way more because of the royalties he received for his role as songwriter.

Bernie tried hard to redeem himself with Flynn, but Flynn wasn't having it. Anyone close to them could see their relationship was strained. In public, Flynn was the seasoned professional, who waited patiently while Bernie said his piece, and ignored him completely in private.

By the time opening night arrived, I was excited. I couldn't wait to see Flynn perform live. The band's first stop was Baltimore. We arrived early afternoon and had five hours until show time, so we were taken directly to the venue. I'd never been to a large rock concert before, and the first one Major ScAlz had was at Pier Six Pavilion.

By the time the guys reached the stage, their crew had obviously been working for many hours. Sound checks and positions were walked through, and once they had finished, we were all led backstage through a maze of corridors, to their dressing room.

Long platters of food were placed on white linen-clad tables in the green room, and I realized that I hadn't eaten since breakfast. Simone and I went straight to the table to grab some food. Excitement ran through me at the thought of watching the guys play from the vantage point of where roadies and band members got to enjoy the concert: side stage. While I was eating, Tyler showed up with two girls and disappeared into a room off to the side from where we were sitting.

"Who's that with Tyler?"

"Who cares?" Simone shrugged her shoulders.

When I looked confused, she raised her eyebrow and exhaled in an exasperated sigh. "Groupies, Valerie, they're groupies."

Even though I'd heard about the reputation of bands on tour, I was still shocked at Tyler's blatant behavior. We'd only been there a few hours. Both girls looked about the same age as me, and I felt sick that they were with someone like him. From the way he spoke, he had no respect for himself, never mind anyone else. I had the urge to go and warn them how gross their idol was. It took a heap of mental restraint not to do that.

I had the horrible thought, *What if they are inexperienced?* I shuddered, because if that were the case, I doubted they'd receive the same attention I had with Flynn during my first time.

"Still on the love list this week, I see?" Tommy said, as he came up next to me. Sarcasm distorted his face with the smirk he gave me. I ignored him and continued to fill my plate with food.

"Don't look so smug, honey. See how you feel when you're left out front until we're all done being blown after a gig. They won't let you back here until we're all … nice and relaxed. We'll see who feels so sure of themselves after that."

"Why don't you go fuck off, Tommy. I could use some entertainment," I spat back at him. Tommy rolled his head back, facing the ceiling, and laughed loudly. Flynn instantly turned, in search of me, and left the group he was talking to.

Bending to kiss my ear, he whispered, "Are you okay?"

I nodded and gestured at Tommy. "Tommy was kind enough to remind me what an asshole he is, weren't you, Tommy?"

"Speaking of assholes, did you know your man has a thing for anal? We used to swap notes about the anal rides we'd had on tour. Isn't that right, Flynn?"

"Enough, Tommy, get the fuck away from her."

"Touchy, Flynn, I think I struck a nerve there … or was it a gland?" Tommy said, smirking wickedly.

"No, Flynn, let him talk. He thinks he's embarrassing me. You and I know differently," I replied.

"You think? You have a lot of explaining to do, Flynn," Tommy elaborated, trying to rile us up.

I was thankful for the interruption of Dennis, the PR guy who entered the room at that point. His arrival couldn't have been timelier, because the look on Flynn's face was murderous. Dennis waved a clipboard, and the band members stopped what they were doing and went to listen to what he had to say.

Less than half an hour before they were due on stage, Simone and I were ushered out and led to our seats for the performance. I saw a handwritten roadie sign that said:

Reserved for Band Members' Wives, Girlfriends, and Guests

My heart pumped quicker. It was hard to comprehend that I was one of those chosen few.

Once seated, I shook my head in disbelief as I stared out around the massive auditorium and saw all the tiny heads and bodies that had gathered in one space to see the man I loved. Settling down in the front row nearest the stage, I pulled out two of my cameras. Simone's eyes went wide at my serious hardware. "Oh God, Flynn has his own personal paparazzi," she said, and chuckled. I giggled at her comment and sat patiently, waiting for the show to start.

Focusing my camera at the audience, I began to record some images of the crowd and wondered why it seemed strangely quiet, considering the number of people in the vast auditorium. No one was shouting or screaming like they had when I'd watched concerts filmed for TV, and although there were thousands of people present, it wasn't particularly full at that point.

The opening band came on, and the atmosphere changed considerably. The crowd politely joined in when the band interacted, and their music was loud. If I'd heard any of their songs before, they weren't memorable. The concert venue still had tons of empty seats and the floor space was half empty. I took some shots of the band called Fireburn, but personally, I'd never heard of them.

Ten minutes from the band's scheduled appearance, the hall was transformed. The seating filled up, and the floor space suddenly came to life with hordes of music lovers. Every seat was occupied, and the massive setting buzzed with anticipation.

On stage, guys in black outfits ghosted across the stage, placing drinks and checking equipment, and once the last roadie had vacated, the whole concert hall fell into darkness. This coincided with an incredible roar of appreciation that seemed to build in at the back of the venue and rush forward to the front, as the crowd responded to the impending appearance of the band.

Within seconds, Tyler's bass blasted out from the massive black speakers that were stacked on either side of the stage. The vibrations rumbled through my body and resonated in every fiber within me. My mouth and fingers tingled, and I realized the excitement running through me was adrenaline.

Fans immediately swarmed in from both sides, congregating as close to the catwalk part of the stage as they could get. They screamed hysterically, everyone chanting in unison. Arms held above heads swayed to the music or waved in the hope of catching the attention of one of the band members.

I concentrated on the followers because I knew that once my attention was on Flynn, everything else would pale to insignificance. I wanted to experience the music as a fan before I experienced his performance as the man who held my heart.

The reactions of some were extreme, from fainting and sobbing, to screaming and singing along. Most fans were bobbing up and down, caught up in the frenzied pace of the song, hypnotized by Flynn's voice and fast-flowing lyrics he sang.

Occasionally, I found one person who stood completely enthralled, oblivious of the claustrophobic huddle of bodies all around, while another stood with his eyes closed. I knew he was simply feeling the beat. He didn't need a visual performance to appreciate the genius he was listening to.

I'd taken about forty frames when I swung my camera lens in the direction of the stage, and my heart almost stopped at the sight of Flynn. Dressed in his everyday attire of jeans, white t-shirt, and red Chucks, he should have looked like my Flynn, but up there on stage, he seemed completely different. He was magnified by the huge live video feed behind him. I looked up and saw two more screens on either side of the stage, and the enormity of his fame hit home. Flynn was a worldwide superstar, and his popularity grew daily. And by the look on his face, he thrived on it.

Swaying his hips, Flynn clutched the mic and ran his hand down the microphone stand, as if he were caressing a beautiful woman. My eyes darted back to the female fans who were in awe as he sang his heart out to them. Singing everything from fast, raw, rock tunes, to softer rock ballads note-perfect, he smiled widely. I could see why he commanded the level of adoration he received. He had the ability to make the audience feel like he was singing just to them. That was a real gift.

When Flynn sang "Thinking in Black and White," he knew exactly where I was in that massive hall. He turned and ran up the small ramp directly beside us and caught my wrist as I reached out to him over the security bar.

His concentration was effortless as he sang, let go of me and played his guitar, negotiated the stage, and grabbed my hand again. Before he let me go for the final time, his mouth brushed my fingers and he mouthed, "I love you." He ran back to the center of the stage grinning, while the complex little riff Craig played, led to the bridge of the song.

If I'm honest, I missed the rest of the song because it had taken everything I had inside to control the positive energy running through my shaking body, and to still my haywire heartbeat. Excitement and arousal went hand in hand. Flynn's sex appeal was contagious. He was appealing to most of the people in front of me, and that gave me a twinge of fear for our future. I wondered if I was mad to contemplate even trying to make him happy.

Self-doubt creeped in, and suddenly the happy faces in front of me became potential enemies—people who may take Flynn's attention from me someday. I fought the feeling and lifted my camera. They say a camera never lies, so I began to record the people who had made the crowd so animated by the music they played.

Tyler wasn't a good subject. I only captured three images. He seemed like a one-trick pony because he only struck repetitive poses, and he wasn't as confident on stage as his personality would have one believe.

Craig was a natural performer, like Flynn, but his stage presence needed some work. With a bit more experience, I was sure he could be much better. Tommy... he looked like someone possessed, sitting behind his huge, messy-looking drum kit. His long, black, curly hair swung in a frenzied haze as sweat poured from his brow. Looking at him made me uncomfortable.

Then there was Flynn. My camera clicked incessantly. Each time I pulled it away to watch the man outside the lens, my heart almost burst out of my chest with desire. I listened to his words and stayed behind the camera to capture as many memories as I could from my first rock-concert experience.

When the set finally ended, disappointment overcame me. Even the encore hadn't satisfied my, or the crowd's, thirst for the talent on stage. The lights came on, and sadness filled the air. The atmosphere switched from one thick with the pheromones expelled by the crowds, to one of resignation that the high was over.

My heart empathized with that of the crowd, and I considered myself fortunate I only had a short time to wait to be with Flynn. The fans leaving would have to wait another year for a glimpse of the man I was lucky enough to call mine.

Simone helped me pack away my equipment and, after a few minutes, we made our way back to our men. We passed the pit where the technicians were tearing their set down, and only got about twenty feet further before we were stopped in our tracks by security.

"Sorry, ladies, no wives or girlfriends for an hour after they've come off stage."

Simone tried to push past the huge, burly guard with the knife-proof jacket. "Bullshit, get Craig Southers. This is Flynn fucking Docherty's girlfriend, and I'm Craig's, you moron. I've been on two tours and never heard of this before."

"New tour rules, I've been told."

"Who the fuck said that?" Simone asked.

"Bernie Laker. I'm just doing my job, ma'am. If you ladies would like to go back and sit over there, I'll make sure you get some refreshments while you wait. Bernie said there were to be no spouses or girlfriends present for the meet-and-greet sessions during the tour."

Simone shook her head. "Well, I'll be giving Bernie a ration of shit as soon as we get back there," she said, but resigned herself to waiting. No matter what argument she gave, once Bernie had spoken, everyone worked their instructions to the letter, or so it seemed. Turning back, we took our seats again and waited for them to let us in to the meet-and-greet room. Simone muttered under her breath, but as I had nothing to gauge this by, I accepted that someone would come and get us when they were ready.

"This is fucking humiliating. I'm not having this. Wait until the guys hear what Bernie did to us. Flynn's gonna bust a blood vessel."

"Listen, Simone, maybe Bernie wants confrontation with Flynn, so perhaps we should play down the fact that we were excluded from this part of the night and not feed into what he wants."

Simone smirked. "Fuck, there are no flies on you, Valerie. I'd have gone in there and created havoc. You're right, that would just have fed into his sick little game. A watch-and-wait approach will have him seething if he gets no reaction," Simone said, as she jokingly rubbed her hands together in evil glee over the idea of how to play Bernie at his own game.

Chapter Thirty-Three

WORKING IT OUT

$\mathcal{I}$t was over an hour and a half by the time Craig's girlfriend finally persuaded one of the security guys to ask Craig to switch his phone on. We were still waiting for access to the dressing room, and Simone had been texting Craig from the moment we'd sat down again. Admittedly, I was a little confused as to why Flynn nor Craig had found us when we didn't show after the gig, but I'd sat, distracted by the images I'd taken from the concert. I hadn't realized how long we'd sat there.

Ten minutes later, the guard came back, looking more than a little uncomfortable. Bernie said you're free to go back there, but I'd think about that. It's not pretty in there. I don't think you ladies are going to like what you see.

Simone pushed off her seat and stood up before jumping the short distance down to the stage level. She turned to look up at me. "Come on, Valerie, I don't know what the fuck is going on, but I'm going to see for myself," she stated as she turned to look in the direction of the dressing room.

Once I was down beside her, we went to find everyone. When I pushed the door open, the first person I saw was a young girl giving Tyler head. I was mortified, but I knew I had to ignore it if I wanted them to believe I was capable of staying with Flynn. I wasn't happy that Flynn was comfortable around that kind of exhibitionism. My head wouldn't accept that he'd be tolerant of the raw indecency of their public display, while knowing I'd be arriving at any moment. Or was it that I was too prudish for this?

My eyes quickly scanned the barely lit room, and my heartbeat faltered in shock when my eyes found Flynn. Slouched down on another sofa, he was bare-chested with his pants undone, passed out. Further along the same big leather couch, Craig also appeared drunk, and he was naked from the waist down.

A naked blond girl was lying tucked into Craig's side with her head on his chest, and a leg cocked over his one nearest to her.

"What the fuck is going on?" Simone flung her arms out wide and screamed at no one in particular as she stomped over to Craig and whacked him hard across his face. The sound was so loud it made me flinch. Craig groaned and rolled his head to the side, but he didn't wake up.

The girl in his arms pulled away from him and straightened up a bit to look at Simone. "Hey, what the fuck do you think you're doing?" she said, her face distorting angrily.

"I think that's my fucking question. He's my fucking boyfriend, you whore," Simone yelled hysterically, her temper rising with every second we stood there. "Get the fuck off him," she shrieked, as she pulled the girl by the arm and dragged her away.

Rising to her feet, the girl grabbed Simone by the hair, and I thought mayhem was going to develop, but Tommy stepped forward and caught the girl's wrist to stop her from doing any real damage to Simone. "Enough, you got what you came for; it's time for you to leave." Tommy nodded to a guy I'd never seen before, and he took care of throwing her out of the room.

Tyler turned bleary-eyed and gave Simone a contemptuous smirk, and then rolled his head away from her as the girl on her knees continued to work his dick in and out of her mouth. "What the fuck did you expect? You think these guys can ignore all the lure of knowing there are hundreds of girls prettier than you who want to fuck us? That's a pretty naïve assumption on your part, don't you think?"

I'd only been in the room for a couple of minutes and was trying to get my head around everything I saw. Inside, I'd wanted to scream. The debauched scene was beyond my comprehension. Simone was arguing with Tyler. They were cursing and name calling, while I stood silently trying to assimilate the situation before me.

My rational side wouldn't allow me to think for one minute that Flynn would have made such a stand to his band mates about me, and then had sex with someone else, but I couldn't deny his appearance on the couch.

But appearances could be deceptive. *Am I so naïve I never saw this coming? What do I really know about Flynn?*

Martin's stern and protective planning around Flynn and me sprang to mind, but it was quickly contradicted by all the beautiful words in the songs Flynn had written about me. Confusion and hurt flooded my body and collected heavily in my stomach. It made me sick. My emotions were changing inside as quickly as I scanned the images I'd taken of the band's concert a few minutes prior to entering the room.

For a fleeting moment, I allowed myself to accept that I'd only seen one side of Flynn and wondered if his public image was, in fact, more true to life than he'd admitted to me. Instinct and reason pushed that thought aside. At the very least, I knew Flynn wasn't stupid enough to let anything happen while I was in the same building.

A checklist of possibilities ran through my mind. *Something's definitely off here. Where's Lee?* Lee was always where Flynn was, yet I hadn't seen him since we'd arrived at the venue. Craig used the band security, and there was no one else specific to ask. "Where's Lee?"

Bernie turned and sneered at me. "Yeah, where *is* Lee?" he chuckled to himself and moved in on me. I scowled at him and swallowed down my fears that someone had gotten the guys into this state deliberately. Bernie raised his hand and tried to move a strand of hair away from my face. His closeness, coupled with the stench of whiskey on his breath, made me cringe.

"Looks like your guy's a little ... worn out over there. What do you say we get to know each other a little better?"

His fat hand grabbed my upper arm, but he'd underestimated me. My knee connected with his balls, and he crumpled up in pain, but didn't release his grip. As I struggled, I felt the weight of a hand adding to the pressure on my arm. "Off. I won't tolerate that. I never agreed to fucking with her," Tommy said sternly.

I crossed the room and crouched beside Flynn, shaking him hard. No response. I patted his jeans pockets for his cell and found it. It was password protected. I cursed myself for not having Lee's number on mine and hit the emergency-call-only button, and held it to my ear.

"I have an emergency, please," I stated, before Bernie reached me and knocked the cell from my hand.

Simone grabbed the phone off the floor and fought Bernie off. She spoke with the 911 operator, naming the venue, exactly where we were and who we were with, before Bernie managed to grab it out her hand and cut her off.

Fighting back my fears, I glanced down at both men, and even though both were breathing steadily, they weren't conscious. I grabbed some towels from the bathroom and covered Flynn's naked upper body to keep any heat in. It had dawned on me that they'd possibly been drugged by someone in the room. At that point, I'd been thankful for the first-aid course I'd taken when I was setting up my studio.

Bernie and Tyler were suddenly on their feet, Simone and I forgotten as they cleaned up the place like the cops were coming to inspect it. I knew at that point they'd had a hand in what had happened to Flynn and Craig, but my main concern was keeping Flynn alive until help arrived.

"What the fuck did you give them?" My voice was cold and controlled. I knew if I showed them how frightened I really was, they'd use that against me, and any chance I'd had of protecting Flynn from them would be gone.

Bernie shook his head but continued to push stuff from around the room into a plastic bag. I sounded so controlled, addressing the rest of the band.

"If you don't tell me so I can help them, and something happens, it could be the death penalty for all of you. What's been going on here was obviously premeditated, or were you planning on killing all of us to achieve whatever sick plans you had?"

"This had nothing to do with me, honey," Tommy quickly offered.

"Bullshit, Tommy, you were here. I remember what you said to me before the gig. You knew something and saw what was going on, and you did nothing to stop it. I'm not sharp on my knowledge of the law, but I think that makes you an accomplice, if I'm not mistaken," I threatened.

Tommy's eyes widened as he held his hands up. "Like I said, I've got nothing against your boy. These two planned it. They thought it would be easy to get you out of the picture once you thought Flynn had been fucking other girls."

"Look at him, Tommy. The girls would have to be into necrophilia to fuck him. The only thing Flynn's doing voluntarily here is breathing," I commented dryly.

"Simone, come over here and help me get them to a sitting position. Grab a couple of those towels and their jackets. Flynn's skin is icy cold and clammy to touch; we need to warm them up."

Bernie opened the dressing room door and disappeared down the corridor, past the two security guys there.

"Anyone got Lee's number? Where the fuck is he?" I shouted.

"Bernie sent him back to the bus to get something. I've got his number here." Tommy reached into his jeans pocket, and Tyler squared up to him. "You heard her. You're in this as much as the rest of us, Tommy. You did nothing to stop us. Remember that."

Simone cramped Tyler's personal space. "What the fuck were you all thinking, anyway? 'Oh ... I know, let's drug our lead singer. That'll make him see clearly? Are you all out of your fucking minds?" Simone strutted back and forth in front of them, and I lay a protective hand on Flynn's head to feel his temperature.

Tyler and Tommy stared helplessly at each other, both suddenly looking like two scruffy guys no one would look twice at, instead of the rock stars they'd appeared to be on stage just an hour before. Tommy's ashen face was a measure of his understanding of how grave the situation was. Tyler... I doubted he'd ever had any empathy for anyone. He was insular and self-serving, and probably evoked the strongest feelings of anger from me, of anyone I'd met in Chicago, apart from Iria.

Loud voices spoke urgently as a commotion in the hall drew nearer, and then four policemen and an ambulance crew crammed into the room. My immediate concern was for Flynn, and as soon as I saw the medics, my emotions rose from my chest to my throat, and I burst into tears. The panic I'd been swallowing down for the previous fifteen minutes bubbled over. My body shook violently, and it was only then I allowed myself to face the gravity of the situation with Flynn. *I can't lose him.*

Once the thought he might die was in my head, I was practically inconsolable. I refused to allow Flynn into the ambulance without me, and as they were closing the door, I saw Tyler being led to a police patrol car.

"Please, baby, don't leave me. Please, God, help him," I begged and prayed as I sat opposite Flynn. I couldn't see his face anymore. A medic leaned over him and hooked up the electrocardiograph machine to the pads dotted around his body. He hooked them up to the battery pack in the back of the ambulance, and connected the wires to the monitor that hung above his head.

Flynn was covered in heavy, red blankets after they wrapped his body in a silver foil one. An oxygen mask had been placed over his mouth and nose. Finally, a clip attached to his index finger made the oxygen saturation levels appear on the same screen as his heart rate and respiratory count.

"He's stable. We just need to find out what he's taken, then we'll hopefully be able to counter that," the ambulance attendant said.

"He hasn't taken anything voluntarily," I defended.

"That's the usual response," he countered dryly.

"Maybe, but I'm telling you, the guys in that band have grudges. What you see here is a crime. We were held back from seeing him and Craig. Bernie Laker and Tyler Chisolm had something to do with this. They were talking about it. Tommy even told me it was them because he got scared, and said he wanted nothing to do with it. You might want to add sexual assault or indecent exposure or something to your charges as well; I doubt Flynn was in the state of undress I'd found him in when he passed out. Craig neither."

When we reached the Emergency Room, they whisked Flynn straight through on the gurney, still attached to the monitors, but I was left in the waiting area. They needed space to work on him, they said. I didn't protest, I just let them take him, and sat down heavily with my head in my hands. I couldn't face the possibility of being there if something went wrong. I felt completely helpless and alone—the same feeling I'd had when my parents went to Las Vegas when the boys died.

Twenty minutes later, there was still no news, and when I heard the automatic doors swish open behind me, I turned my head to see Lee striding in my direction. "Fuck! Valerie. Is he okay? Where did they take him?"

"What the fuck happened? You were supposed to be keeping him safe," I screamed, as I jumped up and beat my fists on his chest.

"Whoa, Valerie. I'm sorry. I never wanted to leave him, but Flynn insisted I do what Bernie wanted. Bernie had new cells for all the guys and said they'd be getting updates about the tour on the new number. Flynn and Bernie argued because Flynn said he didn't see the point of yet another cell phone. Eventually, Flynn sent me to Bernie's bus to get it because Bernie wouldn't stop going on about it, and Flynn didn't want anything to affect his performance."

"Where was I when this happened?"

"You were in the restrooms with Simone. Anyway, I went over to the bus, and five guys were waiting inside for me. I got kidnapped, and they handcuffed me to the table bolted to the floor, until the police came and found me."

I was suddenly overwhelmed, learning that Flynn had people close to him who wanted to hurt him. Planning to separate him from Lee was a deliberate attempt to hurt Flynn and Craig. What I couldn't understand was what it was supposed to achieve. Unless it was to get rid of Simone and me, or maybe Bernie had an insight that they had planned to leave the band. They had to know Lee, or myself, or someone would figure it out. It was a stupid plot.

I turned to face Lee and made it three steps toward him before I collapsed into his arms. I was a sobbing wreck. "Don't worry, honey. He'll be okay. Flynn's a fighter. I'm ashamed I wasn't there for him today. Don't worry, Valerie, I'll make sure they pay for what they've done."

Chapter Thirty-Four

FUNDS

*W*e heard footsteps coming down the corridor, leading from where they'd taken Flynn. As they drew closer, my heart raced, and I had to swallow the panic that made me feel like I was going to vomit. The door leading from the hallway opened, and a small Asian doctor appeared. She gave me a sympathetic smile.

"Valerie?" I nodded and fought back tears as Lee put a protective arm around me. "Hello, my name is Dr. Kaur." She shook our hands. "Mr. Docherty is awake now. We had to give him Narcan, an antidote drug to counteract the opiates in his system. He's a very lucky man. Flynn was very close to having a respiratory arrest by the time the paramedics got him here."

Relief washed over me, and my heart felt weightless in my chest. My legs gave way, and my body sagged into Lee when I knew Flynn was okay. She agreed we could see Flynn and told me he had asked if I was okay as soon he had regained consciousness.

She led the way into the ER and Flynn was sitting, propped up by pillows, still on a gurney. All the wires had been removed, but a clear bag of fluids with a label on it was being administered into the vein on his left hand. He appeared much more like Flynn, instead of the almost-lifeless man I'd found a couple of hours earlier. Considering what he'd been through, the effect of his appearance still made my heart flutter.

Flynn smiled softly and reached out a hand for me to go to him. "So, is there no end to the talents you possess, Valerie? I hear I have you to thank for me being here."

As soon as I heard him speak, I dissolved into a teary mess. I loved him so much my heart squeezed tightly and relief flooded my veins. I rushed to his bedside and buried my face in his neck, crying hard. "God, Flynn, I thought you were going to die," I blurted out, unable to be strong any longer.

"And leave you here on your own? Not a chance, babe. You're mine, and I promise you I'm going to stick around and love you until I'm so old I'm peeing my pants, and we're interviewing retirement homes together," he said, chuckling. The low timbre of his voice and his rumbly laughter against my face felt like the warmest hug.

When I started telling Flynn about what happened, he said that he'd started to feel weird as they went on for the encore, and by the time he'd gone back to the dressing room and sat down on the sofa, he was passing out.

"It was weird because I was tired, but the last thing I remember was being so thirsty, and my heart was racing. Initially, I just thought it was an adrenaline rush. I'd carried the water bottle from the stage to the dressing room, and I drank all of that, and..." Flynn sat, staring into space, and then looked back at me, confused. "Nothing. I don't know what happened after that."

Flynn stopped his thought and threw his hands up, looking at Lee. "Where the fuck where you?"

Lee explained what they'd done to him, and Flynn's lips formed a line as he bit back his anger for not seeing any of what they did, coming. He sent Lee to find out how Craig was doing. I hadn't mentioned anything about him, but then again, he'd known it was me who'd found him, so I guessed the doctor must have brought him up to speed that Craig was involved as well.

"My guess is it was something to do with Bernie or Tyler, Valerie. Whoever did that to me could've fucking killed me. What were they trying to achieve? I'm not going back. I'm done."

"It was them, and I've got some thoughts about that, Flynn. I wonder if they thought drugging you and making it look like you were in a compromising position would run me off. Your zipper on your pants was undone and the way I found you, it looked pretty damning, if I didn't trust you. Poor Craig wasn't so lucky. Simone found him naked from the waist down with a nasty groupie hanging all over him."

"Fuck, Valerie. I don't get it. What the fuck went through their minds when they tried to pull shit like that? I'm sorry you had to see it. Do you know where my cell is?"

"Sorry, it's probably still in the dressing room. I hit the emergency button and called 911, but Bernie knocked it out of my hand."

"Can you call my legal team and ask someone to come over? I want to press charges."

Lee came back into the room, and Flynn's attention turned to him. "Call Clinton, Lee. I want you to get me out of my contract. I'm not going back."

Lee stood at the end of the bed. "Already done, boss. There's more. Bernie has released a statement that you and Craig almost died tonight, due to a drug overdose. Clever fucker said the band stands united behind you and Craig, and that you're in rehab."

"What the fuck is going on? He's fucking crazy. He's trying to kill my reputation. I want to press charges, but how do I prove they did it?" Flynn asked.

While we were talking, a nurse arrived and checked Flynn's vital signs, and he asked to be discharged from the hospital. Everyone advised against it but, after a few arguments with various doctors, he insisted on signing a disclaimer, and Lee chartered a plane to take us home.

My cell rang as we were leaving the hospital. My parents had been contacted by the paparazzi and were naturally frantic about Flynn and the drug statement. Once I'd assured them it was a pack of lies, my father released a statement of his own.

Bernie was obviously still meddling from a distance and, the way the story was being spun, it sounded pretty damning for the both of us. From what Dad said, it seemed they were saying Flynn had corrupted me, and I'd run away from home to move in with a rock-star drug addict.

On the way home, Lee rang Craig and Flynn told them that when Craig was released from the hospital, they should come to stay with us at his place, where the security was better. When he was informed that he'd be out the following day, Flynn instructed Lee to arrange a plane for them.

Fifteen minutes after we made it home, Clinton arrived. His legal team had been informed of the details, and his advice was to go public and give the press Flynn's version of events. Once the public saw for themselves that Flynn wasn't strung out on drugs, and safe at home, they'd realize that Bernie was out to damage his reputation.

"Think carefully about what you're doing if you leave the group. They could bankrupt you by suing for damages and lost revenue from this tour," Clinton warned. "Don't you want to wait until you know what this is about?"

"I'm personally liable? Even if criminal charges are brought?" Flynn asked.

"You aren't just under contract to the band, Flynn. You have contracts with all the venues, PR, the merchandise company, radio stations ... not to mention the record label and all the contracts for TV and festival appearances."

Flynn sat, staring out the window with his elbows on the kitchen countertop, his chin resting on his hands. I sat and studied my beautiful man and wondered what was running through his mind. I saw worry etched on his face. A frown creased his brow, and his eyes were focused straight ahead. He began to register those thoughts visibly, as his breathing became faster and shallower. Finally, he spoke.

"We've got insurance for this kind of event, right? Fuck. You know what? I don't care. I've lived on nothing before, I can do it again. Let them take the money, and when it's gone ... they can't get blood out of a stone."

"We do have insurance, Flynn, but you could still find yourself penniless," Clinton advised.

Grim faces stared pointedly as Flynn, and his lawyer went head to head about how he should play it. As far as Flynn was concerned, clearing his reputation and mine were his priority. He'd deal with all the rest when the time came. I saw his strength and strong sense of right and wrong in that.

"You sure you know what you're doing, Flynn? You don't want to sleep on this? You've been through hell tonight," I prompted.

I had some money. Nothing near the wealth he was used to, but enough to keep us going for a couple of years, if we lived moderately. I stared at him, wondering how someone like Flynn could fit back into normal society.

"Nope, but I'm doing it anyway. As long as I have you, Valerie, I don't care what else happens. The house is ring-fenced, in a way, so they can't take that. Not sure how they did that, but I suppose it's a security thing for events such as this. Is that right, Clint?"

"Yes, Flynn, but I really think you should think harder about this. It's my duty to advise..."

"Alright, you advised," he said, and growled in frustration. "Just get the fucking press release ready; we're going to the front gate to make a statement. I'm out. I won't line those bastards' pockets for another minute. The companies will get their money back eventually. Royalties come in steadily, for the most part, and I can write for other people if I don't have a record deal anymore."

Flynn rang Craig to tell him of his decision, and when Craig heard what he had to say, he was naturally in agreement that they should both leave together. Flynn had promised Craig he'd keep him with him if a new band was formed, but that he'd try to protect him from the fallout of the decision he was taking. Craig told Flynn to do what he needed to do and that he was with him one hundred percent.

Decisive and resolute, Flynn was determined to brave it out and kill the contracts he'd committed to. As we were being driven to the gate, my heart was in my mouth and I felt a mixture of pride and fear at the same time. I glanced at Flynn, and he squeezed my hand. "You okay, babe?"

I knew I'd been quiet. He'd worked so hard to get where he was. "We're still alive, and we have each other, Valerie; that gives us a fighting chance in life. Everything will find a way of working itself out."

Flynn tugged my hand and eased me out of the car. Wrapping his arms around me, he dipped his head and leaned in to place his forehead on mine. "We're solid, Valerie. No one is going to take us down, as long as we have each other, right?"

Reaching up on tiptoes, I kissed him like my life depended on it. Breathless, we broke the kiss, and he rewarded me with a wide, loving smile. "Ready to watch your sexy rock-star boyfriend commit professional suicide?" he asked with a wink. There was no hint of nerves from him, and I thought he was the bravest person I'd ever known at that moment.

Nodding his head, Lee signaled to the guard and the metal gates ground opened. Instantly, cameras were flashing relentlessly, and I shielded my eyes but noticed that Flynn stood still, confident in his decision about disappointing not only all the supporting industries, but his fans as well.

A barrage of questions came thick and fast, as reporters sought their pound of flesh from Flynn, and the cameras flashed as they continued to click loudly. Flynn stood motionless and waited until he decided to speak. He was in control of his future. After a minute, he raised his hand, and everyone fell silent.

"Thank you for coming over this evening. I hope you are all well. Forgive me, but I've had a very long day, and I'm not taking questions. It's 3:45 A.M., and I've had a hard day at work."

The media crews all laughed, and Flynn commanded their attention. He knew exactly how to handle them. When the laughter died down, he narrowed his eyes and drew a breath, and my feelings for him ran deeper for what he was about to tell them.

"I'm here to issue a statement and to allow you all to see that I am here in the flesh, not in a drug rehabilitation clinic, as my *ex*-management would have you believe. Let me make this clear. Despite what is being reported in the press, I do not take drugs of my own free will. Yes, I can confirm that earlier I was taken to a local ER in the Baltimore area after I somehow ingested narcotics. The method of administration is being criminally investigated. I am not going to speculate as to how that happened. That is for the police to decide." Low murmurs rippled through the reporters as Flynn quickly pressed on.

"As you can see, I am fit and well as I stand before you. Today was the first day of what was to be a sold-out tour of many dates for Major ScAlz, the band of which I am the lead singer. I am announcing tonight that I am no longer a member of this band." One reported began to ask a question, and Flynn held up his hand.

"For reasons that will become clear over the following weeks and months, I cannot discuss what has prompted my decision, nor has this been taken lightly. To my fans, I am deeply sorry. I have worked tirelessly to earn your respect as a musician and performer, and I am very thankful for your support and love. I hope you understand that if there were a way to resolve this issue without leaving the band, I would do that. Unfortunately, there isn't." Flynn commanded the media's full, silent attention by that point.

"Irreconcilable differences mean that Bernie Laker, Tyler Chisholm, and Tommy Alzaci will no longer be working in partnership with me or my Major ScAlz bandmate Craig Southers. To clarify who will be dealing with any correspondence regarding Craig or myself, my law firm—namely Clinton Bright—should be contacted in the first instance, until my new public relations team are identified. Contact on a personal level will be directed via my lawyer's assistant for the first twenty-four hours until further arrangements have been made." Just as Flynn looked like he was done, he leaned back toward the microphone and added one more thing.

"The last point I'd like to make is there has been much speculation about my relationship with my girlfriend Valerie Darsin. Only a week ago, most of your press offices had to issue a retraction around us. Make no mistake. This time, if there are any derogatory personal remarks levied toward Ms. Darsin or myself, there will be no leniency to the offenders. Another press release will be issued when we have clarified the situation. Thank you."

As soon as Flynn stopped talking, the questions became a blanket of noise as hundreds of reporters shouted at the same time. Flynn bowed his head to them, turned and reached for my hand, then slowly walked back behind the gate. The reporters continued with their onslaught, but Flynn lifted his hand, waved, and the tall black gates ground mechanically until I heard the dead bolt lock into place. I realized they were sound-reduction gates, because all I could hear was a muffled buzz from behind them.

Flynn squeezed my hand and smiled reassuringly. "How did I do? Was I sexy? Did that turn you on, all that masterful behavior?" He smirked wickedly, wiggled his eyebrows like what he'd done was fun, and pulled me into his side. "Fuck everyone. Fuck music. I don't need any of it as long as I have you, Valerie. I could have died tonight. I was lucky I didn't. Knowing you're here and standing beside me no matter what, tells me we'll do just fine."

By the time we got back to the house, Flynn was in a more somber mood. He spoke to Lee and Niamh, and both said they'd stay with him, without pay if necessary. Pulling out a pad, I started to jot down some of the most basic things I could think of that we could work on, and wondered how to find Flynn new public relations. There was no doubt he'd be discarded by his PR team as soon as they'd heard his statement. *But then again, hadn't he just dumped on them?*

Flynn's legal team speculated about the potential losses, and they said the extent of the financial damage to Flynn would be huge. They also said the final total of compensation wouldn't be known for many months, while legal negotiations took place.

At 6:00 A.M., Simone called Flynn to inform him that Craig was being released, and he told her Lee had arranged a plane to bring them back to Chicago.

My cell rang once the statement was aired on TV. It was my dad. He spoke to Flynn and told him he was very proud of his approach and professionalism, despite what happened to him only hours before. I saw him swallow roughly at my father's praise. Flynn went off to talk to Lee while I continued to talk to my dad. I explained how worried I was about keeping Flynn safe if all his money went into paying for legal proceedings. Dad went quiet, and I had the feeling he had something on his mind.

I was prepared for a lecture about not using my money, because he knew I had a couple of hundred thousand dollars sitting in the bank, and more tied up in investments. My royalty check was due any day again, and my disposable income could well have doubled by then. My business was doing well. As I prepared to defend myself for how I used my money, what he said stopped me dead in my tracks.

"Listen, Valerie, I have something very important to tell you. We didn't say anything because we weren't sure quite how to tell you, but I guess Martin and Adam have decided it's time."

The mention of my brothers' names while my emotions were raw, made me choke back tears that suddenly sprang to my eyes. I swallowed everything down, inhaled deeply, and forced myself to respond.

"It's time? Time for what, Dad?" I said quietly. My heart raced from the squeeze of pain I felt at remembering their loss again.

"When you were kids, your grandad kept harping about getting life insurance for you all. Well, we had these policies and the bank just kept taking the money. Anyway, it was something we thought we'd never need." Clearing the emotion from his throat, my dad pushed on. "They paid out on the deaths of my boys, two-hundred-fifty thousand each. But that's not all, Valerie. Ziggy's father sued the river rafting company for reckless endangerment and wrongful death. They settled out of court three weeks ago. It isn't public knowledge. Ziggy's dad had a long battle, but as the rafting company was found guilty of negligence, Ziggy's parents were awarded money for his wrongful death. In a closed-court hearing, a judge awarded the same to the families of the others who lost their lives as well."

"Money isn't going to bring them back, Dad."

I heard a smile in my father's voice when he answered, "I know that, baby girl, but we had no idea how to use it. We felt it should benefit something, and Kayden thought some should go to better safety training for outdoor activities staff, so we've earmarked ten percent for that. We don't want it to buy any houses or fancy cars. My boys died, and that money should be used for something appropriate. I've spoken to Kayden and your mom. Kayden doesn't want any of it."

I wasn't sure where he was going with the conversation, but my head was buzzing with the sad fact that my brothers had earned my family money with their deaths. I zoned out for a moment, then tuned back in to the sound of his voice.

"So, we figured this: We leave this house and land to Kayden when we're gone, and you use the money to start over with Flynn. This money came from a lack of protection, and you both need to be protected from any backlash Flynn's band members or manager may be concocting. Let Flynn pay his debts with what he has. Once he's done that, it's up to you how you spend your money, but we feel it's appropriate that it's used to protect you both in the future."

I thought my dad had flipped, trying to give me extra money like that, and I was about to refuse until he spoke again, "It may sound insane, handing over a large sum of money to an eighteen-year-old and a rock star, but your mom and I have watched you two over the years. Despite what we said before you went away, we figure you two have a special bond that will survive most things, and you'll work it all out together. I've gotten to know Flynn, and I have faith in him. Your mom and I were your age when we got together, so we know love can be real no matter how young you are. You may only be a slip-of-a-girl, Valerie, but if you apply everything I've taught you about business, I know this money will only continue to grow. You're feisty and passionate. Use those skills and, with the money behind you, we're confident you'll put Flynn and yourself in a much better place in life."

My heart raced because he was placing his trust in us, and treating me as an equal. "Dad... I don't know what to say." My heart thumped wildly in my chest at his and my family's selfless generosity, and their belief in me.

"It's not being given without conditions, Valerie, but you've proven yourself as a great little businesswoman. You're shrewd, and you're not easily fooled in the business world. With the right people behind you, you'll fly. Flynn's your partner, and he's already proven himself in his field of work."

My dad had been a small businessman for thirty years, running his successful little garage. He could have done things on a much larger scale, but he wanted to see his children grow and not spend all our childhoods as a slave to his business. He'd survived slumps and recessions, so I was awed that he thought I had the ability to help Flynn.

"Thank you for believing in me, Dad, but running a small business isn't the same as taking care of a rock star. I doubt a couple of million dollars would even buy enough to produce and promote a CD these days," I said, feeling the weight of responsibility about that.

"Valerie, hon, I'm not talking about two million. The total amount in the bank is around twelve-and-a-half million. The tour company had big liability insurance." My heart stopped. I'm sure for two beats—it stopped.

I thought I'd misheard him. "Excuse me? What did you say?" My hands shook and my head spun as the sum sunk in.

When he'd said it again, I almost choked for real. I'd always thought my dad was a quiet genius, but his decision to give that kind of money to me made me think he'd finally fallen on the insanity side of the wall.

"Take your time. Absorb what I've told you, and what you're being offered. We'll talk again in a couple of days, honey. Stay strong."

I concluded the call and wandered back into the room where Flynn was sitting. My mind was going a mile a minute, and I wondered how to tell Flynn. He had switched on his huge TV screen and was sitting in the dark, apart from the TV glow. He was deep in thought and not watching anything in particular.

Being near him was the only thing that had seemed to center me, so I climbed on the couch and snuggled close to him. Immediately, his arm slid around my shoulder, and he pulled my head to rest on his chest. We didn't speak, and I just sat in his arms for about forty minutes, while we mulled everything over in our minds. Eventually, after a period of consolidating my thoughts, I raised my head to look at him.

"They'll catch Bernie and Tyler and then what, Flynn? Do you want to keep performing?"

"I don't see any way I can, babe. Not without funds. Even if they do catch them, the damage taking time out does in this industry would just make me yesterday's front man. It would take years for someone to take a chance on me after this ... if ever."

"What about me? What if I took a chance on you, Flynn?"

He chuckled and shifted, then he took my face in his warm hands. "Valerie, you are so fucking adorable. You're definitely my number one fan, huh?"

I pushed away from him, trying to be taken seriously. "You don't think I'm capable of managing a rock star?"

"Valerie, I think you are capable of just about anything, except murder, but knowing how to run a business and loving me isn't going to get us very far."

"I came here with you because I trusted you. I went to the press with you because I trusted you. Now I'm asking you to trust me, not only to help you recover from this, but to be bigger and better than anything Bernie Laker did for you. What do you say to me learning to manage you? If I can get the right team behind me, I believe I can do it."

Flynn sat up and ran his hands through his hair. "Do you even know what you're trying to take on, Valerie? These people are slimy bastards. There's so much cut-throat..."

"I'm taking on a whole heap of shit, I expect, but I've never taken anything on I've not managed and made a success of. It'll be a steep learning curve in muddy waters, but I'd do it to the best of my ability. You asked me to trust you. I do. Do you trust me?"

Flynn gave me a soul-searching look, then nodded. "Of course, I do."

"Do you want me to take you on, Flynn? I'm ready for you, just like you told me I had to be. Question is, are you ready for me?"

Flynn stared through me for a few seconds and grinned. "Fuck yeah, with a manager with the balls you just showed, how can I not be ready? Bring it, Valerie. People are going to say I'm crazy to trust my career to some girl from nowhere, but they have no idea who you are or what you're going to be in the future. I'm in."

Without knowing the financial power behind the words I'd said, Flynn placed his life and his career in my hands. The feeling was indescribable to have that level of trust. I had to ensure I'd make the most of it.

Bernie and Tyler could wait. I knew we'd get them and that they had only days of freedom left, at the most. However, it was important to Flynn's and Craig's futures that I told no one about the money until the financial shit storm they were facing, had passed. Then my plan was for Flynn Docherty to rise from the ashes of his previous band, much bigger and better.

Martin and Adam died, and their legacy made them a part of what

I was about to do. They'd always protected me, and somehow even after their deaths, they were continuing to do that. The money from the company that hadn't kept them safe meant nothing to us in material terms, but it could teach the Bernies of the world that they can't manipulate, control, and monopolize people. And if it could achieve and protect someone else in the future, then I'd use every penny of it.

First, I wanted to protect my father until the time was right, because if anyone knew he had passed all that money to an eighteen-year-old girl to manage a rock star, they'd certify him. They could also say Flynn manipulated me to use it for his own gain as well.

Flynn stood and stretched, kissed me tenderly, then told me he had some calls to make, and I knew I had no time to lose. Reaching into my oversized bag, I pulled out my detachable keyboard and notepad, and fired it up. Flynn had to be seen to be still buoyant and resilient, and a positive professional profile had to be maintained.

My business brain was already in action, and I was determined Flynn would come back fighting. At best, I'd have a few months to rebrand him, learn about the music business and how things got done, and to build a loyal team of experts around us. We'd have to be clever about how it was all done and, once we had our plan in place, we'd sit waiting in the wings.

Meanwhile, I was a photographer, and made videos, so I'd cover Flynn's PR but find a public spokesperson to act on his behalf. I could easily pay for that. Flynn could write new material that we'd copyright after his solvency issues were settled, and he'd be free of all ties. We'd find a recording studio, or better still, build one in my old studio at my dad's place. No one would have to know about it.

Opening a Word document, I smirked and titled the file: *Rock bottom to Rock God: Shortcut for Beginners*. It was a tongue-in-cheek title, but my intentions were deadly serious. The first rule in business is to believe in the product you have, and I had no hesitations about that. I believed in Flynn.

I had no nerves or doubts about Flynn's come back. All I needed was the right skill-set for the job. The financial backing was secure. Once the time was right, I'd tell him about the money. My guess is, if he knew, he'd object. My intention was only to use what we needed, when we needed it. If my plan worked, Flynn could pay it back, and we'd decide how to donate it in the future.

In the meantime, I knew I'd have to prove myself from the get-go if I were to make him feel confident in my hands. There was no doubt in my mind he loved me, but placing trust in me to deliver him back to the public was a massive risk. I felt the weight of that reality in my hands as I began to record my first thoughts, and prepared for our future—or more importantly, Flynn's rock-star return.

End of Part One

OTHER TITLES BY K.L. SHANDWICK

THE EVERYTHING TRILOGY

Enough Isn't Everything

Everything She Needs

Everything I Want

Love With Every Beat

just Jack

Everything Is Yours

LAST SCORE SERIES

Gibson's Legacy

Trusting Gibson

Gibson's Melody

READY FOR FLYNN SERIES

Ready For Flynn, Part 1

Ready For Flynn, Part 2

Ready For Flynn, Part 3

OTHER NOVELS

Missing Beats

Notes on Love

ABOUT THE AUTHOR

K. L. Shandwick lives on the outskirts of York, UK. She started writing after a challenge by a friend when she commented on a book she read. The result of this was 'The Everything Trilogy'. Her background has been mainly in the health and social care sector in the U.K. Her books tend to focus on the relationships of the main characters. Writing is a form of escapism for her and she is just as excited to find out where her characters take her as she is when she reads another author's work.

FIND K. L. SHANDWICK ON SOCIAL MEDIA

- **KLShandwick.com**
- **Twitter**
- **Facebook**
- **Bookbub**
- **AllAuthor**
- **Instagram**
- **Amazon**
- **KL's Hangout Group**
- **KL's Newsletter**

Printed in Poland
by Amazon Fulfillment
Poland Sp. z o.o., Wrocław